Dora Freeman's (Un?) Eventful LIFE

Dora Freeman's (Un?) Eventful LIFE

Christiane Zander

ASHWOOD
PUBLISHING

ISBN-paperback: 978-1-7636921-2-1
ISBN-epub: 978-1-7636921-5-2

Published by Ashwood Publishing, Cradoc, Tasmania.
ashwoodpublishing.com.au
info@ashwoodpublishing.com.au

This is a work of fiction, and the persons, events, and locations depicted herein are either fictitious or, in the case of real locations, persons, or organisations, are used fictitiously.

Cover design: Susan Young
Mannequin image Lordeer/Shutterstock.com

A catalogue record for this work is available from the National Library of Australia.

The work of Ashwood Publishing is nurtured by the beautiful country of the Melukerdee people in the Huon Valley in southern Lutruwita / Tasmania. We acknowledge and pay respect to the traditional owners and continuing custodians of this place.

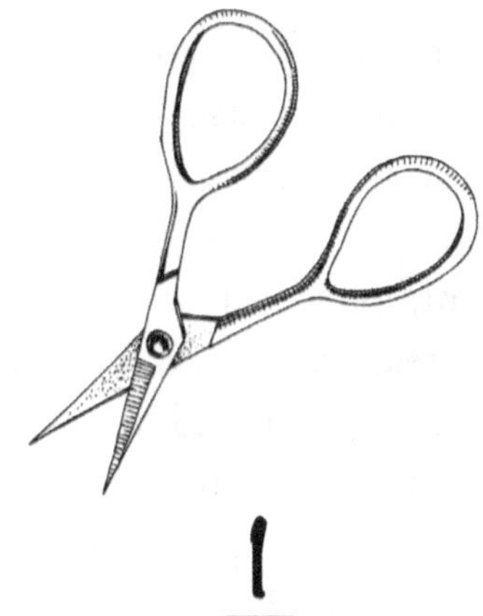

1

26 February 2024

The day of Harry's death, early morning

DORA RAN DOWN THE GRAVELLY path as fast as her sixty-three years and slippery old thongs would allow. Out of breath, she reached the unofficial, grassy car park and let her bunched-up skirt drop down again to her ankles. Her car was still the only one there. Thank goodness! The unusual heat must have kept the regular dog walkers and joggers away. Why did it have to be so hot, right this very day? A nice cool day would have been much better.

The summers in Tasmania really could drive a person crazy. Every so often there would be a run of three or four warm, if not hot days, deceiving everyone into thinking that finally, finally, they were in for a beautiful summer. Then, seemingly out of nowhere, cold, cloudy days would strike. To add to the unreliability of the weather were randomly interspersed rainy days that seemed to serve no purpose whatsoever. They never produced enough water to be of any benefit to the garden. Windy days were the worst, especially when the wind came straight from Antarctica, so that even on what was forecast to be a warm day, you could feel freezing cold. But this particular day, of all days, it had to be stinking hot!

For a short moment, Dora leaned against the driver's door of her car to catch her breath and calm her heavily pumping heart. Strands of damp hair hung limp and heavy on her shoulders. Her cotton shirt was glued to her sweating body, her face was on fire.

What on earth had just happened? What in God's name had she done? To her horror she realised that her urine-soaked underpants were still firmly enclosed in her left hand. She dropped them in disgust.

Wriggling one of her feet out of its dusty thong, she saw what she had suspected: the soft flesh between the first and second toes had been rubbed red raw by the plastic toe post. That was all she needed, blisters between her toes! Gingerly she slipped her foot back into the thong. It was no good thinking about blisters now.

Only then did she bend down and feel with her fingers along the inside of the metal above the front wheel. There were her keys. One car key and one house key. She quickly unhooked them from the small screw that Harry had put there. The slightly bent screw was meant to hold the spare keys, in case she lost the ones she normally used or accidentally locked them in the car. He didn't know she had actually lost those very keys, most likely flinging them from her handbag together with one of the many mysterious items she carried around with her. Anyway, they were irretrievably lost and now she was always using the spare that was meant to be for emergencies only. She unlocked the boot and retrieved one of her shopping bags. Picking up her underpants with the tips of her fingers, she threw them into the bottom of the bag.

Suddenly she stopped. The shopping bags! She had told her neighbour that she was going shopping. Stella Sticky-Beak from next door would be suspicious if she caught Dora coming home without any shopping. And she would see her, no doubt about it. She was always in the front yard singing to her vegetables. If only old Mr Tomlinson could see what she had done to his English lawn. Halved it and made the rest into vegetable beds!

The shopping! Could that be her alibi? She could swear she had been nowhere near the Alum Cliffs track. That she had no idea what had happened up there. Yes, she had gone shopping. Of course she had, like she did every Monday when Harry went for his walk. Her heart was still racing at a million beats a minute, but mixed into its panicked beat was now a tiny glimmer of hope.

Dora stared at the empty bags. She would have to fill them with something. Stella would surely ask questions if she came home from the shops with empty bags. Dora looked around frantically, then rushed across the car park towards the edge of the bush. There, a few small rocks and some gravel for a bit of weight. Handfuls of dead gum leaves for some volume. All at once, Dora was filled with optimism. This could work. She broke some smaller branches with thick fresh leaves in half, then in half again. More volume. The bags were nearly full!

For a moment Dora felt sorry to see her home-made bags, sewn from beautiful cotton and linen material, dirtied and possibly torn by the gravel and jagged branches. But no, she could not allow herself to think about that. She had plenty of material at home and could easily run up some more bags. This was the least of her problems!

What else could she throw into her bags? Maybe the box of tissues and that roll of toilet paper she always kept in the car.

Perfect! And the half-empty packet of wet wipes in the glove box. She would place them right on top just in case anyone should cast their eye over her 'shopping'.

The bags safely stored away in the boot of the car, Dora fell into the driver's seat, exhausted and out of breath. Sweat ran down her back and the inside of her legs. She could feel the blood pumping crazily through her body. Blood! Immediately she thought of Harry. My God, where was he now? Was he still lying on the rocks below the cliff, the water washing over his body? Yes, yes! Where else would he be? He wouldn't have got up and walked away. You couldn't walk away after a fall from that height. If he wasn't dead, he would be seriously injured. All his bones broken, his body smashed up. In all likelihood, blood everywhere. The incoming tide would carry his body out into the ocean. The swirling blood attracting all sorts of sea creatures, maybe even sharks.

Heaven help her, she mustn't think about this!

'Turn on the air conditioning,' she told herself. Within seconds cold air was blowing into her face. Would she be able to get away with this? What if someone, for whatever reason, discovered she had bags full of gravel and leaves and twigs in her car? For example, if she had an accident and the paramedics pulling her out from the wreck saw what she had in the car? They would think she was crazy. She could only hope to be dead if she had a car accident. Because if she wasn't, she would have to answer some very awkward questions.

'No, stop it!' Dora chided herself. 'Your imagination is running away with you. Nothing is going to happen. You will drive home. There won't be an accident.'

She lowered the sun visor and looked into the mirror. God, she looked a mess! Her face was streaked with sweat and dirt, strands of her hair glued down on one side of her face and crazily fanning out on the other as if she had suffered an electric shock. She jumped out of the car again and retrieved the packet of wet wipes.

Checking her reflection in the side window, she carefully wiped down her face and hands. Then she brushed her fingers through her hair and knotted the damp strands into a bun as best as she could. If no one looked too closely she could get away with the way she looked. But what about her legs? Phew, the urine had already dried on her thighs. She probably smelled to high heaven. Luckily, there was still no one else in the car park, so she lifted her long skirt up and wiped her legs down with the last of the wet wipes. Lastly, her dust-covered feet and thongs. What a mess! What a mess!

At least this frantic activity had distracted her mind from Harry. It would serve no purpose to think of him now. She must not think of him! Dora collected the used wet wipes, stuffed them into the shopping bags and knotted the handles of the bags together. That way no one could see what was in them. Just in case she had an accident after all on the way home.

Right, and now she would drive with her 'shopping' down this narrow road, turn into her street and then await whatever might happen next.

*

To her great relief, Stella Sticky-Beak was nowhere to be seen when Dora pulled into her drive. The short ride home and the car's air conditioning had calmed her down considerably. She could nearly convince herself that she had this strange situation under control. Or that the events up on the cliff hadn't happened. Maybe she had just imagined it. And Harry would be home in no time at all.

Dora jumped out of the car and placed the shopping bags onto the drive.

'Hey, Mrs F,' a voice suddenly called out behind her. 'You wanna hand with that?' Startled, Dora swung around and spotted the two young men who lived in the near-derelict house on the other side of the road. As usual, they were sitting on the front veranda with cans of beer in their hands.

'No, thanks,' she yelled back. 'I'll be alright!' That was all she needed, now that she had come this far, for someone to see what was in her shopping bags!

When she got to her front door she turned around again and gave the young men a wave. Then, without stopping, she walked straight through her house, out the back door and into the garden. The large compost bin was located in the furthest corner by the thick hedge. Dora opened the heavy wooden lid and emptied both bags into the bin. Rocks, gravel, twigs and leaves. She didn't care. She would deal with that later. The only thing she fished out of the mess was her underpants. They went straight into the washing machine.

After a shower and a fresh set of clothing she nearly felt her normal self again. A cup of coffee, that's what she needed. And then she would decide what to do next. There was no point deceiving herself into thinking that Harry would soon be coming back from his walk. Because she knew that he wouldn't. So what was the next step in a situation like this? At some point, surely, she would have to go to the police and report Harry as missing. Usually, it took two hours at the most for him to return. So if she gave it, say three or four hours before ringing the police, would that be too soon? Should she wait until the evening? In those crime shows she liked watching on TV, the police were never overly worried about a missing adult. Not for the first few hours, anyway. It was different, of course, when a child went missing. Then they sprang into action straight away. She could tell them that Harry had started behaving like a child more and more over the last however many months. Or she could mention that he possibly suffered from dementia, even though it was undiagnosed. God, it was not easy making a decision.

Of course, there was always the option to ring the police right now and tell them the truth. Tell them what had happened on top of the cliff. Would they understand? Most likely, no one would believe her. There were no witnesses. But the police would certainly spring into action and then detain her as the main suspect. The only suspect.

Having watched a never-ending series of those crime shows, she was also aware that most murders were committed by family members. She would be questioned and questioned again to describe how events had unfolded that morning, until she got herself into such a muddle she forgot what she was saying. Would she need a lawyer? She didn't know any lawyers.

With her hand shading her eyes, Dora rested on the couch. A full cup of coffee sat untouched on the table next to her. What on earth had she gotten herself into? This needed to be thought through very carefully, very carefully indeed. Except that her thoughts were zip-zapping through her mind like out-of-control laser beams. Her running along the track like crazy, the heat, their argument, and Harry, oh God, Harry! And she had wet herself. It was unthinkable that something so embarrassing could happen to her.

She sat up abruptly, as if stung by one of her sharp sewing pins. Her clothes were still lying on the bedroom floor! She leapt up off the couch. Quickly gathering her dirty skirt and the sweaty top, she threw them into the washing machine to join those unspeakable underpants. If Harry had seen this years ago he would have had a fit. Turning the machine on for only three items of clothing!

'What a waste of water and power!' he would have complained. But then he had started doing it himself. Harry, who had never used a washing machine in his life, had suddenly started washing a few items of clothing. Once he had set the water level on high for a couple of handkerchiefs. And then that business washing his favourite pillow in the machine! If that hadn't been a sign of a spongy mind, then she didn't know! Well, she hadn't known at the time. There were so many things Harry had done that should have stopped her in her tracks and made her think. But they hadn't.

But no, she couldn't worry about that now. She had much more important things to concentrate on. And Harry wasn't there to notice anything anyway. All things considered, it was a relief that he couldn't see what was going on.

Right at that moment she decided not to call the police. As far as she was concerned, Harry was out for his walk and she, Dora, had just come back from the shops. With two heavy shopping bags filled to the brim. She would just have to wait and see what would happen from here on.

Back on the couch, and after a few sips of lukewarm coffee, Dora felt a tiny little bit better. Even her feet didn't hurt that much anymore. The antiseptic ointment she had smeared between her toes seemed to help. With a bit of luck she wouldn't get any blisters. She closed her eyes and thought about one of the first times she and Harry had gone on that Alum Cliffs track.

*

A long time ago, when they were just married, Harry had taken her for a walk up along the cliffs, some of the highest in Tasmania, to show her this beautiful, wild area. He had pointed out the many different trees to her, but later she only remembered the coastal blue gums and the silver banksias. The place she had found most enchanting had been the dark, cool fern gully they had descended into. Man ferns lined the path, and at the lowest point a rickety old timber bridge led across a tinkling brook.

Climbing up to the top of the cliffs again, Dora had recalled an article about the geology of Tasmania she'd recently read. According to the article, nowhere else in Australia was there such a preponderance of dolerite. Tasmania was a dolerite island, it stated. Dora loved the solidity and density of that rock. As if nothing could move it.

She had pointed to the cliffs and said with a proud smile, 'Dolerite!'

But Harry had shaken his head and with a slight trace of sharpness in his voice said, 'No, not here. This is Permian mudstone, 250 million years old.'

Mudstone. That had sounded much more crumbly than dolerite. So maybe not that solid and immovable after all. A bit disappointing, really, but Dora would not allow that to distract her from the beautiful landscape, and so she kept walking.

In some parts along the Alum Cliffs track were a number of rocky overhangs that had possibly tempted the odd daredevil to climb down towards the water. Quite often trees were growing on those overhangs, desperately clinging to the rocks. Scraggly trees they were, with skeletal, twisty branches and curled-up leaves, starved for water and desperate for some stability. But there were other sections where the cliffs dropped straight into the sea. There were no overhangs or trees that could potentially break someone's fall. It was a sheer, straight drop into the swirling waves.

When they had come across this spot, this one particular spot, Dora had walked right up to the edge and stared down into the water. A bright red fishing boat was bobbing up and down on the waves right below them, a blue and white flag indicating that divers were in the water. Probably looking for crayfish or snatching some abalone in these already depleted waters.

Nevertheless, the image was breathtaking. All around them, gum trees were gently swaying and whispering in the breeze. The sky was a sparkling blue, the water a mixture of emerald and cobalt. The red fishing boat way down below in the water completed the picture.

She had felt elated and happy. Her eyes shining, she had turned around to Harry and said, 'If ever I wanted to commit suicide this is where I would do it. This would take me straight to heaven.' She had laughed and kissed him. Nothing was further from her mind than killing herself. Her life had only just started. She had just finished her course at the technical college and started working in her own business. Her own sewing business! And she was a little bit in love with Harry. Or so she had thought then. It had taken quite a number of years to accept that she had fooled herself about that one.

Ever since that first walk they had called this particular place the 'suicide spot', and often they would stop there, admire the view and have a bite to eat. Sometime in the past the council had put a wooden bench there, as if to invite a possible suicidal person to sit down and have another think before making the jump. For Dora and Harry it just made their tea break more comfortable. She had often thought that the council should have fenced off the top of the cliff to prevent anyone from falling or jumping, but the cliff edge remained unsecured, and the view into the distance unmarred.

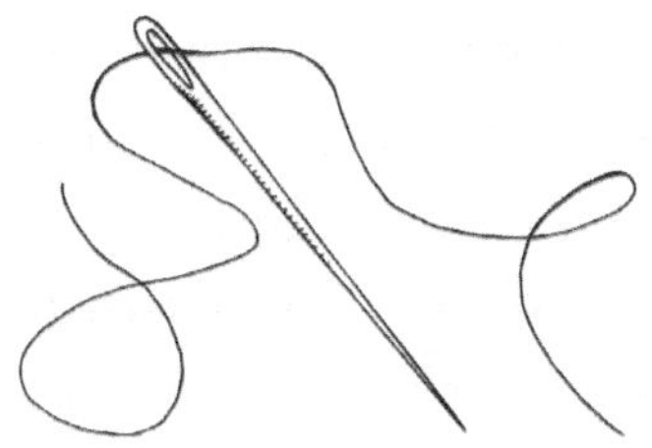

2

26 February 2024

The day of Harry's death, late morning

THE NOISE OF A CAR stopping right outside her house disrupted the quiet of Dora's morning. She jumped off the couch, upsetting the cup on the table and spilling some of the cold coffee over her new tablecloth. Barefoot, she walked into the kitchen to get a better look at the street and the car. Through the lace curtains on the window, she saw that it was a police car. Two officers in uniform got out, took a casual look around, then walked up her drive. Dora clasped her hands over her heart. It was suddenly beating like an out-of-control drum.

A quick look at the kitchen clock stopped her breath. Nearly half past eleven. She must have fallen asleep on the couch. How on earth could she have fallen asleep after everything she had been through that morning? And how, for heaven's sake, did the police get here that quickly? Had they come about Harry? Had someone seen her after all? Suddenly she felt faint. Her legs only just held her upright.

This is it then, Dora thought, her breath shallow, her temples throbbing slightly. I've got to deal with this. The decision has been taken from me. Now I just have to stay calm. *Stay calm!* she urged herself as she opened the front door.

One male and one female officer flashed their badges at Dora, much too fast for her to ascertain whether they were fake or not. You just didn't know these days. But considering her situation – she had half expected them – she had to assume that they were real.

'Mrs Freeman?' the female officer asked. Dora nodded. She felt unreasonably reassured by the fact that the officer seemed to be of Indian background. The officer instantly reminded her of that nice Indian taxi driver she'd had so many years ago. He had been a lovely man.

'I'm Sergeant Sharma and this is my colleague PC Miller,' the officer continued. 'Can we come in, please? We need to talk to you.'

'Yes, yes, of course. What's happened? Is my daughter alright?' Now that was quick thinking! Worrying about her daughter rather than Harry. It was a relief to know that her synapses were firing like little rockets, despite this stressful situation she found herself in.

'Let's sit down first.' All three of them took a chair at the kitchen table. PC Miller kept a watchful eye on Dora but so far had not uttered a single word. It was obvious that the lovely Indian sergeant was in charge. Dora felt herself relax. Everything would be alright. Of course, she knew that her daughter Sophie was alright. Nevertheless, she was glad that this question had popped into her mind at this point in time. Just like a suspect would do on TV to show their ignorance. Or their innocence.

'Mrs Freeman, is your husband's name Harry?' Sergeant Sharma asked.

Dora nodded, hoping that the expression on her face would pass as perplexity with just a touch of anxiety.

'We're sorry to tell you that we found a body we believe to be your husband's.'

Dora let herself slump into the back of the kitchen chair. 'Harry? But he's out walking. Up on the Alum Cliffs track.' Did she have an appropriately incredulous look on her face?

For the first time, PC Miller spoke. 'He was found at the bottom of the cliffs by a man who was fishing in the area.'

'Fishing?' Dora repeated uncomprehending. Now that had her stumped. She couldn't recall seeing any boats nearby. She sat up straight. No, she hadn't seen a boat, but she had heard the engine of what could have been a boat. Dear God! Her heart started beating even faster. Had she been seen up there? Together with Harry? Or on her own? After …?

'The man and his son were in a dinghy. They said they drifted around the rocks and saw a body lying on the rocks just at the edge of the water.'

'Are you sure it's Harry? How do you know it's Harry?' Dora asked. Her eyes were suddenly filling. Was Harry really dead? The enormity of this hit her like a fist in the face.

Sergeant Sharma stood up and after a quick look around, retrieved a box of tissues from the top of the fridge. 'We found his senior's card and ten dollars in the back pocket of his track pants.'

Dora dabbed her eyes, then blew her nose noisily. Yes, Harry always carried that stupid senior's card with him. She could hear him right now saying that you never knew when you might need it. What on earth could you possibly achieve with that card on the Alum Cliffs track? Absolutely nothing!

Dora gave a start and suddenly the tears were flowing. 'Oh God,

Harry!' she sobbed. All at once she felt overwhelmed by everything that had happened that morning on the cliffs and by everything that was happening right now.

PC Miller stood up. 'Mrs Freeman, is there someone we can contact? You said you had a daughter?'

'Yes, our daughter Sophie. She lives in Launceston. Her number is in my purse, over there.' She turned around and pointed at the hallway stand. Several jackets and handbags of different sizes hung off the tree-like branches of the stand.

'Oh, my God, Sophie! She will be devastated!' Dora cried. She watched PC Miller as he handled the different bags. 'Not that one!' Dora called out to him. 'The big leather one over there!' Her favourite handbag, the 'bad conscience' bag. No, she couldn't afford to think about that now. Not with the police in her house.

Flustered, Dora turned back to Sergeant Sharma. 'Sophie and her dad were close. He taught her everything. Everything to do with mathematics. He had such a head for numbers! Sophie was ahead of everyone in her class. Right through her primary school years and high school.' Dora blew her nose again. Was she rambling? 'Do you know the value of each of the angles in a hexagon?' she asked PC Miller as he approached with her handbag. She fixed him with her swollen eyes, waiting for an answer.

Perplexed, PC Miller exchanged a quick glance with his sergeant. Both shook their heads.

'I thought so,' Dora exclaimed, then gave a sniffle. 'Hardly anyone knows. But Sophie already knew at the age of ten. Its 120 degrees! You'll remember that forever now!' she sobbed.

'Mrs Freeman, your daughter's phone number, please!' Sergeant Sharma reminded her gently but firmly.

'Yes, yes. Here!' Dora extracted a thin notebook from the side pocket of her purse.

'I'll ring her and inform her,' PC Miller volunteered.

'And Harry's brother, Andrew, and his wife! Their number is in the book, too.' Dora burst out crying again and felt the tension that had been holding her together completely disintegrate. A memory of a silly old science room skeleton falling off its stand at school came to mind. The skeleton had just collapsed into itself. That's how she suddenly felt. So much for the synapses!

In the hallway, Dora could hear PC Miller speaking to her daughter. Very businesslike, but not unfriendly. She could even hear his voice soften a bit towards the end of the call. Just like on TV, she thought as she sniffed into her handkerchief. Very professional, to the point, but not without empathy. She really had to get herself together. Lift that crumpled skeleton up and hang it on its clip again.

'Your daughter will be here in a couple of hours,' PC Miller said on his return to the kitchen. 'I can stay with you until then.'

'No, no, please! I will be perfectly alright. What I mean is, there's nothing you can do here. There's no need to stay. You must have other jobs to go to!' she protested. Oh, God! The thought of the police being in her house for all that time! Surely they had crimes to solve, fining skateboarders riding on the footpath, or chasing speeding cars. Maybe notifying other wives or husbands of a death. No, she did not want them in her house for longer than was absolutely necessary.

Sergeant Sharma regarded her critically. 'Alright,' she finally said. 'But before we go … I'm sorry to have to do this but it's purely routine. Where were you this morning, Mrs Freeman?'

'My husband goes on his walk every Monday morning and I use this time to do the shopping,' Dora answered.

'Every Monday morning? So this was nothing unusual?'

Dora shook her head. 'No, nothing unusual. He's trying to keep fit and he likes looking out for the sea eagles.'

'The sea eagles?' The sergeant looked surprised.

'Yes. He loves them. All the raptors he loves. The hawks, the wedge-tailed eagles, but most of all the sea eagles. They come every springtime, a pair of them. We see them flying over our house sometimes. But their nest must be somewhere near the cliffs.'

'So your husband goes up the cliffs for a walk, trying to find the nest?'

'Yes, they sometimes nest on cliffs, or in the forks of large trees. But it has to be near the water, I think. He's never found a nest, though.' Talking about sea eagles was helpful. Dora sat up straighter in her chair.

PC Miller had pulled out a small writing pad and was taking notes. 'Back to you, Mrs Freeman,' he said. It was apparent he was not interested in a lesson on sea eagles. 'So you went shopping?'

'Yes, I went to the shops.' Dora gave another little sniffle. There, she'd done it now. No going back. She'd just missed her last chance to tell the truth. Her stomach dropped just a little bit.

'Which shop did you go to?'

'First I went to the fruit and vegetable place near the shopping centre, here in town. Then the wholefood shop. I always get our nuts and grains from there, even though it is a bit more expensive.' She really had to stop rambling. 'After that I went to the super-market for a few bits and pieces.' Dora was praying they would not ask her for the sales dockets from the shops. Or for her credit card. Did they have a way of instantly checking whether she had used her credit card? Surely, they could just ring her bank. And what about CCTV cameras? Nearly every shop had them now. The police could easily look through the tapes of those cameras and check whether she had been to any of the shops. Anyway, she would have done all of that if she'd been a policewoman. Evidence, it was called. Most important evidence. But, to her relief they didn't mention it. She breathed a bit easier.

'Did anyone see you?'

Dora shook her head. 'Obviously there were lots of other people there, but no one I knew.'

'So no one saw you?' Sergeant Sharma asked, taking over the questioning again.

'No. Yes! I mean, not in the shops but Mrs Fulton from next door saw me leave and the two young men opposite …' Dora vaguely pointed towards her front door. 'They saw me come home.'

'Okay, thank you. We'll go and have a word with them.' Sergeant Sharma stood up. 'We have to do our job,' she added apologetically. Both relief and dread flooded through Dora as she saw the police to the front door. For the time being they were gone, thank goodness. But they were sure to return. What was going to happen then? Surely she was not that easily let off the hook.

*

Only a couple of hours later, Dora heard Andrew's car pull up in her driveway.

'Dora,' Andrew said and hugged her. Over the years he had become a man of few words but just hearing him say her name made Dora burst into tears again. She left a few wet spots on the shoulder of his nice-smelling shirt.

'Dora, I'm so sorry,' Leah said, hugging her too. It was a surprisingly firm embrace for such a fragile-looking woman.

'What on earth happened?' Andrew asked, bewildered. 'The police rang but they only told us Harry passed away today. An accident, they said. I can't believe it!'

Dora sniffled and blew her nose. 'Yes, he did. He did pass away! He fell off the Alum Cliffs this morning. Oh, Andrew,' she sobbed. 'Someone found him in the water. I don't know any more than that.' She sank into the couch. By lying to the police, she had set something in motion that could easily veer out of control. And now she had to continue with this lie, looking her brother-in-law and his wife in the eye and spinning them a story she had not at all thought through. How easy it would be to say the wrong thing and get caught out. What if she accidentally mentioned that she had been up there on the cliff looking for Harry?

It would be the wisest thing to continue pretending she didn't know anything more than the police had told her. Her mind was befuddled by the visit of the police and the mess she had got herself into. She had to get her thoughts sorted and get the story into a clear and believable sequence. For example, when exactly Harry had left the house to go for his walk. And when exactly she had left to go shopping and at what time she had returned.

'I'm so sorry, but I don't know any more.' Dora blinked, willing her face not to give away the truth. It was cruel to withhold the little bit she could possibly tell Andrew about Harry's death. People had a right to know why and how someone close to them had died.

Avoiding his eyes, Dora scrunched up her soggy handkerchief. 'Sophie is coming later tonight,' she said after a moment's silence. 'He meant everything to her.'

'Would you like us to stay with you until she comes?' Leah asked. Sitting next to Dora, she put her arm around her. 'I mean we could even stay the night.'

'No, no. That won't be necessary. No, thank you for offering. Unless you absolutely want to.' She turned to Andrew in question and scanned his face. For the first time she noticed how pale he was. His eyes were red. He was trying hard not to cry. Dora chided herself for having been so thoughtless and selfish, thinking only of herself and what she had been through that day. She had completely forgotten that with Harry's death, Andrew had lost his only brother.

She moved to get up. 'Would anyone like a drink?' she asked. Leah shook her head. Andrew stopped Dora with one movement of his hand and disappeared into the kitchen. He clearly needed a few minutes to himself.

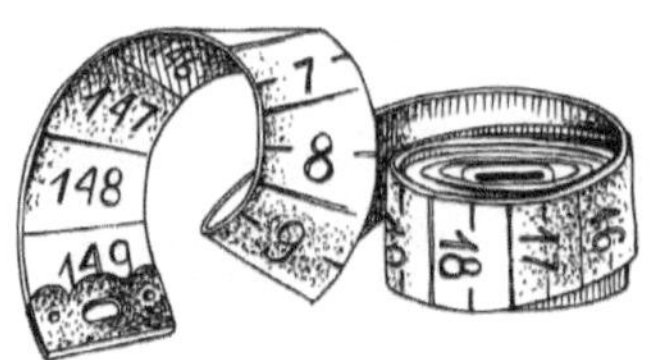

3

26 February 2024

The day of Harry's death, evening

S OPHIE'S ARRIVAL A FEW HOURS later did not start another flood of tears as Dora had initially feared. After saying goodbye to Andrew and Leah she had had some time to compose herself. She had sat silently, staring out into the garden, concentrating on breathing in and out slowly to calm her nerves. Seeing the gum trees sway lightly in the sea breeze always relaxed her. A few small birds, a group of fantails and a couple of robins were flitting from one tree branch to another.

Dora wondered whether the life of a bird was punctuated by more or less difficulty than her own. Certainly birds wouldn't squabble over jackets hanging on kitchen chairs. Or whether one of them was contributing more to the household than the other.

Was it possible for birds to get dementia? She'd never heard of it. But a bird's life was probably harder than hers in other regards. There would be dangers out there for a small bird that she could only guess at.

Maybe it had been the sheer relief that the interview with the police had gone so smoothly that made her start to feel better – the first big hurdle had been overcome. Tick that. Or it could have been the fact that with her daughter's arrival there was someone who needed her now. She did shed a few tears when she opened the door to Sophie, but it was more because Sophie was so distraught; it was immediately obvious that she had been crying all the way down from Launceston. Dora could not help but cry a little bit in sympathy with her.

After a hot drink and a sandwich, both mother and daughter lay on the big bed in Dora and Harry's bedroom, holding hands. Dora and Sophie had never been particularly close. Sophie had always been a daddy's girl ever since he had discovered in her a love for numbers. He had nurtured her mathematical brain in challenging but often surprisingly fun ways. For a man who could be so ruthless with his clients' tax returns and company audits, he was obsessed with finding ways to make number problems enjoyable for Sophie. Sometimes Dora suspected he also used this to side with the daughter against the mother. Measuring dress fabrics, working out arm holes or the exact spacing of sixteen tiny buttons on a Victorian dress that Dora had made obviously didn't hold up in her husband's eyes as a mathematical skill. But then, all of that changed shortly after Sophie's thirteenth birthday. Not that Dora wanted to think about that awful time. Not now.

She turned her head to regard her daughter. Sophie's eyes were closed, her eyelids swollen and her cheeks wet. The thick blond hair Sophie had inherited from Dora was cut into one of those asymmetrical modern styles: shaved on one side, the other side in layers nearly down to her shoulder. Her students would definitely think that she was cool. Dora could see that. No wonder Sophie's maths classes were popular. If anyone looking so cool taught maths then surely maths must be cool, too.

It was clear that her daughter had come straight from work. She was still in a skirt and some fancy top that only young women could wear, her jacket on the floor beside the bed. Dora stared at her daughter's stockings. Black with thousands of sparkly dots woven into them. So unlike her own old maths teacher, Mrs Whatever-her-name-was, who had always dressed in something drab. Drab and boring like her lessons. No wonder Dora had not turned into a maths genius.

'That stupid old bugger,' Dora suddenly heard Sophie murmur, her voice thick with tears. 'To die on us like that! What was he doing on that track all by himself, anyway?'

'That stupid old bugger, your father, always went walking on that track by himself. Regular as clockwork,' Dora replied, slightly piqued that her daughter would use such an expression. Even though, truth be told, she thought exactly the same. He was a stupid old bugger. 'He could have done that walk with his eyes closed. He never once asked me to go with him. I couldn't stop him. You know him. He did what he wanted. Always.'

Dora turned towards the window. The sun was still fairly high in the sky. In mid-summer the sun seemed to be up there all day long, shining down into her garden. And yes, the days were so long now. It started to get light at four thirty in the morning and it wouldn't get really dark until ten at night. Dora loved these long, and sometimes hot days. They were the exact opposite to those short winter days when you got up in the dark, did one round of the house and garden, and before you knew it, it was dark again.

Sulphur-crested cockatoos screeched somewhere nearby. In all likelihood they were sitting in Harry's favourite tree again, that spruce thing whose name she could never remember. Probably spitting pine kernels all over the lawn. Harry hated the cockatoos as much as he loved the sea eagles.

Anyway, for all she cared the two young men across the road could chop that tree down. At least she would not have to argue with Harry over it ever again. From now on she could do whatever she wanted.

Surely, it is only early evening, if that, Dora thought. Good heavens, how can so much happen in such a short amount of time? Only a few hours ago her day had started as it always did, same old, same old … Then, within the blink of an eye, Harry was dead, the police had come knocking on her door and now her daughter, whom she hadn't seen in God knows how long, lay on the bed beside her.

Dora strained to listen to Sophie's breathing. Was she asleep? Sophie's nose was making a funny noise, whistling and snorting. It was probably blocked up from all that crying.

'Sophie,' she said quietly. Something important had just occurred to her. 'You may have to postpone your wedding.'

'Doesn't matter,' Sophie replied without opening her eyes. She took a few forceful breaths to clear her nose. 'We've already changed the date once because of Tom's parents.'

'I didn't know that.' Dora was surprised. 'Why was that?' She lifted her head and looked at her daughter.

'They'd already booked a holiday for exactly the same time. It was easier to change the wedding than the holiday.' Did Dora hear some sarcasm in Sophie's voice? They sounded like difficult people, these soon-to-be parents-in-law.

'Doesn't matter,' Sophie repeated. 'We can change it again.' She sat up suddenly. 'I've completely forgotten to ring Tom!' Then she sank back into the bed amidst another flood of tears. 'Dad would've loved Tom!'

'What makes you think that?' More than anyone else, Dora knew that Harry didn't love people. Not love! He would put up with them. Very occasionally someone even impressed him, not that he would ever admit to that. But love? No. Generally he thought most people were useless or ridiculous.

'I told you Tom is in cyber security, didn't I? You wouldn't think it, but mostly he deals with maths. Numbers, patterns, sequences … you name it. He and Dad would have had a lot in common.'

'Huh,' Dora replied, but she wasn't convinced. Her head sank back into the pillow. She couldn't think of anyone who had much in common with Harry. No, it was rather that she couldn't imagine Harry wanting to have anything in common with useless and ridiculous people.

'Speaking of marriages … just a sec.' Sophie pulled a tissue box towards her and blew her nose. 'Speaking of marriages, you and Dad would have been married forty years this year. That's right, isn't it?'

'God, yes! Forty years and I was only twenty-four. So young! And to think I was in love with Andrew, your Uncle Andrew!' Shocked at herself, Dora stopped talking. Now where had that last sentence come from? It had just flown out of her mouth. She had never intended to share that information. With anyone! Least of all her daughter, who thought her Uncle Andrew was the best thing since mathematics had been invented.

Sophie lifted her head in surprise. 'You were in love with Uncle Andrew? I never knew that!' She rolled over onto her side, her elbow supporting her upper body. Within a nanosecond she had forgotten about ringing her soon-to-be husband, Tom. She blew her nose forcefully and wiped her eyes with a clean tissue. Her tears had stopped flowing. Expectantly, she stared at her mother. 'Come on, tell me about it!' she demanded, her voice still thick. 'What about him? Was he in love with you?'

'Mmh, yes, at least I think so. No, he was. He definitely was,' Dora replied. She had opened a can of worms but so what? Why not tell Sophie everything? Or nearly everything. What did it matter after all these years?

'We were both nineteen, madly in love and wanted to go to Europe together.' That seemed a good-enough abbreviated version.

'Europe? But I thought he went by himself?' Growing up with relatives living close by, Sophie had heard snippets of Uncle Andrew's European trip and how he had met Aunt Leah. But Dora had always avoided mentioning that she was the one who was meant to go with him. So really, she was the one who should have come back married to Andrew. But no, once out of sight, halfway around the world, he had quickly forgotten about her. Out of sight, out of mind, she thought with lingering resentment.

'He went by himself because your grandmother, my mother, wouldn't allow me to go.'

'Wow!'

Dora could see that Sophie was probably considering for the first time that her mother had had a previous life as a young woman, full of idealism and unfulfillable dreams. *I wasn't always old and married to your father, you know*, she wanted to say.

'Come on, tell me!' Sophie repeated with more urgency. Dora would tell her. Just for a few minutes it would be good to distract Sophie from her father's death.

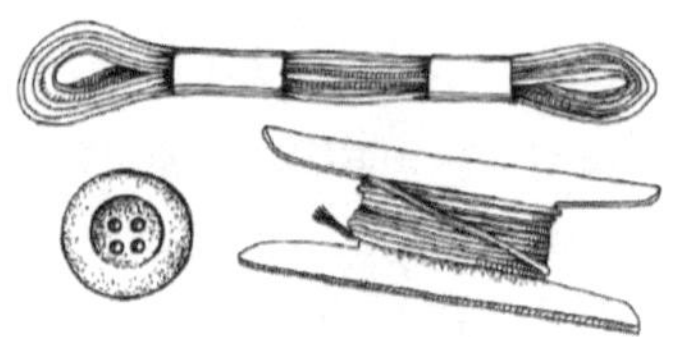

4

Early March 1979

Dora's mother puts her foot down

'YOU ARE NOT GOING!' PRONOUNCING every word slowly and in an infuriatingly exacting manner, as if she were rehearsing a stage play, Dora's mother was standing by the open bedroom door, her hands on her hips. 'You have just started your second year at the university and you've got no money!'

Dora lay sprawled on her bed, surrounded by textbooks and bunches of scrunched up sheets of paper. She was pressing a teddy bear against her chest, shooting killer looks at her mother.

'You'd better finish your degree first before you go gallivanting around the world! Or do you want to end up like me?' Mrs Hanson swung around and pointed at the three wash baskets behind her.

They were full of clothing belonging to other people, patiently waiting to be ironed.

Exasperated, Dora closed her eyes. How often had she heard that one? Yes, her mother worked in a café all day long and took in other people's ironing to make ends meet. And no, that was not what Dora wanted for herself. But her first year at university had not been as thrilling as she had expected. Most of her lecturers were as old as her parents, or even older. Their lectures were as boring and tedious as a basket full of ironing. And having to write essays all the time was no better than the homework she had struggled with when she was doing matric.

Ok, it was fun hanging around the Refectory, the university club, chatting to the other students, laughing and feeling intellectual. But that was really only a feeling and nothing more. Going to all the parties on the weekends was what she enjoyed the best. Drinking, dancing, meeting new people. She loved it. Dora was a great dancer and she had even had a few dances with Harry, Andrew's brother. He was one of the older students, already in his last year of accounting. Andrew, on the other hand, had never gone with her to these parties. 'But you're my boyfriend,' she had begged. 'Not my thing,' was always his response. Dora did feel a bit resentful about that. It wouldn't have killed him to come just once or twice to have a dance with her. But she did understand that he probably felt awkward among all those university students, considering he himself had never set a foot in that institution.

And now Andrew was about to go to Europe for a year and Dora was dead set on going with him. If it weren't for her mother. And the money.

'Finish your degree first.' Mrs Hanson voice cut through Dora's thoughts. 'And then you can do whatever you like.'

'I'm nineteen!' Dora yelled. She sat up abruptly, causing some of her books to crash to the floor. 'I can do what I like right now!'

'Good luck then!' Mrs Hanson turned around to leave just as her younger daughter Freda squeezed past her into Dora's room. 'Do as you please!' She picked up one basket of ironing while pushing another one with her foot into the lounge room, heading for the ironing board. Defiantly, Dora stuck her tongue out at her mother's back, but those sarcastic last words had stung.

'Sis, darling …' Freda moved towards Dora's bed holding up a pair of jeans. 'Look at these! They are much too wide, totally old-fashioned. Can you please, please do the seams for me? All the way from top to bottom? I want them super tight. Bell bottoms are so out of fashion!' She flopped onto the bed and passed the jeans to Dora.

'No problem!' Dora jumped up, grateful for the distraction, and dislodged the loose sheets of paper on her bed. With a gentle rustling of relief the sheets slid onto the floor to join the textbooks. 'Put them on so I can pin them!' For the time being, the argument with her mother was forgotten. This was what she loved, stitching and sewing and undoing and sewing again. She had changed nearly all of Freda's and her own worn-out clothes to make them fashionable and like new. This was what made her heart beat faster, not boring lectures and writing essays on impossible topics.

While Freda was getting into her jeans, Dora picked up some of the papers that had ended up on the floor. Two essays were due soon. Too soon as far as she was concerned. With a frown she read the title of the history essay: 'Post WWII – The pros and cons of establishing an independent Jewish state in Australia.' She had no idea that something like that had ever even been discussed, here or overseas. In all likelihood she'd missed that lecture. Or she'd been dreaming about something, probably Andrew, when the old professor was droning on in his sleep-inducing voice.

In despair, she threw the paper onto the floor again and read the other essay topic: 'Human beings are insignificant and there is no purpose to their existence. Discuss in view of the extracts below by Nietzsche, Kierkegaard and Jacobi.' This one was for her philosophy course on existential nihilism. Dora already knew without even glancing at those extracts that she wouldn't understand a word.

'Oh God,' she groaned, pulling a face. 'I'm just going to write 'NOTHING'. That should say it all, don't you think?' she addressed Freda. 'That fits with nihilism. That's one thing I've learned!' But Freda ignored her and, with the patience of a saint, waited for Dora to start pinning the seams of her jeans.

As soon as Dora knelt in front of her sister, a box of pins at the ready, she forgot about all the things that annoyed and upset her. Her mother's sarcasm, her university courses, not really knowing where she was going in her life. Because this was where the magic started for her. She put her heart and soul into every seam and every stitch. She even forgot about Andrew and that he would probably be going to Europe without her.

With a critical look she examined the pinned seams. Then she ordered Freda to take the jeans off so that she could get to work on them with her sewing machine. She'd had this machine since her thirteenth birthday, first making simple drawstring pyjama bottoms for everyone in the family, whether they wanted them or not. Then, over the years she'd advanced to skirts, then bright summer dresses and crazy costumes for dress-up parties. It wasn't long before her friends were asking her to do some sewing for them. Dora took up skirts for girls whose mothers refused to do it for them. She made fashionable vests for a number of boys in her school. Out of leftover fabrics, she made tiny pants and dresses suitable for dolls and teddy bears.

Over the years her sewing enterprise earned her a considerable amount of extra pocket-money. Unfortunately, money always flowed through her fingers like water. And now she didn't have enough to go to Europe with Andrew.

*

'Wow!' For some strange reason this seemed to be the only exclamation of surprise her otherwise clever daughter knew. 'And then what? He went to Europe and came back with Aunt Leah! How did you feel about that?'

Dora sat up. 'We've been lying here for ages. Aren't you hungry, or thirsty?' she asked her daughter. Right at that very moment she didn't want to talk about the feelings she had had for Andrew all those years ago. As a matter of fact, those feelings she had thought would be there for eternity, had changed so much over the years. She could hardly remember the electric jolts anymore that she had felt, just looking at him. The electric jolts had dulled, faded and then one day disappeared completely. Probably because Andrew had become her brother-in-law and she saw him that often, her feelings towards him had lost their meaning. Just like a song that used to make you cry. The more often you heard it, the more it lost its power over you, until you couldn't remember anymore the heavy meaning it had once carried.

These days she regarded Andrew as more of a very good friend. Someone she'd once been in love with. An innocent, all-encompassing, totally trusting, you'll-never-disappoint-me kind of love that only teenagers could experience. Well, so much for that. That was definitely gone.

That night on Bruny Island had been a slip-up, an aberration. Dear God, she was glad that nothing had actually happened that night. Another thing she didn't want to think of. Not now. She suddenly realised that there were lots of things she didn't want to think about.

30

'Hungry no, thirsty yes. What have you got?' Sophie disrupted her slightly bitter musings.

'Coffee, tea, a bit of orange juice. Or I could make us a hot chocolate.' She glanced at Sophie, hoping that a hot chocolate didn't sound too childish. Dora herself was quite partial to hot chocolate even though Harry was convinced it made her put on weight. Too right! It was definitely the hot chocolate that had added the extra few kilos.

To her surprise, Sophie nodded. 'Sounds good. And I could also do with a glass of red, maybe. Have you got any?' Of course Dora had wine.

Sitting on the couch, each with a mug of hot chocolate and a glass of wine, Dora noticed that Sophie had taken off her sparkly stockings and replaced her work skirt with an old pair of Dora's shorts. 'Hope you don't mind, Mum,' Sophie said pointing at the shorts. Dora shook her head.

Sophie tucked one of her legs under her and took a long sip of red wine. 'A bit strange, hot chocolate together with wine! A weird combination and the perfect recipe for a migraine.'

Despite herself, Dora had to smile. So Sophie did remember what Dora had told her years ago. One night, her teenage daughter had watched Harry drink a glass of wine while Dora had a hot chocolate. 'Have you ever had the two together?' Sophie had asked. 'Sort of all mixed up in one cup?' A typically silly suggestion only a teenager could come up with. And Dora had pointed at the wine and the hot chocolate and said, 'You try it! It would be a perfect recipe for a migraine.' Not that she knew whether that was actually true.

'You could mix them in together!' Dora said now, letting her daughter know that she, too, had not forgotten. It was lovely to smile at each other and remember those small, shared moments from the past.

'So Mum, to get back to what I asked you before … What was it like for you when Uncle Andrew came back from Europe a married man? And you really didn't have a clue the whole time?'

'No, of course not. It was a bit different in those days, you know. Phone calls cost an arm and a leg and letters took weeks and weeks to get there. I had only a very vague idea where he was or what he was doing. There was no internet, remember?'

'So, tell me.'

It was hard to resist her daughter's persistence. And it made her glad that Sophie suddenly showed an interest in her mother's life.

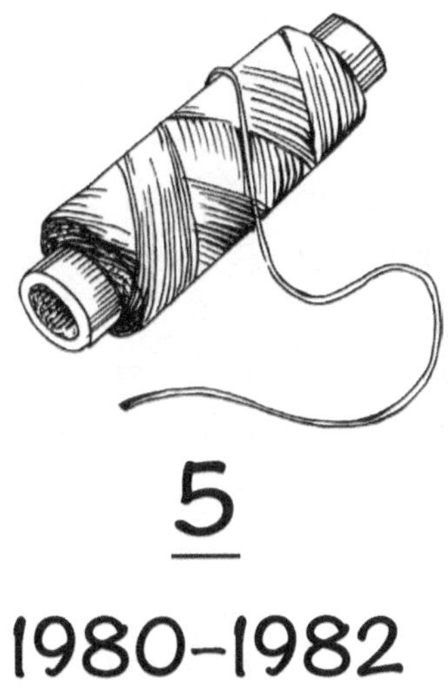

5

1980-1982

Harry makes a serious appearance in Dora's life

I T WAS MAINLY ANDREW'S OLDER brother Harry who kept Dora up to date about Andrew's whereabouts. Even though it was exorbitantly expensive, Andrew rang up his parents once in a while to tell them he was alive and well. And she had to admit that she hung around Harry more than usual in order to be the first one – after the family, of course – to find out what Andrew was up to. She just couldn't wait for him to return from Europe.

The day she saw Andrew walk up the short main street in Cygnet just as she left the bakery, her heart fluttered like an excited New Holland honeyeater. She nearly dropped the loaf of bread in her eagerness to run up to him. Only to stop dead when she became aware that there was a girl by Andrew's side. Was it intuition or the sheepish look on his face that told Dora straight away that this girl was not just an acquaintance?

Instead of folding her, Dora, into his arms – an event she had so long envisaged – he actually took a step back and then stiffly introduced this girl as his wife. His wife! It took Dora a moment to grasp the fact that he wasn't speaking a foreign language. For God's sake, he was only just twenty and he was married? No one got married anymore! It was a conservative notion that belonged to her parents' generation, the era of the Stone Age, not hers, the young, modern, hip era!

Dumbstruck, her eyes jumped from Andrew to this wife-girl and back again. Then the blood shot into her face. What a fool she'd made of herself! She had been so stupid to expect that he would come back to her, unchanged after all those exotic experiences that she could only guess at. How could she have been so naive to think that they could pick up their relationship as if those intervening months hadn't existed? If they'd ever had a relationship. She suddenly doubted that holding hands and stealing a kiss here and there constituted a relationship. What a baby she was! Humiliated, Dora ran off home and cried for a week.

When she came out of her stupor of pain she realised that she was still able to breathe and that her heart was still beating. It hurt, but it was beating. Something came to her mind that she had read not too long ago. Something about pain not being about getting a thrashing or cutting your foot on glass and getting it stitched up. The author of the book ... who was it again? Dora was wracking her brain trying to remember his name. Someone called José Mauro de ... something. He had written that pain was when your heart hurt so badly you couldn't even talk about it. When you lost all energy and strength and the will to even lift your head off the pillow. When all you could do was cry and when all that was left were tears.

José Mauro de Vasconcelos! That's who it was. What a name! Her brain was still working. José Mauro de Vasconcelos, Brazilian writer, 1920–1984. Thanks to her English teacher at high school, Mrs Jones, Dora had developed a habit of always looking up the origins and the dates of an author whose book she was reading. It put the novel into a historical context, Mrs Jones had said. Very helpful indeed!

She was convinced that what he'd written about pain and grief was all about her, Dora. He understood. Unlike Andrew, who seemed completely oblivious to how much he'd hurt her. Books could be such a consolation.

*

But after a while, Harry became her friend. Before, his only purpose had been to keep her informed on Andrew's whereabouts. Then one day, without her realising, he was suddenly a solid presence in her life, even though she did not need or want his services as a messenger anymore. Everyone in Cygnet, except for Dora, was aware that Harry was making a big effort with her. It was touching how attentive he was. On the weekends he took her to the local milk bar on the main road. Mostly they were on their own, sometimes Andrew and Leah joined them. Dora had to try hard not to show how awkward she felt around those two. She preferred not to see too much of them. After a milkshake, Harry and Dora would sometimes go for a walk along the river. At other times, Harry took her for a drive in his new car. He earned good money in the accountancy firm in Hobart and had saved up enough to buy himself a brand-new Audi 100. In a small town like Cygnet where utility trucks and rusty old Holdens were the norm, it was impossible to ignore this car. Bright orange and polished to a blinding shine, it made everyone turn their head, no matter whether it was zipping along the main road or parked outside the milk bar. Many an eyebrow and the odd middle finger were raised in its wake. Speculation ran wild in the town as to where on earth Harry had bought this car. Nobody had ever seen anything like it in any of the showrooms in the city. But, as Harry was a man who liked to keep a secret, they had to keep guessing.

*

It was even less impossible, in a place where everyone knew everyone else's movements at any time of the day, not to notice that Harry and Dora were suddenly walking along the river hand in hand. Or that early one morning she was sitting next to him in this orange rocket of a car on the way to the city. Or that from then on she was sitting next to him in the car *every* morning! There was no need to speculate where they were going together. In a small place like Cygnet, the fact that he took Dora to her sewing classes at a technical college in Hobart was accepted without question.

Dora herself sometimes wondered how she had suddenly become Harry's girlfriend. It seemed to have happened without her realising. Had she that quickly overcome her heartbreak over losing Andrew to some English girl? When she had waited for him for so long and then cried her eyes and her soul out when he returned from Europe with a wife? A wife, for crying out loud!

Even more intriguing was the question of why Harry had chosen her, over all the other girls in their small town. They were pretty enough, and they were certainly willing to be considered by him. Yet, he showed no interest in them. At least not as far as Dora could tell. Not that she knew what Harry was up to every minute of the day.

And what about the successful, beautiful girls he surely must be running into in the city? He could have had his pick of these worldly, sophisticated young ladies. After all, he had that Tom Cruise look about him. They had just seen 'Endless Love', a romantic drama, and Dora had loved the young Tom Cruise. That slightly chiselled face that nevertheless had some softness about it that all the girls seemed to swoon over. A face that said, 'Trust me, everything will be fine.' Except that Harry was taller than Tom Cruise, which was a bonus, and maybe he was even more charming and more caring than this smooth actor. Obviously Dora didn't know what Tom Cruise was actually like, but she had experienced Harry's charm and deference towards her. It was very pleasant to be surrounded by all that attention.

And on top of that – how could it be otherwise? – Harry was a football player. He was fit and strong, 'a packet of muscles', Dora's friend Cindy reckoned. It was not important at all that Dora couldn't stand football. That small fact could easily be overlooked. As a matter of fact, a type of sport she liked hadn't been invented yet. But she didn't mention that. What she did mention was that she liked his voice. It was strong and clear, the voice of a man who knew what he wanted and who could make himself understood. It appealed to her because she often struggled to make herself understood. Unfortunately, she discovered much too late that this voice did not lend itself to whispers of seductive nonsense.

*

So why was Harry attracted to her? What could she offer that was desirable? She had the natural blond hair and light skin colouring from her Swedish heritage, and a pretty face, she knew that. Her parents and even her sister Freda had always called her their 'little doll'. People insisted that she was pretty, but hopefully it was her personality, rather than her looks that made her attractive to Harry. She was an amenable kind of person, someone who liked to have fun and disliked arguments. She would rather give in than have a big fight on her hands. Maybe Harry could sense that in her.

Most likely it was a combination of her looks and her personality. Surely it couldn't be her intellectual powers. After all, she had thrown in her university course because she couldn't handle it. She couldn't handle the old professors, the boring topics, the time she was wasting being unproductive. Instead she was taking courses in dressmaking and fashion design. Was that something an accountant, a man with brains and ambition, would find irresistible? It certainly didn't seem to worry him that she had chosen a rather doubtful career. If you could call it a career.

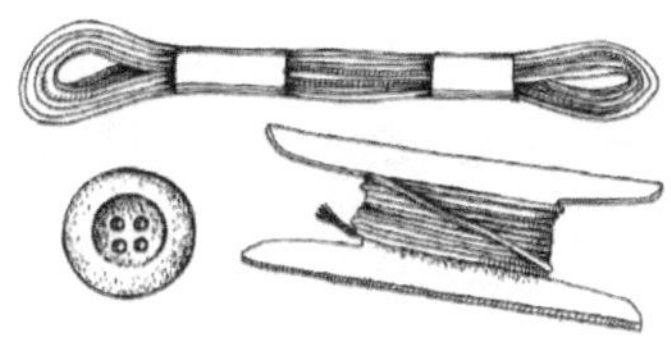

6

26 February 2024

The day of Harry's death, late evening

'**M**UM, I JUST CAN'T BELIEVE you and Dad were driving around in that car! And going to milk bars!' Sophie exclaimed. 'It sounds so … so … so sixties,' she finally finished her sentence. 'You know how in the sixties they all drove around in their cars just for fun. I've seen it in the movies. Elbows hanging out of the side window, whistling at the girls!'

'Well, it was a bit like that,' Dora nodded. 'You're thinking of American movies from the sixties and seventies. We were probably lagging a few years behind. So it was still going on here in the early eighties.'

'Did you have sex with him?' Sophie and Dora had never talked about sex. Not since Dora had explained love and sex to Sophie when she was a child. Dora's stomach contracted a little with surprise to hear that question coming from her daughter.

'Heavens, no!' she replied with a hint of embarrassment. 'I think I was a bit backward about it all. That whole feminism and "my body belongs to me" and "I have sex with anyone I like" business somehow totally passed me by,' Dora explained. Well, there was no denying that she had been completely naive. Backward, indeed! Some of her more adventurous school friends could have confirmed that. Her old friend Cindy certainly would have some stories to tell.

'Don't tell me you thought you had to get married first!' Sophie's eyes widened with incredulity.

'Well, yes, maybe. I can't quite remember, to be honest. That's just the way it happened.'

'I assume Dad fell on his knees when he asked you to marry him?' Sophie spread her arms out wide. 'Tada!'

'Not exactly,' Dora sighed. 'He never actually asked me. But I didn't realise that until many years later.' After a pause she added, 'But somehow that wasn't important. We got married and that's all there is to it.'

Sophie stared at her mother, her forehead knitted. 'Let me just come back to something here,' she said. The concentrated expression on her face told Dora that Sophie's brain was whirring like the insides of a computer, analysing something, working on the additions and subtractions of her mother's love life.

'You were in love with Uncle Andrew, right?' She didn't wait for Dora to answer. 'But basically you just went off and married the brother of the guy you were in love with, didn't you?' Sophie looked stunned. 'The whole thing seems a bit weird to me! Sounds like an act of revenge. Were you even in love with Dad?'

'No, I didn't just go and marry your dad because I had been jilted by his brother, for God's sake!' Sophie's comments had stung a bit. Probably because she was right. Because she was exactly right. Andrew had abandoned her. It was just that the whole marriage thing did not happen straight away. And somehow it had felt like the right thing to do at the time.

'Remember, there were four years in between. Four years between Uncle Andrew coming back with Aunt Leah and your dad and I getting married,' she clarified. 'We got to know and like each other during that time, and only got married when I was twenty-four. At that age, four years feels like a lifetime. It's only when you're looking back decades later that it seems things happened quickly.'

Sophie nodded but there was doubt in her eyes. She emptied her wine glass in one gulp. 'You say "like" each other, so were you in love with him? Did you actually want to marry Dad?' With a louder than necessary bang she placed the glass back on the table. There was a challenge in that bang that made the table quiver with anticipation.

'Of course I was in love with him. I was much more mature at that stage. Uncle Andrew and I ... it had just been a crush, nothing serious.' Dora took a careful sip of her hot chocolate. She should have put more sugar in.

No, it had not been a crush. She had been seriously in love with Andrew. For many, many years. Many years. Forever. But she had succumbed to Harry's charm and attention. She had been so flattered that he had chosen her over all the other girls. So she had been a little bit in love with him because of that.

*

Again and again, after all these years, Dora asked herself what Harry saw in her. She had a pretty face, there was no denying it, but it was hard to believe she was the daughter of a tall, slim Swedish woman. Dora was short with a full figure, rather than

41

being trim and willowy. Only her hair, long and blond, attested to her Swedish background.

And because she had thrown in her university course, she felt intellectually inferior to him. Harry, on the other hand, knew all there was to know about everyone and everything. After all, he did finish his university degree. And in his work he came across all sorts of interesting people. Men and women who ran companies, who had invented things, who had amassed fortunes in real estate and businesses and whatever else. Clever people who he talked to and who widened his outlook on life and the endless possibilities it offered. Whereas she, Dora, was ensconced in her sewing room, at home, alone. There were no earth-shattering intellectual exchanges with anyone. Unlike Harry, she did not even read the daily newspaper. Only through the news reports on TV did she even know what was going on outside her 'habitat'.

Only a short time into her marriage did she notice how Harry had started to lecture her on current affairs or philosophical issues or whatever interested him at that particular moment. Her general knowledge seemed flawed and her contributions to discussions or arguments juvenile and badly thought out. At least that's what she seemed to glean from his disappointed facial expressions.

And then there was the financial aspect of their relationship. She knew she would not be able to contribute much financially as a dressmaker. If anything at all. Harry earned plenty of money, more than enough for the two of them. And as he had said all those years ago in his flashy orange car, it didn't seem to worry him that he would be the main provider. It was his money that bought their beautiful house near the beach in Kingston, their two cars and the very occasional holiday. But generally he preferred to spend his holidays at home and have Dora fuss over him. So overall, she should be pleased he indulged her passion for dressmaking.

What then was Dora's contribution to this marriage? Sometimes she wondered whether he needed someone who would look up to him and admire him. Someone pliable, not very worldly, someone he could steer and shape? She asked herself whether other potential girlfriends had seen something in his character that made them wary of him.

And what about Dora herself? Had she only married him because he was the next best thing to Andrew? Or because she could see how much Harry could offer a woman? Was she really that selfish? Or was it true that she wanted to get her own back on Andrew?

There, I don't need you. I can do very well for myself. Was that what she was saying? Had she wanted to show Andrew and his *wife* that she was just as capable of doing what they had been doing? Was Sophie right in suspecting it had been revenge after all? An 'eye for an eye' sort of thing?

*

Right from the beginning of their marriage Dora suspected she had been overthinking this 'love and relationship' business. She was not unhappy. She liked Harry, she liked his family. It was just not what she had always imagined. She certainly had not imagined there would be all these little niggly things that tended to upset her. Harry's jacket for example. Why would he always hang it over a kitchen chair when he came home from work? Why not hang it on the clothes stand in the hallway which he passed on the way in? God, it was annoying! No amount of telling him had achieved anything. In the end there was only one thing to it and that was for *her* to put the jacket away and to get on with life as it was.

Not that she would ever say any of that to Sophie. Sophie wanted to hear that she, Dora, had loved her dad and that's what she would tell her.

'Of course, I loved your dad,' Dora said. 'He loved you and he loved me and he was a generous man.' She reached for her glass of wine and emptied it in one big gulp. 'Enough of this. I need a rest.' She stood up and headed for her bedroom. At the door she looked back at her daughter. She was glad she hadn't told her everything.

'I loved your dad!' But there was more than one occasion when she could have killed him. And now he was dead.

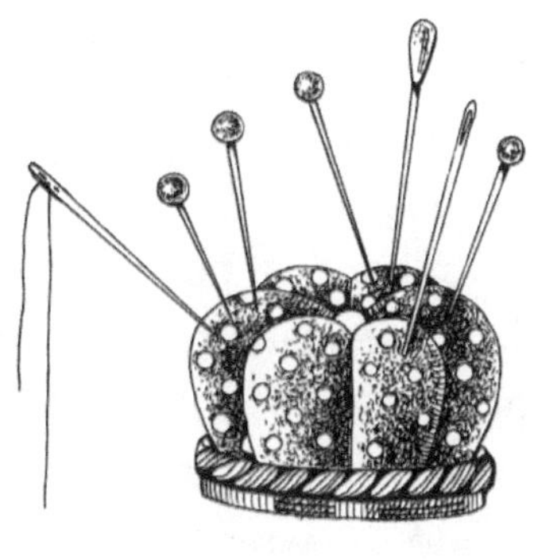

7

August 1983

Harry has a proposition

ONE RAINY AFTERNOON HARRY AND Dora were sitting in his Audi by the banks of the Huon River. Grey clouds hung heavily over the apple orchards and the fields. The other side of the river was only just visible in the mist. Dora was firmly sucking on a straw, slurping the last drops of her strawberry milkshake out of the bottom of the cardboard cup, when Harry turned to face her.

'If I were to get married,' he said slowly. 'I would state my expectations well before asking someone to marry me.'

Dora's straw fell from her lips into the cup. 'Expectations?' she repeated obtusely. Was Harry thinking of getting married? What was he talking about?

'I think one needs to set some parameters when one thinks about getting married,' he answered.

Parameters! And 'one'! Did he think he was the King of England? Dora had noticed before that sometimes he did sound a bit pompous. She didn't like the impersonal 'one' very much. Who did that 'one' apply to? Why not say that he was talking about himself? But she was a tolerant kind of girl. To gain some time and to figure out a reply she fumbled in her coat pocket and pulled out a bar of chocolate. Good God, her hands were shaking!

'Would you like some?'

'Do you always carry chocolate around with you?' Harry grinned and took it off her to undo the wrapper. A big piece of chocolate disappeared into his mouth.

Dora shook her head. 'No, very rarely actually.' Somehow this bar of chocolate had found its way into her pocket while she had been waiting for Harry to pay for the milkshakes. If you took four bars of chocolate into your hand, as if to figure out which you would like best and then only put three back onto the shelf … well, it was no surprise then that one bar might end up in your pocket.

It was a 'system' she had tried once or twice before. It worked perfectly and she had never been caught. *One gets a bit of a thrill out of it*, she thought, silently mocking Harry's pompousness.

Harry swallowed his chocolate, took a sip of his milkshake and faced Dora. 'So, what do you think?'

'About what?'

'Parameters! Expectations! You know, things you would want to happen in a marriage and others you wouldn't want to happen,' Harry explained slightly impatiently.

'Yes, no, of course not,' Dora stammered. It seemed obvious to her that there were certain rules in a marriage one – one! – had to adhere to and that there were behaviours that were either acceptable or unacceptable. Did all of that need to be stated? Stated in writing with both parties signing off against those rules? She crunched up her cardboard cup and put it on the floor next to her feet.

'Don't do that!' Harry reproached her. He turned around and fished a paper bag from the back seat. 'Here, put your cup in that. I don't want the last few drops on the carpet. You can never get milk stains out and they stink to high heaven.' He took the bag with the cup off Dora, leapt out of the car and a moment later was back minus the bag.

'Phew,' he said. 'It's getting really wet out there.' He brushed his hands through his damp hair, then settled comfortably back into the driver's seat. Dora looked out her passenger window. She couldn't see a rubbish bin anywhere. Had he thrown the bag into the bushes? Well, she wasn't going to ask about that. Not with this ominous, unfinished conversation still hanging heavy in the car.

'So what do you think about discussing expectations concerning marriage?' he took up the topic again. Dora had a strong sense of foreboding. Something was going to happen here in the car, but she wasn't sure whether it was something she was ready for. Was Harry thinking of asking her to marry him? She wondered if Tom Cruise would have gone about it in this manner. Sitting in a car, in the rain, discussing this potentially life-changing issue as if it were a new law to be presented to parliament.

Instead of answering his question she decided to deflect his attention away from her. 'What are your expectations? You've obviously thought about it,' she said. 'Give me an example or two.'

Harry interlinked his fingers behind his head and looked out the windscreen. Not that he could see anything there. The raindrops were pelting down heavily on the glass now, transforming the landscape in front of them into a greyish blur. The sound of the rain on the roof of the car was also making it quite difficult to hear.

'Say I wanted to marry you,' Harry started. He dropped his hands onto his lap. Suddenly Dora's heart was racing. She, too now, stared out the windscreen into the invisible landscape. Her pulse was thrumming in her temples, her reflection in the window taking on the exact same shade as her strawberry milkshake.

'Say I wanted to marry you, I would expect that you would look after everything involving our household. The shopping, cooking, cleaning et cetera. The children, should we have any.' He still wasn't looking at Dora. 'My work already takes up every minute of the day and every brain cell I have. And there will be more work in the future because I have plans. But that's not relevant now. So I would need you to do all the other things outside of my work.'

The noise of the rain on the roof of the car and the windscreen had increased to a metallic roar. Nearly in concert with Dora's heart. Harry raised his voice so that Dora could hear him. 'In return I would provide for you. I mean share my income, no questions asked, let you get on with your sewing and whatever else you do.'

He turned to Dora with a sudden, suspicious glint in his eyes. 'Unless you've become one of Germaine Greer's disciples and you think that all of this is humiliating for the modern woman. Maybe you think you should be the one with the job and the income. The one climbing the ladder.' Dora stared at him, eyes wide open. Naturally, she wanted to work and earn money, yes. Otherwise she wouldn't have been doing those courses at the tech college, but she had never thought about the nitty-gritty of it all. How it all fitted in with being married, having children, running a house. Whether certain jobs needed to be shared equally. Or not.

'No. God, no,' she replied hastily. 'I'm not a fan of Germaine Greer. I haven't even read her books. No!' she said emphatically. As she hadn't read the books she didn't know Germaine Greer's birth and death dates either. Maybe she was still alive? Dora would look it up. Or maybe not.

Slowly the noise from the rain abated. Harry turned on the windscreen wipers to clear the windscreen. The sky in front of them was still grey but the clouds had drifted higher up, allowing the first golden threads of sunlight to shine through.

'So hypothetically,' Dora said into the sudden stillness, 'if I became your wife I could still do my sewing and everything associated with it, as long as I looked after the house. And you,' she added.

Harry nodded. 'From where I stand,' he said with conviction, 'you would do very well out of it. You can do whatever you like and I will pay for it. You wouldn't ever have to worry about money again.'

Dora felt a slight cramping in her abdomen. She thought about Tom Cruise again. And Andrew. Would they have talked about marriage in this way? Sorted out the parameters, as Harry called it, before proposing? Listed the advantages for both parties involved? It was sounding more and more like a business transaction. There had not been a single mention of love. Did Harry actually love her?

As if he'd read her thoughts, Harry suddenly said, 'I think you're the right woman for me. I do love you, you know.'

And that did it. Dora's doubts were swept away by a tsunami of emotions. Harry loved her! Of all the girls in the world, this successful, charming, Tom Cruise look-alike loved her! She could suddenly see herself married to him, happy, confident, looking after him and at the same time nurturing her own business. All of this without any financial worries.

'Harry,' she said. 'In all seriousness, are you asking me to marry you?'

He nodded. 'Would you say yes, if I asked you?'

'Yes, yes,' Dora repeated, her heart about to burst. 'Yes, I would marry you!'

Harry leaned over and kissed her. 'That's done then,' he said with a satisfied smile. 'We're getting married!'

Dora did not notice that Harry hadn't actually asked her.

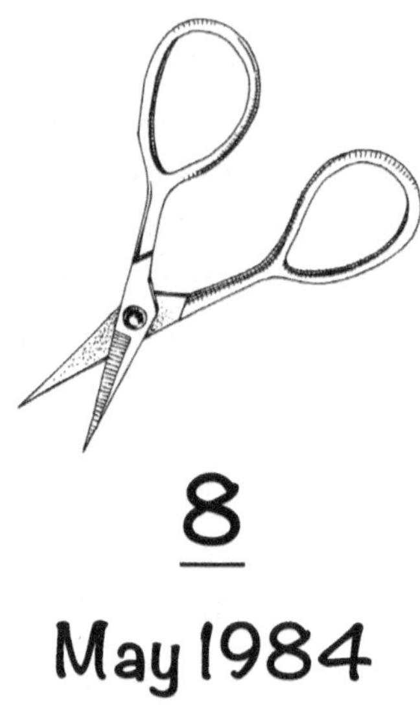

8

May 1984

THE UNEXPECTED SILENCE IN THE car stopped Dora's breath. Behind her eyes, red warning lights were flashing erratically. Why was no one talking?

She had just clambered awkwardly into her father's car, gathering the bulky skirt of her wedding dress in one hand so it wouldn't brush against the dusty sides of the car. She could feel her mother's impatience as she struggled into her seat. It had angered Dora's mother no end that her father had refused to wash the car for the wedding. She kept a tight rein on her daughters and her husband and didn't like to be crossed. Why on earth wouldn't he wash it, she had demanded. Was he trying to make some sort of point? But he hadn't replied, and he hadn't washed the car.

Not only was Dora wrestling with her dress, she was also juggling a heavy bouquet of red roses. No one, it seemed, had thought of assisting her. When she pulled the seat belt over her shoulder it snapped against the long-stemmed roses, beheading two of them. The two flowers rolled clumsily down the side of Dora's wedding dress into the dusty legroom of the car, never to be found again. Quickly, Dora stuck the bare stems right into the middle of the bouquet, hoping that no one would notice.

Out of breath, she made herself as comfortable as possible in the passenger seat next to her father, her white skirt ballooning around her. Dora had wanted to sew her own wedding dress. After all, that was what the bulk of her work consisted of, sewing wedding dresses for women who couldn't or wouldn't find anything suitable in the local shops. She had to agree that the choice, even in the city, was not the best.

But Harry had insisted she buy a wedding dress. What would people think if his wife had to sew her own wedding dress? The whole situation had the word 'poverty' or maybe 'stinginess' written all over it. It did not occur to Harry that Dora and maybe her parents should have a say in the matter, rather than him making the decision regarding an appropriate dress. No, he wanted to have his say. He gave her what she thought was an inordinate amount of money and told her to choose the best dress. Meaning the most expensive.

So she had gone to the city with her sister Freda to buy one of those dresses that her own clients had rejected. At least that's how it felt when she really thought about it. But she didn't think about it much. Harry had been generous. He had to be given credit for that and she should be grateful.

Dora took in deep, silent breaths to slow her pulse. A funereal silence was emanating from the back seats. Her mother sat stiffly in a brand-new dress and ridiculous hat, her body held upright by tension. She never talked much when she found herself in impending formal situations, reserving her energies for the moment of impact. Normally Freda, at least, would be chatting away excitedly. The opposite of her mother, Freda let everything that happened in her mind tumble out of her mouth when she was anxious or excited. But even from her, nothing.

Dora glanced across at her father. Dressed in his best suit, he sat staring out the windscreen. He hadn't even turned the engine on. During endless seconds the four of them sat in the car like wax figures in an abandoned museum.

'Peter!' Dora's mother finally broke the silence, her voice demanding his immediate attention. Dora's father pretended not to hear, but he turned his head towards his daughter as if awakened from a dream.

He gave a small cough. 'Dora,' he started slowly. 'This is your last opportunity to back out. You don't have to get married. But when I turn on the engine it will be too late.' Dora had rarely heard her father say three continuous sentences. Particularly not sentences so heavily laden with meaning. For him to speak about emotional matters was like stepping onto quicksand. He had always preferred to keep his feet on solid ground.

Hearing these words, Dora's heart was suddenly overflowing with love for her taciturn father. She blinked away threatening tears that would surely ruin the make-up her mother had insisted she put on.

'Peter!' Dora's mum shrieked from the back seat. 'What on earth are you talking about?' Springing into action as if a key had been turned in her back, she threw her upper body forward towards her husband, dislodging her hat.

'What on earth are you talking about? We've got people waiting for us at the church. Everyone is already there! Everyone! Stop that nonsense and get going or we'll be late!' Exhausted by her outburst and the unthinkable possibility that her daughter's wedding could be cancelled, she sank back into her seat. She and Harry's mother had organised the whole wedding circus, as Dora described it to herself. All of it, from the guest lists to the final wave-goodbye at the end of the evening. Everything! It would all be for nothing if her daughter climbed out of the car now. Worst of all, their family would be the laughing stock of their small community.

Unperturbed by his wife's outburst, Dora's father regarded his daughter steadily. 'Well?' he finally asked. There was a collective intake and holding of breath as everyone awaited Dora's answer. In the back seat, Freda's eyes moved from one person to the other, her mouth agape. This was one of the rare occasions when Dora's talkative younger sister had lost the power of speech.

It was no secret that her father was opposed to the marriage, but Dora hadn't understood how strongly he felt about it. He had never said as much, but the slightly raised eyebrows whenever Harry or the wedding had been mentioned should have told her. Again, her eyes filled with love for her father who had never openly expressed his disapproval. And she knew that once he turned the engine on he would never mention it again. Not washing the car had been his way of protesting against his daughter getting married to this ambitious young man.

In the weeks before the wedding she herself had occasionally felt that little needle inside her, pricking her as if to ask whether she really knew what she was doing. Asking herself whether she really wanted to commit herself to Harry for all eternity. That did sound scary. Driving around with him in his car, going to milk bars, holding hands and kissing was all very well but this … this was a different dimension altogether.

But she had pushed those thoughts aside and attributed the needling inside her to nerves. She was nervous. This was a big thing. Of course she was a bit frightened. It was only normal that she sometimes thought of backing out, running away and forgetting about it all.

Her old school friend Cindy had felt exactly the same before her wedding. 'That's why we have a hens' night and get completely sloshed,' Cindy had explained to her as if to an imbecile. 'You want to drown your brain in alcohol so it only works at quarter-strength on the day. Or even better, not at all. So you don't have the wherewithal to change your mind.'

Dora didn't want a hens' night. She didn't want to get sloshed. There was a feeling in her that, unlike Cindy, she would change her mind if she *did* get drunk. Things she couldn't say when sober might burst out uncontrolled. No, she wanted her brain to work and to be fully alert on her wedding day.

'Let's go, Dad,' she said softly to her father. 'This is what I want.' She lowered her head into the bouquet of roses and took a deep breath of the heady perfume. There was doubt in her father's eyes, but he turned the engine on without another word and put his foot on the accelerator. A loud sigh of relief emanated from the back seat.

'You've cooked your meal, now eat it!' her Swedish grandmother would have said. So much better than the English equivalent, 'You've made your bed, now lie in it.' Blushing, Dora turned her head and looked out the side window. She didn't want to think of lying in a bed. Harry's bed.

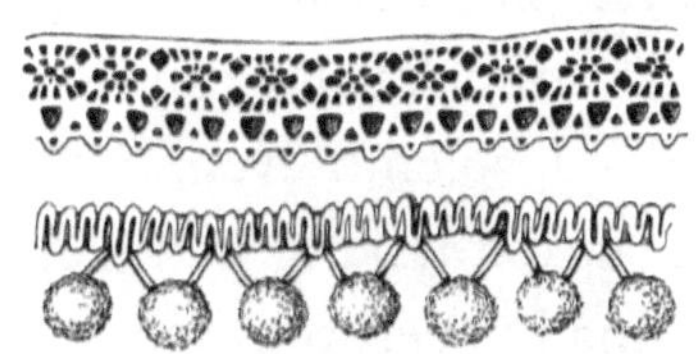

9

26 February 2024

Dora relives her wedding day

Now, lying on her and Harry's bed, Dora tried to conjure up the images of her wedding. But when she thought about her wedding day, nearly forty years ago, she could hardly remember what had happened. This was meant to have been her special day, the most important, unforgettable day of her life and now she could only recall a few arbitrary moments.

It was strange that her memory of the day was so fuzzy when she could actually remember that her mind had been so acute on the day, so sharp, that it had made her head ache. All her senses had been ringing as if on high alert and everything around her had played itself out in an exaggerated manner.

The light around her had been so bright, so blindingly bright she had wanted to snap her eyes shut. Like that night when Freda had woken her and shone a torch into her eyes to check out the reaction of her pupils. She really had been blind for a few minutes after that.

And the sounds enveloping her at the wedding … they had been like one great raging torrent of noise. The actual ceremony had been pleasantly subdued, solemn even, but afterwards everyone had jumped up and started talking and laughing like a flock of cockatoos that had finally been released from a cage, fluttering around her and Harry. She hadn't even been able to make out what her guests were saying. Their voices had been loud and shrill, their words hyper-pronounced, the inflection rising and falling like a roller-coaster. Her eyes brilliant and her mouth set in a smile of concrete, Dora had walked around and seen and heard everything and nothing. Maybe she should have followed Cindy's advice after all and drowned her mind in alcohol. Maybe that would have taken the hard edge off everything. The whole wedding day had left her with a ferocious headache anyway, even without the alcohol.

She could remember a couple of things very clearly. Her wedding night, for example. Presumably, nobody ever forgot that. She had indeed made her bed and lain in it. With Harry. Who had been more than surprised to find that he was her first lover.

'So you've never … you know, with Andrew?' he had said. 'Or any other man?'

Dora had shaken her head. 'No, never.'

'Well! Well, who would have thought?' Harry had pulled Dora towards him and whispered, 'Then you are truly mine. I knew you were the right woman for me!' Dora hadn't liked the sound of his voice. He seemed so pleased with himself, like he had become the owner of a precious piece of jewellery that now could never belong to anyone else.

You may think I'm yours, Dora had thought, but I certainly have to teach you a few things. She wasn't quite sure what exactly she had to teach him or how to go about it, but she knew that what had happened in their bed that night needed a lot of work. Especially if it was going to happen for the next however many years.

The other thing she did remember was something her mother had said to her. It hadn't been on the wedding day but shortly after. In a hushed voice she had told Dora to start an emergency fund. Dora had no idea what she meant.

'Every so often, put a bit of money aside for yourself. You never know when you might need it. Save it and don't tell anyone about it,' her mother had advised her. Dora was astonished, imagining her mother squirrelling away money, keeping a secret from the man she was meant to share everything with. Things seemed to be happening in marriages that were inconceivable to her young mind.

Initially, the thought of hiding away money struck her as an absurd idea, something disenchanted wives might do. Or wives preparing an escape. She was not disenchanted and she certainly did not consider escaping. She didn't want this wedge of distrust driven into her marriage.

Nevertheless, the echo of her mother's words stayed with her and a few months into her marriage she had started her own emergency fund. Maybe her mother had been right. If she continued on with her sewing she would never earn enough to stand on her own two feet. She would always be dependent on Harry for money. And you just never knew. One day she might need those reserves.

So Dora had 'hoarded' money and it had come in very handy over the years. Not that much of it was left. Sometimes she had used it for expenses that Harry would have vetoed, sometimes expenses that Harry regarded as unnecessary or those that he didn't need to know about. The two young men across the road came to mind. They had been the recipients of quite a quantity of that secret money. Despite the heat, a shiver ran over Dora's back. All those secrets, all those lies. Mostly over trifles, nothing big and earth-shattering.

To her mind, Harry had a strange attitude to money. Being an accountant, he kept a record of all their incomings and outgoings. As he did their yearly tax returns, he had access to Dora's bank account and knew where and how she spent money. Except, of course, for the odd fifty or even hundred-dollar note she had squirrelled away. But generally, he didn't question her expenses. He only got his back up when he thought certain items or services were overpriced, or unnecessary. Anyway, Dora didn't want to think about any of that now. So many things she didn't want to think about. And yet, they forced their way into the front of her mind, asking to be finally disinterred.

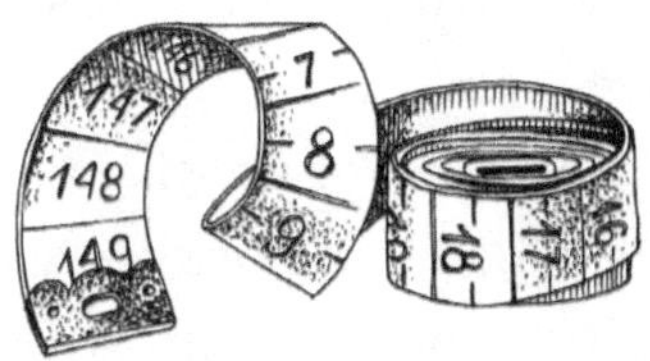

10

27 February 2024

One day after Harry's death

DORA HAD HAD A SURPRISINGLY good night's sleep. The excitement of the previous day, if you could call it that, combined with all the crying she'd done and that nice glass of red wine, had knocked her out quite pleasantly. As a matter of fact, she felt rather refreshed. Unlike her daughter, who looked a mess, poor girl. Dora only just caught a glimpse of her as she stumbled out of the guest room into the bathroom. Dressed in an old bathrobe, her eyes puffy, she looked like she had spent the night crying. Her smart, sharp haircut did not look in the least sharp anymore. Reminiscing about the past and sharing all those memories with Sophie had distracted both of them for a while.

But during the night, the reality of her father's death and the tragic circumstances obviously had overwhelmed Sophie.

Andrew and Leah arrived early that morning. As promised, they had returned to be with Dora and Sophie. And Dora was ready to talk to them about Harry's fall. As much as she could allow herself to. Seeing Andrew and Leah, Sophie burst into tears again and sank into the free armchair.

Dora noted with the tiniest grain of satisfaction that Sophie's businesslike, confident shell had noticeably cracked. It was good to see that her daughter could be thrown off balance. All your expertise in long divisions and convoluted algebra meant nothing in the face of life-defining moments like this. But immediately, Dora chided herself. This young woman, her daughter, had just lost her father. Of course, she was devastated. Dora would have been appalled if Sophie's reaction had been anything less than emotional.

Andrew patted the seat next to him on the couch, and at once Sophie changed places. He put his arm around her and pulled her close.

'What in God's name happened on the track?'

'The police told Mum that he most likely slipped and fell down the cliff.' Sophie's voice was shaky. She reached for the table and pulled a handful of tissues out of a box.

'You know that place with the wooden bench? Above that narrow cove?' Dora took over the explanation. 'They said it happened there, but they're still looking into it.' Without waiting for a reply she stood up and walked into the kitchen to put the kettle on. Beyond the kitchen window she could see her neighbour, Stella Fulton, walking along her rows of vegetables, bending down here and there to pull out a weed.

Someday soon someone will steal her vegetables, Dora thought disapprovingly. Who'd ever heard of putting vegetable beds right in the front yard? Where everyone could see what's growing? And then help themselves to whatever they needed for dinner.

Sometimes she wished old Mr Tomlinson still lived next door. She remembered vividly introducing herself to him just after she and Harry had moved into their new house. Being only in her mid-twenties, she had been convinced the little old man who opened the door would have to be somewhere between seventy and eighty years old. As he died a bit over twenty years later, she had overestimated his age considerably.

Old Mr Tomlinson lived by himself and appeared to be a recluse. He was only ever seen outside when mowing his extensive lawn or hurrying to his car. Initially very reluctant to let Dora into the house, he slowly warmed up to her and her regular supply of home-made snacks. Even though they remained neighbours for a number of years, Dora could never bring herself to call him by his first name, Robert. An aura of old-fashioned distinction surrounded him, which demanded respect and forbade such familiarity. It took a long time for Dora to discover that his wife had died very young. The only son had moved to the mainland but had no contact with his father. It was a sad story.

And now Stella Sticky-Beak Fulton had transformed Mr Tomlinson's lawn into neat rows of vegetable beds, talking and singing to her vegetables every day! Seeing her bent over the broccoli plants checking for aphids, Dora was reminded of those helicopter parents who hovered over their precious children every minute of the day. Supervising their every move, not giving them any breathing space. No wonder so many children suffered from depression and anxiety these days. They were suffocating! Dora wouldn't be surprised if her neighbour's vegetables were infused with anxiety inducing hormones. Peeking over the fence, Dora had spotted some carrot greens drooping resignedly, probably begging weakly to be left alone, if just for a couple of days.

Dora carried a big tray with her best cups and the full coffee pot back into the lounge.

'The police rang early this morning,' she said as she placed the hot coffee pot onto a protective mat on the table. She sat down opposite Leah and only then noticed that no one had offered to help her with the coffee. Someone should be doing this for me, she thought. After all, I'm the grieving wife! – *Widow*, she silently corrected herself.

A little put out, she poured the first cup for herself. 'The police said they would be keeping Harry's body for at least a week, until they're satisfied that everything's in order.' She pointed at the coffee. 'Help yourself,' she said.

'What does that mean?' Andrew frowned. 'Everything *is* in order, isn't it? He fell, didn't he?' He took the coffee pot and poured a cup for everyone.

'Obviously they can't be a hundred per cent sure, but it's most likely that he fell,' Dora answered. 'They said they had to ascertain that there was no foul play.'

'Foul play?' Sophie cried out, tears flowing again. 'Are they saying someone killed him? Someone pushed him over the edge?' If Dora hadn't been sitting on the other side of the table she would have taken her daughter in her arms and rocked her. Exactly like she used to do when Sophie was a little girl and upset about a broken toy.

'Sophie, darling …,' she started but stopped. In vain she tried blinking away her own tears which had started again. It was terrible to see one's child so distressed. Dora pulled a handkerchief out of the back pocket of her slacks and blew her nose. Had she really just thought 'one's child'?

'They have to make sure that nothing untoward happened to him. The nice police lady even asked if he left a note before he started off on his walk this morning.'

'You mean a suicide note? That's ridiculous!' Andrew burst out. 'Harry wouldn't kill himself!'

'No, of course not. Not Harry,' Leah agreed with her husband, calm and composed as usual. 'Of course he slipped. That's all there is to it. He probably got too close to the edge of the cliff looking for the sea eagles' nest.' Everyone in the family knew about Harry's obsession with the cliffs and the sea eagles. It got quite tedious listening to him going on about it.

'The police always have to make a fuss.' Leah turned to her sister-in-law. 'We'll probably never find out what exactly happened, but that's what I think.'

Well, Dora thought, as a matter of fact … she knew exactly what had happened. No, she needed to push that thought far, far away. Otherwise she might slip up and say something that was best left unsaid. She blew her nose again, then turned her head and looked out the window into the garden.

Good God! Dora nearly jumped out of her chair. There on the clothesline, fluttering in the wind, was her long skirt! Very early that morning she had hung out the skirt and the top together with those wretched underpants. They would forever remind her of the day she had followed Harry onto the Alum Cliffs track and of everything that had happened there.

Deep in thought, she frowned. Maybe she should get rid of them? But no, she had done that once before and thrown out a perfectly good skirt. All because she couldn't bear to be reminded of another horrible incident. One that had happened many years ago.

Abruptly, Dora turned to her visitors. 'We'll just have to let the police do their job. Everything will sort itself out.' She gave a sniffle and wiped her eyes again.

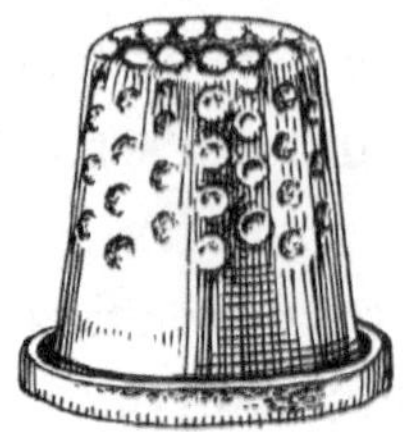

II

27 February 2024

Still one day after Harry's death

THE REST OF THE DAY passed in a blur. There was more speculating about Harry's death, more crying, someone found another bottle of wine. At one point Dora went to lie on the bed, where she nodded off for a bit. She couldn't remember eating anything, but Leah had brought a quiche, which she had heated up in the oven. They must have all had a piece or two because the quiche dish was empty that evening when Andrew and Leah left.

All those people in the house, all that activity … but the one person she really needed was her sister Freda. She could have told Freda everything, the whole truth. She always did. No pretending or masquerading with her. Dora should pick herself up and write a letter to her sister, her friend, her only confidante.

*

Now, with her letter written, Dora sat on the deck in a rattan chair, her eyes closed, a light blanket thrown over her legs. The sun had disappeared behind the hills, leaving behind a faint chill in the air. That was the thing about Tasmania. It could be as hot as an oven during the day – not that it happened very often – but in the evenings the temperature always dropped. You opened your windows and a cool breeze would flow through the house. Quite unlike the mainland where there never seemed to be a reprieve from the heat, not even at night. No wonder Tasmania had suddenly become a popular refuge for those heat-affected mainlanders.

A blanket of fatigue settled on Dora. So much had happened in the last however many hours and she felt utterly drained. Talking to Sophie had brought up all sorts of memories. Some of those she hadn't wanted to ever think about again. Huh! So much for that. She had done nothing but.

Strangely though, it had been a relief, too, to talk about herself as a young woman. She had never been asked by her daughter about her past. Children could never believe their parents had been young once. It was ridiculous to think that she had been so much younger than Sophie was now, when all that business with Harry occurred. She had been so innocent and immature, and despite that had made all those life-changing decisions. What a baby she'd been! Thinking she knew it all!

If she could change one thing it would be that moment in the car with her parents on her wedding day. If she could have that day again she would listen to her father and jump out of the car faster than an Olympic sprinter. Despite that bulky wedding dress.

Her relationship with Harry had been a conundrum. She hadn't been unhappy. Her life had been comfortable. She could pursue her work. She lived in a nice house, in a nice neighbourhood. She could spend all the money she wanted. Within reason. Harry had never made much of a fuss over money. He didn't drink, he didn't sniff cocaine, or whatever you did with cocaine. He wasn't a monster. He just had to prove all the time that he was better than anyone else. More educated, more informed than anyone around him. She had at times wondered what his colleagues thought of him. Had he been the same at work? Had he been the man who had the answers to all the problems? It was highly likely. It would be tiresome to work with someone who had to be top dog all the time. Yes, she knew it *was* tiresome! And how did a person like that react when he was put in his place?

Like a sharp sting, the memory flashed into her brain again. It was the first time she had thought herself capable of killing him. The first time it occurred to her that she had made a big mistake marrying Harry. He had done something that seemed so out of character. So unexpected. Something he had never done before.

His language could be aggressive. He would at times attack her verbally, accuse her of something that was a banality. He could get loud, swear and stomp around the house like a soldier of the French Foreign Legion. Usually, it was more like letting off steam, rather than anything else. It was unfortunate that she was the one who had to listen to his ravings, but over time she had developed a thicker skin and learned to ignore him.

Yet, up to that point he had never shown any signs of physical violence. He had never pushed her, pulled her by the hair or arms or restrained her. Dora had heard and read many stories of women who were treated appallingly by their husbands. There were probably things happening everywhere that she couldn't even imagine.

But apart from his occasional verbal aggression, Harry was not like that. Not at all.

Every so often he would make her feel inferior. Especially when the topic of money crept into a conversation. He rarely questioned her expenses, like he had promised. Nevertheless, he let it be known to her and anyone else who happened to be present that he was the one keeping their *boat* above water. It irked her because he chose to ignore the fact that he only kept one half of the boat afloat.

'Harry,' she had once said, pointing her sewing scissors at him, 'you may have bought the boat but who—' Her voice low and ominous like distant thunder over the ocean, she continued, 'Who do you think keeps the engine oiled and the decks scrubbed and the sails mended? Now, please, shut up about it!'

Without giving him a chance to reply she pivoted on her heels and, long skirt fluttering behind her, she sailed out of the room. Yes, sailed! The *boat* was never mentioned again.

At other times Harry belittled her sewing skills, as if it didn't require much of a brain to produce a wedding dress or one of her costumes. Well, she would have liked to see him design and sew a wedding dress or one of those elaborate Baroque dresses! Work out the design, size the different bits and pieces to make sure they all fit together. Calculate the metres and metres of material needed. Use his fine motor skills – if he had any – for cutting, folding, basting, stitching. Let him try to put in a long zip or do an invisible hem or cover buttons with miniscule bits of silk by hand. Just let him try!

Dora's eyes snapped open. Her heart was racing. Good God, her blood pressure would be off the scale. Why had she allowed herself to get so worked up over issues she thought she had come to terms with a long time ago? All because one thought always led to another and this had led her to that one time when he had become physically violent, that's why!

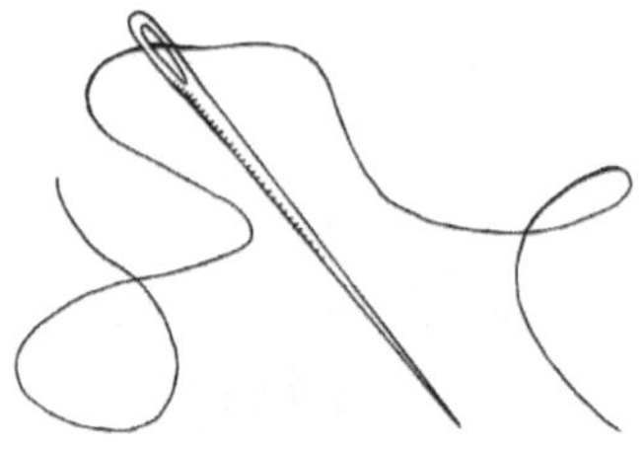

12

The Slap

March 1988

S HE SENSED STRAIGHT AWAY THAT something was wrong when he slammed the front door shut behind him that night. His briefcase flew into a corner in the hallway; she could clearly hear it hit the wall. He came looking for her in the kitchen, flinging his jacket over one of the chairs, before storming into the lounge room. 'Those idiots gave the job to someone else!' he yelled. He pulled at his tie to make room for his throat, red and bulging. 'Do you know how they justified it?' His eyes wide and furious, he stared at Dora.

Carefully, Dora folded the silk underskirt she had been pinning up. There was a slight tremor in her fingers. She hoped the pins wouldn't snag on the fragile material. She placed the skirt on her lap and looked up at him.

'No,' she answered, keeping her voice even. 'What did they say?'

'What did they say? What did they say?' Harry threw himself down beside Dora and thumped the arm of the couch with his fist. A small glass vase gave a little shiver on the side table by the window.

'They said I was too young! Too young! I'm fucking thirty-four, I have studied three years of accounting, two years of commercial law and have worked in this shit firm for however many years, but they want me to have more experience. Those arseholes!'

Aha, that's what it was all about, Dora thought. She recalled Harry telling her that his firm needed someone to audit a couple of companies on the mainland. Unfortunately, she had never listened properly when he talked about his work. She knew virtually nothing about it. Bits and pieces, though, she could remember. Fragments about tallying assets and debts, reconciling accounts, predicting future incomes. Heaven only knew what it all meant.

Dora stood up from the couch. Her breath had become rather shallow and her pulse was beating a little too rapidly. Best to remove herself and make a drink. She took a few steps towards the kitchen, taking the half-finished underskirt with her. You never knew where it might end up if it was left on the couch with Harry.

'I'm making us a drink,' she said. 'What would you like?'

'Nothing!' he growled. 'They gave the job to some old fogey. I know him. He hasn't got a clue how the book-keeping of big companies has changed in recent years. Probably still uses an abacus!' Harry raised his voice so Dora could hear him among the clattering of cups and the boiling kettle.

'I would think they'll soon figure out that he is useless,' she called back in what she hoped was a consoling tone of voice. 'And then they'll give the job to you.' She switched off the kettle and reached up for the tea. This role as peacemaker did not come naturally to her, but she was learning fast to suppress the fire she sometimes felt in her belly.

'You haven't got a clue how these things work!' Harry suddenly appeared in the kitchen door. 'All the backstabbing and skulduggery and favouritism. It's not as simple as making a cup of tea or cooking dinner!' He moved towards her and lifted the underskirt off the kitchen table. His face was contorted with disgust, as if he were holding up a dead cat.

'Look at you! What are you doing all day? Playing with those dresses! You're living on a pink cloud! You have no idea what the real world looks like!' he snarled.

'Harry,' she said, her voice ominously quiet. Her day hadn't been particularly easy or productive either. She had had to undo this underskirt because it didn't sit right on the mannequin. It had been a tricky job to get all the stitching out without ripping the delicate fabric. Then she had to pin it up again. And couldn't finish it because Harry had come barging into the house like Napoleon into Germany. If only he would put the underskirt back on the table. She didn't like the look of it in his hands.

As she said his name she realised that she had not managed to contain the fire inside her after all. Instead, the hissing flames in her stomach shot up uncontrollably. She pushed the tea caddy towards him.

'Harry, if it's that easy, then why don't you make your own drink?'

The last word was still hanging in the air as his open hand connected with her cheek.

It was so unexpectedly violent that she crashed onto the kitchen floor before she even registered what had happened. When she managed to look up at him from the floor, she could see his mouth moving. Spittle flying, he was yelling soundlessly. What on earth had happened to her hearing?

Her body lay crumpled against the fridge, her legs in a strange position. Absurdly, it made her wonder about this flexibility she didn't know she had. It brought to mind Freda's marionette, that old puppet-on-a-string with the sad clown face. If you didn't manipulate the strings properly or, heaven help, you dropped the puppet, its arms and legs would collapse all over the place, ending up in the most twisted, unnatural looking position. And the sad clown face would take on resigned, helpless features, as if it knew that it was at the mercy of some incompetent handler.

Dora's eyes moved from her legs to the rest of her body. Her left arm was wedged behind her back. Looking down she noticed that her favourite skirt, the dark blue, pleated one, had somehow ended up above her hips. It had taken her ages to make that skirt because of the many pleats in it. Every pleat had to be measured exactly so.

Dora loved that skirt because of the way it swung lightly and naturally around her legs with every movement. When she wore it she felt light and beautiful, like a ballet dancer. But now this skirt exposed her shapeless white legs and her underpants. More humiliated by this than the brutal slap, she tried to pull the skirt down over her thighs. Luckily, her arms were still working.

Dora shifted her legs and pulled herself into an upright sitting position. Her back was sore, having crashed against the corner of the fridge, but overall she felt uninjured. For the moment she remained seated on the floor, pulling her skirt further over her legs, as far as it would go. As soon as she could, she would throw this skirt into the rubbish bin.

For the first time she thought she would be better off without him. If he died she would surely be better off. Because she did not want to end up with that same resigned look on her face as Freda's marionette.

From her position on the floor she could see Harry's legs, her unfinished underskirt dangling from his hand against his thigh. He was still standing by the table, probably watching her. Never before had he hit her. And the worst thing was that she couldn't even remember now why he had done it. What had they been arguing about? What had aggravated him so much that he had struck her? The minutes before the slap had completely disappeared from her brain. The memory instantly erased. Strange, that she could think about the whole incident quite calmly. As if she hadn't really been involved. As if a film had been put on pause to give the viewer time to assess the situation, before continuing with the performance.

Holding onto a chair, she pulled herself up until she stood on shaking legs. Harry had stopped yelling. In the silence Dora noticed the humming of the fridge and realised with relief that she could hear again. Somehow that gave her the strength to face Harry.

His face was red, pounding with the heat of anger, but there was also a flicker of uncertainty in his eyes, as if he knew that something irreparable had just happened. And as if he was unsure about the next step in these unscripted proceedings.

The side of Dora's face where he had hit her was red hot. Her eyes were burning but to her own surprise she was not crying. She thought she must be in some state of shock as she hobbled up to him. She was standing so close to him she could feel his breath on her face.

'Don't you ever, ever do that again,' she said in a controlled voice. Her eyes had turned into small, narrow slits. The burning coals in her belly flickering low, but viciously hot, hotter than flames. 'I swear I will leave you if you ever do that again.' For a short moment she stood staring at him, as if daring him to hit her again. Then she tore the underskirt from his hand, ripping it in the process. She turned around and gingerly walked to the bathroom.

She locked the bathroom door behind her and was suddenly

swept away by a wave of laughter. It just broke out of her hysterically. Such a ridiculous threat! Don't ever do that again or I will leave you! Laughing insanely, and then finally crying – oh what a relief! – she faced the mirror.

'Maybe I should kill him,' she said to her reflection. 'Or at least leave him right away.'

How often had women used that same threat and never acted upon it? Countless times, for sure. Violently, she pulled the last few pins out of the underskirt and wet it under the cold tap – it was ruined now anyway – then held it against her burning cheek.

For her, though, this lame old sentence held some power. She knew that Harry would be devastated if she left him. Not necessarily because he loved her and couldn't live without her. No, she didn't have romantic illusions like that. By now she knew him too well. It was rather that being divorced didn't gel with the image of himself that he had so carefully built up, that of a reliable, capable and trustworthy man. For that, he needed a stable marriage and not a divorce which, as he had once explained to Dora, was a reflection of a weak character and people's inability to overcome difficulties. Divorce was not an option for Harry, oh no. In his marriage, problems were solved and figures added up perfectly, just like a spreadsheet. Let that be an example to his colleagues! If he played his cards right, he would be a senior auditor one day rather than just a lowly accountant, despite the present setback, and after that maybe a financial controller. She had remembered that much about his ambitions. It wouldn't surprise her if he ended up running the company. And for that he needed a nice, pretty wife and a smooth-running marriage.

Dora put the wet underskirt under the cold water again. Now she remembered. That's what Harry had been upset about. He'd missed out on his first promotion! Huh!

Weeks ago, he had proudly told her that he would soon cast his critical eyes over the books of big companies. Not just here, but all over the country. There would be a lot of travelling involved and a lot more money. The big, important auditor-to-be could not afford to be left by his wife.

Right now, she felt some satisfaction in the fact that she could balance the power in their relationship with that particular bit of knowledge.

'Served him right that he didn't get that job after all. Huh!'

But Dora had her own reasons for not leaving him. Practical, selfish reasons. First of all, she didn't want to lose the house they were living in. She was well aware it was a deplorable reason and that she should be ashamed. It didn't exactly bear witness to a strong character, but the house was important to her.

As soon as the real estate agent showed them through the house in Kingston, Dora just knew that this was it. This was the house she wanted to live in. She felt at home straight away, even though the house was empty and hadn't even been given one last goodbye-clean by the previous owners. Sitting on a level block in a quiet cul-de-sac, the house bordered onto the bush. The rooms were light and spacious. Double doors gave access to the garden from the main bedroom and the lounge room. It was a house that could be opened to the elements, the heat of the sun, the breeze from the ocean, the smells from the eucalyptus trees nearby.

Dora was not going to give up this house. She and Leah had painted its walls and washed it from top to bottom. Dora had sewn its curtains and furnished all its rooms. There was a bit of her everywhere in this house. And most importantly, working together with Leah had cemented their initially very fragile and tentative friendship. Incredibly, this house had brought them together.

But Dora knew she could never keep the house and maintain it if she lived there by herself, without someone who paid for it all. Which really was her second point. Money.

Dora sat down on the toilet lid. Now she could only see the top of her head in the mirror above the hand basin opposite. Maybe she should cut her hair. Harry was proud of her thick, blond hair. He would have a fit if she came home from the hairdresser's with a really short haircut. It would serve him right. But no, she wouldn't do it. It would be such a juvenile reaction. Vindictive. And she was not really like that.

Her thoughts returned to her financial situation. While she was earning quite a bit of money at the moment with her sewing, it would definitely not be enough to keep this house. In fact, she should bear in mind that she earned quite a bit of money at certain times only. Not always. Only when a well-heeled client paid her enough for the dresses she created.

Indeed, there were times, weeks on end, sometimes whole months, when she earned no money at all because there were no commissions forthcoming. At times she made costumes for the local theatre company or the high school in their area that could only pay her a pittance, if anything at all.

The third reason she was not going to leave Harry was … his family. Having a family was important to her, and the Freemans had become hers now. There was Andrew, yes. She still had a soft spot for him, but no more. And she and Leah had become close over the painting and decorating of the house. Sometimes she suspected Leah was her only friend, because she hardly saw any of her old school friends anymore. Cindy, for example, had long ago moved to the mainland.

Then there were her parents-in-law. John was a bit of a phantom, hardly ever there, always away working in the paddocks. She liked his quiet ways, his stoicism. There was not much that rattled him. He reminded her a little bit of her own father. They were men of few words. They spoke when something needed to be said and that was all there was to it.

Her mother-in-law, Barbara, was the kind of woman who grabbed life with both hands. Full of energy, she ran her household like a military institution. When Harry and Andrew were young, they had small jobs to do before school: feed the chickens, collect the eggs, count all the new-born lambs ... Barb made sure they were busy. After those jobs were done, the boys had to make their beds and turn up at the breakfast table showered and fully dressed, their school bags ready at the front door. She would never allow anyone at the breakfast table unwashed and in their pyjamas. After school, it was time to do their homework, feed the animals, help with dinner preparations and wash the dishes. Before bedtime, after all the animals had been dealt with and all the gates around the farmyard were secured, they always played cards together. As a reward for the hard work during the day, the family came together to enjoy each other's company in the evenings.

Once a week, Barb transformed herself from a farmer's wife into a lady about the town. She went off at night on her own, to play bingo. Her hair meticulously curled, fingernails freshly painted and dressed in her best slacks and a matching jacket, she could have been any of those women with too much time on their hands. Those who played bingo and had weekly appointments with the hairdresser and manicurist out of sheer boredom.

Dora loved her mother-in-law. Her dry sense of humour made Dora laugh and there was an unspoken sense of complicity between them when Barb made some acerbic comment about her eldest son.

'Oh, just listen to Mr Haughty Harry!' she had once exclaimed when Harry insisted that anyone who had any sense should keep an exact record of their finances, the incomings and the outgoings, no matter how small. Like he did.

'People always complain they haven't got enough money. They blame the government all the time for their own incompetence.' He had put on a very unbecoming, whining voice. 'Everything is so expensive … I can only afford one packet of cigarettes a week now … The price of liquor has gone up … Heaven help me, I have to file my own fingernails … I really need those rally tyres for my Mazda 2 …' Once Harry got going on other people's senseless expenses it was hard to stop him.

'I think,' Barb once said with raised eyebrows, 'I think they mixed up the babies in the hospital when he was born. He is like no one else in this family! Where did he come from?' Her eyes had followed her eldest son as he stormed off outside. 'How can one son be so even-tempered and down-to-earth and have so much empathy for others when the other is the exact opposite? Bad-tempered, impatient, self-righteous Mr Know-all!'

She had looked sideways at Dora. 'Maybe I shouldn't say those things. He's your husband after all.' Dora just shrugged her shoulders. Deep down she had to agree with Barb's assessment of her sons, but it would be disloyal of her to admit as much. She didn't want to be disloyal to her husband. Also, there was another side to him, something insecure and vulnerable. Sometimes he struck her as an anxious little boy who was constantly scrambling to prove himself and to get to the top of the heap. It often made her wonder whether his parents had sub-consciously always preferred the little brother. Barb's comments undoubtedly attested to that. At times she felt great empathy for him and would envelop him in her arms as she would a dejected child.

Admittedly, there were moments when Dora didn't recognise Harry. He would fly into a temper over nothing, or say very unpleasant things about his colleagues or their neighbours. The tone of his voice implying that whatever had caused his anger was someone else's fault. And often enough Dora's fault. At least, that's how it appeared to her. But Dora was an understanding person. She had a lot of empathy. She could see that every so often Harry felt overwhelmed and needed to let off some steam.

Nevertheless, at this juncture, she would not feel any pity for him. He had hit her. She needed to come to terms with that. She would stay with him, but if he hit her again she would leave. She would leave.

Dora unlocked the bathroom door and stepped into the hallway. The house was eerily silent. Maybe Harry had gone to walk off his anger. Well, that suited her just fine. She would go to her sewing room and write a letter to Freda, telling her what had just happened. She knew already what Freda would advise her to do, namely pack her bags and disappear. But not everyone could just up and leave like Freda had done, living somewhere on some Galápagos island looking after heaven only knew what exotic type of animal.

Of course, letters to the Galápagos Islands took ages to arrive. It would be weeks before Freda would get Dora's letter. By then Dora would probably have forgotten about this upsetting incident. Or maybe not. If only she could ring her sister, but not even a proper phone service existed over there, and of course it would be too expensive anyway to ring and talk for hours. No, instead she would write Freda a letter as she often did. Afterwards she would feel a lot better. This dreadfully demeaning and hurtful incident might fade away once it had been put to paper. If she were a person who harboured deep resentments her relationship with Harry would most certainly deteriorate. But she couldn't allow that to happen. She needed to make this marriage work. Freda had once said it wouldn't hurt her to feel a bit of resentment. It would give a person fierceness, something she thought Dora was definitely lacking.

Be that as it may, for the time being it would have to suffice to watch Harry more closely and learn to better read his moods.

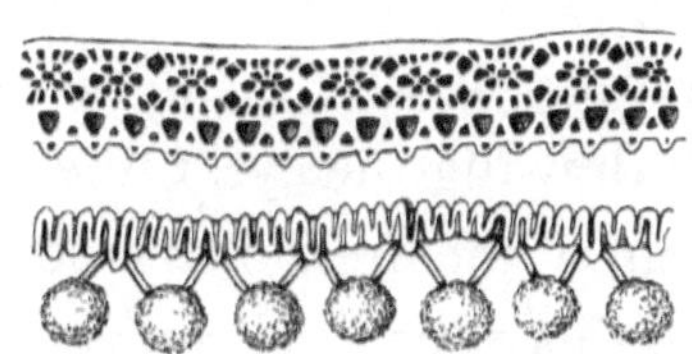

13

May 1988

A dress for 'The Great Gatsby'

THINGS CHANGED AFTER THAT DAY. For the first time, Dora noticed that Harry hardly took any interest in her work. She had often shown him the finished wedding dresses and more than once they had laughed together about her clients' ideas over what constituted a nice dress. When she started making costumes he raised his eyebrows in doubt.

In her letter to Freda she mentioned that she had taken a step away from Harry after that incident in the kitchen. That she looked at him differently now. She hoped Freda would understand what she meant.

Shortly after, she received a commission from one of the bigger theatre companies in Hobart. An old school friend, whose wedding dress Dora had sewn, rang her. She was a drama teacher in the local high school with connections to this particular theatre company. They needed a special dress for a play set in the 1920s and asked Dora to design and sew it.

Immediately, visions of elegant, slim-line dresses flitted through her mind. Sleeveless, of course, with a voluminous feather boa wrapped around a long, slender neck. Something in the hair, understated but still drawing the eye. Other things drawing the eye, maybe to the hem of the dress or the décolletage.

Harry's reaction to this offer had been deflating. 'Don't get any illusions of being some high-profile designer,' he had said dismissively. 'They'll just use you, pay you a pittance and then you'll never hear from them again.'

Even though his comments had hurt, Dora went ahead designing and sewing the dress. Stubbornness and excitement over this project drove her to create a stunning piece.

Months later, Dora received free tickets for the premiere, but Harry refused to accompany her.

'What's the play about anyway?' he had asked.

'It's called *The Great Gatsby*, set in America in the 1920s. You know, the jazz age, rich people driving around in those old fancy cars and all of that,' she had offered.

Harry had looked at her sideways.

'You've seen the dress I made for that play,' Dora explained excitedly. 'That really narrow shift-like dress with the décolletage going right from the neck to nearly the belly button. They wore some extravagant dresses in those days.'

'Décolletage? Since when do you speak French?' If Harry had raised his eyebrows any further they would have jumped off his head.

Dora blushed. 'It's just one of a few terms we learned in the dressmaking course,' she replied. 'Décolletage means—'

'Honestly, Dora, I know what it means! But you still haven't told me what the play is about.'

'I don't really know. I've never read the book, even though it's a classic.' She really should make time to read that book. She had only read *Tender is the Night* by the same author. F. Scott Fitzgerald, she thought, 1896–1940, American writer. 'Mainly I'm going because it's one of the first public shows where someone is wearing one of my dresses,' Dora said proudly.

'So you're actually just going there in order to see a dress? Surely you know better than anyone else what that dress looks like!'

'Well, yes.' Dora felt a bit put out by Harry's questioning. What was wrong with her wanting to see one of her creations 'in action' so to speak? Up to that point most of her work still consisted in making wedding dresses as well as the odd costume for some minor theatre company. Recently she had made children's costumes for a local high school's annual play, *Oliver Twist* by Charles Dickens, and the costumes had been fun to make. Old rags sewn together, making them look like they had been worn by generations of poverty-stricken children. It was harder than she had thought to find old fabrics in second-hand shops or even just really old clothes that she could resew. How do you make something look old when you're just sewing it this very minute? She had enjoyed this little challenge. Charles Dickens, Dora remembered, 1812–1870, British writer. She had read *Oliver Twist* and *Great Expectations*.

Her heart, though, was in the design of women's dresses. Extravagant dresses, that called for her artistic and sewing skills. This particular one in the upcoming play had cost her a lot of time and a lot of sweat. She definitely wanted to see it worn on stage! It was, after all, one of her first more elaborate creations.

Harry turned and walked off to his study. 'I'm not going anywhere just to see a dress,' he called out over his shoulder. 'You'll have to go by yourself.'

Dora stared at his closed door.'My vocabulary extends far beyond words like "décolletage", she mumbled grimly. 'Thanks to my grade nine French teacher it includes words like *détester* and *irriter* and *décourager*, but I won't let you discourage me, no way!'

Disappointed and angry, she reached for her sunglasses on the hall cupboard and slammed the front door behind her. She needed some fresh air and a few moments to herself!

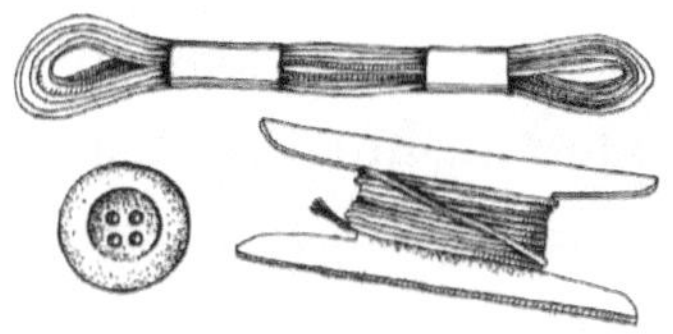

14

27 February 2024

One day after Harry's death, the evening

IN SOME WAYS, HARRY HAD been right in what he said. The theatre company hadn't paid her much for that first dress. And they hadn't rung back for another one for months. She had nearly given up hope ever hearing from them again. But then, eventually, they had asked her to do more work for them. They had been more than impressed with her creation and had increased their payments to her. What Harry didn't understand was that in her line of work she couldn't expect to be busy eight hours every day. Commissions didn't come in regularly. There were days – no, weeks – when she had no wedding dresses and no costumes to work on at all. She remembered sewing nearly all of Sophie's clothing when she was a child, just because she had no other work coming in.

Dora opened her eyes and sat up on the rattan chair. The sun sat low in the sky. She shivered. It really was getting a bit chilly now. She folded up her blanket and went inside. She could hear Stella next door mowing the lawn again. Their lawn must be growing twice as fast as ours, she thought. She should suggest to her neighbour to get rid of all the lawn and put in vegetable beds everywhere. At least they wouldn't hear that blasted lawnmower anymore.

She could hear Sophie washing the dishes. Sophie hated dirty cups and glasses with dried-up coffee or wine residue in the bottom.

Apart from Freda, she would never tell anyone else, especially not her daughter, about that day when Harry had hit her. It had been the worst moment in their relationship. Strangely enough, though, it had also given her some stubborn determination. She would not let this happen again. She could look Harry in the eye now and challenge him. Try me, you just try me! There was some power in that. New parameters had been set. Too right! Parameters!

Harry had never hit her again. In fact, over the years they had developed quite a pleasant way of living together. He went about his work as usual and, astonishingly, he had refrained from making any further fuss about the auditor's position he'd missed out on. A position he got anyway a few years later, just as Dora had predicted. And with much better remuneration. Dora could still see that triumphant look on his face.

But it wasn't just Harry who had achieved certain goals. Dora, too, had finally started to make a name for herself in her own small business. It was surprising how many women suddenly wanted a custom-made wedding dress. Even more surprising how much they were prepared to pay for it. That, and the growing order from the local theatre group, filled her with pride and confidence. It was proof that her designs were good, maybe better than just good! Dora loved working on the costumes, especially if she was given complete freedom in regard to the design.

So, apart from the occasional outburst of anger on Harry's part over a trifle, and Dora's stubborn refusal to engage with him when he threw a tantrum, all was well. Now she ignored his biting comments about others and only rolled her eyes at his pompous remarks. She had even managed to make their love-making a much more pleasurable experience. After her initial embarrassed hesitation and some bumbling, stumbling attempts, she had managed after all to guide him. In such a way that he hardly noticed. Harry had been quite willing to accept Dora's suggestions, if you could call it that. All in all, things were not too bad.

*

It was actually quite nice to reminisce, Dora thought. For a long time she had taught herself to look ahead and ignore the past. Mainly in order to forget the unpleasant bits. Everyone always seemed to say: don't look back. You can't change the past anyway.

Well, it might do her good to ignore that advice and to have a closer look at her past. After all, the next few days were days of waiting. Days in suspense, until the police had concluded their investigation. It could be a time of recalibration. God, what a word! Resetting things, maybe.

Dora peeked around the door into the kitchen. Her daughter was drying the cups and wine glasses, then putting them away into the cupboard in neat rows. All lined up with perfect spacing between them. Yes, Dora thought, only just preventing herself from rolling her eyes. A mathematician cannot allow a crazy jumble of crockery.

Silently, she grabbed her blanket again and stepped back into the garden. With the blanket wrapped tightly around her she stood under her favourite tree. The two young men across the road had done a good job shaping this old blackwood tree. It used to be tall and straggly but after several years of pruning it had grown a lovely thick canopy. Now you could sit under it in the shade. Not that she needed the shade at this time of the evening, but it felt cosy to have the branches suspended above her like a roof. Soon she would get them to cut down that old spruce thing she hated.

The washing-up noise emanating from the kitchen was hardly audible here. It was a surprise to Dora that Sophie hadn't simply thrown the dirty dishes into the dishwasher. It was evident she needed a mind-numbing activity. Dora wondered how long Sophie would stay with her. Her daughter didn't particularly like to sit around and do nothing. And who knew for how long they would have to do exactly that. Until the police had concluded their investigation and Harry's body was released. Obviously! The thought made Dora shudder. Best to push that thought away. Best not to think about what was to come. She really was contrary. One minute she told herself not to think about the past, the next she wanted to avoid thoughts of the future.

Leaning against the trunk of the tree, Dora looked straight across to the external door of her sewing room, the studio as Harry always called it. She recalled well the night the idea of the sewing studio was born. For one, it happened after their tense and distant relationship had started to mellow again. Something had been lost after Harry had hit her, but both of them tried to recover some understanding and intimacy between them.

The second reason she remembered it well was because the sewing studio had been her idea.

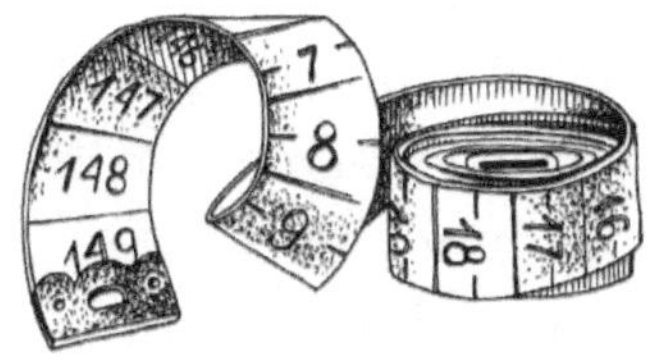

15

1990

All is well between Harry and Dora, sort of ...

THE FIRE WAS CRACKLING HAPPILY in the wood heater, filling the room with warmth and the fragrant smell of orange essential oil. Despite Harry's warnings, the fire-proof bowl containing the oil always sat on the top plate of the heater.

Dora was snuggled up against Harry on the couch, her knees pulled up to her chest, her head resting on Harry's shoulder. He had one arm around her, pulling her close and distractedly playing with a strand of her hair. His mind was focused on the history program on TV.

For Dora it was an effort to keep her eyes open. The warmth of the fire and the rather monotonous voice of some archaeologist praising the wonders of the Egyptian pyramids had lulled her into a pleasant half-sleep. As if from far away, she heard the mention of an Egyptian pharaoh's name, a name she would never remember even if she had paid attention. Then something about the decorated royal chamber this pharaoh had built for himself inside the pyramid … and then Dora drifted off completely letting the sounds of the TV wash over her.

'Easy for them to build a monument like that!' Harry's voice snapped her back into the lounge room. 'If I had all those slaves available I could do the same thing!'

Yawning, Dora sat up and wriggled her toes inside her thick woollen socks. She blinked several times and tried to focus her attention on the TV screen and the meaning of Harry's words. Rows and rows of muscly, sweating slaves digging in the desert, cutting and carrying huge blocks of stone.

'They had to work from sunrise to sunset,' Harry continued, oblivious to the fact that Dora was just catching up on the story. 'Day in, day out, year after year, no letting up. Just like me!' He turned to Dora. 'Did you buy any potato chips?'

Well, Dora didn't think that Harry's work was at all comparable to what these slaves did. Working from nine to five Monday to Friday, with weekends off, was surely not quite the same. Those slaves did not earn the equivalent of Harry's salary either, or get paid holidays and sick days. If they fell ill they'd probably get their heads chopped off. No, Harry had no reason to feel sorry for himself.

When Dora returned with a packet of potato chips, Harry had spread himself out on the couch. Dora squeezed into a corner of the couch and placed his feet on her lap. Harry muted the TV and ripped the packet of chips open.

'Day in, day out,' he repeated, flakes of chips floating onto his jumper. 'Always the same and no one to give you any thanks.' He passed the bag of potato chips to Dora. 'What do you do all day? How do you keep yourself busy?' He regarded her curiously.

'You mean apart from cooking and cleaning and shopping and washing and ironing and gardening?' Dora replied, incensed. 'And apart from sewing the odd dress?'

'You have to admit that you lead a comfortable life. You're always at home,' Harry said. 'You can eat when you want, have a little snooze, look at the flowers in the garden. I would have thought that to be quite a pleasant life. Apart from the fact that you never see anyone and that nothing ever happens.'

Dora pushed Harry's feet off her lap. What on earth had gotten into him? Had he never considered before how she was spending her days? Who did he think was washing his clothes and cooking his meals?

Of course, to a certain degree he was right. She could organise her days whichever way suited her. Certainly she didn't spend eight hours every day engaged in those household tasks she had just listed for him. There were times when three rounds of the house and garden did not provide her with any work. Whole mornings or afternoons when she had nothing urgent to do. But she always found something to keep her occupied. For weeks now she had been working her way through a book on creative dress design and costume making that she'd borrowed from the library. There was also a big tome on her table waiting to be read, on the history of clothing. Not that any of that interested Harry.

So, was it really true that nothing ever happened in her life? Did Harry mean to say that she was boring? What happened in other women's lives who did not go out to work? Did exciting things happen to them? Did they have lots of friends?

'Harry, I do see people,' she said. Why did she have to justify her way of life? 'Leah, for example. I do go out to the farm occasionally and visit her and Andrew. Or they come here.' That was stretching the truth a bit. Her in-laws hardly ever came to Kingston to visit.

'But you wouldn't even know them if it weren't for me,' Harry insisted. 'They're my family. You don't have any friends of your own or people you do things with!'

That was true. Dora had never had many friends, simply because she didn't need them. She had Freda and she did have one very good friend once, Cindy. But Cindy had married and moved to the mainland. As she had never been much of a letter writer, that had put an end to the friendship.

Dora had quite a bit of contact with old Mr Tomlinson next door. Supplying him with scones and fresh farm eggs allowed her to keep an eye on this lonely old man. He was probably not what you would call a 'friend' though, so she thought it best not to mention that.

'I see my customers,' she defended herself vehemently. Admittedly, there were very few.

'For all of five minutes, I suppose,' Harry said. She could not help but notice that deprecating look on his face.

'No, for God's sake, Harry! Initially they come to discuss with me what sort of dress they want. So we look through my patterns or my sketch book. And then I might sketch a custom-made design for them. I show them all my fabric samples and believe me, there are many.'

'Sketch book? You have a sketch book?'

'Yes, of course! It contains all the wedding dresses I've designed. And occasionally I play around with some designs for period costumes!' Her sketch book also contained drawings of some very early skirts and jackets she had made for Freda and herself. Such a long time ago!

'Do you want to have a look at my book?'

Harry shook his head. 'No, don't bother.'

Upset, she scrunched up the empty packet of chips and threw it onto the coffee table. 'Usually my customers take ages choosing the design and the fabrics they want. Then they come back at least twice for a fitting. And then finally to pick up the finished dress and pay me! So I do talk to people. For more than five minutes!' The sour-lemon look on Harry's face told her that something had just occurred to him.

'Are you saying that all these strangers come traipsing through my house?' He untangled his legs and sat up.

Our house, our house, Dora thought but refrained from commenting.

'You make it sound as if hordes of people are coming through every day. It's only ever some bride-to-be and her mother or her best friend. Or should I talk to them on our driveway for everyone to see?' Dora was really getting worked up now.

'I don't like it. Having strangers come through the house, checking everything out,' Harry insisted. God, he really could be querulous. How did he think she'd been dealing with her customers these last few years?

Exasperated, Dora fell back into the couch. 'If you don't like it, then build me a sewing studio in the backyard. There's plenty of space. Or an extension to the house with a separate entrance. That would keep people out!' So there! Let him digest that!

To her surprise, Dora saw a flicker of interest cross Harry's face. 'An extension?' he repeated with narrowed eyes. Already his brain had moved into top gear. 'That's not actually a bad idea,' he said slowly. 'Why didn't that occur to me? Let me think about it and do the figures. It would cost a bit.' He nodded to himself. 'I'll think about it,' he repeated. 'It'll take a bit of time to figure it all out.'

Harry took Dora's hand and pulled her towards him. 'Sometimes you have some good ideas!' he said before he kissed her. 'I knew I'd married the right woman. No more lost pins and scraps of fabrics in the lounge room and mannequins hiding in the corner!'

Rare praise from Harry, despite the fact that he had to allude to the occasional mess in the lounge room. Which irked her a little bit. Dora let out a deep, slow breath. In all likelihood she was too sensitive, too easily riled up. It didn't matter much that things weren't always perfect. She could live with the odd argument or the fact that he didn't take any interest in her work. She hoped she was not the kind of person who bore a grudge. And if she thought about it, she would have to admit that she didn't care much for Harry's work either. What did she know about tallying assets and debts? Or reconciling accounts? Absolutely nothing.

No, she was quite content with her life. Harry was not a bad husband. Therefore, the events on Bruny Island the following summer came as a bit of a surprise. They'd often used Barbara's shack on Bruny for a weekend or the Easter break, just the two of them, but that particular time they were not alone. The whole family stayed in the shack. Andrew, Leah, Harry, Dora and Barbara, her mother-in-law.

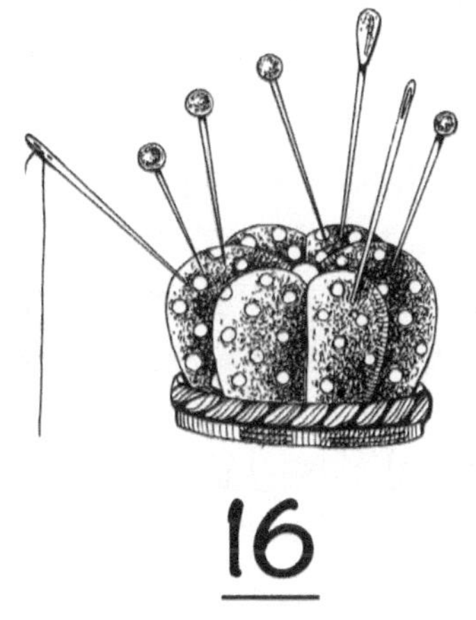

16

February 1991

Holidaying with the family on Bruny Island

ANDREW DROPPED THE PAPER BAGS full of groceries on the kitchen bench. To the left of the kitchen, in the lounge room, Harry sat in front of the TV. He was slouching on an old bean bag with his long legs stretched out in front of him. The flickering images of the TV were reflected in the window, and it was just possible to make out that Harry must be watching a cricket game. The sound had been turned off. Sometimes Harry couldn't stand the inane comments and constant references to games statistics the commentators were making. So he sat there in silence, occasionally calling out a score to anyone who was interested. No one ever was.

Barb and Dora were lying on deckchairs just outside the open lounge room door. Barb, in her bathers, was wearing a wide-brimmed hat, protecting her face from the sun. She was reading a women's magazine. Dora lay off to the side so that her head was in the shade. A light sarong covered most of her body. Even though she loved the sun, she knew that her pale skin did not agree with it. Only a few minutes in the full sun were enough to turn her into a freshly cooked lobster. She held a book in her hands but her eyes were closed.

By the beach, Leah was walking knee-deep in the cool water, occasionally bending down to pick something up. Already most of the windowsills in the shack were covered with shells, mostly cowrie shells, rarer than the usual limpets, periwinkles or scallop shells. Leah did like the scallop shells, even though they were common. Like small, solid fans, she had stuck them into most of her pot plants. Her dream, she'd said, was to one day find a large conch, preferably a Queen Conch, but Andrew had told her that finding one of them would be an impossibility in Tasmania.

He waved at her and called her over. When she stepped onto the deck, again with a few cowrie shells in her hand, Barb looked up from her magazine. Dora, too, was stirring in her chair. Through her dark sunglasses she regarded her sister-in-law. Leah was not much taller than her, definitely not over five foot six. But while they were the same height, the shape of their bodies was quite different. It annoyed Dora that people always thought anyone of Scandinavian origin should be tall, slim, blond and sexy. She was blond, but definitely not tall and slim. Her body was solid. Not fat, no, but well upholstered, as her sister Freda had once described it. Well upholstered, huh! Making her feel like a big cumbersome armchair. But no, Freda had meant that all her curves were in the right places. So could that mean sexy? She didn't dare hazard a guess at what others thought of her in that regard. Although already in her early thirties, thinking of her appearance made her feel like an insecure teenager again.

Dora's thoughts returned to Leah. Now here was someone slim. She was looking positively fragile in that thin cotton dress that floated around her like a veil. The slightest breeze would knock her over. The only robust thing about Leah was her heavy red hair. Right now it was twirled up on top of her head with loose strands sticking out here and there. Untameable, that's what her hair was, and much too weighty for that slender body of hers.

'Hey, listen everyone!' Andrew interrupted Dora's musings. He lowered his body gingerly onto the edge of Barb's deckchair, aware that his weight might topple the chair over. 'There's a film on tonight. I saw a notice in the shop window. The Bruny Island Progress Association is putting on an open-air movie. Let's all go!'

'What's the movie?' Harry called out from the lounge room without turning away from the TV.

'*Casablanca* with Humphrey Bogart and Ingrid Bergman.'

Harry groaned. 'That bowler is totally hopeless! They should have let him go years ago!' He leaned back in his chair to catch Andrew's eyes. '*Casablanca*? That old thing? No, count me out but if you all want to go I'll give you a lift and pick you up again. Yes, finally!' he yelled. 'Finally! That young one is good!'

'What time does the movie start?' Barb was clambering awkwardly off the deckchair. She flung her sunhat through the open door into the lounge room.

'Ten pm, it said on the notice. They have to wait until it's dark.'

'And where?'

'Seven Rowlands Street, I think.'

'Ah, that must be the Lawlers' place. Yes,' Barb nodded. She pulled a dress over her bathers. 'Old Lawler is in the Progress Association. I reckon they're showing it in his paddock behind the house. Lots of room there for cars.' Barb slung a belt around her dress and pulled it tight. 'There's no denying I've put on weight!' She patted her stomach. 'No, it's too late for me.' She looked up at Andrew and burst out laughing. A loud, gravelly laugh. 'I meant the movie, not my weight! Ten pm is too late for me. It won't finish until eleven thirty or so. Way past my bedtime!'

'I won't go either.' Leah walked into the kitchen and started putting away the shopping that was still sitting on the bench. 'We need to get a bigger fridge. It's absolutely chockers!' She slammed the fridge door shut. 'I can't go because I'll be eaten alive by the mozzies if it's outdoors,' she said as she reached up to put the biscuits away above the stove. 'You know how they love me!'

Andrew turned to Dora. 'Are you coming or do I have to go by myself? Come on, someone! It's a fundraiser. Ten dollars for a good cause!'

'What cause?' Harry called out to him.

'It did say on the notice, but I've forgotten. Something to do with birds I think.'

'God help us if birds are more important than the crappy health centre,' Harry growled. The difficulty of retaining medical staff on the island was a hotly discussed topic in the Bruny Island community. For several years now, there seemed to be problems retaining either the nurses or a new doctor or some locum. It was impossible to get staff on a permanent or even semi-permanent basis. But the medical facilities, too, were sub-standard in Harry's eyes, run-down buildings in urgent need of an upgrade.

'You realise that your beloved raptors are birds, too? They will probably benefit from this as much as any other bird,' Barb said sharply.

'S'pose so. Here you go.' Harry pulled his wallet out of the back pocket of his shorts. 'Here's ten bucks, my contribution.' With a flourish he put the bank note on the coffee table and turned back to the cricket on TV. He would have rather donated the money to the health centre. Nevertheless, if some of the money went towards protecting the sea eagles, the ten dollars was not altogether wasted.

Dora blushed. Did he have to sound like a condescending old man? For heaven's sake, what an old fuddy-duddy, she thought indignantly. He was only in his thirties, not his eighties. Next, he'd want a medal for being so generous.

With one swift move she turned to Andrew. 'I'll come. It'll be nice sitting outside in the dark and watching a movie.'

'If it doesn't rain,' Harry grumbled.

Barb raised an eyebrow at her older son. 'No rain forecast for at least a week.'

*

It was a calm night. For a few short minutes the roar of departing cars followed Andrew and Dora down the road. As it was past midnight already, they had left the Lawlers' place straight after the movie had finished. In no time at all the cars vanished into the distance. Suddenly there was silence all around. Even the sea breeze that had come in during the afternoon had disappeared. The air was so still Dora hardly dared to breathe as they walked. A full moon cast its light onto the road and the trees on either side of it. On the surface of the ocean its reflection quivered, shimmering in the gentle waves like liquid silver.

She put her arm through Andrew's. 'Let's walk home along the beach,' she suggested, her voice hardly audible. Andrew nodded and steered her away from the road towards the wide sandy beach. They walked silently, in step with each other, the sand crunching under their feet.

He should have been my husband, Dora thought. We could have walked like this many times. Just the two of us, arm in arm.

She looked up at him, wondering what he was thinking. Did it make him uncomfortable walking like this with Dora, his brother's wife? Or did he, too, wish that things had taken a different path ten or so years ago? Dora groaned internally. Had it really been more than a decade since Andrew had come back from England with a new wife? And she, silly Dora, had waited for him all that time while he was overseas. Months and months she had waited. An eternity when you're only just nineteen or twenty.

She pulled her arm out of Andrew's and bent down to take off her shoes. 'It's easier to walk barefoot,' she said without looking up at him.

'Let's sit here for a while.' Andrew lowered himself onto the sand. 'I want to look at those two moons. One above, one below.'

'You sound like an old romantic,' Dora teased him.

Andrew turned towards her. 'You know I'm an old romantic. Used to be, anyway.'

With a sudden movement he put his arm around Dora and pulled her towards him. Holding her tight. 'I'm sorry,' he mumbled into her hair. 'I'm sorry for what happened. I've never said anything about it, but I'm so sorry.'

Dora's heart was pounding. Pressing her face into his shirt she breathed in his scent. Yes, it was still the same clean, indescribable smell, still familiar. For such a long time she had wanted to be held by him. But more than that she had wanted him to say something, anything about what had happened when he was overseas. She needed to know how it had been possible for him to forget her that easily.

She freed herself of his embrace and leaned away from him. 'Will you tell me what happened?' she asked. 'Back in those days, in Europe?'

By the light of the moon she saw him nodding. 'But not now,' he replied as he pulled her close to him again and kissed her. Instantly she was a teenager again, nineteen years old. Mostly they had held hands and kissed in those days. Both had been inexperienced and had practised kissing on each other. Sometimes his hand had strayed but he had been shy, not sure of himself, so his hand had never strayed far. Dora had liked that. She had always felt safe with him.

Her body softened and gave in to the rush of blood that swept through her. Somehow they were both lying on the sand now. She was not a teenager anymore. He was not shy and inexperienced anymore. The moment was full of possibilities. The possibility of rewinding time by a few years and doing what they should have done all those years ago. Doing whatever it was that would have kept them together.

She felt the heat of his body on her chest and the cold of the damp sand on her back, seeping through her shirt. And then, instantly, she sat up and shook him off.

'We can't do this!' she cried out. 'What were we thinking?' Without responding Andrew rolled over onto his back, both hands covering his face.

'What were we thinking?' Dora repeated, her voice shaking. 'I'm married to your brother, for God's sake! And you …' She left her sentence unfinished. 'I would never be able to face Leah again. She's my friend!'

Andrew sat up and rubbed his face. 'Yes, yes, you're right,' he said quietly. 'You are so right! It's much too late for this. Too much has happened.' He groaned and stood up abruptly. 'We got carried away by … I don't know what! We need to forget about this.' He held out his hand and helped her up. 'Come, Dora, let's go back.'

'And not a word to anyone!' Dora warned him as she brushed the sand off her skirt. 'You'll still tell me what happened all those years ago, won't you? When you were in England?' she asked, her voice rushed. 'I really want to know whether you married Leah in some moment of madness. Maybe you weren't thinking straight or maybe you were feeling lonely or something.' It was embarrassing how these words, whole sentences, flowed out of her without any filters. She was behaving just like Freda, always talking without thinking first. 'Or maybe you really loved her? Love her?'

'Stop!' Andrew said, drowning out her last question. But her flow of words only came to a halt because she didn't dare ask if she herself had been that forgettable. That really would have been pathetic. Pitiful.

Andrew held up his hand. 'I will tell you all about it sometime later, but not now.' Dora nodded. She really didn't want to hear the answer to her last two questions.

Silently they walked up the narrow sandy path to the road. Under the first streetlight Andrew stopped. His face looked garishly yellow in the artificial light as he turned to Dora. 'Are you happy?'

Surprised, she looked up at him. 'Happy enough,' she answered with a shrug. The image of Harry hitting her zapped her body like lightning.

'Happy enough? What does that mean? What sort of a shitty answer is that?' The forceful tone of his voice, the unexpected swear word came as a surprise.

'Well, that was a really shitty question!' Dora stared at him. What was it he wanted to hear? That she was happy so he could be absolved of any guilt? That she was unhappy? Then what? So he could continue to stew in a soup of bad conscience? Surely, they were too old for games like that.

'You're right. It's none of my business. Come, take my hand! And no more talking.' Walking back to the shack in silence, Dora thought of Freda again. She would be most frustrated to read of this in her next letter. Knowing Freda, she would have let things take their course.

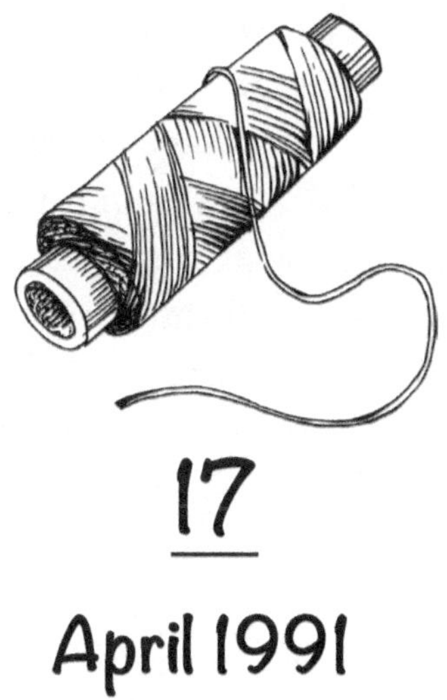

17

April 1991

I T WAS ONE OF THE last warm days that saw Dora sitting in Andrew and Leah's sunroom on their farm in Cygnet. Dora could smell the change of the seasons. Autumn always had that fruity, slightly overcooked smell about it, like stewed plums, still hot in the saucepan. Here and there, a few impatient deciduous trees had already lost their leaves in anticipation of winter, their dead leaves turning into mushy compost on the ground.

While Andrew busied himself in the kitchen, Dora reached across and pulled the cushion from the armchair to put it behind her back. She wanted to sit straight against the back of the old couch, a worn-out, saggy thing rescued from a second-hand shop. It certainly wasn't the most comfortable, but she needed as much support as she could get. She didn't want to slouch in it like some spineless soft toy. 'Hold yourself straight and people will show you more respect,' her mother used to say when she, Dora, had been in her early teens.

If she turned sideways she would be able to see the garden. Well, it was more like a small acreage. When Andrew and Harry's father John died, the old family farm was sold. Harry had never had any interest in farming and Andrew could not manage the land by himself. Rather than employing someone, they had all decided to sell up. The money was shared three ways between Barbara and the two sons. Harry had put some of his share into the house in Kingston and invested the rest. Andrew and Leah had bought this small hobby farm. Small, but big enough to keep quite a large number of beehives and an even larger number of noisy chickens.

Fortuitously, the house had an annexe, a self-contained little flat, into which Barbara had moved. The rent she paid and the income from the free-range eggs and honey, plus some extra from a vegetable stall at the weekly market, gave Andrew and Leah sufficient funds to live a pleasant life. All in all, it was a comfortable arrangement that suited everyone.

Barbara now spent two or three nights a week playing bingo. She had become one of those ladies with time to kill and because she had enough money and more than enough time to do whatever she wanted, she had relaxed her previously rigorous lifestyle. Enjoyment without rules and pressure, she once said, was what she wanted. And that included a couple of glasses of brandy in front of the TV before bedtime.

Just at that very moment, when Dora was reminding herself to get some eggs and honey before going home, she spotted Leah coming out of one of the large chicken coops. At times she was still surprised that Leah, this woman who had flown in from halfway around the world like a lost migrating bird, was her sister-in-law. That they were part of the same family.

She had watched Leah like a hawk for many months after her arrival in Tasmania. Dora had been on the lookout for signs of malice or Schadenfreude in Leah or at least some horrendous character flaw. This girl-who-took-away-her-boyfriend. The one who got the man. The early bird who caught the worm. Dora had been too late. That's what happened if you hung around and waited. She should have thrown all reason overboard and jumped at her chance, instead of listening to her mother. That was exactly what Freda would have done.

But there was nothing defective in Leah. There was no malice, no Schadenfreude, no significant character flaw. Leah was as lovely as she looked with her slim figure, porcelain skin, and thick red hair that glowed in the sun. She was quietly self-assured without any need to flaunt her privileged upbringing and first-class private school education. Leah had nothing to prove.

Andrew was still clattering about in the kitchen, so Dora kept her eyes on her sister-in-law. Leah was wearing a long-sleeved, dirty old shirt over stained jeans and a pair of black gumboots. The shirt, which looked like a cast-off of Andrew's many shirts, reached down to her knees. Her hair was tied up under a floppy sunhat. It looked like she was cleaning out the chicken coop. Annoyed chickens and dust and feathers all fluttered around her as she lifted out the dirty smelly straw with a garden fork that looked much too heavy for her to carry.

Leah did what she always seemed to be doing when she was working: singing some Joan Baez or Bob Dylan song. What a lovely voice she had! Dora could hear it clearly through the half-open window. And when she was not singing she seemed to be meditating while working. Completely concentrated on the one task she was doing, so fully immersed in the moment of digging up potatoes or pruning some apple tree that nothing else around her mattered.

It was inconceivable to Dora that a girl of Leah's background – rich parents who had supper with ministers and royalty – who could easily have married into some British aristocratic family, would end up working on a farm in some god-forlorn country town in Tasmania, and by all appearances loving it. With chicken shit on her boots and dirty, broken fingernails.

And the strangest thing of all: she loved Dora. Had pressed her to her chest with so much warmth when Dora and Harry got married and had somehow become her best friend.

But now Dora was sitting in Leah's sunroom, wondering how this English girl had managed to make Andrew forget all about her. Of course, Dora knew that they met while on the hippie trail. She'd heard the story many times, the sanitised version, the one you told your parents. She'd always suspected there was more to it than Andrew and Leah just being swept up by the adventure of an exciting trip through exotic countries. She stubbornly refused to believe that Andrew had just fallen in love and forgotten all about the girl who was waiting for him halfway around the world. Surely, she wasn't that forgettable? she asked herself yet again.

Finally, Andrew returned to the sunroom, a bottle of home-made raspberry juice and two glasses on a tray. Some ginger biscuits on a small plate.

'Dora,' Andrew said as he filled both glasses with the pink juice. 'Dora, before I tell you about my trip to Europe I want to say that I'm sorry about that night on Bruny. That was just stupid of me. I don't know what came over me. Too much time has passed to carry on like that, like an immature teenager. Luckily, you are a more sensible person than me.' He gave her a crooked, apologetic smile. Then he took a deep gulp of juice and bit into a biscuit.

Dora waved away his apology. 'Don't worry,' she said much more casually than she felt. 'I sometimes forget, too, that I'm not a teenager anymore.' As a matter of fact, she hardly ever felt like a woman in her thirties. A 'sensible', married woman who owned a house and who had started a small business. And she was clearly not one hundred per cent over Andrew. Otherwise she wouldn't be sitting here questioning him about Leah.

'Let's just forget about it,' she said lightly. 'Tell me about you and Leah instead. Was it a matter of out of sight, out of mind for you when you were overseas?' She looked at him with a smile, hoping she was not blushing. 'Did you ever tell anyone you had a girlfriend at home?' Dora feared she sounded pathetic, but she was desperate to know whether she had been important enough to Andrew to acknowledge her existence.

For a moment they regarded each other in silence. There was no doubt at all that Andrew and Harry were brothers. Both had the same dark hair and brown eyes. They were even the same height but Harry was probably a little heavier. They could nearly be the same age, Dora thought. But Andrew's skin would be ageing faster than Harry's if he kept working outside in the sun.

Andrew shook his head. 'No,' he admitted. 'I wanted the others to think that I was completely committed to this hippie trail thing.' He shrugged his shoulders apologetically. 'Admitting to a girlfriend back home … it would have sounded so conservative, so fettered. I wanted the others to think I was as carefree as them.'

That explanation did sting a bit. Dora lowered her eyes.

'But I thought about you every day,' Andrew added.

Now Dora really was blushing. Her cheeks felt as red and hot as freshly bottled tomatoes.

And then he told her of the brightly painted old hippie bus, of the other five young people, one of whom was Leah, and their two leaders. They were all just as excited as him about going overland from England across Europe and via Afghanistan and Pakistan to India. He told her of Carlo, their bearded leader and driver who ever only wore shorts. He had done this trip many times together with his girlfriend; 'my woman Mia', he used to call her. The gypsy with the long black hair. The two of them knew the ropes and they knew it would probably be the last trip ever. Things were heating up in Afghanistan, politically. It was not a hundred percent safe anymore to go through these Eastern countries, but maybe that's what made the trip special. It could possibly be the last one. The young travellers felt the magic and were exhilarated.

The group were sleeping on the bus or camping under the stars. They swam in rivers and lakes and bargained with stallholders for food in markets. They made music together and sang by the campfire.

Andrew stopped talking and laughed. 'Talking about it now it seemed such a cliché! All of us wanna-be hippies together, feeling free and crazy, smoking dope,' he said. 'You should have been there.'

Yes, Dora knew. She should have been there. But she remained silent and waited for him to continue.

Andrew nodded to himself. 'I was okay with everything, you know. I enjoyed it.' He looked at Dora wanting her to show that she understood. 'But I didn't like the whole free love business so maybe I wasn't as carefree as I tried to be.' Again he stopped. Then he said, 'I was thinking of you every day and I didn't want to …'

'I understand,' Dora interrupted him. She really did. She hadn't wanted to … either with anyone else.

'That's when I noticed that Leah was keeping to herself more and more. She rejected Carlo's advances and he didn't like it. He said to her it was all part of the experience. But she stood up for herself and told him what she thought. I really liked that. I liked that she felt the same as me about the free love thing. So she and I spent more and more time together and distanced ourselves from the group.'

So that's how it started, Dora thought. She bit into a biscuit. Home-made by Leah, she was sure. Leah was a great cook. Dora was not certain whether she needed to hear any more. Now she knew how it all happened. Most of which she knew anyway, except that Andrew had always told his parents the clean version without the dope and the sex.

'One thing led to another and suddenly Leah and I were a couple. And frowned upon by the others,' he suddenly said and laughed out loud. 'You should have heard Carlo. He said to us: 'We don't do that ownership thing here.' As if Leah and I owned each other! The guy was an idiot. Particularly since he kept calling Mia "my woman". Now there's a contradiction!'

Dora nodded, but she wasn't particularly interested in what Carlo did or didn't say. Her attention had drifted to noises outside. She could hear Leah shifting something. Something heavy was clearly being dragged across the pavers, then there was a thump. Andrew seemed oblivious to the activity outside. He filled his glass again and twiddled it round and round in his hand, watching the swirl of the pink liquid.

'The one thing we have never told anyone is what happened in Pakistan.' He looked up at Dora, his voice much quieter than before. Maybe he was aware after all that Leah was doing something just outside the sunroom where they were sitting. 'And you have to swear not to say anything to anyone. I don't even want Leah to know that I've told you. I promised her.'

Dora's head spun around to him. A sudden chill crept up from her feet. She put her glass on the table.

'What happened?'

'Leah discovered she was pregnant. By me.' Andrew put his head in his hands at the memory and let out a deep breath. 'She fell pregnant and she didn't want the baby.'

There was another thumping noise outside and the back door

flew open. Leah came in but stopped at the door. Her feet were bare, the dirty shirt hanging from her arm. 'Dora, hi!' she called out. 'I won't hug you! I'm covered in dirt. Those bloody chickens! They make such a mess!' Dora gave her a little wave from the couch. For a frightening moment she wondered whether Leah had heard them. But no, she was beaming, her face open and unsuspecting.

'How is the extension going?' Leah wanted to know. 'Have you told Andrew all about it? When will it all be done?'

'Not for a while,' Dora answered. 'We'll have to live with the chaos a bit longer yet.'

'You're a lucky woman!' Leah said. 'I wouldn't have thought that Harry would build you a sewing studio.'

'Only because he was sick of all my stuff lying around in the kitchen and the lounge room and everywhere else.' Dora suddenly laughed out loud, relieved that the conversation had taken a different turn with Leah's appearance. 'He was always complaining about it but you know what topped it all?' Expectantly, she looked at Leah, then Andrew. Both were shaking their heads. 'One night when he came home late he ran into my mannequin! It frightened the living daylights out of him!'

'And I imagine he's done a cost-benefit analysis anyway,' Andrew said with more than a hint of sarcasm. 'He knows that the extension will double the value of the house.'

'Yeah, I'm sure you're right,' Dora conceded.

'I'm off to the shower. See you in a moment,' Leah called out before she disappeared upstairs.

There was silence in the sunroom, then the old water pipes started rattling as Leah turned on the shower.

'So, she didn't want the baby?' Dora picked up the conversation again, as difficult as it was. She couldn't imagine Leah not wanting a baby. But maybe the timing hadn't been right for her.

Andrew shook his head. 'No. Even though I tried to convince her we'd manage somehow. But she went to Mia and told her about it.' He paled at the memory. 'We were in Pakistan, for God's sake, and Mia sent her to some midwife who gave her a backyard abortion. Literally, a backyard abortion. In a shed.' He took a deep breath. 'Leah wouldn't stop bleeding. I had to take her to a hospital. They did what they could but told us Leah would never be able to have children again.' Andrew stood up and walked towards the window. His hands were in his pocket, and he did not turn around when he continued speaking.

'We flew home from Pakistan as soon as Leah was able to. Her parents paid for the flights. We never made it to India. When we arrived in London, Leah took weeks to recuperate. We told her parents she'd had a severe case of food poisoning in Pakistan. That's why she had been so sick. We never said anything about an abortion or the fact she would never have children.' Andrew was silent. Holding her breath Dora watched him, waiting for what was to come.

'When she was fully recovered I told her it was time for me to fly back to Australia. She said she wanted to come with me. Her life in England was finished.'

Andrew turned to Dora. 'How could I not take her with me?' he asked vehemently. 'I had basically destroyed her life.'

So there it was, now she knew. How easily things could take an unexpected turn. The arbitrary and unpredictable ways of fate filled her with melancholy.

After a few long seconds Dora nodded. 'I think you did the right thing,' she finally said. Her stomach was knotted up and her breath laboured. She could imagine how guilty Andrew would have felt, obliged to make up for that terrible mistake. 'You did the honourable thing.'

Good God, had she really just used this old-fashioned, mean-ingless phrase? That's how Harry would have expressed himself.

With a shrug of his shoulders Andrew added, 'And for immigration purposes it was easier to marry Leah.'

'I suppose. Yes. And you're lucky, Leah is a good woman. She's a very good woman.' Dora finished her glass of raspberry juice and stood up. 'I'll think I'll go now,' she said. This was as much as she could take. 'Thank you for telling me.'

At the front door she turned to Andrew. 'Tell Leah I had an appointment and needed to leave, ok? But before I go … have you got any spare honey? Two small buckets?' One for her and Harry, and one for Mr Tomlinson, such a lonely old man. Dora's eyes were welling up in pity for him. Or maybe for herself.

'Of course, of course!' Andrew jumped up and walked into the large pantry. He was on safe ground now. But for Dora the floor was swaying.

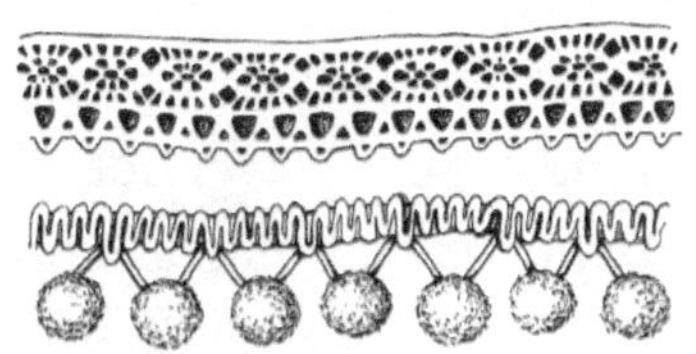

18

April 1991

Dora needs to go shopping

H ER ARM OUT THE WINDOW, Dora waved at Andrew as she headed down their long drive. Once out of sight, she drove straight to the Huon River. Not far from the entry into town was a lovely park right where the river wound its way around a headland. Often fishermen could be seen on the banks of the river, or families enjoying a barbeque.

Facing the river, Dora sat in her car and stared at the gentle motion of the waves. It was a calm, peaceful day. She was surprised that there were no kayakers on the river. There were usually a few appearing unexpectedly around the corner from behind the headland. But on this day, all was quiet.

She was glad to be on her own for a while. Even though on the outside she had stayed calm and composed during the telling of the story, her insides had been dug with a big shovel. For a moment she feared she would throw up.

It had been a shock to hear of Leah's pregnancy and abortion, and subsequent impossibility of ever having children. What a terrible thing to have to go through and live with for the rest of your life.

Andrew had been right to say that they had been so very young. It had been such a long time ago. When she looked at young people that age now, they struck her as children. They were so innocent and had no idea of the machinations of the real world. It was frightening to think that the things you did when you were young could determine the course of your life forever. And how could you have such strong feelings at that age? How come those feelings could influence your whole life?

Maybe, she thought, you could only feel that strongly when you were young. When none of the shutters had come down around your heart yet. When your heart was still open to give and receive. Sadly, Dora shook her head.

As far as her own disappointed teenage feelings for Andrew were concerned, she would treasure them and she would keep them stored away somewhere. All at once, one of her favourite quotes by Simone de Beauvoir came into her mind. Not that she could ever exactly remember the quote by this famous existentialist writer, or any writer for that matter, but it went something like, 'Even if you forget me, our relationship *did* exist.' It was a consolation to Dora that at one stage Andrew had had feelings for her, and she for him. The feelings had existed. They could not be denied or erased. Simone de Beauvoir, Dora thought. 1908–1986, French Existentialist.

That was existentialism for you, she thought. She liked it. Not that she knew much about the whole philosophy of existentialism, if she were honest. After all, she had never completed her philosophy course at the university, or any of her other courses, and thank God for that!

Dora took a sip of water from her water bottle. Her stomach had settled down. Her head was clearer. Truth be told, she felt quite comforted. She would drive into the city and do some shopping. There were a few bits and pieces she needed for her latest costume, a Viennese dress from the early 1800s. High cut, with a small lacy collar, the waist also high, sitting just under the chest. Sleeves narrow, ending in frilly cuffs which covered half of the hands. At the back, a number of small buttons. Apart from the hat, which was covered in artificial flowers, the outfit was quite understated. Luckily, a milliner on the mainland would construct the hat.

So, buttons and some lace maybe. Who knew what else she might find in the city.

*

Dora's first and, as it turned out, only stop in the city was the large fabric and haberdashery shop. It wasn't exactly her favourite place. A big, cavernous hall, it felt more like an aircraft hangar rather than a place for home crafts, but it was the only shop of its kind and generally it had everything Dora needed for her work.

As she walked into the store her senses were instantly assaulted by the glaring lights, the inane music that was meant to make shopping a more pleasant experience and the sickly, plasticky smell that hung in the air. One quick look around told her straight away that the store had yet again been rearranged. From the front door, anyway, nothing looked like it had the last time she'd been there. It really was annoying to have to go searching from aisle to aisle every time she entered this place.

Luckily, she spotted someone sitting at the check-out right at the entrance. A young girl, her head buried in a magazine. Clearly, she did not have much to do. Dora would ask her for help.

'Excuse me, where do you keep buttons?' she asked the dyed head of hair. Slowly, the head lifted from the magazine to reveal a very young shop assistant, probably in her late teens. Her face heavily made up, eyelashes like tarantula legs, the downward sloping line around her mouth indicating that she would rather not be disturbed in her reading.

'Buttons? Over where the fabrics are,' the answer came lazily. The tarantula legs dropped down towards the magazine.

'And where would the fabrics be?' Dora asked sweetly. She would not be fobbed off by this insolent young thing. Two could play this game.

'Opposite the bedding.'

'And that would be where?' Dora's voice had taken on the high pitch elderly ladies reserved for toddlers in a pram.

Her eyes only half open, the young shop assistant looked up at Dora with contempt. The tarantula legs were fluttering alarmingly. 'There.' With a vague gesture she indicated towards the back of the store.

'You have been absolutely marvellously helpful.' Dora smiled sweetly. She had very little hope that her sarcastic remark might reach the inner workings of the shop assistant's brain, but you never knew. It was easy to misjudge people by their looks.

Well then, Dora would make her way through the cavernous store, past the artificial flowers, and the cheap candles which smelled as if infused by nuclear waste. Not that Dora knew what nuclear waste smelled like, but it couldn't be any worse than those candles. Then past the fabrics, no stopping! But, ooh, her trained eyes spotted some lovely material there she could use for the costume she was planning to make. A beautiful dark green that could be used as a contrast fabric for what she already had. A metre or a bit more would be sufficient.

The green fabric safely in her shopping basket, she steered towards the bedding on the right and there, opposite, just like the young shop assistant had indicated, was all the sewing paraphernalia. The pins and needles, the zips, the laces and the buttons!

The shopping basket with the material hung in the crook of her elbow as she critically examined the rows and rows of clear plastic tubes filled with buttons of all sizes and colours.

Right away, her practised eye discovered the perfect buttons for the dress. She pulled the tube off the shelf and was immediately appalled at the price. How was it possible that buttons were so expensive? She had to be a little careful with this particular costume. The small local theatre company couldn't pay her as generously as some other, bigger companies with a larger budget might. She sighed as she slid the tube with these beautiful, pearl buttons back in its place. She would have to make do with plastic replacements.

But when she looked at the cheaper plastic buttons she couldn't bring herself to buy them. They just didn't feel right. The pearl buttons were so much better. They were the ones she wanted. For a second time she pulled the tube with the pearl buttons from the shelf. She opened the lid, even though she knew you weren't meant to do that, and removed one of them. Holding it up to the light she confirmed that these were just perfect for the costume.

She pretended to look along the many rows of buttons. Her forehead was knitted in concentration, as if she were incapable of making a decision. In fact she was looking up and down, left and right, scanning the area around her to see if there were any customers nearby or, heaven help, the assistant with the eyelashes. But no, only one elderly lady fiddling with zippers a few metres away. No danger there.

Dora quickly turned the tube on its head and let several of the buttons fall into her hand. Then she slowly and carefully let them slide into the sleeve of her jacket. Lifting her arm she felt the cool buttons snuggle right into the crook of her elbow. She bent her arm to prevent the buttons from coming back down and shifted her shopping basket into the crook of this elbow. They were safe now.

Finally, she took another three buttons out of the same tube and placed them on top of the fabric in her shopping basket. The tube back on the shelf, Dora made her way to the cash register, to the very helpful shop assistant.

The tarantula legs flew upwards as the young girl looked up from her magazine. She was not at all pleased when she spotted the three buttons nestled loosely on top of the fabric. 'You're not meant to take them out of the tubes!' She frowned, her heavy eyebrows disappearing behind her fringe. 'Now I have to go and check how much they cost.' She snapped her magazine shut and grabbed one of the offending buttons to take with her to the other end of the store.

Well, sorry, Dora thought. Her eyes followed the girl as she disappeared behind a big stack of boxes. So sorry to get you away from your magazine and make you do your job! She was slowly losing her patience with this sulky, heavily made-up girl who acted like the world owed her something.

While she waited, she carefully patted the sleeve that was holding her buttons. All still there as far as she could tell. Or feel. She smiled at the thought that she might just be a little cleverer than this young thing who obviously thought every customer was a nuisance. And then the shop assistant returned, flying back into her position behind the cash register.

'Six fifty each!' Her eyes challenged Dora to protest the price but she got no reaction from her difficult customer. With a smile

Dora swiped her credit card. 'Hope you haven't lost your page,' she said, nodding towards the magazine.

What a silly girl, she thought. But I'm the one who came off better in our little encounter. These buttons will look just lovely on that dress!

*

Satisfied with her shopping, Dora made her way home. It had been a thrill *acquiring* those buttons. She hadn't done anything like it in years. Not since those days when bars of chocolate mysteriously appeared in her coat pockets. Now, just like then, she felt a little twinge of guilt, but she enjoyed the satisfaction of having done something outrageous.

It was particularly pleasing that for the whole time she'd been in the shop, she had not once thought of Andrew and Leah. Come to think of it, what he had told her had not even been all that extraordinary. Young people on a journey together, falling in love … that was all pretty normal. Even getting an abortion at a young age was not that unusual. It was more than a bit out of the ordinary that it had happened in a backyard shed in Pakistan but, well … she had to be realistic. As far as she was concerned the 'goose was cooked', 'the meal eaten' or whatever the saying was. All of that was now in the past.

And suddenly she remembered something else. Something else she had not thought of the whole day. She was two months pregnant! She had been as sick as a dog very early that morning and then the knowledge of her pregnancy had floated straight from her mind. Boy, was she glad she hadn't surprised Andrew and Leah with her news! Sooner or later she would have to, but not now. Not after what Andrew had just told her about Leah's abortion.

Nevertheless, she could tell Freda about it. She would write to her and tell her all about the conversation with Andrew. She would also relieve her slightly bad conscience by confessing to Freda that she had stolen those buttons. It was such a stupid thing to do but it made her feel so good, if only for a short time. So, yes, in hindsight, Dora was a tiny bit ashamed, but Freda would understand.

She would share her big secret with Freda. Not even Harry knew yet that she was pregnant. Freda would be the first one to find out. She would be so thrilled to find out she was going to be an auntie. Auntie Freda. It sounded good. Considering the fact that it probably took weeks, if not months, for her letter to get to the Galápagos Islands, Freda could be an auntie before she knew it. Well, there was nothing Dora could do about that.

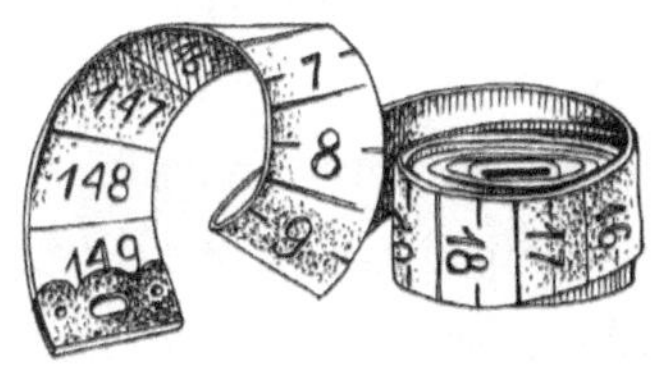

19

May 1991

Dora gets her first big commission

SLOWLY DORA CARRIED THE DIRTY dinner dishes into the kitchen. Her plate was still half full. Meatballs in an Italian tomato sauce all mixed up in a small pile of cold, sticky spaghetti. Her stomach turned again looking at the food. She was three months pregnant and nearly every day she felt nauseous. Luckily, she had only thrown up a few times, otherwise there would soon be nothing left of her. The sight of food alone made her ill but for the baby's sake she forced herself to eat light soups at least and to drink vegetable juices.

Suddenly Dora was grateful that her mother-in-law Barb had given her a juice maker one year for Christmas. The third prize in a raffle, which Barb had rejected. She would have preferred the first prize, ten days in Bali. Or at least the second prize, a massage and a facial at one of the better beauty salons in the city. 'Who would want a juice maker?' she had asked indignantly.

But now it came in handy. Dora roughly rinsed all its bits and pieces under the kitchen tap. Then she put it back together and quickly juiced up some carrots and apples. That drink was all she could ingest right now.

She was leaning against the kitchen counter sipping her vegetable juice when the phone rang. Damn, she'd forgotten Michelle was going to call! Michelle had introduced herself to Dora – 'I'm a location and props scout' – some time ago in a theatre in Hobart. By pure chance she had been there to see a re-run of *The Great Gatsby* and had been impressed by the 1920s dress Dora had designed. Dora, too, had been there to see her dress, yet again on stage. Afterwards, Michelle had approached her wanting to talk about the costume. She had been interested in the daring design.

Dora swallowed the last of the juice, ran her hands through her hair and cleared her throat.

'Michelle,' she said. 'How are you?'

'I'm fine, honey, and I need to talk to you about a project, a new commission.' Dora hated to be called 'honey', but she appreciated that Michelle was a woman who came straight to the point. No faffing about with small talk. Michelle had contacted Dora shortly after their first meeting. Then, a bit later again, she had a business proposition. At that time she had been looking for a dressmaker with a passion for costumes. Would Dora be able to show her the sketches of all the costumes she'd made and if they liked her designs, would she be interested in a few commissions for Upstage, a theatre company in Sydney? Again, there had been no time wasted with pleasantries. Since then, Dora had made a couple of elaborate dresses for a play set in eighteenth-century France, all commissioned by someone Michelle was working for. Metres and metres of material had been needed, lots of lace and lots of gold thread. It had not been an easy assignment, but from the moment Dora had sat down at her sewing machine, she had been hooked. And according to the director of the play, the costumes were just what he had wanted.

Dora pulled a kitchen chair towards her and sat down heavily. The juice she had drunk made her stomach gurgle like a blocked sink. She'd probably drunk it too quickly, because she could feel her stomach heaving again. She closed her eyes and tried to concentrate.

'What is the new project, Michelle?' she asked. She rubbed her stomach with her free hand, hoping to settle the upheaval in there.

'Honey, this is exciting!' Dora realised that the usual unflappable Michelle really had been stirred up by something. 'Those costumes you made for me last year have come to the attention of – no, doesn't matter. Anyway, next year a movie will be shot in the outback of Queensland. Set in the mid-to-late-1800s and the director wants a unique dress. Something very special. Stunning. I recommended you to him, honey.'

'I would have thought there are hundreds of them everywhere in theatre wardrobes and wherever these film companies keep them.' But already, even though Dora sounded hesitant, images of an evening dress started to take shape in her mind. Something made of cotton and silk, and lace. A very narrow waist and a voluminous skirt. Contrasting threads of fabric pulled through the bodice. And beads. Yes, glass beads of various sizes that would reflect the light and the colour of the fabric with every movement. Simple but effective. Eye-catching.

Dora's heart was beating with excitement. 'I—' she started but before she could finish her sentence Michelle's voice pulled her back.

'Yes, honey. There are lots of dresses from the 1800s but the director doesn't want anything that's been seen before. He wants:

unique, stylish, desirable. He wants the female viewers to be green with envy and wish they were born a hundred and fifty years earlier.'

With the phone at her ear, Dora walked through the lounge into her sewing room. She stopped in front of the mannequin and brushed her free hand over the wedding dress she had recently started. If she accepted Michelle's offer she would be able to give up sewing wedding dresses, and mother-of-the-bride dresses, and whatever else. Best of all, she wouldn't have to do exactly like her demanding customers wanted. She would be able to be creative. Yes, it was worth considering. For a long time now she had wanted to get into costume making full-time. Unfortunately, the few bits and pieces she had sewn for local theatre companies had not always brought in much money. On the contrary, sometimes she had only been reimbursed for her expenses. Only occasionally had she received a satisfactory paycheck. The 1920s dress had paid well. So had the Viennese one.

'Honey, are you still there?'

'Yes, yes. I'm thinking about it,' Dora answered hastily.

'I need an answer by early next week. Just remember, if the director likes what you're doing, you've got it made. For quite some time anyway. He's got big budgets and he's willing to spend every penny. It's either you or someone else who will benefit.'

Well, maybe she had it made. Michelle words resonated in Dora's mind and made her heart jump with excitement. But she suspected that Michelle could be exaggerating. It was a tough business, and Dora was a careful kind of person. She would not get carried away by her first really big commission.

20

August 1991

Dora buys a painting

THERE HAD NEVER REALLY BEEN any doubt in Dora's mind that she would accept Michelle's offer. It was one of those opportunities that had to be grabbed because it would not come again. Fortunately for her, it took a few months before all the details of the contract and the required work had been settled. It gave her time to finish the few commissions she still had pending for wedding dresses and other bits and pieces. But after that, if it was at all a viable option, she would only accept costumes for film and theatre. This was her passion. This was what she had always wanted to do.

At the moment her life could not have been better. She finally had the work she wanted. It was one contract only, but it was a big one. There was no certainty that more would be coming her way. But she put that thought aside. It was important to get this one special commission right. She wanted to make a name for herself. She wanted her name to be on top of the list when film or theatre directors were looking for a costume designer. And now she had her own sewing studio with everything she needed. The extension that had been started months ago was finally finished. The timing couldn't have been better. She could now close the door and concentrate on her work. No more setting up the sewing machine in the kitchen or lounge room. No more collecting all her paraphernalia together at the end of the day and storing it away in a corner somewhere. No more mannequins in the corner of the lounge room to frighten Harry.

Now she had a large rectangular table right in the middle of the room. She could finally walk around her patterns rather than always shifting them into position when measuring or cutting fabrics. There was plenty of room for the two sewing machines and three overlockers. Three! With different coloured threads in each so she wouldn't have to go through the complicated threading process all the time. Harry had been amazingly understanding when she'd explained the situation to him. Without blinking an eyelid he had accepted the withdrawal of funds from his account for this oh-so-essential acquisition.

In the corner, two mannequins stood ready to be dressed and her filing cabinet was filling up with patterns. It had been such a relief to move all her sewing paraphernalia out of the lounge room into this brand-new sewing studio. There was even a small ensuite attached to it. Harry thought that sometime in the future the studio might be turned into a guest bedroom, so an ensuite was a must.

Her pregnancy was no hindrance to her work now. She was past the stage where nausea had been governing her daily activities and already the baby made its presence felt, moving inside her, pushing and kicking. Dora felt strong and confident and was convinced that she could manage a baby and work.

Harry, too, had been in a surprisingly good mood for weeks now. The prospect of becoming a dad had definitely cheered him up. He seemed relaxed and content. Dora hadn't been aware that he was that keen to have children. It was a bit strange that it had taken such a long time for her to fall pregnant. Right at the beginning of their marriage they had decided not to use contraceptives. It had always been part and parcel of being married that one day there would be children.

*

On the spur of the moment, Dora decided to drive into the city and do some window-shopping. The first few months of her pregnancy had prevented her from venturing outside the house much. She had felt weak and apathetic, but now that the nausea had subsided, her strength had returned. It didn't take her long before she had bought a new pair of shoes and a painting.

A painting! Surprised at herself, she had been drawn into an art gallery by the vibrant colours of a seascape in the window. It was an abstract, but there was no doubt in her mind that it depicted the ocean on a hot summer's day. Dora could see what she would have called a light celeste blue on one side, a strong turquoise with hints of purple and green in the centre, azure and midnight blue blending into each other in the furthest corner. She was captivated by the swirls of colour moving the waves along from one side of the painting to the other. And here and there she discovered thin golden strands where sunlight penetrated the water.

Dora's heart was pounding as she opened the door to the gallery. This was the painting she had always wanted for that bare wall in the lounge room. It would look magnificent! The price tag stopped her breath for a moment. It was way more than she would have ordinarily spent on an item whose purpose was purely decorative, but she felt elated. Soon, she knew, more money than she could have hoped for would come to her from the film company. This painting would signify the beginning of a new phase in her life. She was going to buy it.

*

'What on earth have you done?' The blood was pulsating violently in Harry's face. 'What is that meant to be?' He stood in front of the new painting, his hands on his hips, staring at the seascape. It had only taken Dora a few minutes to find the exact right spot for the painting and, although heavily pregnant, she had climbed onto a kitchen chair and hung it up herself. All afternoon she had walked in and out of the lounge room and admired the painting.

Why was Harry so angry? Something must have happened at work. For weeks, if not months, there had been no signs of frustration or anger from him. Her hopes that the imminent arrival of the baby had somehow settled his emotions were instantly dashed.

'It's the ocean.' Dora could hear her voice shaking. 'Can't you just imagine being at some hot tropical beach and diving into those waves?'

'I can't see any fucking waves!' Harry raised his voice. 'All I can see is a bloody mess of paint!'

'But look here, all the different blue tones, how they blend into each other, how they make the waves move.'

'If you'd wanted something like that I could have thrown a few pots of paint onto a piece of cardboard.' Harry was yelling now. He was furious. Turning towards Dora, he stared at her with blazing eyes. 'I know pregnant women do crazy things, but I can tell you I'm not having that in my lounge room!'

Dora felt a flutter in her belly. She thought about the time Harry had hit her. She knew how unpredictable he could be, his mood changing dramatically from one second to the next. Her face burned at the memory. Would he do it again? The baby moved and kicked again, upset at what was going on in the outside world.

At that moment, Dora knew that she would hit him right back if he dared raise a hand against her. And the baby. She gently stroked her belly. *Stay calm*, she told herself, her eyes fixed on Harry's hands.

'If you don't take that shit down, I'll throw it out myself!' Without another glance at Dora, Harry turned on his heels and left the room.

Her legs shaking, Dora sank into an armchair. Her hands were freezing cold. A sharp needling sensation in her left temple started to spread down towards her cheek. My face thinks it has been hit, she thought. Was that possible? Could the body have a memory of a violent act and react like it had done previously, even though this time nothing had happened? She rubbed her temple and her cheek vigorously. Then she glanced up at the painting. Yes, she would take it down. She would not allow Harry to throw it in the rubbish. She would hide it in her sewing room and every so often, when he was at work, she would look at it. She would keep that painting because it meant something to her.

And she would make no attempt to find out what had upset Harry so much. Let him deal with it himself.

*

'What did you do with the painting?' Harry asked Dora a few days later.

'As you can see, I got rid of it.' Dora was still smarting. She had taken the painting off the wall, wrapped it in some paper and stashed it behind the filing cabinet in her sewing room. The hole in the bare wall, left by the hook, gave her a sense of grim satisfaction every time she looked at it. She was not going to fill that hole.

'Did you get the money back?' So he thought she'd returned it to the gallery!

'Yes,' she lied and bent over the pot on the stove so he wouldn't see her burning face.

*

When Sophie was born at the end of the year, she became everyone's focus. Harry was crazy about this little creature who was waving her arms and legs about in her crib. Or stretching out her fingers and regarding them as if they were something extraordinary. Which was exactly what they were. He tried to convince Dora that Sophie was counting her fingers. First the ones on the left hand, then the right hand. He could see it clearly and he recognised the concentration on her face. She was definitely dealing with numbers, trying to figure out whether she had exactly the same number of fingers on each hand.

Dora was not too sure about it. After all, Sophie was only a few months old, but she didn't want to discourage Harry's interest in his daughter. He just knew that his daughter would be very clever one day.

Andrew and Leah were just as smitten by this little girl as Harry and Dora. Knowing what she knew now about Leah and her inability to ever have her own children, Dora shared her daughter freely with her in-laws. When they came to visit, Dora busied herself with the coffee and the biscuits, pouring the milk from the two-litre container into a little jug, filling up the sugar bowl and fluffing about with serviettes. All unnecessary activities just to give Andrew and Leah time alone with their little niece. The brand-new aunt and uncle became a second set of parents for Sophie.

As Sophie got older, she even spent the odd night on the hobby farm with her aunt and uncle. She loved the chickens and chased them all around the yard, flapping her arms and squawking as if she were one of them.

Sophie also became a favourite with Mr Tomlinson next door. He always called out to her over the fence when she was playing in the backyard. Sometimes Dora found new toys lying in the grass. 'Mr Tomli gave them to me,' Sophie explained to her mother with a serious expression on her face.

From the age of three, Sophie was allowed to go across to their elderly neighbour, holding on tightly to a small wicker basket. She would deliver Dora's freshly baked scones or a small jar of honey, sometimes half a dozen eggs she had collected at Andrew and Leah's farm. Dora would watch her daughter from the driveway as she stood patiently in front of Mr Tomlinson's house, waiting for him to shuffle from his kitchen to open the door for her. He would let her in and several minutes later she would emerge with a handful of lollies in her little basket. Sometimes Dora would lift Sophie over the low fence back onto her driveway. Other times she watched her daughter skipping down old Tomlinson's drive, swinging her basket to and fro, and then back up their own driveway. One day she proudly told Dora that Mr Tomlinson had called her 'Little Red Riding Hood' but that she did not have to fear the big, bad wolf. He would always watch out for her.

21

October 1994

Dora's dress makes its film debut

L ATE IN 1994, TWO TICKETS to the preview of the outback movie came in the mail. It had taken nearly three years for the filming to be finished. With a young child in the house, Dora had just about forgotten that she had created a stunning dress for this film. There was so much to do, her mind often flitting from one thing to another.

The preview was to take place in Sydney, and Dora was desperate to go. Would she take Harry? She hadn't forgotten his deprecating comments when she had invited him to see *The Great Gatsby*. No, she wouldn't ask him. He could look after Sophie while she either went on her own or with Leah. She would definitely ask Leah.

The movie was set in colonial Australia sometime in the mid-nineteenth century. A young English woman had come out to marry a poor but ambitious squatter who had promised her future wealth in this land of plenty. But to start with, her life consisted of neverending work and unimaginable hardship. Living in a log cabin somewhere far removed from the elegant society she was used to, she felt exhausted and defeated by this hostile land. Then, one day she received a box from an aunt in England.

At this point in the movie, Dora's breath stopped and she grasped Leah's hand. This was the scene she had been waiting for. In the box the young woman finds bed linen, tablecloths, soap, big tins of tea, writing paper and ink wells. And finally, from the bottom of the box she pulls out this exquisite evening gown. In the movie, her dirty hands and broken fingernails are clearly visible as she holds the dress up and starts wailing.

Dora's brief had been to create an unforgettable contrast between the deprivation the young woman suffered in her current life and the life she had left behind. 'Yes!' Dora quietly rejoiced in her seat. 'Yes!'

The shiny, burnt-orange cotton and silk gown with the delicate lace trimmings had achieved everything it was meant to do. In the candlelight of the rough cabin, the glass beads were shimmering and sparkling as the young woman turned the dress from one side to the other. It was a blindingly beautiful object that had dropped out of the sky into a dull, desperate situation. And it was this dress that gave the young woman hope and the courage to keep going. It held the promise of a better life.

*

Later, in the hotel room she shared with Leah, it took Dora an eternity to calm her excitement. Luckily, the minibar was fully stocked. She had a couple of small bottles of gin with cold water to settle down the incessant fluttering that had taken possession of her whole body. When she finally lay in bed her mood took a dramatic change. It was a great disappointment to her that Harry felt no desire to share her triumph, that he saw no purpose to her work. All of a sudden she felt deflated.

'Harry thinks my work is an indulgence, something that contributes nothing essential to society,' Dora confessed to Leah. 'He sees himself as my great benefactor who lets me play with my toys.' In the dark of the hotel room it was easy to share her feelings with her best friend, her sister-in-law. Never before had she spoken to anyone about this.

'You're an artist,' Leah replied. 'And when you look at it from that perspective, then Harry has a point. The arts can only flourish in a rich and benevolent society.'

A sharp intake of breath came from Dora's side of the room. Did everyone think her work was of no consequence? She pulled the blanket up to her chin. Her eyes felt heavy. The gin had made its way into every little crevice of her body.

'Think of countries where people are scrambling around in the dirt trying to feed their children.' Leah broke the silence. 'Trying to survive in countries where the governments are completely blind to the needs of their people. There's no time, no money, no energy and no mental capacity for the arts.' Leah lifted herself up on her elbows and in the dark looked across at Dora. 'Exactly by the way, like the main character in this film tonight. But ...' Leah sat up straight in her bed. 'But just like your dress in the film, it's the arts that give us hope and strength and insight, and help us get through difficult times. The arts force us to look at the world differently and make us aware of all the different possibilities life has to offer that we would have never considered otherwise.' Leah sank back into her pillow. 'Don't let Harry's attitude discourage you. He's a difficult man with a one-track mind. Don't let him squash you.'

'He's not a bad man,' Dora said into the darkness.

'No, he's not, you're right. Just difficult. Anyway, it's a consolation of sorts that he doesn't appreciate anyone else's achievements either. It's nothing to do with you, Dora, nothing personal.'

He did appreciate Sophie's achievements, Dora wanted to object, but all at once she was too dispirited to continue the conversation, despite Leah's encouragement. Nevertheless, it was a comfort to her that at least he acknowledged their daughter's accomplishments. Sophie was just a toddler and already she could count to fifty. She even seemed to understand small additions. In the dark, a smile passed over Dora's face, remembering Harry's pleasure at teaching Sophie how to add three mandarins to five mandarins. Yes, at least she had that consolation.

In the ensuing silence in their room, Dora became aware of the noise outside. It had probably not been a good idea to book a hotel in the middle of the city. The traffic was incessant. It was well past midnight by now, but still, cars could be heard accelerating, slowing down, accelerating again. Late revellers were calling out to each other on the footpath outside the hotel. A bottle was thrown against something metallic. A light pole maybe?

Dora turned on her side and closed her eyes. To sleep, to sleep, perchance to dream, she thought. Shakespeare? Yes. If memory served her right it was from *Hamlet*. William Shakespeare, English playwright, 1564–1616.

But sleep would not come. Instead, the film passed through her mind again. In the end, the young woman and her husband had climbed the colonial ladder and had become rich, influential personalities. The sort of people who were invited by the governor to dinner. That's where Dora's dress had been seen for the first time in public. The young woman had made a dramatic appearance in Dora's dress, to the envy of all the other invited women. More than anything else, the dress said, 'Look at us! We've made it!'

The more Dora thought about the film, the less she liked it. It had been such a 'poor-white-settler-does-good-in-untamed-wilderness-at-the-end-of-the-world' story, it made her cringe. There had hardly been any mention of the Aboriginal people whose land had been taken, or of the cruel treatment and of their killings. It had been all about how to get them off their land and get rich. Not an inkling of their suffering and unspeakable demise at the hands of exactly those people that the film celebrated.

We should be ashamed, Dora thought. Of what we did in the past and how all those lies were still perpetuated to this day. She couldn't help but feel that through her dress, she had participated in keeping alive these outdated clichés. It would certainly have been against Freda's principles to watch a film like that. Best not to mention it when she wrote to her next. Anyway, it was a consolation of sorts that she, Dora, had only gone to see her dress.

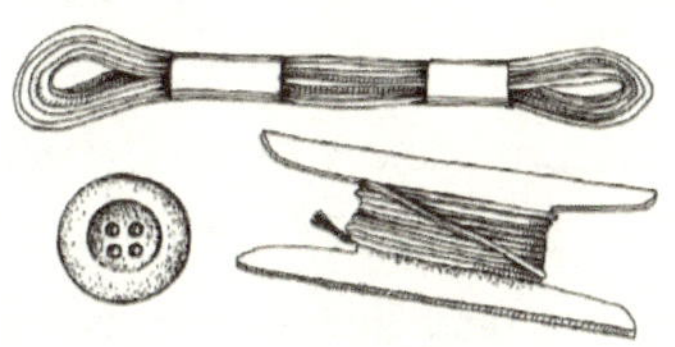

22

February 1997

Sophie's first day at school

WHEN SOPHIE STARTED SCHOOL, DORA had felt bereft. Every day for the first week she had taken her little girl to school to see her disappear into a classroom with so many other little girls and boys. And throughout those days, by herself at home, Dora had felt restless. Sophie's absence had left an unexpected vacuum in the house. Dora found herself walking from room to room, surrounded by silence. Whereas in the past five years Dora had ever only been able to snatch two or three uninterrupted hours at her sewing, she now had nearly the whole day to herself. Strange, how she so often had wished for this but suddenly she had difficulty deciding what to do first. Tidy the house? Do the shopping and prepare meals? Get down to her sewing straight away so she could get those dresses finished that were patiently waiting? Even though she had all the time in the world, she had not been able to settle down to do any sewing. At the slightest sounds she jumped up from her chair, thinking Sophie had dropped something or had cut herself. She would run into the lounge or Sophie's bedroom to check. But no, the house was empty and quiet.

She just couldn't concentrate. A noise drew Dora to the kitchen window. Peeking through the lace curtain she could see old Mr Tomlinson make his way across the front yard to his flower bed. Awkwardly he bent down and started pulling weeds. For the first time, Dora noticed how much he had aged in the last few years. His hair was thin and white, his back curved.

Not long now, Dora thought, and he wouldn't have to bend down. He would be on the same level as his plants. Instantly a guilty feeling shot up in her. No one, as far as she could remember, had visited him in months, if not years. His only son and daughter-in-law had long ago moved to the Northern Territory. They couldn't have gone any further if they'd tried, she thought with a frown.

Since Sophie's birth she had had more contact with him than ever before. The old man had been surprisingly delighted that a child lived next door. It was not long before he came over with a present. It had since become a regular occurrence. For her first day at school he had left a small parcel containing a colouring book and coloured pencils as well as an eraser in the shape of a unicorn. The eraser had been a great hit with the little girl.

In his mind he had probably adopted her as a substitute grand-child. Dora narrowed her eyes. What was he doing now? While she had been reminiscing he must have lost his balance. He was flat on his back, his arms and legs stretched out in a crooked star shape.

Good God, was he dead? No, after a few long moments he slowly rolled over onto his side. Should she go and help him up?

Too late, he was already on his knees. Finally he managed to pull himself up. Relieved, Dora watched him for a few more minutes. He looked frazzled but seemed to be alright.

Watching her elderly neighbour, Dora wondered whether Harry would turn into a doddery old man one day, holding onto the furniture to get from one room to the other. Forgetting to do up the buttons on his clothes and sloshing soup all over his face. Right at this time he seemed to be in his prime, only forty-three years old, so it was unimaginable that he would one day be too frail to hit her. Hit her! There, she had allowed that nasty thought into her mind again. For years she had pushed it away and nearly forgotten about it. Lucky for him that it only happened once! Huh, her successful husband! She couldn't care less about his achievements.

But she gave him credit for being a good father. He was absolutely enchanted by his daughter and spent as much time as he could with her. He didn't believe in fairy tales or pony club stories or colouring in. That was Dora's area of expertise. Harry explained that he would create a balance in his daughter's mind by teaching her maths. He didn't want the right brain hemisphere to take over. So he started teaching her maths and geography when she was only three or four. Geography! Dora didn't even know he had an interest in geography. Harry insisted, though, that everyone needed to know the capital cities of as many countries as possible. It was just as important as the basics of mathematics. And so he started teaching his daughter. Every morning from then on at the breakfast table there was a little test. It usually started with, 'Good morning, little sparrow. The capital of Italy?' Of course, Sophie's brain had been soaking up everything he'd taught her, so she knew the answer. 'Rome!' she called out.

'And twelve divided by three?'

'Four!' Her face was beaming.

At only four, five or six years old, Dora was not sure whether

Sophie actually understood what she was learning. Did she even know what a capital city was? But after that, breakfast could start.

By the time Sophie was nine she knew her times tables up to twelve. She didn't need any time to work out the answer when Harry did his mini-tests with her. The answer just shot out of her. Additions, subtractions, multiplications and divisions had become a game that she and Harry played together. It was fun and she rarely got the answer wrong. She also knew the capitals of countries Dora had only vaguely heard of. Some she wasn't aware even existed. The capital of Brunei? Bandar Seri Begawan, of course!

23

28 February 2024

Two days after Harry's death

Dora had taken Sophie on a little tour through their garden. She had been in desperate need of some fresh air and thought Sophie, too, would benefit from stretching her legs. Neither of them had felt like eating any dinner, but they had finished another bottle of wine.

The sun had slowly started its downhill slide. The sky was covered in pink streaks, the air still and fragrant with the smell of jasmine. New Holland honeyeaters were chirping and chasing each other.

Dora loved these long summer evenings. You could still sit outside after nine o'clock and pretend it was only mid-afternoon.

'Dora!' a voice called out to her from the other side of the hedge.

'Dora!' Dora grimaced and rolled her eyes at Sophie's questioning look.

'Yes?' she replied. She should have thought of that. As usual at this time of night, Stella Fulton was in the garden putting her vegetables to bed. Dora approached the hedge. She was determined to make this quick. She gave Sophie a little wave indicating for her to sneak back into the house.

'Dora, I'm so sorry to hear about Harry! It's such a … I'm so sorry, I don't know what to say! I can hardly believe that he's … I'm so sorry,' Stella repeated. It was rare to see this woman so flustered. 'The police were here,' she continued. 'Did you know? The police came to see me. I've never had any dealings with the police before!'

Well, I didn't send them, Dora thought, but she only nodded without speaking. Any explanation would be pointless, and she knew that Stella Sticky-Beak would not even give her half a second to respond.

'They wanted to know whether I had seen you that morning. That awful morning! When was it? Yesterday? Or the day before? Of course, I had seen you! "Hopping into the car to go to the supermarket," I said. I even told them I reminded you to take your shopping bags with you. Everyone always forgets their shopping bags and then they have to buy bags at the cash register. So I told them you were going shopping. I saw you leave in your car a bit after Harry set off for his walk.' She suddenly stopped and stared at Dora, as if waiting for her to confirm that she had told the police the right thing.

'You did right,' Dora replied. 'I went shopping. You probably saw me coming back, too.'

'Actually, I didn't. I mean I didn't see you, but I heard your car. So in a way you could say I saw you come back.'

Dora nodded. 'Yes, you could. You could say that.' She turned away from her neighbour. 'I'm sorry but I'll have to go inside. I've got my daughter with me and we're both quite upset as you can imagine.'

'Oh, of course, of course. Can I bring some vegetables over for the two of you? Maybe tomorrow morning? Yes, that's what I'll do. I'll pick them in the early morning so they're fresh for you! And my condolences again.'

'Thank you, Stella! Goodbye.'

*

'Wow, that woman is quite something!' Sophie had been standing by the open lounge room door following the one-sided conversation. 'I suppose she means well.'

'Yes, she does. She has been supplying us with vegetables ever since she and her husband moved in years ago. I have to say, I'm a bit surprised that you've never made an effort to meet your tenants.' Dora raised her eyebrows at her daughter in disapproval. 'They are the ideal tenants. Mind you, half the time she's on her own. Her husband works on some ship or other and is away for weeks on end. Anyway, you couldn't have wished for more.' Dora couldn't avoid a tiny hint of criticism in her voice.

'I would have wished for old Mr Tomlinson to still live there,' Sophie countered. 'I loved that old man.'

'Well, he would've been over a hundred by now, I reckon,' Dora said. 'Do you think we should ring for a pizza? We may not last the night without any food.'

Sophie nodded. 'Did you know that he was going to leave the house to me? Had he ever mentioned anything along those lines?'

'No, it was a total surprise to all of us,' Dora replied as she fished her mobile out of her handbag. 'But he always liked you. You were like a grandchild for him.' Dora dialled a number and ordered two pizzas. 'Twenty minutes,' she told Sophie.

'Yeah, a bit tragic that his only son didn't want to have anything to do with him.' Sophie followed her mother back into the kitchen.

'You should have seen your dad's face when we were told that Mr Tomlinson had left the house to you! His eyes were popping out of his head when he read the letter from the solicitor!' Dora smiled at the memory of seeing her husband, the man who was never lost for words, look like a stunned mullet. He had waved the letter around, his mouth half open, then finally managed with a croak, to ask if the letter was a joke. No, it had not been a joke and Mr Tomlinson's only son did not contest the will, either. So the house was Sophie's.

'I have a memory of Dad not particularly liking him. Do you remember, Mum …?' Sophie had opened the pantry door and pulled out another bottle of wine. She examined the label before unscrewing the top. 'Do you remember, Mum, that it was a sort of secret? I mean, me going over there and visiting Mr Tomlinson?' Sophie poured herself another glass. 'Dad didn't like him giving me lollies.'

'Yes, he always gave you lollies when you went over there, but that was not the reason for not telling your dad.' Dora put her hand over her glass and shook her head. 'Not yet. I'll wait until we have the pizza.'

'Wasn't it? Why didn't he want me to go and visit Mr Tomlinson? It's not as if I was there for the whole day. Just to drop off something for him to eat.' Sophie looked at her mother with a frown and took a sip of wine.

Dora sat down opposite her daughter. The two women scrutinised each other, one because she was used to getting her questions answered, the other because she wondered what had become of that little girl who had called herself Little Red Riding Hood whenever she walked next door with a basket of food. She had morphed into a confident young woman, a popular maths teacher at a private girls' school, and soon she would be getting married.

'One afternoon your dad saw you in Mr Tomlinson's backyard. He was probably showing you his flowers or something. I was in my sewing room when he came storming in. He was nearly apoplectic. "What is Sophie doing next door? I don't want her there by herself!" he yelled. I said, "Calm down, he's not a murderer. He's just a lonely old man. Sophie took him some cake." But your dad went completely off, telling me he wasn't talking about murderers. He was talking about lonely old men being the worst of the paedophiles and I wasn't to let you out of my sight. Otherwise he'd go over there and smash his face in.'

'Wow, I never knew that!' Sophie said stunned. 'I mean, Dad had a bit of a temper but to go off the rails like that …'

'Anyway, he calmed down and your visits to Mr Tomlinson became our secret. There, now you know.' She didn't tell Sophie that from that day on, she had made sure Sophie never stayed next door for more than ten minutes on her own. Dora would always find a reason to go and get her. Sometimes she joined her and they would sit in Mr Tomlinson's dining room or on his deck together. After all, Harry had put that worm of suspicion into her mind. Because if you weren't actually there yourself, you really couldn't know what was going on, could you?

As if she'd read her mother's mind, Sophie suddenly said, 'Just to reassure you, he never did anything, you know? He really was just a lonely old man.' She finished her wine and stood up. 'I'm having a quick shower before the pizza arrives.'

While Sophie was in the bathroom, Dora put out some plates and cutlery. Even in a time of crisis you should eat properly, she thought. Eating pizza straight out of the box and with your hands was one of her pet hates. Somehow, mysteriously, the grease always made its way from your fingers to your face. And when you rubbed your nose, it would itch for ages. With perfect timing, there was a knock on the door just as she set down the knives.

*

Sophie had just washed down the last of the pizza with some more red wine, when she suddenly jumped up off her chair. 'I can't believe it!' she cried. 'I still haven't rung Tom!'

'Go, go,' Dora shooed her away from the table. 'Go into my sewing room. You can talk in private there. I'll clean up here.'

It would be interesting to finally meet this young man. Sometimes Dora thought that Sophie kept her private life a bit too private. Surely, sometime soon Sophie would have to introduce him to her, particularly considering everything that had happened these last two days. You would expect this young man to come and support his wife-to-be during this difficult time. So hopefully Dora would make his acquaintance well before the wedding, whenever that would happen now, but she did not like her chances. She hadn't even known this young man existed until Sophie rang her and told her they were getting married. Come to think of it, she had ever only been introduced to a boyfriend once. And that had been years ago! Her daughter was thirty-two! Surely she would have had more than one boyfriend before this … this Tom.

She did remember the call, though, and she remembered very clearly Harry's relief at finding out that his daughter was not a lesbian!

*

Sophie decided to drive back to Launceston early the following morning. She wanted to apply for more time off and prepare some work so that a substitute teacher could take over her classes. Then she would pack a bag, come back to Kingston and stay with Dora until the funeral.

So on the third day after Harry's death, Dora found herself alone in the house. Gingerly, on bare feet, she wandered from one silent room into the next, scrutinising the walls and the furniture as if she hadn't seen them in years. As if they belonged to someone else.

In the past, when Harry was still working, she had often been alone in the house, sometimes for several days, when he was away on a business trip. But she had always known that he would be coming back. Now he was gone forever. Yet, somehow his presence was still there in the house. His shoes stood neatly lined up on the shoe rack, his car keys and mobile phone in a small wicker basket on top of the hall cupboard.

Through the open door of his study, Dora saw a pile of paperwork on his desk. Probably someone's tax return he hadn't quite finished. She would have to contact that person and tell them to find someone else. For a while now, she had had her doubts over these tax returns he did privately. His mind had not been as sharp as it used to be and someone had come back to him once, pointing out a mistake he had made. Oh well, his death had put an end to all of that.

On the floor next to his desk lay an old jumper. Even in summer it could get cool at night, but Harry refused to turn on the panel heater they had had especially installed in his office. He preferred to put on an extra jumper. Dora frowned. She stepped into the office and retrieved the jumper. It belonged in Harry's wardrobe, not on the floor.

And there, behind the jumper, pushed halfway under the desk were the shoe boxes with all those family photos she had asked Harry to sort. Dora bent down and opened the boxes. Well, why was she not surprised? Harry had done absolutely nothing with those photos. He probably hadn't even opened the lids. With her foot she pushed the boxes even further under the desk and left the study.

On her way to the bedroom she passed the lounge room, where her eyes immediately fell on Barb's old chair. She loved that chair, but she hadn't taken any notice of it in a long time. With her finger tips she traced the carvings on the timber back and the seat. Why would anyone put carvings on a seat? They were uncomfortable to sit on and once you sat on them you couldn't see them anyway. How silly! Not that she or Harry had ever looked on it as anything other than a decorative object. But that chair would stay. Years ago she had made a nice thick cushion for it to make it more comfortable. Yet, the cushion always sat on the floor beside it because Harry said it spoilt the look of the chair. Dora bent down to retrieve the cushion, gave it a vigorous slap to clear the dust off it and placed it on the chair. Well, one day soon she would sit on it.

Some other things would have to be more rigorously dealt with, though. For example, Harry's dark green recliner chair, that looked like a dead dinosaur, would definitely have to go. Right from the beginning, when the store delivered it, she had hated that recliner. It took up a whole corner in the lounge room and Dora hadn't even known Harry had bought it! It sat there like it had lost its way into the jungle and accidentally ended up in her house. Maybe St Vinnie's would take it. They had a salesroom somewhere in the city specifically for second-hand furniture.

Idly, she walked into the bedroom. The window was still open from this morning's airing and the bed was unmade. Dora opened the door on Harry's side of the wardrobe. Carelessly, she folded the jumper and shoved it onto one of the shelves. A number of suits, mostly in different tones of grey, hung resignedly on their hangers, as if they knew they would probably never be worn again. Who would want them? Sophie's new man? Unlikely. Andrew? Dora had never seen him in a suit.

Harry's shirts offered a bit more variety in colour than the suits. There were some blues, some greys, a number of white ones, even a couple of lavender tones. His ties hung right next to the shirts, folded neatly over a special tie hanger. Dora ran her hand over the ties. Here were some bright checks, paisleys, some dots. Some time ago, someone had given Harry a really silly tie, pink elephants on a dark blue background. She pulled the elephant tie off the hanger and knotted it up. This one could go straight into the rubbish bin. Harry had never worn it anyway. But what would she do with the rest of his clothes? The suits, the shirts, they all came from the best shops. The discount stores made no money out of Harry. It looked like she would have to take everything to the charity shops. They would have a field day with these clothes. But not now. There was time for all of this. Dora slammed the wardrobe door shut again.

She looked towards the unmade bed. With a swift movement she swept the rumpled doona aside and sat down on the edge. Soon she would have to make some important decisions and Harry's clothes would be the least of these. She would have to organise a funeral. Whatever paperwork needed to be done for that would, without doubt, be left for her to deal with. She would have to contact their solicitor and sort out the will. Also Harry's retirement fund, to release the money to her. At least the bank account was no problem. She had always had access to it. One thing could be said about Harry and that was he had always given her access to his accounts and rarely questioned her expenses. But at the moment there was nothing she could do, nothing at all.

Unless the police took her away for questioning or – God forbid! – worse, she would have at least a week or two of doing nothing, a short period of living in a vacuum. If she were sensible she would use this time to finish off the dress she was in the process of sewing. At the moment it hung half-finished on one of the mannequins.

It was definitely a priority, as the opera company in Sydney could not wait for her personal dramas to conclude.

And maybe, just maybe, she should be dealing with a few other things. Stored away in the recesses of her mind were a number of significant events from the past that she had so far successfully ignored. Telling Sophie about her teenage crush on Andrew and explaining why she hadn't been allowed to go to Europe with him, had released something in her. As if a valve had been tentatively opened to let out some very stale air. Dora had felt strangely relieved to share those snippets of her life with Sophie. Maybe she should sort through her memory and examine a few more events. She might not have Harry's or Sophie's genius mathematical brain, but she had a very good memory. Very good, indeed. So with a bit of luck, some of the more unpleasant memories that were lingering in her mind might evaporate, and if not completely evaporate, at least the sting could be taken out of them.

But where to start? Should Sophie be her sounding board? No. Dora shook her head. Sophie didn't need to know everything. She lifted herself off the side of the bed. It would probably be best to start with the letters she had written to Freda. For decades now she had told Freda in letters about all those momentous events that had happened in her life. If she read them out aloud it would be like reading them to Freda. What a good idea!

She crossed over into her sewing room and opened the grey filing cabinet. All her patterns were neatly folded up inside large yellow business envelopes and labelled on the outside. *Sarah MacQueen, wedding dress, 1989.* God, some of those patterns were decades old but she couldn't bear to throw them out. She'd kept them all, together with her sketch books. Quickly she rummaged around the envelopes. *18th C, Baroque dress, Melbourne Rep Society, 1997.* No, not that one. *Hunting suit, Robyn Hood, Huonville Theatre Co., 1986.* No, not that one either. Finally she found the one she was looking for, right in the middle. A large yellow envelope like all the others, labelled *For Love or Money, EF.*

No one looking through the envelopes in her filing cabinet would think that this was anything else but another pattern for a play by that title and for a company called EF. Only she knew the 'company' was called Emergency Fund. Dora opened the envelope. In it were a number of letters and however many hundred-dollar notes. Good God! She only glanced at the money. It was the letters she wanted to check. Yes, all still there. Every single one. But the desire to read them had completely left her.

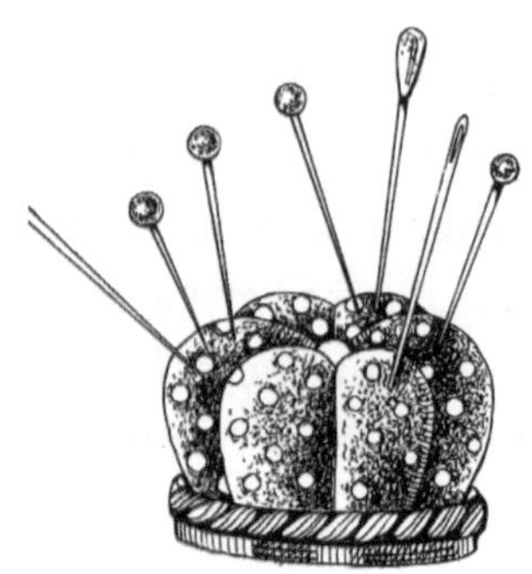

24

29 February 2024

Three days after Harry's death

Towards the afternoon, Dora decided to get back to the dress she was sewing for the opera company in Sydney. She hadn't had many commissions recently and wanted to do a particularly good job with this one. The opera company was waiting, and she needed to keep busy and distract herself.

She pushed one of her mannequins into the corner behind the door. It was the old one, the first one she'd ever bought, the one that had stood in the lounge before they had the sewing room built. The one that had been the impetus for the extension because it had so often frightened Harry when he walked past it in the dark. Well, she didn't need it at the moment. It was old and you couldn't adjust the width and length of anything on it. Really, Dora only kept it for sentimental reasons. It was an old friend reminding her of her early years as a designer and seamstress.

Dora pulled her chair out and sat down in front of her sewing machine. Without moving, she stared at the black cotton string making its way from the reel on top of the machine all the way down in many wondrous curves to the needle. Into the needle hole it went and then sat there waiting for the machine to start and to be entwined in a perfect pattern with the cotton thread that came up from the bobbin.

Just like life, Dora thought. Everyone going up and down in crazy movements, sometimes in perfect harmony with one another, forming a beautiful, neat seam. At other times dealing with snags or big tangled knots that could only be undone by an enormous amount of patience or the cruel snip of the scissors.

Dora didn't believe that she was much of a philosopher. No, she was much too practical to contemplate airy-fairy concepts. Generally, she didn't like to think too much of things that she couldn't deal with directly. If something needed to be done, she would do it. If there were problems, she liked to solve them. If a dress needed to be sewn, she would sew it. And that was all there was to it.

Nevertheless, she thought, there were always things that surprised you by their inability to be understood or resolved. It did hurt to realise, for example, that your own children could become unknown entities as they grew up. To think you didn't even know your own children! At least she thought she didn't know her daughter. Not like she used to imagine she would when Sophie was growing up. She'd had that notion that there would come a day when Sophie and she would be best friends. But that didn't happen. Inconceivable that something coming directly from your body could be so different from you and so unknowable. Surely she was not the only person with such a dilemma. What were others thinking about all of that? She only seemed to know people who were either showing off with their children's achievements, all those doctors-to-be, lawyers-to-be and so on, or people who were avoiding the topic. Maybe their children were unemployed or drug addicts, something that you couldn't show off with.

With a sigh, Dora put her foot on the pedal and started up her sewing machine. Leah, her sister-in-law, had confessed to her once that she couldn't have children. Not that she said why. She hadn't realised that Dora already knew. But Dora had promised Andrew never to mention it and so she hadn't.

There was a sadness that darkened Leah's eyes when she saw Dora play with Sophie. Sophie, the baby. Sophie the toddler. Dora would kiss and cuddle her, blow raspberries on that oh-so-soft skin on her daughter's belly to make her scream with pleasure and wriggle like a big grub and cry out for more. 'More rabby!' Sophie would call out. 'More rabby!' and lift her tummy up to her mother's face.

'Rabby, rabby, raspberry,' Dora would sing out to her in response. She could have eaten her daughter up.

At moments like these, Dora could feel Leah's pain and sadness. When Sophie lay snuggled up against her mother's chest, fast asleep, making those sweet sucking noises that only small children could make. When she could nearly convince herself that this small creature was back in her womb, warm and safe. Leah would never experience this mother-daughter union.

But now her situation was not so much different from Leah's. You couldn't snuggle a grown woman in her early thirties to your chest or blow raspberries on her belly. A woman who turned out so differently from her mother, so separate. A woman with a doctorate in mathematics and a partner of seven months and twenty-five days, neither of whom wanted to contribute to the overpopulation of the planet. Well, that's what her daughter had told her in no uncertain terms!

Dora took her foot off the pedal and the machine came to an

instant stop. She narrowed her eyes as she inspected the fabric under the needle. The stitches were much too long, much too loose. She would have to go over the seam again. It was clear that she was not in the right frame of mind for this. It was too soon after Harry's death. Good God, what was she thinking? A quick snip with her scissors and the fabric was liberated. She pulled it out from under the machine and started the seam again.

Five minutes later, she cut the black thread and regarded the seam on her fabric. There, double-stitched now. Bomb-proof. Just like her love for her daughter.

*

Turning towards the kitchen door, Dora caught sight of her daughter's photo on the fridge. Sophie! Where had that rosy, kissable baby gone? The little girl who pulled Aunt Leah's radishes out of the ground? Oh, the delight when she discovered the plump red radishes at the end of the greenery she held in her chubby little hands! That little girl was now in her thirties! It was unthinkable.

Michelle's phone call all those years ago when Dora had been pregnant had changed her life. She had accepted Michelle's contract and had worked on that very special dress for the film that was being shot in the outback. The contract had enabled her to limit sewing never-ending replicas of some princess's wedding dress or creating an outfit for someone's silver jubilee that would have looked better on a woman thirty years younger.

So, despite her pregnancy, and despite being the main carer for her daughter, she had embraced this new work and had been able to make a name for herself in certain theatre and film circles. Not quite as much as she had dreamt of all those years ago. It was clear that she had not moved to the top of the 'desirable designers' list as she had once fantasised. Nevertheless, her dress designs were authentic, creative and imaginative, and she was proud of them.

*

Dora walked into her sewing room and regarded the fabric she had spread out on her cutting table. Several metres of a dark green georgette were waiting to be cut. When she had first come across this fabric she had not liked working with it. At the technical college, her teacher had given her a piece of silk georgette that ran through her fingers much too quickly. She had not been able to control the fabric. It had a mind of its own and slid around under her machine every which way. Compared to her classmates she was already quite an experienced dressmaker, but the fabrics she had used had been heavier than this. They had been mainly cottons or cotton-polyester mixes. It had been easy to work with them. In the technical college she had struggled with the softer, sheer fabrics, the silks and satins and georgettes. Since then, though, Dora had come to like and manage them. The light and sheer fabrics flowed around the wearer like a gentle sea breeze on a hot summer's day. They were perfect for that special skirt or dress!

Dora ran her hands over the fabric. At times she thought it was a shame to cut beautiful material into pieces. It should remain uncut, whole, only the edges tidied so they wouldn't fray.

Sitting back on her stool, Dora looked around her sewing room. Two mannequins, a cupboard whose doors would not close anymore. Every shelf inside the cupboard full of fabrics and cotton reels and all sorts of bits and pieces. On the opposite side a small filing cabinet containing numerous dress patterns, some shop-bought, others of Dora's own design.

On the wall next to the filing cabinet hung a pin board. It was covered in notes that Dora had scribbled to herself and a couple of pictures of dresses she had cut out of magazines. A whole row of family photos was neatly pinned to the board, running down the right-hand side. The three of them on the beach in Bicheno, on the Tasmanian east coast. It had been a two-week summer holiday, spent in a cottage owned by some work colleague of Harry's.

Another photo showed Sophie as a five-year-old on a swing, her hair flying, her face looking ecstatic. Dora couldn't remember where that photo had been taken. They must have discovered a playground on one of their many walks.

Dora and Sophie in sun hats and bathers in a third photo. This had been Sophie's shell collecting phase. There were always shells on Kingston Beach, right near their house.

And here, Harry and Sophie at the kitchen table, their heads together, the expression on Sophie's face full of wonder. She was nearly eleven when Dora took that particular photo.

Dora stood up to take a closer look. She remembered the day this particular photo was taken very clearly because she had learned something, too, and because she realised then that Sophie was completely hooked on numbers. Harry had taught her a multiplication trick: how to multiply numbers between eleven and nineteen with each other in a very simple way that no one but he knew. He had winked at his daughter, whispering that this particular trick was a family secret. And now she was old enough to be initiated into the circle of the few people who knew this trick. He had it made sound like magic. Then he had assured her that with a bit of practice, she wouldn't even need to write down the process of working out the answer. She would be able to do it in her head.

He had given her an example: 12 times 16. Add the unit of the second number to the first number: 12 + 6 = 18. Add a 0 to make 180. Then multiply the units of each number. In this case 2 x 6 which equals 12. Add 180 and 12 to get your answer: 192!

It probably only took Sophie two or three attempts on paper

before she could do it in her head. Sophie then tried the method with numbers larger than twenty but as her father had warned her, it only worked with numbers between eleven and nineteen. Dora remembered Sophie beaming at her father. She was absolutely thrilled. Of course, in her maths classes at school she showed off with it. Asking everyone to test her. And always getting the answer right. Apparently she had never told anyone how she could do the multiplication that quickly. She had kept the family secret.

Harry was her god. He was clever and showed her that she, Sophie, was just as clever if not better. It amused both of them no end to set Dora maths problems or ask her if she could name the capital city of some obscure country. The two of them ganging up on her. She didn't resent it. She was pleased at the close connection the two of them had. It was just that occasionally she felt left out. Of course, everything changed shortly after Sophie's thirteenth birthday. The day when her god showed his malicious and churlish side and did not even spare his daughter.

The day when Dora could have strangled him.

25

November 2004

Sophie's thirteenth birthday

WHEN SOPHIE TURNED THIRTEEN, UNCLE Andrew and Aunt Leah were invited to a birthday afternoon tea. As usual, they brought Gran Barb with them.

Barb, at the age of seventy-five, was still a feisty lady. Somehow she seemed to have become much younger and much livelier since her husband's death many years ago. For a while she had seemed lost after John died, but in time she recovered and took her life in hand. She transformed herself from a farmer's wife into a well-dressed, well-coiffed lady about town. She looked after herself better. Her clothes were not exactly elegant, but always of good quality, neat and clean. Every Friday now she went to her hairdresser for a trim that didn't seem to be necessary. Her short, layered hair always looked exactly the same.

And that was not all. Twice a week she made her way in her zippy little car to the casino, where she played bingo or the pokies. Elegant, with manicured fingernails and painted lips, she slipped coins into the slot machine with a satisfied smile and a complete absence of a bad conscience. Her two greatest pleasures in life, she once confessed to Dora, were spending all her money before she died and seeing her only granddaughter, Sophie, grow up.

Sophie brought so much joy to Barb, just like she did to old Mr Tomlinson. For her thirteenth birthday he had given her a fifty-dollar voucher to her favourite stationery shop. Sophie must have told him how much she liked the boxes of colourful pencils and the notebooks covered in what looked like antique paper but probably wasn't. For quite a while she had also had her eyes on a leather-bound address book, which was exorbitantly expensive. As soon as the guests had left, Dora would go next door with Sophie to thank Mr Tomlinson for his generous present.

From her Grandma Barb, Sophie received a small box wrapped in silk fabric.

'I know what's in it!' Sophie held up the box excitedly for everyone to see. 'Well, not exactly but I have an inkling!' They all knew what was in the box. She had told everyone that she wanted a pair of earrings from Grandma Barb. They had looked through a catalogue together and Sophie had picked out two pairs that she liked. She had said to Grandma Barb, 'I would like one of these but you can pick which one to get. Surprise me!' Andrew smiled at his niece's enthusiasm. Even Harry looked pleased. His daughter knew what she wanted but she was open to surprises.

Carefully, Sophie removed the silk fabric, then she opened the little box. A small sound escaped her as her eyes grew bigger and bigger. She snapped the lid shut again and flew at her grandmother.

'You really are the best!' she cried as she kissed Barb noisily on the cheek.

'Come on, show us!' Even though Harry didn't really care about jewellery one way or the other, he wanted to know what his mother had bought for his daughter. Sophie ran over to her father and opened the box again. Everyone was leaning over Harry to have a look and soon the room was filled with 'oohs' and 'aahs' and 'how beautifuls'.

'She's bought me both pairs!' Sophie was dancing around the room, her eyes sparkling. 'I got both pairs of earrings!'

Raising his eyebrows, Harry looked at his mother. 'You're spending your money like it's going out of fashion.' He stared again at the earrings. 'At least they're real gold. They won't lose their value.'

Barb put her hands on her hips. 'And what did you get your daughter?' she challenged her eldest son.

'Well, there is something,' he said with a mysterious smile.

Everyone looked up expectantly. Even Dora was surprised. She had bought a voucher for Sophie from one of the clothes shops that were so popular with teenage girls. She was always the one who organised presents for everyone, so she was astonished to hear that Harry had something else in store for his daughter.

Harry shook his head. 'I'm not telling. Sophie is getting her surprise from me when you've all left.' There was a collective sigh of disappointment in the lounge room, but they knew Harry. It was no good pushing him so the next best thing to do was to leave him be and cut the birthday cake.

*

'Now, listen, you two,' Harry said to his wife and daughter in the evening. The guests had gone home and Dora had been busy cleaning up. She also had a pot of Bolognese sauce simmering on the stove for their dinner.

'I have a surprise for you,' Harry continued. 'As a matter of fact it's a surprise for all of us, not just the birthday girl.' For a quick moment he scowled at Dora, who was dressed in her apron, holding a wooden spoon in her hand. Tomato sauce was dripping onto the floor.

'Put that spoon back and sit down here for a second!' he ordered her. 'I want to tell you something. Something important. Because this is my birthday present for Sophie.' He pulled Sophie to his side and waited until Dora sat down opposite him.

'First of all,' he said to his daughter with a twinkle in his eye, 'what is eighteen times fifteen?'

Sophie moaned and rolled her eyes. Without thinking she said, 'Two hundred and seventy!'

'Well done!' Harry praised his daughter proudly. She knew her times tables upside down and back to front. At the age of thirteen she could have put many a university student to shame.

'And the capital of Benin?'

A few seconds of hesitation. 'Porto-Novo?'

'Excellent! And how about the capital of—'

'Dad, stop it! What about my birthday surprise?'

'Well, then, here it is,' Harry said magnanimously. 'In a few weeks, the school holidays are starting and I have taken ten days off work during that time. I think we can all do with a holiday, so we're going to go away somewhere nice and warm. What do you think?'

Surprised, Dora exchanged a quick glance with her smug-looking husband. She could not help but think that this had been a rhetorical question. He was not actually asking her opinion, was he? Or Sophie's?

'And because it's Sophie's birthday I thought that she could decide where we should go. And that would be my birthday present to her!' Harry said triumphantly. Dora could definitely sense something boastful in this pronouncement, but she immediately chided herself for being so suspicious. What Harry had suggested was really generous. Unusually generous. She could only assume that he had finished some difficult audit or other and received a nice bonus.

'Now, I have to put a small proviso on this,' Harry continued. 'When I say, Sophie, you can choose where we're going, I don't mean something extravagant like Europe or South America. I'm talking about something a bit closer to home. After all, we only have ten days. So maybe Noosa or Broome. Even Thailand or Malaysia would be alright. It's not too far and those places are not all that expensive.'

Sophie flung her arms around her father's neck. 'Oh, Dad, that is so cool! That is the best birthday present I've ever had!' she cried out. 'And I know exactly where I would like to go. Bali!' She pulled away from Harry and looked from him to her mother to gauge their reaction. 'Would Bali be alright?" she asked excitedly.

'Well, that was fast!' Dora pushed her chair aside and walked over to the stove to stir the Bolognese sauce. 'Why do you want to go to Bali?'

But Sophie had already turned back to her dad. 'I think Bali would be the best! And it's not expensive! And the flight doesn't take that long!' she exclaimed breathlessly. She kissed Harry on the cheek. 'I'd love to go to Bali!' she repeated.

'Well, well,' Harry said. 'Indecision is not a problem with this little girl.'

Sophie leaned away from him. 'Not so little, I'm already thirteen,' she reminded her father. 'And no, I'm not indecisive. That's really where I want to go, Bali.' She hesitated for a moment. Her forehead wrinkled, she seemed to contemplate something.

'Annabelle and her parents are going to Bali in the holidays. For a week. I could meet up with her there. We would have such a cool time together.' Her voice faltered slightly. She knew that her father did not particularly like her best friend's parents. They were artists, people who did not contribute anything constructive to society. People who were supported by the taxes of those who worked hard. People like him.

'I will ask Annabelle when exactly they're going. Maybe we could coordinate our time over there,' Sophie continued, suddenly desperate to convince her father that that was a great idea.

When Harry spoke there was a trace of hardness in his voice. 'If we're going to Bali, we will definitely not go on someone else's timetable,' he said. 'I'll check flights and accommodation and book something that suits us best, and not according to what suits the Desmans best.' Tension flooded the kitchen as he stood up. 'Leave it with me. I'll organise something.'

*

From the kitchen, Dora could hear the door slam. According to the clock next to the kitchen dresser it was a quarter past five. She had only just started preparing dinner, thinking Harry would not be home before six. Not to worry. He could wait.

Harry entered the kitchen and flung his briefcase onto one of the chairs. Why could he not carry it into the study? It was only a couple of steps more. But then Dora saw the big smile on his face and her annoyance evaporated. It was so rare to see him come home from work in a cheerful mood that she didn't want to spoil it by making a fuss over his bag.

'Is Sophie home?' he asked as he loosened his tie.

'Yes, in the lounge, I think. Doing her homework.'

'Good girl. Hey, little sparrow!' Harry called out. 'Come here, your dad's home!' There was no doubt now in Dora's mind that he was in an excellent mood. He only called Sophie 'sparrow' when all was well in his world. Which was not very often. Maybe he had finally finished the books for that company that had been giving him a big headache. She hadn't dared mention it again after one of his outbursts of anger when she had inquired about it some days ago.

Sophie came skipping into the kitchen. She was still in her school uniform, but her blouse hung out of her skirt and her feet were now in her favourite fluffy slippers instead of the heavy black uniform shoes. She had retained the blond hair she was born with and that she had inherited from Dora. Her French plait must have come undone on the way home from school. It now hung loosely around her shoulders.

'Look at you, little sparrow,' Harry said as he pulled his daughter towards him. 'You're looking quite dishevelled. Had a hard day or has someone attacked you?' he asked jokingly.

Dora took a bottle of water from the fridge and turned towards Harry. He really was in an exceptionally good frame of mind.

'Now, tell me,' he said to his daughter, 'what is the value of each angle in a hexagon?'

'A hundred and twenty degrees,' she answered.

'And what is the sum of all the angles in a hexagon?'

'Dad, you're annoying!' she complained. 'Seven hundred and twenty degrees!' Sophie pulled away from him and sat down on a chair.

Dora poured a glass of water and put it on front of Harry.

'You would not believe it,' he started as he wriggled out of his jacket and hung it on the kitchen chair behind him. Another thorn in Dora's eyes but she refrained from saying anything. This was not a good moment to mention the jacket. As a matter of fact, there was never a good moment. She would just have to put it in the wardrobe herself. As usual.

'I mentioned to some of the guys at work that I'm about to book a holiday to Bali and one of the accountants, Rob, says, "If you want you can have our apartment in Fiji."'

Sophie stared at him in surprise. 'Fiji? Why Fiji? It's nowhere near Bali!'

Harry ignored her and took a large sip of water. 'Rob has talked about that apartment before. It's usually let out but someone cancelled and so it's available in the holidays. How fortuitous is that? And best of all, he'll let us have it for nothing!' Pleased with himself, he looked from his wife to his daughter. 'We'll only have to pay for the airfare!'

When he finally stopped speaking, a silence hung in the kitchen. Dora and Sophie were looking at each other. Dora to gauge Sophie's reaction to this announcement. Sophie to will her mother to say that they didn't want to go to Fiji, that they had agreed to go to Bali.

'I don't want to go to Fiji!' Sophie suddenly yelled. 'You said I could choose where to go and I said Bali and you agreed!'

'At that point I didn't know we could have an apartment in Fiji!' Harry had raised his voice, too, but was not yelling. Silently, Dora gave him credit for trying to control his impatience. 'Can't you see what an opportunity this is?'

'Harry,' Dora ventured carefully. 'This was meant to be Sophie's birthday present, and she chose Bali. Bali is cheap. I'm sure we can afford to pay for the accommodation there.' As soon as the last sentence had escaped her lips she knew she shouldn't have said it. Harry hated sarcasm, even the slightest hint of it. Particularly when it was directed at him.

In the silence, Harry stood up. 'Right then,' he said very quietly. His face was white, his lips contracted into thin lines. 'Right then. Forget it. The holiday is off. We're staying home. I'm not having you tell me where we can and can't go.' Without another look at his wife and daughter he disappeared into his study.

Sophie's whole body tensed up. Distraught, she clenched her hands into fists and said, 'I didn't know Dad could be that mean.'

She burst into tears, ran into her room and slammed the door shut behind her.

Mean? Dora thought. Vindictive is more like it. She knew then that something had been broken between Harry and his daughter. It was the first time that he had exposed his ruthless side to Sophie.

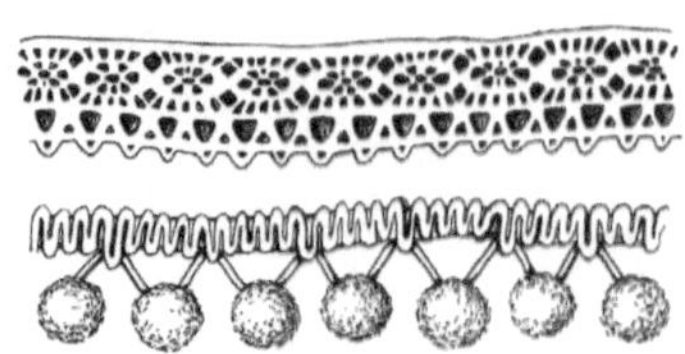

26

1 March 2024

Four days after Harry's death

THE SOUND OF HER MOBILE phone tore Dora from those upsetting memories. Where was the blasted thing? She ran into the hallway. There, on the hall table.

'Mum, I can't come for another couple of days,' Sophie said, as always without a preamble. 'There are things happening at school and they can't get a replacement for me until the day after tomorrow. But I'll come as soon as I can, okay?'

'Yes, darling, I understand. Just come whenever it suits. The funeral won't be for another week or two anyway.'

'Okay, Mum. Bye.'

In a way, it was a relief to have another few days to herself. There would be no interruption to her work on that dress that was nearly finished. If only she could sit down and finally complete it, she wouldn't have to think about it all the time! Anyway, she didn't have to stop for meals now that Sophie wasn't coming, or waste time on conversations or walks or whatever else one did when there was another person in the house. Not that she usually minded, but at the moment everything was piling up on top of her. She really needed to get a grip.

With a determined sigh, she sat down and got to work on the dress. There really wasn't much left to do. A hem, quickly done on the machine. The lace around the neck tucked in and fastened here and there with a few stitches. One of the buttonholes needed tidying up. There, all done. To finish it, Dora ironed the creases out of the dress and hung it up. It was another dress for the theatre company in the city. The severe, black dress of a grieving widow. Even the lace around the neck and the wrists was black. Huh, Dora thought. I should be wearing this. She brushed the dress down with her hands like she always did when she had finished a project. A caress and a goodbye to yet another one of her creations.

Dora knew, though, that her rest was short-lived. Another pattern lay waiting on top of her filing cabinet. She'd already prewashed the fabric for this new dress. All was ready to go, but she just couldn't get started. It would have to wait a day or two until she felt more settled. After all, she had other more important things to deal with right now.

She needed to start sorting out a few things around the house. Take another look at Harry's clothes and decide what to do with them. Rearrange some of the furniture. The green recliner would definitely have to go.

Suddenly she was hit by an idea! She would ask the two young men across the road whether they wanted it. The sad-looking couch they always sat in had most likely come from the tip. They could do with something more civilised. As long as they didn't argue over it, but that was not her problem.

Above everything else it would be some form of atonement for her own misdemeanours. She just didn't understand why she occasionally acquired ... no, not *acquired*. She should be honest with herself. She stole things. She stole. Did she have some mental problem? Why did people steal? When she was young it had just been the odd bar of chocolate or a bag of lollies. Just for the fun of it. Just to see if she could do it without getting caught. Did that mean it was some sort of power play? That she had something over those shop owners? For God's sake! She didn't even know them. Well, she hadn't *acquired* ... stolen anything in a long time.

Dora swore to herself she would never do it again. Harry was gone and this habit of hers would go too. Getting rid of the green recliner chair would symbolise the end of her silly habit. Harry gone, that dinosaur of a chair gone, her stealing gone. The chair would go to the two young men as some sort of penance and the marker of a new beginning for her.

*

Good God, she had completely forgotten about the two young men! Had the police spoken to them? They had seen her come home with her shopping bags. What had they told the police? Now she had two very good reasons to go and talk to them. Get rid of the recliner chair and find out what they had said to the police.

Dora walked to the kitchen window and stared through the lace curtains at the dilapidated house across the road. No, there was no one sitting on the veranda. They must be out working somewhere. She would just have to wait. In the meantime, she could start thinking about this new dress.

Thinking only, she told herself. The actual work can wait. It can wait!

She walked back into her sewing room and spread the fabric out on her cutting table. Running her hands over it, she smoothed it out carefully and took a critical look. You're only looking at it, she reminded herself as she walked around her cutting table scrutinising the floral pattern of the fabric. Peonies in all shades of red, alternated with yellow day lilies. Coiling around them were tendrils of ivy in delicate tones of green. A very colourful piece of fabric. A bit of care was required with the positioning of the pattern pieces if she wanted the flowers to alternate along the side and back seams of the dress. It was no good having two peonies or two day lilies meeting at the seams. Only looking!

*

Yet again, Dora was pleased that she was on her own in the house. It was lovely not to be distracted by visitors or thoughts of Harry. Oh Harry! It was difficult to grasp how quickly he had disappeared from her life. He really did some very unexpected things sometimes. Like that time when he decided, completely out of the blue, that he was going to join a card group. Dora hadn't even known he was still interested in playing cards. Her mind wandering into the past, she took her box of pins and started pinning the pattern pieces to the fabric …

27

2005-2008

The neighbourhood is changing

IT HAD BEEN SHORTLY AFTER Sophie's thirteenth birthday, and the fiasco of the abandoned holiday, that Harry had walked into Dora's sewing room late one evening. He didn't come into this room very often. The jumble of fabrics on the big table, the cut-offs underneath it and all the bits and pieces that Dora had lying around everywhere, pins and measuring tapes and reels of cotton … he couldn't deal with what to him looked like utter chaos.

Harry critically examined the mannequin, which was wearing a half-finished wedding dress. One of the sleeves had been pinned on, the other was missing completely. With his knuckles he tapped it on the head. 'Hollow, I think, like most people's heads.' Then he turned to Dora. 'I've been thinking that I would like to start playing cards again.'

'Cards?' Dora was surprised. She knew that Harry's family had been playing cards together ever since the two boys were young. Thanks to his mother they could play just about any card game. Poker, canasta, bridge … anything. Barb had been a bit of a gambler all her life. Harry had definitely inherited his competitive streak from her. More than once he had told Dora that if you wanted to be 'top of the heap' in business you had to be ambitious and a tiny bit ruthless. Something he had been taught at the card table as a young boy.

'You haven't played cards for years,' Dora said. She finished threading her sewing machine and frowned at Harry. 'What brought that on?'

'I've missed it and someone from work told me about the Kard Klub in the city. I might check it out. It's just a social thing. No money involved. Are you interested?'

'God no!' Dora sighed. 'It's never really been my cup of tea. And I've got enough on my plate with all this work.' With one sweep of her arm she indicated the mess that surrounded her.

'Sure?'

Dora waved him away. 'Yes, I'm sure. You know I'm not keen on cards. But you go. Might do you good having a hobby.' She really had been sick of seeing him in front of the television every night, swearing at whatever he was watching. 'When is it?'

'When is what? Express yourself properly!' Impatiently he tapped the mannequin's head again.

'What I mean is: what day and at what time are these card games on?' Surely it had been obvious what she was asking. He could be such a stickler for correctness.

'Every second Thursday night from seven thirty to nine thirty.'

'Okay, that's good. Check it out. You might like it,' she said breezily. She pulled a piece of fabric towards her and folded it in half. Every second Thursday night he would now be out of the house. She could work in peace and quiet. No more annoying noise from the television and no more grumbling and swearing from Harry. For at least two hours. It sounded like bliss.

Dora turned back to Harry with what she hoped looked like an encouraging smile. 'I mean it. It sounds like a good idea.'

Dora was relieved that he had found the card group and that he seemed to enjoy the company of other players. Much later, when she asked him about the games and the other players he never said much, but his satisfied smile told her that he probably won more games than he lost.

*

The year 2007 saw a couple of major changes in the small cul-de-sac. First, Dora and Harry's old neighbour, Mr Tomlinson, died of a heart attack. Alone, in hospital.

Shortly after his death, Harry and Dora received a letter from a solicitor asking them to attend the reading of Mr Tomlinson's last will and testament. At first they were confused. What was his testament to do with them? They visited the solicitor's office to discover that he had left his house and contents, as well as a small sum of money, to Sophie. Mr Tomlinson had specifically stipulated that nothing was going to go to his son.

'Could the son contest the will?' Harry had asked the solicitor. The solicitor granted that it was definitely a possibility, but in the end it never happened. As a matter of fact, the son contacted the solicitor to confirm he was not interested in any of his father's belongings, and with that, the house belonged to Sophie. As she was only sixteen at that stage, Harry looked after it for her. He handed it to a real estate agency, which rented it out to a middle-aged couple, the Fultons. Very soon after, Harry and Dora discovered that Mrs Stella Fulton was one of the nosiest people they had ever come across. She wanted to know all about the Freemans, as well as everyone else in the street, and within a few weeks she knew and spread more gossip than any of the other residents. Very quickly Harry dubbed her 'Stella Sticky-Beak Fulton'. For once Dora had to agree with him. The name he had given their new neighbour was completely justified.

*

Secondly, the old couple, the Wilsons, across the road from Harry and Dora, moved into a nursing home. They had been in their house forever, right from the beginning when the houses on that side of the road had been built, some time in the early sixties.

Harry and Dora lived on the northern side of the road, where the building blocks had been levelled before construction of the houses began. Most of the homes there were only single-storey, the front and back yards nice and flat, easily managed. Beside each house stood a garage, conveniently enabling access to the house through an internal passage from the garage or alternatively, from the roller door to the front door.

On the southern side, where the Wilsons lived, the houses were older. No one in those days had had the foresight to carve out level building blocks. Instead, the houses had been set halfway up a gentle incline, overlooking the street. There were no garages on that side because nobody had predicted the rapid rise of car ownership. All vehicles had to be parked along the street. To get to the house, owners and visitors had to march up an inclining pathway through the front yard. A set of steps led from there to the front door.

Dora remembered the elderly couple well. Through her kitchen window she often observed them lugging their shopping up the path, then stopping at the bottom of the steps to catch their breath before clambering up the stairs to their front door.

In the early years, when she and Harry had just moved into their house, there had been a lot of activity around the Wilsons' place. Mr Wilson had somehow anchored a swing set into the sloping front yard, catapulting an ever-growing number of grandchildren out into the soft grass amidst loud shrieks and a lot of laughter.

The Wilsons had spent every free minute in their garden, putting large numbers of flowering shrubs and trees into the front yard and vegetable beds into the larger back yard. Even as they crept up into their eighties, they could still be seen working in their garden. It was noticeable, though, that over the years gardening had become an arduous task for them.

First, they moved around the place at a much slower pace. Then the shrubs and trees, which had previously been regularly pruned, grew out of control. The lawn with the unused swing set grew masses of dandelions in summer and large patches of moss in wet winters. Much later, a gardening service could be seen occasionally giving everything an indiscriminate, ruthless haircut. Then even that stopped. And one day a removal truck arrived, carrying the furniture and the old couple with it, erasing all signs of a life lived over forty years.

For reasons she could not quite explain, Dora had never befriended the Wilsons. They had been older than her, their children already grown up when she and Harry bought the house opposite them. Everyone had been so busy with their own lives.

Only when the Wilsons' house was empty and devoid of all life, did it become obvious that the house had been as neglected as the garden. The paint was peeling off the weatherboards, the gutters hung loose on the western side, the veranda post closest to the wooden steps had a dangerous lean on it, only just managing to hold up the alsynite roof above it. The house stood empty for over a year after the Wilsons had gone, falling further into dereliction.

'The whole place is a job for a bulldozer,' Harry snarked often. 'An eyesore! A stain on the whole neighbourhood.' He was concerned that the dilapidated house would decrease the value of all the homes in the street.

The birds loved the deserted house. Swallows nested under the eaves, sparrows gained access via the gutters to the roof space where they raised their young, and blackbirds built nests in the daisy bush that leaned into the western wall of the house. The black-and-yellow New Holland honeyeaters flitted in and out of the grevilleas, competing with the Eastern Spinebills for nectar.

*

Early one Saturday morning in 2008, several battered utility vehicles pulled up noisily outside the old Wilson house. A number of young people violently slammed car doors shut, sending shock waves across the road. Laughing and calling out to each other, they began to lift boxes and an odd assortment of things off the backs of their utes.

Harry and Dora had just finished their breakfast. The kitchen smelled of toast and fried eggs and coffee. At the noise, Harry jumped off his chair to peek through the lace curtain on the kitchen window.

'Good Lord, Dora! Just look at that! I think we're getting new neighbours!' One hand on his hip, the other holding the lace curtain aside, he frowned. 'This doesn't bode well. Dora!' He turned to his wife and beckoned her over. 'Just look at that lot! I hope they're not all going to move in there!'

Dora stood beside him. Drying her hands on a tea towel, she

counted the young people. Seven, and a small dog tied to the back of one of the cars. Good God, seven people in that one house really seemed too much.

'Maybe they're just helping someone to move,' she ventured.

'I sure hope so, otherwise it'll be music and parties and heaven knows what every night,' Harry grumbled as he observed the activities across the road.

The young people seemed to be in their late teens, maybe early twenties. They were a rough-looking lot, sporting tattoos and sloppy clothing, their laughter harsh and loud.

'God help us,' Harry moaned. 'Surely they couldn't afford to buy a place like that. Even in the state it's in. Dora!' Harry raised his voice even though Dora stood right next to him. 'Dora, have you seen a for sale sign on that place?'

'Maybe they're just renting,' she suggested.

'God help us,' Harry repeated even though he was not in the least bit religious. He narrowed his eyes. 'Look at that girl over there! That girl carrying the basket! She's half-naked!'

Dora had long worked out that it was best to ignore some of Harry's comments. 'You know, Harry, my guess is they're renting. They might not be here for all that long. You know what those young people are like, always moving around, particularly if they're students.'

'Don't be silly, Dora. Do they look like students? More like a carload full of social refugees! They don't want to participate in our society but are more than happy to receive the dole, or whatever it's called these days!' Harry turned away from the window and sat at the table again. 'Is there any more coffee?' He held up his cup. 'I'm sure Stella Sticky-Beak next door will find out soon enough what the story is with that lot. You'd better have a word with her in a few days or so.'

Harry was right. Within days, Stella from next door knew

everything the neighbourhood needed to know about the new residents in the dilapidated old house. Most important was the fact that only two young men were living there, not the whole gang that had helped with the move. What a relief for everyone, she suggested.

The dark-haired young man was one of the Wilson grandsons and was looking after the house. Dora was flabbergasted. She had watched the Wilson grandchildren running around the street or playing in the front yard for years, but she would have never recognised this young man as being one of them. Maybe she had never looked closely enough.

The other one appeared to be the dark-haired man's cousin. He was renting a room and sharing the expenses. As to what work these two did, if any, Stella had no information as yet. So far, she could only confirm that they came and went at all hours in their rusty utilities. But as sure as eggs, she would keep an eye on them, she confirmed.

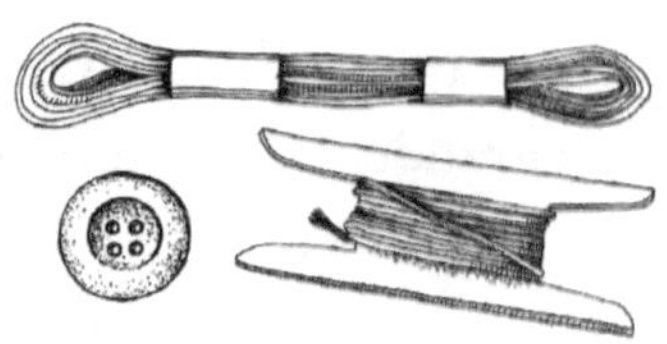

28

July 2008

The Kard Klub

DORA HAD NEVER ACTUALLY KNOWN where exactly in the city the Kard Klub was located. Funny name, that. She had not really been interested to find out where this place was that Harry had been going to every second Thursday night. It had been several years by now. He enjoyed playing cards and the company, and he always looked content and relaxed when he came home. That was enough for her.

Dora spotted the illuminated sign above the front door of the Kard Klub accidentally. She had had a late meeting in Hobart with a theatre director one night and on the way home she had driven straight past it. A group of people stood outside, some already leaving. Spur of the moment, Dora decided to stop and talk to the card players. Maybe they had an evening set aside for beginners. She should go and try it out. Playing cards couldn't be that hard, surely. Later, when she got a bit more experienced, she could possibly join Harry's group. It would be something they could do together. They didn't really have a hobby that both of them enjoyed. They were busy with their own work and it was hard to find time together.

It took her a while to find a car park further up the road and she had to rush back to the Kard Klub, hoping that not everyone had left. An elderly lady was the only one left of the group that had only moments ago stood there chatting and laughing.

'Sorry, love,' the lady said. 'We're closed. I've just locked up.' As if to prove she was telling the truth she held up a bunch of keys to Dora.

'No, it's alright,' Dora replied. 'My husband has been playing cards here on Thursdays and I was driving past and suddenly thought maybe I could start playing. If you have groups for total beginners,' she added apologetically.

'Yes, of course we cater to beginners. We're always happy to get new players. On Mondays we have experienced players come in and teach beginners. Just drop in next Monday and we'll sort you out.'

Monday night. Dora bit her lip. She had hoped she and Harry could go together the same night. 'So you don't take beginners on Thursdays?'

'No, love. We're closed on Thursdays. There!' She pointed to a small sign next to the door. 'Monday to Wednesday, 7.30 pm to 9.30 pm.'

'But my husband has been coming here every second Thursday for years.' Dora was genuinely puzzled. 'Have the days changed recently?'

The lady shook her head. 'No, it's been the same forever. You see, we're only renting the premises and those three nights' – again she pointed at the sign with the opening hours – 'Those three nights are our nights.'

'Is there another place somewhere where people go to play cards?'

'Not that I know of. It's possible, of course. Maybe the casino? They have card tables there.'

Dora shook her head. No, Harry would not go to the casino. Ever since they had allowed in people wearing jeans and checked shirts the casino had been a thorn in his eye. Not that he would go there anyway. They had once had a meal there that had seemed so exorbitantly expensive that Harry swore never to set foot in the casino again.

'Well,' Dora said deliberately casually to hide her confusion. 'I will just have to ask him. Thank you.'

Dora sat in the dark car, her hands and feet freezing cold. The street was empty and quiet. Here and there lights peeked through curtains and blinds in the houses to Dora's left. She noticed a cat on a low garden wall, motionless and watchful, one ear turned to a barking dog.

Dora had turned the engine on and had the heater running on high, but she was still shivering. She needed to think this through. Harry was definitely going to card nights every second Thursday. He never said much about it, but over the years he had told her little snippets. Wilma, for example, he had mentioned several times. A little old lady with a pink perm. More than once he had made fun of her. Wilma who could hardly remember her children's and grandchildren's names but who played bridge like a champion. Or Mike, also elderly. Deaf as a post, Harry had said, but he heard everything he needed to hear when he played. There had also been mention of a young autistic man. Nobody could ever beat him.

In all likelihood Harry had wanted to play cards at the Kard Klub. But when he found out they only played early in the week he went somewhere else. He had probably forgotten to tell her about it. Or had she forgotten that he had told her? Sometimes, when her thoughts were on a particular sewing problem, she did not listen properly to him.

Should she ask him about it? Ask him where exactly he played cards? He would probably fly into a rage and insist he'd told her more than once where he went and who he was playing cards with. He would accuse her of never listening to him. Harry could be so impatient. So easily frustrated with her.

Dora turned the headlights on and put the gear lever into first. She would drive home and for the time being not mention that she had been to the Kard Klub. If she let all of this settle, she might find a way of figuring out what was going on.

*

Of course, it was easy enough. All she had to do was follow him next time he went out on a Thursday night, but not in her little yellow car. He would instantly recognise it in his rear-view mirror. It didn't bear thinking about what he would do if he suspected that she spied on him. No, she needed to do this differently.

A week later she had her plan worked out. Sophie was spending a night with a friend so she, Dora, didn't have to explain why she was going out. Not that Sophie cared much anymore what her mother was up to. She had her own life which was much more important than that of her parents.

Dora had ordered a taxi, and she had asked for it to wait in the laneway outside her back gates. As soon as Harry left in his Mercedes she would fly through the backyard and jump into the taxi. If she got the timing right, Harry should drive past the laneway just after she had hopped into the taxi. Then the taxi would follow him.

When she heard the garage door go down, Dora rushed out the back. She was wearing her black coat, and on her head sat a strange-looking hat. It was big enough to cover all of her blond hair and part of her face. It was a hat meant for a play, but no one would mind if she borrowed it just for tonight. She felt ridiculous wearing it.

A young Indian man was leaning casually against the taxi, waiting for her. When he spotted her running down the backyard, he opened the back door of the car like a well-trained chauffeur.

'No, the front!' Dora panted as she ripped open the front passenger door before the taxi driver could react. She needed to have a clear view of Harry's car. Puzzled, but without comment, the taxi driver gently clicked the back door shut and took his seat behind the steering wheel. Even though he seemed to be young, no more than in his early thirties, he had probably seen all sorts. Even women wearing strange-looking black hats that belonged to a different century. Not much could surprise a man of his experience.

For a short moment, Dora stared out the window. Then she spotted Harry's car driving past.

'Follow that car!' she ordered the driver breathlessly. Only then did she sink back into the seat. She did not want her face right on the windscreen when Harry looked into his rear-view mirror. He had a keen eye, and her large black hat might not be enough to make her unrecognisable.

'Are you a detective?' the driver asked without taking his eyes off the street and Harry's car. In the semi-dark of the taxi Dora shook her head.

The driver, Dora could now confirm, was undeniably Indian. Even though he had only spoken a few words, she recognised that melodious Indian accent immediately. His taxi seemed to be Indian, too. On the dash lay an unmistakable garland of colourful plastic flowers and Lakshmi, the goddess of wealth, dangled from the inside mirror. The smell inside, sandalwood, was surprisingly pleasant. With relief, Dora felt her breath slowing.

The young man was a capable driver. His taxi flowed smoothly along the dark highway, and when he needed to brake he did so slowly and gently. So unlike Harry, who often jumped on the brakes with all the force he could muster.

The taxi wove in and out of the traffic, following Harry's Mercedes just close enough not to lose sight of it. Like a secret agent working for some intelligence service, the driver made sure there was at least one other car between them. Once, for a short heart-stopping moment, a large truck squeezed past the taxi and settled behind Harry's car, obscuring their view.

'Oh, don't lose him!' Dora cried out.

'Do not worry yourself, lady,' the driver said soothingly. 'I will not allow him to disappear from under our eyes.'

Despite herself, Dora had to smile. His voice was warm and confident, his English … what? A bit colourful, maybe? Dora was suddenly tempted to engage him in conversation, but for the life of her she couldn't think of anything to say. Her mind was too preoccupied, all of her senses focused on Harry's car.

When they got to the city it was immediately clear to Dora that Harry was not going to the Kard Klub. He had turned off the highway well before it and was now heading in the opposite direction, right into the city centre. Why there? Dora wondered. She sat up straight and narrowed her eyes to see better out the front window. There were mainly offices and shops there, some cafés and restaurants and a few private residences.

Finally, Harry pulled the car into a small lane. 'Go down a bit further,' Dora whispered, sinking back into her seat. 'I don't want him to see me.'

When he had switched the engine off, both the driver and Dora sat in silence, watching Harry approach the open front door of a two-storey red brick house. There was no hesitation in Harry's walk. It was obvious from his determined step that he had been there many times before.

If Dora's memory served her right, this was a Federation house, built around the 1900s. In the dark she could just make out a tall chimney rising out of heavy terracotta tiles. A light above the door threw shadows onto the leadlight in the windows to either side of the entrance. There was no doubt that this house was well cared for.

As there were no signs anywhere to indicate what this place was, Dora wondered if it was a private home. She suddenly felt silly. This would be where Harry was playing cards, in someone's home. It was nothing unusual. Book club meetings, craft meetings and a lot of other interest groups met in private homes. She should be going home right now and forget this miserable spying mission.

On a sudden impulse she turned to the silent taxi driver. 'What is this place? Do you know?' Taxi drivers knew everything, didn't they?

'Oh,' he replied in his melodious accent, nodding knowingly. 'It is a *house of ill repute.*'

'Pardon?' Dora was not sure she had heard right. Or understood what he meant.

The young man fastened his soft brown eyes on her. 'Some would call it a house of bodily bliss.' He looked away from her. Despite his unusual way of expressing himself, Dora now perfectly understood.

'A brothel?'

He shook his head reprovingly. 'Such a harsh word.' With his little finger he pointed at the house. 'This is a high-class establishment. Everything is clean, lady.'

If this had been an attempt to reassure her, he had failed. It was no consolation to Dora that this was not a grotty harbour-side brothel. His comment made no difference to the sudden hollowness that had opened up inside her. Whether it was the cheapest – whatever you called these places – or this high-class establishment, it did nothing to shake off the sense of unreality she felt.

She kept staring at the open door, unable to believe that Harry had just disappeared into the hallway of that house. Maybe the taxi driver had been wrong. Maybe it was not a *house of bodily bliss*. There were so many two storey Federation-style houses in this area that it was surely possible to confuse them. But why would this lovely young Indian man not know exactly what this was? He had probably taken more than one customer to this place. No, he knew what was going on here.

Dora didn't dare imagine what was happening behind those lovely leadlight windows. Her husband, Harry, what was he doing there? All at once, she sat up straight in her seat. Whatever it was, surely it would not take two hours, would it? Harry had always come home at the same time, roughly two and half hours after he had left to go to these card games. So what was that all about? On the spur of the moment she decided she would wait this out. She wanted to see Harry come out of that house.

'Your man?' The young taxi driver's voice broke the silence. When Dora nodded, he shook his head at her in sympathy.

'Would you mind if we waited here for a while?' she asked. And with a quick glance at the meter, which already showed quite a horrendous amount, she added, 'I will pay you, of course.'

'We shall wait, and I shall turn the meter off.' He pressed a button on the taximeter, and instantly the dollar amount on the screen stopped rolling over. Then he flashed a beautiful smile at her. The warm, sympathetic look in his eyes nearly broke her composure. Quickly she blinked away the tears which were threatening to fall.

'You're going to get into trouble for that,' she said, thinking of his boss in some taxi headquarter somewhere.

'Oh no, lady.' He shook his head and proudly added, 'This is my taxi. I can stop it whenever and wherever my mood takes me.'

Again, Dora felt his thoughtfulness and understanding would overwhelm her. Such a generous young man!

As they sat watching the door of the *establishment*, the young man told Dora about his home country. He described the landscape, the work he used to do there and his reasons for coming to Australia. Although she was only half listening, she was grateful that he filled the silence with his soft voice, distracting her with his stories and his funny, at times stilted, expressions.

Suddenly, forty minutes later, Harry emerged under the front door light. Without looking left or right, he headed straight to the laneway. He sat in his car for a few minutes but in the darkness it was impossible to make out what he was doing. Then the car reversed out of the laneway.

'Follow your man?' the taxi driver asked. Dora only nodded. She had come this far, now she wanted to know what was going to happen next. To her surprise Harry only went around the block and then stopped in front of a restaurant. An Indian restaurant of all places! Again the driver stopped at a distance, keeping Harry's car in their sights. Both he and Dora watched Harry enter through the double doors of the restaurant. Dora's sense of unreality only increased. Was this really her husband? As far as she knew, he had never expressed a desire to eat in an Indian restaurant. What was his reason for going there?

As if he'd read her mind, the young driver suddenly declared, 'I shall go and investigate.' He turned his engine off and opened the door.

'Oh God, no! Stop!' On an impulse Dora held him back by his arm. 'What are you doing? You can't go in there! Do you know the restaurant?'

'I know the place, but not the owners,' he explained seriously. 'But we Indians are all one family. In a few minutes I shall know them all. Wait here!'

Somehow it felt like this young driver had become her accomplice. They had been in this taxi together for only a little over an hour, but to all intents and purposes it seemed he understood her perfectly. Before he closed the car door behind him he smiled at her reassuringly. In the ensuing silence she noted that the meter in the taxi was still switched off.

Even though it felt like an eternity, he was suddenly back in the taxi holding a steaming paper bag in his hands. 'Naan bread, freshly cooked. It's delicious. Here!' He passed her the bag.

'Now you may wonder what I found out,' he declared. Without waiting for a response he said, 'The owner of the restaurant comes from an area in India I'm not familiar with. But we still had a good talk. Your man' – he reached across and took the warm bag of naan bread from Dora – 'Your man comes here every second Thursday. He is a regular customer. He walks in, he orders, he eats and he leaves. Always alone.' The driver took a big bite out of a piece of bread and chewed with obvious pleasure. 'He has enjoyed the delights of the food for many, many years now.'

Incredulous, Dora stared at her young companion, her accomplice, her ally. 'For many years?' she repeated senselessly. He nodded, mouth full. He looked at her as she tried to come to terms with this information. Was he wondering how she would react? Would she start sobbing uncontrollably? Or run into the restaurant screaming the house down? In his job he had seen it all. So what type of woman was she?

Dora did neither. She sat paralysed in her seat. She felt like Lot's wife, this tragic figure from the Bible, who was turned into a pillar of salt for being disobedient. Except she, Dora, was not the one who should be punished for disobedience. She was not the one who had done something wrong. It was not she who had enjoyed the restaurant and the delights of the *house of ill repute* for years. So what did all of this mean for her, her future and her marriage?

No, she stopped herself. That could wait. What was important was what she had to do right now, this very minute. 'Take me home,' she finally said to her accomplice, her ally, her only friend. There was no need to sit around here and wait … for what? She needed to get home.

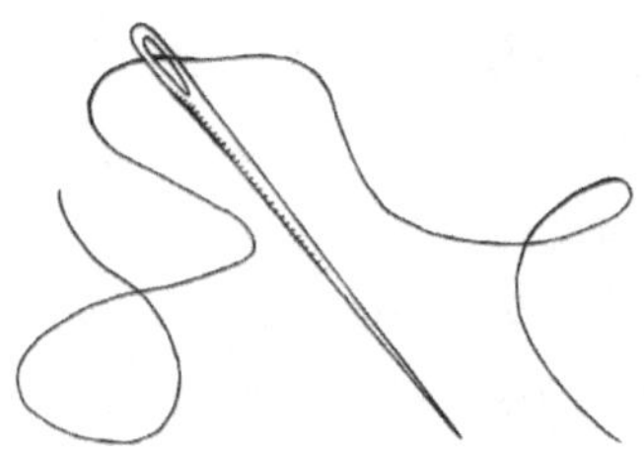

29

July 2008

Dora needs to go shopping again

DORA HAD PAID THE YOUNG driver twice the amount shown on his taxi's meter. He had accepted the money gratefully and without a word. Instead, he had touched the goddess of wealth on his mirror with two fingers. 'Lakshmi has been good to me,' he said.

'And you have been good to me,' Dora replied. She was tempted to hug him but it seemed inappropriate. Nevertheless, she waved at him when he drove off as if for a departing relative.

Once inside the house, she got undressed and went straight to bed. It would not be long now until Harry would be home. In the meantime she wanted some time to herself, without distractions, so she could think through everything that had happened that night.

Dora wrapped her doona tightly around herself. She was glad she had insisted early on in their marriage to have separate doonas. At first, Harry had grumbled but at least there was not pushing and pulling and fighting over the quilts.

Eyes wide open and wrapped up like a mummy, Dora lay on her side of the bed. Slowly she replayed the events of the evening. So Harry had been visiting a … a *house of ill repute* all these years. As regular as clockwork, every fortnight. Except, she supposed, for those times when he was working on the mainland. And afterwards he had always gone to this Indian restaurant. All by himself. It was obvious he had never set foot inside the Kard Klub. Right from the beginning everything had been a sham. None of the other card players he had occasionally mentioned existed. Not the lady with the pink perm, or Mike who was deaf but heard everything he needed to hear. Not even the autistic boy. How could Harry have made all of that up? Maybe they were people he had come across in the course of his work. Yes, that would have been it. They could have been clients, or possibly family members of Harry's colleagues.

So what, Dora asked herself, was wrong with all of this? To frequent a *house of ill repute*? Harry had betrayed her and lied to her without the least indication of a bad conscience. That's what was wrong with it. But if she were honest she would have to admit that she had been relieved when their sexual relations had cooled over the years. The whole thing had sometimes just been too much for her. Well, now she knew why Harry had been less ardent than in their early years. She had just assumed it was a normal situation with married couples. But obviously, he had found another … another outlet.

Her pride was hurt, yes. There was no denying that she suddenly felt undesirable. And maybe incompetent. Heaven only knew what these ladies in the *house of ill repute* offered that she, Dora, had no clue about. Remembering the taxi driver's words, she should perhaps at least be grateful that this brothel was a *clean* house. She assumed it meant that the ladies there had regular medical check-ups. So hopefully, none of them had any diseases or were drug users. Or what else was the meaning of a *clean* house in that regard? Dora sighed. She was such an innocent creature.

So, now the question was how to deal with it all. Should she confront Harry? Tell him what she had seen and how she felt about it? Now that she had calmed down a bit she had to admit that she did not feel all that much anymore. She would get over that little bit of hurt pride and the fact that he had lied to her. Lied for years.

Well, what else was there? She had always believed in adhering to certain rules in a marriage. Like, treating each other with respect, supporting each other, allowing the other person to develop and grow. Not betray each other. Not lie to each other. What about keeping certain things to yourself? Was that acceptable in a marriage? Thinking about that envelope in her filing cabinet made her wonder whether she had been as secretive and cheating as Harry. Harry had not told her about Thursday nights. She had not told him about the envelope.

No, she would not confront him. Let it ride, she thought, forcing herself to ignore the tension in her stomach. Knowledge was power. She now knew what he was up to and she would watch him. Who knew where it would lead.

But she would tell Freda all about it. She would conjure up her sister, imagine the two of them in her sewing room, Dora measuring some skirt of Freda's, pins between her lips, Freda standing patiently, listening to her describing Harry's visits to the *house of ill repute*. Two adult women discussing how to deal with a husband's indiscretion. Maybe even having a little laugh about it. Yes, she would conjure up Freda.

*

But then she, too, did a shameful thing. A day after finding out about Harry's *misdemeanour*, she felt the urge to go shopping again. Or maybe just go for a drive. Or both. She knew a beautiful old shop in Huonville that she had visited several times on her way to Andrew and Leah's place.

Homewares and Moore, the shop was called. A very clever name, Dora thought, as it sold homewares and the owners were Mr and Mrs Moore.

Huonville used to be a neglected outpost just south of Hobart. Neglected by tourists, mainly because all there was to see were apple orchards. They were extraordinarily pretty when they flowered, not unlike the famous flowering cherry blossoms in Japan which attracted tens of thousands of tourists every year. Somehow apple blossoms did not compare when it came to tourist attractions.

But neither was Huonville the most desirable area to live for people who were not associated with agriculture and apple orchards. Those who worked in Hobart or Kingston certainly did not want to move their families into this country area where nothing ever happened and where education did not quite compare to the city schools.

Only recently, when house prices went sky-high in Hobart and Kingston, did people consider more remote areas like Huonville where houses were still affordable. Following an increase in population came an increase in shops, cafés, restaurants, and beer and wine bars, so that the small country town of the past converted itself into quite a hip place, as Sophie would have called it. Old-fashioned milk bars and small, dusty corner shops had given way to these new upmarket places where the in-crowd met on a Friday night.

Yet, Dora's favourite shop, Homewares and Moore, still persisted and was one of her go-to places when she came through Huonville. She'd dropped in many times before on her way home from Andrew and Leah's place and always bought a little something. The shop was crammed full of an indescribable array of goods. Dora had bought a silver soup ladle once, a purchase she regretted because she constantly had to polish it to prevent it from turning black. But the small wicker basket had been just right for her dried flowers in the guest bathroom.

One of her favourite purchases had been an embroidered peasant blouse, similar to one she'd worn in the last of the hippie days. She'd smuggled it into the back of the wardrobe and only wore it when Harry was out. In the past he had only shown contempt for anything associated with those days.

'Dirty, long-haired, cannabis-smoking, good-for-nothings,' he had once called those happy, carefree young people who only wanted to make the world a better place.

It would have done Harry a world of good to smoke a bit of cannabis occasionally, Dora thought grimly. She had wanted to be one of those young people but somehow it hadn't happened.

The prices at Homewares and Moore were reasonable, but if Dora were truthful, she would have to admit that this old-fashioned shop had other advantages. For one, she loved to see the old cash register in action. It was probably a relic from the 1950s or sixties. Mrs Moore would punch the price into the old register, press down some buttons and with a heavy *ker-chang* the money drawer would spring open, always catching her in her well-padded stomach and making her roll her eyes.

There was no electronic scanning of items in this place and therefore no need for the price tag to have any of those black and white squiggly barcode things. In this shop, price labels were hand-written and dangled off the goods on thin pieces of string. Dora did wonder, though, how much longer the shop could get away with that. The only concession to modern business transactions was the provision to pay by credit card. If the customer preferred the quick swipe with a plastic card, then so be it. Without this,

Homewares and Moore would have long gone under. Dora herself always paid in cash so she could watch Mrs Moore or her husband operate the old cash register.

She walked along the aisle with the kitchen goods but nothing took her fancy. Her kitchen cupboards held plenty of tea towels and the old potato peeler had just last week been replaced with a brand-new one. Her eyes fell on a bright red fly swatter. No, definitely not. She could already envisage Harry using it like a scythe, swishing it madly from left to right in pursuit of some poor fly.

Looking up, she discovered an array of colourful scarves hanging from a swinging rail towards the back of the aisle. The scarves were gently swaying from side to side, set in motion by the draught coming through the open back door. Dora touched one of them, lovely and soft, but no, she already had more than enough in the hallway cupboard.

On a shelf just below the scarves, she spotted ladies' handbags. Dora squatted down and pulled a medium-sized black leather bag off the shelf. Yes, she could do with another handbag. This one was lovely, with a convenient side pocket, which was a bonus. You could quickly pull out your mobile phone or a handkerchief without having to undo a zip and rummage around in the main section of the bag. The strap was nice and long, too. It would sit nicely right over her shoulder. Dora checked the price tag and frowned. A hundred and fifty dollars! It was more than she would want to spend on another bag, and it was more than she had in her wallet anyway.

Disappointed, she returned the bag to the shelf and pulled out another, smaller one. By the feel of it, not real leather. Not like the one she had just put back. She brushed her fingers over the bag. Definitely faux leather. She should know. Again she frowned. The only advantage of this bag was the much cheaper price, only

sixty-five dollars. She had enough cash to pay for this one but …
Dora narrowed her eyes and regarded the hand-written tag dangling on the thin brown string. It was fastened to the strap of the handbag by a simple loop. If she loosened it a bit and slipped the tag through the loop she could possibly …

Still squatting by the shelf with the bag resting on her thighs, she focused her senses on movements and sounds in the shop. There was no one nearby, and the shop seemed empty except for Mrs Moore, who was just then calling out to her husband.

There! Done; without quite knowing how it had happened, the price tag on the thin piece of string suddenly lay in Dora's hand. She closed her fingers around it and put the small bag back onto the shelf. Then she pulled the bigger bag out again, the real leather one, the one she liked. One quick movement of her nimble fingers and that tag, too, lay in her hand. Without turning her head, Dora again focused her ears on any sounds around her. Could she hear any steps nearby? Was the little door chime tinkling, indicating that another customer had entered the shop? No, nothing. Only Mrs Moore's voice was audible. She was yelling at her husband, telling him to take over at the cash register.

It only took Dora a few seconds to reattach the switched price tags to the two bags. Then she stood up, holding the bigger bag, the leather one she had liked right from the beginning, over her arm and made her way to the cash register.

'I'll have this bag, thank you!' she said to Mr Moore with a smile on her face. 'Paying cash,' she added. 'Why are wallets always at the bottom of the bag?' she asked as she rummaged around in her backpack.

'Sixty-five dollars,' Mr Moore said. 'That's good value for such a lovely bag.' He wrapped it carefully in tissue paper. For a second, a wave of guilt rose up in Dora. She cleared her throat. 'Yes, I like coming to your shop. You sell nice things.'

Mr Moore laughed as he handed over the carefully wrapped package. 'You women always find something to buy!'

*

Driving home, Dora wondered if Harry would notice her new handbag. Probably not. After all these years, he still didn't have any idea about her hippie shirt that was safely hidden in the wardrobe, rolled up behind her pile of t-shirts. Impatiently, she put her foot down on the accelerator and overtook a truck going up the hill. Andrew had given her the original shirt, decades ago. She was meant to be wearing it during their overland trip from England to India. The hippie trail. It was made of white cotton and had a round neck with a drawstring so that the neck could be pulled tight or loosened. To show more skin. Or a lot of skin. Shyly, she and Andrew had tried out the different variations, tight and loose and very loose.

Dora had loved the blue cross-stitch embroidery that covered the length of the full sleeves and the front of the shirt.

Dora indicated right to turn off the highway. How innocent and idealistic they had all been. At the age of nineteen they had known exactly what the perfect life looked like. They had it all worked out.

But now, here they were. So much older, disillusioned with so many of their dreams. Constantly shifting parameters, huh! Living with compromises and disappointments. Lying to each other and keeping secrets from each other. Stealing from people who could least afford it. Good God, Dora!

The wave of guilt rose up again. She had promised herself not to *acquire* things in shops anymore. But yet again, there, right next to her on the passenger seat lay her new acquisition. What on earth would Freda say if she knew about it? If she, Dora, told of Harry's misdemeanours then surely she would have to admit to her own.

She would tell Freda and then she would promise never to *acquire* things again. This time she would stick to it. It would not be one of those empty resolutions she had made in the past. Feeling lighter already, she headed down the road past the Kingston shopping centre. At the crossing she turned right, leaving the busy streets behind her. Soon she would be home. And the first thing to do was to write a letter. There was so much to tell her sister. Harry's betrayal and her spying mission. Her own inexplicable behaviour. Stealing a handbag she didn't need. Both of them guilty of deceit and subterfuge.

30

September 2011

Dora finds a handyman

'**D**ORA, RING UP A COUPLE of gardening services to get quotes for the garden gate,' Harry called out. She watched him as he took his jacket off the hallstand – the hallstand, not the kitchen chair! – did he ever wonder how it got there? A hundred times, if not more, a good fairy called Dora moved his jacket from the kitchen chair to where it belonged, either the hallstand or the wardrobe in the bedroom. He put the jacket on and slammed the front door shut behind him. Shortly after, Dora heard his car engine start and then he was gone.

The garden gate definitely needed fixing. One of the hinges had come loose, the other was only just holding the gate in place. The slightest breath of air, or someone brushing their hand against it, and the gate would collapse completely. It was a wooden gate, only one metre high, and one of the boards right in the middle looked rotten. Dora was not sure whether to ring a gardener with carpentry skills, or a carpenter who could be bothered with such a small job. It was hard enough to get anyone these days to do work for you. Maybe she should try an IT expert. There seemed to be no jobs for them at the moment.

In the end, she managed to get four quotes: two from gardening services and two from local carpenters. The cheapest quote came in at just over two hundred dollars.

As expected, Harry nearly had a fit when she told him that night. 'I can buy a whole new front door for that sort of money!' he thundered. 'Not just a tiddly garden gate!'

Not quite, Dora thought, but it was not worth mentioning. 'Harry,' she ventured instead. 'You know, those two young men across the road … They seem to be doing all sorts of odd jobs. I've seen them come and go with paint cans and timber and all sorts of things. It wouldn't cost anything to ask them.'

'If their house is anything to go by you'll be wasting your time! Good-for-nothings, that's what they are! Sitting on that veranda day and night drinking beer!'

'Look, we've got nothing to lose,' Dora insisted. 'If they say no we'll think of something else. You never know, they might do it for a carton of beer.' Her attempt at some levity went unnoticed. She regarded her husband, awaiting his response. His hair, she noticed, was nearly all grey now and he was widening out a bit around the middle. It was quite obvious when he was sitting down, letting his body melt all around him. Something, she realised, he had only started to do recently. It was as if his spine was sick and tired of holding him up all the time.

*

The following morning, Dora heard music from across the road floating in through her kitchen window. Someone was home in that dilapidated house! She put a thin cardigan over her blouse, checked her face and hair in the mirror and headed out.

Dora crossed the street and marched through the young men's untidy front yard with more confidence than she felt. The place was a complete mess. The trees and bushes on one side of the garden path had all grown into a wild, tangled, impenetrable jungle. What used to be a lawn, on the other side, was now being 'mowed' by the wallabies. There were wallaby droppings everywhere, forcing her into a little dance, tiptoeing all around them.

A rubbish bin and a recycling bin stood right at the foot of the stairs leading onto the veranda and to the front door. Neither of those had lids, which could at least have eliminated some of the nasty smells emerging from the bins. Dora suspected the young men threw their rubbish straight from the veranda down into the bins. Why bother venturing unnecessarily down those stairs?

She squeezed past the bins and headed up the rickety stairs towards the front door. A deep breath in and she banged the metal knocker against the door.

One of the young men opened the door just wide enough to stick his face through. Strawberry-coloured hair sprang up in mad curls around his pale face. 'Yeah?' he asked sleepily. A pungent, smoky smell escaping from the narrow opening hit Dora in the face.

'My name is Mrs Freeman,' Dora said. 'I live in the house opposite.' She made a vague gesture towards her house. The young man opened the door a bit wider. All at once she was not sure whether this whole thing had been a good idea. She did not in the least like the look of his unwashed face and crumpled, dirty clothes. He'd probably slept in them, she thought Uht with a shudder.

'Yeah, I know,' the strawberry head replied.

'You know?' Dora responded surprised.

The young man rolled his eyes. 'Not your name. But I know where you live.' He squeezed through the gap in the door and gestured towards the old couch on the veranda. Dora shook her head. She did not want to sit down. Not on that couch. It was covered in multiple dark stains and what looked like bits of potato chips or biscuit crumbs. Next to it lay an empty carton of beer. None of that deterred the young man from letting himself drop into the couch.

He couldn't be more than mid-twenties. Despite his dishevelled look and the oversized t-shirt, Dora could see that his face still had some of that innocent puppy look. The skin on his arms and bare legs was smooth and soft.

'I wanted to ask you something,' Dora started.

'Hang on,' he stopped her. He got up off the couch and yelled something through the front door into the house. A couple of minutes later another young man emerged. He was a bit taller and his hair was dark, but he seemed to be a similar age. Early to mid-twenties.

Ah, Dora thought. This must be the Wilson boy. She fixed her eyes on him but could not detect any similarities with the Wilson clan.

The strawberry head dropped back into the couch. The other young man remained standing.

'The lady wants to tell us something,' the strawberry head said.

Dora turned to the dark-haired man. 'I live over there,' she explained again. 'I have noticed that you occasionally go to work ...' She stopped short, hoping she had not implied anything insulting.

'We do, we do,' the dark-haired one guffawed. 'We do occasionally work!' They both laughed.

Dora tried to ignore the laughter and ploughed on. 'It looks to me like you're doing all sorts of jobs.' She had seen them come home with paint splattered clothing or dragging bits of timber or plumbing pipes and whatever else from their old utility. She took a deep breath. 'So I was wondering if you would do a job for me.'

'What sort of job?' the strawberry head wanted to know. Dora explained about the garden gate and the work it involved. Then she waited with bated breath for their reaction. She still didn't know whether she was doing the right thing. What if they said yes? They might come and case her house and within a day or two all her furniture would be gone.

'S'pose we can do that,' the dark-haired man said. 'Not for free, though.'

'No, of course not,' Dora hastily replied. 'Of course, I'll pay you.'

'How much?'

'I'll pay you a hundred and fifty dollars and a carton of beer.' Dora had carefully thought about it beforehand. She hoped the carton of beer would tempt them. Altogether it added up to nearly as much as she would have had to pay one of those gardening services. So it seemed fair. But she was not sure whether they would laugh at that and send her home.

To her surprise the dark-haired man agreed. 'Done,' he said and stretched his hand out as if to seal a contract. Dora was touched by this old-fashioned gesture. 'I'm Mrs Freeman,' she said to him because his mate had failed to introduce her. She shook his hand.

'I'm Luke. That's Boz, my cousin.'

A great sense of relief took hold of Dora. These two were not half as bad as she had thought. And if they could fix the gate, and do a good job of it without stealing her furniture, she might well ask them to do other jobs. But there was no point in getting ahead of herself. First she would have to see whether they could really fix the gate. It was possible that Harry was right and they'd make a mess of it.

'I have one little request,' she then said. Her face was flushing. 'I ... it's a bit ... it's just that ...' She stopped and took a breath. 'Should my husband ever say anything to you about money, I would prefer it if you said that I paid you fifty dollars plus a carton of beer. If you could just tell him that, I would be very grateful. If he ever asks, which I don't think he'll do, but you never know.' She started stumbling over her words. She needed to stop blabbing, right now. Good God, she was embarrassed!

Boz slapped his thigh. 'What the fuck!' he called out and laughed again. Luke just looked at her, one eyebrow raised in question.

'If you don't mind,' Dora pleaded. Somehow they both seemed to understand, but instead of nodding their assent, they shook their heads in disbelief.

'Remind me not to get married,' Boz said to Luke as he got up off the couch and walked back into the house. 'Watch that rotten step,' he called over his shoulder.

*

'I told you they're idiots,' Harry said. He was leaning over the gate, inspecting it from all angles. Two brand-new hinges were holding the gate in place in a perfectly horizontal position. The rotted piece of timber had been replaced and the whole gate had been sanded and then oiled with linseed oil. It opened and closed softly, without the slightest squeak.

'And they did that for fifty dollars? And a carton of beer?' Harry turned to Dora who was standing behind him. She felt her eyelids flutter when she answered.

'Yes. But I did pay for that bit of timber and the oil.' She was surprised herself at how quickly and competently Boz and Luke had worked. And how quickly and competently she could lie.

'Nothing will ever come of those two.' Harry shook his head in contempt. 'They could make a mint if they got their brain into gear. Everyone is desperate for handymen these days.'

*

And so, over the years Luke and Boz did a number of jobs in the garden and the house. Once a month now they came to mow the lawn and do some weeding. Early in summer one year they painted the western side of the house, the side that was more exposed to the rain than the others. Twice a year they trimmed the tall hedge in the backyard. They fixed the drooping doors on the kitchen cupboards.

Once, Dora even took them over to Bruny Island to sand and oil the timber deck of the shack. As the shack belonged to Barb, she paid the two young men the full – and proper – amount. Every other time their official payment, if Harry ever asked, was a carton of beer and anything up to a hundred dollars. Of course, Dora paid them the going rate she would have had to pay anyone else, because her conscience would not allow her to do anything other than that. But every time she opened the envelope holding her emergency funds her heart beat a bit faster. The amount of money was going down fast. And most of it was going to Luke and Boz across the road. Those two were real 'Jacks-of-all-trades'. They could build and repair anything and do a good job of it. The arrangement was perfect for both parties. In order to continue with their services, Dora would just have to 'relocate' a bit more of her household money into the envelope in her filing cabinet.

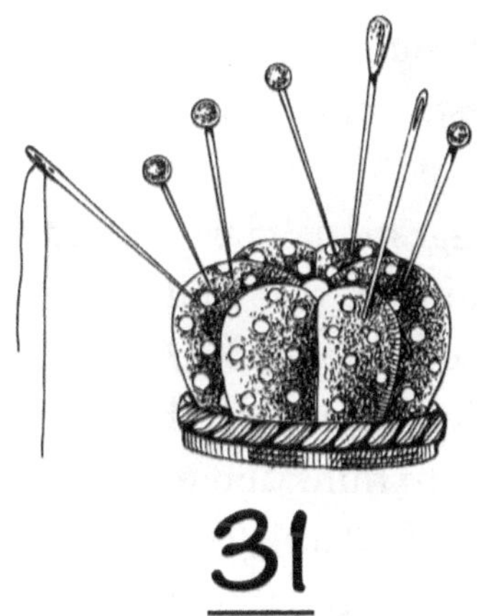

31

December 2017

Sophie's graduation dinner

SOPHIE'S GRADUATION TOOK PLACE A few weeks after her twenty-sixth birthday. After school, she had gone straight to university to do an honours degree in mathematics. Following a short break holidaying overseas, she had enrolled in a post-graduate degree program and was now a fully-fledged Doctor of Mathematics, a DMath.

Harry was walking on cloud nine. 'That's my girl!' he triumphed. 'She's got her father's brain!' For days he walked around with a big smile on his face.

'We're going to celebrate in style,' he announced to Dora. 'When the official nonsense at the university is over,

I'm taking the whole family to a restaurant. A good one!'
he emphasised.

Astounded, Dora dropped the magazine she had been reading.
That was indeed a turn up for the books. They never went to a
restaurant. Except of course, Harry had been a regular customer
at a certain Indian restaurant after visiting a *house of ill repute* all
those years ago!

Well, she had a suggestion. 'Harry,' Dora said sweetly, 'I have
an idea. Maybe we can go to that Indian restaurant in Goulbourn
Street. Do you know the one I mean? It's meant to be good.' But
as soon as the words left her mouth she could have kicked herself.
She had never wanted to think about that restaurant or the *house
of ill repute* ever again. Evidently she was still carrying some lingering resentment, despite the fact that Harry hadn't gone there
for however many years. One day he had just stopped. He was
sick of playing cards, he had said. Huh!

Somewhat vexed with herself, Dora eyed her husband. How
would he react? He sat stumped for a very short moment, then he
shook his head. 'No, we're going to something a bit more upmarket
than that,' he declared.

'How do you know that Indian restaurant is not upmarket?' God,
she just couldn't help herself!

Harry shook his head dismissively. 'I'm going to take you all to
the Red Azalea in Sandy Bay.'

'Chinese?'

'Yes, and the best, I'm told. Very expensive. That's where we're
going. You can tell Sophie. I'm going to ring Andrew. He can
organise Leah and Barb. They'll be impressed.' Satisfied, he
nodded to himself. 'Six people. That is a good number,' he added
smugly. 'Did you know that it stands for good fortune and happiness in Chinese? It's considered excellent for business.' He
rubbed his hands.

Good God! Dora had no idea where that had come from. Was Harry making this up?

As if he'd read her mind Harry said, 'I've had a Chinese client for quite some time now. He has three sixes on the numberplate of his car.' Harry laughed. 'It's brought him luck, I should know. You should see his tax records!'

'Harry, you need to tell Andrew that this dinner is your shout. You know they can't afford expensive meals out.'

Harry waved away her concerns. 'I'll pay for everyone. Don't let anyone say I'm not generous. After all, this is for my clever daughter!'

And mine, Dora thought. And mine!

*

A few days before the dinner, Sophie announced she would be bringing a friend. A very good friend.

'What does that mean "a very good friend"?' Harry frowned. 'Does she mean a boyfriend? I haven't heard her talk about a boyfriend.' He stood by the bedroom door, watching Dora examining the contents of her wardrobe.

Dora shrugged her shoulders. 'I didn't ask any details. You know what she's like on the phone. Always short and to the point.' Dora pulled her favourite outfit, a purple pant suit, out of the wardrobe and gave it a critical look. The jacket was long enough to hide her ever-widening hips, the pants loose and stylish. With a white blouse and her short pearl necklace it would look perfect for the dinner. But what shoes? She had quite a collection, but none seemed to be right for the pant suit. Dora placed the suit on the bed and bent down to have a closer look at her shoe rack in the wardrobe.

'What did you say to her? Dora, I'm talking to you!'

'I said yes, of course. It's her special night and if it's really a boyfriend I couldn't possibly have said no, could I? She probably wants to introduce him to us.'

'But that makes seven of us. So much for the lucky number six,' he grumbled.

Dora pulled a pair black shoes off the shoe rack. They would do nicely. That heel would give her a bit of height and make her legs look just a touch longer. Nice! She straightened up again.

'You might be surprised.' She would give these shoes a good polish. They hadn't been worn for a while. 'Maybe he's a doctor of mathematics, too.'

Harry's face lit up. That was a possibility indeed. Dora could see the wheels turning in his mind. Maybe in the near future there would be two mathematicians in the family! No, three.

*

Two imposing stone lions stood guard on either side of heavy steel doors outside the Red Azalea. The steel doors had been opened to expose a set of glass sliding doors which allowed passers-by and arriving guests a tantalising glimpse inside the restaurant.

Like entering a fortified castle, Dora thought as she stepped past the steel doors to the silently opening glass doors. The interior of the restaurant could have come from a Chinese castle, too. Not that Dora had ever seen a Chinese castle. Dominating the black walls were several wide panels reaching from the ceiling to the floor, all painted bright red. What could have looked stark and intimidating was softened by intricate wood carvings and gilded plates which embellished the panels from top to bottom. When walking to their allocated table, Dora caught a glimpse of a series of carved animals on one panel, on another what looked like traditional warriors standing by a river. Their faces looking fierce, crossbows and long, heavy swords in their hands.

In each of the four corners of the restaurant stood bushy, healthy-looking bamboos in heavy clay pots. Dora noticed that the pots stood on small wheels. She wondered whether they were being wheeled in and out of the sun every day. Otherwise they surely wouldn't survive in the dim atmosphere.

A young Asian waiter led Harry and Dora to one of the six tables in the restaurant. A sign of good luck? Dora wondered as she looked around. All were round and big enough to seat eight people comfortably. It did not escape Dora's experienced eyes that the tablecloths were blindingly white and heavily starched.

Shortly after, Andrew, Leah and Barb arrived, all dressed for the occasion in their best clothing. For Andrew that meant a clean pair of trousers and what looked like a brand-new polo shirt. Leah was in a long-sleeved floral dress which came down to her ankles. Her thick red hair was pinned up, exposing a long, delicate neck. Barb, elegant as ever, sported a dark skirt with matching blazer and all three of her pearl necklaces.

*

Sophie and her 'very good friend' were the last to arrive at the Red Azalea. Harry's body stiffened as soon as they walked in through the door. Sophie's friend was a young Chinese woman!

'Harry, don't stare!' Dora managed to whisper before the two young women approached the table. Yet, Dora was the one who was staring. Sophie's friend was wearing a modern version of a traditional Chinese qipao dress. Instead of the dress being long and loose-fitting with wide sleeves to hide the body, this modern variation was tight and short-sleeved, the length just coming down to below the knees. Nevertheless, it had retained the traditional diagonal buttoned front closure and the unmistakable standing collar. Of red satin fabric, the dress had been embroidered with

209

exquisite colourful floral designs. The sole purpose of its modern design was to emphasise the slim, perfect figure of its wearer. It was stunning.

Sophie walked around the table and in turn kissed her relatives on the cheek. Then she introduced her friend.

'Everyone, this is Mei. We were both in the same post-graduate group at uni. Mei also has a doctorate in mathematics.' At those last words, Dora quickly glanced at Harry, but he sat as if in a trance, staring at Mei. Sophie pointed at everyone in turn. 'My mum, my dad, Uncle Andrew, Aunt Leah and my grandmother Barb.'

Taking the two empty chairs, the young women sat down next to each other.

'I've invited Mei because she's been a really good friend to me,' Sophie explained. 'But mainly I've asked her because she thinks this is the only place in all of Tasmania that serves truly authentic Chinese food.'

Strange that we've never met this friend before, Dora thought. But then, Sophie never talked about personal matters much. Dora was constantly perplexed by the fact that her daughter led a life that hardly ever overlapped with hers. Like a Venn diagram, she suddenly thought. She saw clearly in her mind the image of the two circles side by side, shifting into each other just a tiny bit. That's us two, she thought. Next to each other. Separate. Sometimes crossing over into each other's areas. There now, she was not a totally hopeless case when it came to mathematics. She'd remembered that one from school!

Her thoughts were disrupted by Harry clinking a chopstick against his glass. 'I would like us all to drink to these two young women,' he said. The young waiter had just finished filling up everyone's glass with expensive sparkling wine.

'All I want to say is that I'm very proud of my daughter, and her friend.' Harry nodded his head towards Sophie and Mei. 'To be so young and have a doctorate in mathematics is an achievement indeed. By the time these two turn thirty, they may well be professors at some prestigious university, inspiring many young people.'

'Hear, hear!' Barb called out. Following her example, everyone raised their glass.

'To Sophie,' Harry said proudly. 'And to Mei.' His eyes were moist. It was a momentous occasion for him, but it might have been the rising bubbles of the sparkling wine that had gone into his eyes.

After Harry's short speech, Mei had been instantly engaged in conversation by Barb and Leah. She seemed a vivacious girl, talking and gesticulating in a very lively manner, showing off her slim hands and long fingers.

Somehow, unnoticed by everyone, Mei had become the centre of attention. She was the one who recommended they have the banquet, rather than individual meals. That way everyone could enjoy a cross-section of a variety of foods, she had said.

When the first dish came out, Mei addressed the waiter in Mandarin and sent him away with a wave of her hand before he had a chance to explain what the food was.

'I will tell you what we are eating,' she announced. 'I'm not sure the waiter knows as much as I do. He does not look very confident.' There was no doubting Mei's confidence.

As the different courses were presented, one after the other, Mei held up her plate and pointed at the different food items on it.

'In China, many foods have a symbolic meaning, and I will explain to you the meaning.' She looked at everyone in turn, making sure she had their attention.

'Noodles symbolise long life. So never cut them up!' She turned to Barb with a serious look on her face. 'You may cut your life short.' Barb's fork and knife – she had no patience for chopsticks – remained hovering in mid-air for a shocked moment.

'Duck stands for fidelity,' Mei continued, as the next course arrived. 'All the red dishes symbolise happiness. Red is the colour of happiness.' She laughed and pointed at her dress. 'I'm very happy tonight!'

When the chicken dish was brought out, Mei explained that chicken stood for a good marriage and the coming together of families. 'I feel like I'm part of your family now!' she exclaimed. Everyone laughed, even Harry. Clearly he was much taken by his daughter's vivacious friend, just like the others. His eyes returned to the young girl again and again. She was beautiful, confident and extremely charming. Yet, it seemed to Dora as if there was something worrying him.

Later that evening, Harry winced when the bill was presented, but he pulled out his credit card and paid without a murmur. However, Dora was sure she could see the short hairs on the back of his neck standing up more than usual.

Outside the restaurant everyone was saying goodbye. Without the slightest sign of the Chinese reserve Dora had always heard about, Mei now kissed everyone on the cheek. Her face was flushed, her eyes shiny.

'I'm very happy that you allowed me to join your family tonight,' she said to Harry, facing him.

'Yes, thanks again, Dad!' Sophie chimed in. 'It was a great evening!' She looked at Mei.

'Shall we?'

When Mei nodded, Sophie turned to the others. 'We are going out on the town,' she explained excitedly. 'We're meeting friends.' Without another word she took Mei's hand into hers and the two of them walked off into the night.

'What a stunning girl!' Barb said. 'Beautiful and clever, and I have learned so much about Chinese culture and food. I won't cut up noodles anymore!'

'I just loved that dress!' Leah added. 'Really, she was the only one of us who was dressed properly for the occasion. I felt like a real frump in my home-made outfit. If only I had your sewing skills, Dora!' She turned to her husband. 'Come, Andrew. Let's go home. I'm about to collapse after all that food.'

Minutes later, Dora and Harry were the only ones left standing on the pavement. Harry looked like the air had gone out of him. He carried the nonplussed look on his face of someone who had just been steamrolled.

'Come, Harry, time to go home!'

Once in the car they sat quietly, catching their breath and letting the sudden stillness envelop them. The darkness around them was haphazardly broken by a flickering streetlight nearby. A group of young girls walked past. Their heads together, they chatted in subdued tones as if sharing late-night secrets.

Dora turned her head to look at Harry. He hadn't started the car but sat silently staring out the windscreen. In the flickering light, his face had taken on a ghostly, nearly cadaverous, appearance. Somehow he looked crestfallen. When he lowered his head Dora noticed how rounded his neck had become.

We're getting old, she thought. The young ones have left us and we are struggling to keep things going without them.

'It's been a lovely evening, Harry,' she finally said. Putting her hand out, she stroked his upper arm. 'Thank you! This dinner with the family was a perfect finish to a perfect day.'

Slowly, Harry lifted his head to meet Dora's eyes. 'Do you think Sophie is …?' He hesitated.

'What, Harry?'

'Do you think she is … you know?' Dora took her hand off Harry's arm.

Well, the thought had occurred to her, too, when she saw the looks and smiles her daughter and Mei had exchanged. Did twenty-five-year-old women really take each other by the hand if they weren't what Harry suspected?

'Are you asking me whether Sophie is a lesbian?'

Harry winced and closed his eyes. 'Yes, yes! That's what I mean! You don't have to say it!'

'I think if she is a lesbian …,' Dora said, ignoring his last sentence. 'Well, we would just have to accept that, wouldn't we?'

'I can't imagine …,' Harry groaned. 'I don't want … It's just not what I had expected!' he finally burst out. 'Not my daughter!'

'Harry, you don't have to imagine anything. We don't know what's going on. They may just be very good friends and if they're more than that, so be it!' But she, too, was hoping they were not more than that. She had always wanted grandchildren.

'It seems to me that everyone these days is either a lesbian or a homosexual,' Harry said sulkily.

'Well, we're not!' In the dark, Dora rolled her eyes. 'So let's just go home now.'

Harry appeared not to have heard Dora. 'Everyone pretends it's normal, but I'm telling you, it's not!' He loosened his tie and pulled it over his head. 'Secretly everyone thinks it's weird, abnormal. Call it what you will. But of course, you can't say that or they'll tell you you're sexist and racist and whatever else. So much for freedom of speech in this country!' Harry's voice had risen, his anger bouncing around in the confines of the car.

'Harry, you're getting yourself worked up over nothing. Now stop it and let's go home! If it helps, I'll ring Sophie and ask her.'

'You'll ask her whether she is a …?' Harry's body pivoted towards her.

'Yes, I'll ask her,' Dora replied exasperated. 'I'll ask her if she's a lesbian if that makes you feel better. Now start the engine, please!'

32

December 2017

A delicate phone call to Sophie

ARRY STOOD LEANING AGAINST THE door frame, holding a cup of coffee in one hand. His eyes were fixed on Dora.

'Harry, come and sit next to me,' Dora said impatiently. 'You're making me nervous, standing there watching me like a hawk!' She patted the seat on the couch next to her. 'If you want, I can put the phone on speaker so we can all hear each other.'

'No,' Harry objected. 'I can't stand that speaker thing. Everyone always talks at the same time. You talk to her. I just want to listen.' He remained standing by the door and took a noisy sip of coffee.

Dora gave an audible sigh. Let him hear that she was annoyed with him and herself. Why had she said she was going to ring Sophie? He was the one who wanted to know whether his daughter was a lesbian or not. She should have left it to him to ask her. Truth be told, she didn't really care about the whole thing. It would take some getting used to, there was no doubt about it, but it was not unusual these days for two women or two men to be in a relationship. They could have children. Somehow. It was not unheard of. So she could still have grandchildren.

Come to think of it, she probably would have been better off living with a woman herself. Not in a sexual relationship. No, she couldn't imagine that, but she liked to think that maybe it would be easier living with another woman. Freda would be perfect, of course. If ever she came back to Tasmania, you never knew, there could come a time when the two of them could share this house. Where else would she go? This sister of hers had nothing.

If Dora asked her not to leave her jacket hanging on the kitchen chair, Freda would only roll her eyes and tell Dora she was too picky. Then she would take the jacket and hang it where it belonged, on the hallway stand or in the wardrobe, and if Freda told Dora to do something crazy occasionally, then Dora would laugh and maybe get her hair dyed green. Or get drunk and watch soppy movies all night. Apart from that, they would accept each other as they were, with all their quirks and foibles and inconsistencies.

They certainly wouldn't keep secrets from each other, or dance around each other with bated breath in order not to upset the other person. They would be sympathetic about their emotional ups and downs and support each other. At least that's what Dora imagined. It was probably totally unrealistic. Why should living with a woman, even if she was your sister, be easier than living with a man?

'What are you waiting for? Have you dialled?' Harry's voice disrupted her thoughts.

'Yes!' she replied more forcefully than was necessary. Her musings about living with Freda were unproductive. Nothing would ever come of it anyway. Instead, she should be concentrating on this conversation with Sophie.

God, she was annoyed. And anxious. Would she really be as cool and accepting if Sophie told her that, yes, she was a lesbian?

'Hello, darling!' Dora hoped her voice was sounding chirpier than she felt. 'I haven't woken you, have I?' Frowning, Harry glanced over his shoulder at the kitchen clock. It was early afternoon.

'I've waited especially because I thought you might have had a late night on the town after the dinner.' Dora looked at Harry with raised eyebrows. That explanation is for you, her eyes said. Harry had been waiting impatiently for her to call Sophie all morning. Pestering her!

'Oh, that sounds lovely!' Dora said after having listened to Sophie's reply. She turned her head towards Harry and nodded.

'What?' he mouthed. This time Dora shook her head. Serves you right. If we had the speaker on you would know what Sophie was saying, the shake of her head told him.

She returned her attention to Sophie. 'Yes, we really liked Mei. What an interesting person!' From now on she would just ignore Harry. It was impossible to have a conversation with Sophie and try to decipher the expression on his face.

'Aha. No.' There was a pause. 'You're absolutely right! I did love her dress!' A smile flitted over Dora's face. 'I can never resist a beautiful design as you well know.'

A groan emanated from the door frame but Dora refused to turn around.

'Next week? Ok.'

'Huh!' Dora suddenly sat up straight on the couch. 'You never said anything about that!' Harry stepped into the lounge room and stood opposite Dora.

Again he mouthed 'What?'

'Hang on for a second, darling.' Dora put her hand over the phone. 'Harry, you have to stop interrupting!'

'Tell me what she said!'

'Nothing! You are starting to annoy me!'

Impatiently, Dora took her hand off the phone again. 'Darling, I don't want to sound abrupt, but your dad wants to know whether you and Mei are in a lesbian relationship.' There, now she'd said it. She had not had a chance to ease into the topic like she had planned. She had been abrupt. Harry hovering over her like a vulture ready to pounce, had made her lose her patience.

Pressing her lips together, she listened to Sophie. Then she nodded. 'You are completely right. He is an old fuddy-duddy and totally prejudiced!' God, she was angry now. Let him hear what his daughter thought of him.

'Good luck in Launceston, darling,' she said with as much composure as she could. Then she turned her phone off.

'Harry,' she said with supressed anger. 'Your daughter has just confirmed that she is not a lesbian. No, don't interrupt me!' Harry closed his mouth again. 'She has also said that she is going to Launceston next week because she has a second job interview with a private school there. She has applied for a position as a maths teacher.'

Stunned, Harry stared at her. 'She wants to be a maths teacher in a school?' he finally croaked. 'Teaching little kids? With her degree?' In an instant he had forgotten all about his daughter's sexual preferences.

'Yes. If she gets the job, she will be teaching maths and geography. And they are not little kids. They are looking for someone to teach grades ten to twelve.'

'Geography?' Rarely had Dora seen Harry lost for words. No, it was worse than that. He was utterly deflated. He couldn't have been more surprised if someone had told him that his daughter was going to move to Timbuktu. He stepped around the coffee table and lowered himself onto the couch next to Dora.

'Apparently they were impressed with her knowledge of the most obscure capital cities. Thanks to you,' Dora couldn't help adding. 'And she said she would learn enough of whatever she had to teach in geography to keep one step ahead of the students.'

'What a bloody waste!' Harry suddenly roared. 'She's got a doctorate in maths and should be lecturing at a university!'

'She explained to me that the best teachers should be working in schools. People who know their subject matter inside out and who can inspire the students. Any fool could be teaching willing brains at a university. That's what she said and I think she has a point.'

'It's a bloody waste! That's what it is!' Harry repeated. He tried to heave himself off the couch but sank back into the upholstery.

Seeing Harry's bitter disappointment, Dora's anger evaporated. She could understand that he felt cheated, but it was their daughter's life, not his. If Sophie wanted to teach in a school, so be it. Tentatively, she lowered her head onto his shoulder.

'Sophie knows what she's doing,' she said quietly. 'We should be happy that she's got a good university degree and soon she'll have a good job.'

'She could have had a better job,' Harry insisted stubbornly.

Well, of course, she could have had a better job. At times Dora was worried about the unusual paths her daughter took. When she had finished school for example, everyone else went off to Europe to travel but Sophie had to go to Israel to work in a kibbutz. Dora could not dismiss the suspicion that her daughter had inherited some of Harry's self-righteousness.

Whatever it was, it was clear that once Sophie had made up her mind about something there was no shifting her. She was as stubborn as her father. Dora could not help but think that this attitude might possibly invite trouble in later life. A bit of compliance could go a long way, as far as she was concerned.

'Let's be grateful that she is not a lesbian.' It was a flippant comment, made to cheer Harry up, but Dora herself felt relief that her daughter was not interested in romantic relationships with women. A fact which worried her a bit. Maybe she was not quite as tolerant as she thought she was or should be in this day and age.

'Small mercies,' her husband grumbled.

Well, Dora would not mention any of that in her letter to Freda. She didn't need to know that Dora was no less prejudiced than Harry when it came to same-sex relationships. Instead, she would concentrate on Sophie's success. A Doctor of Mathematics!

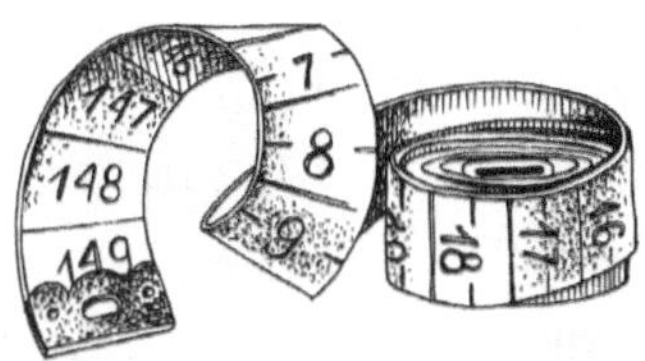

33

September 2019

A retirement party for Harry's colleague

ONE SATURDAY MORNING, HARRY APPEARED at the breakfast table fully dressed in a suit, a white shirt and one of his many paisley ties. Dora had always liked that particular suit. The 'pigeon suit' she called it to herself. It was a velvety, soft grey colour that in a certain light shimmered blue, just like the feathers of a pigeon. If she'd told Harry about that he probably would have never worn the suit again, even though it looked good on him. The smart cut hid his slightly rounded neck and his widening middle. When he was wearing it, you could forget that he was well into his sixties.

Harry pulled one of the kitchen chairs out, sat down and put his briefcase on the chair next to him. 'I need a strong coffee this morning,' he said, rubbing his hands together.

Even though the kettle had not finished boiling, Dora switched it off. It was difficult to have a conversation over the horrendous noise this old kettle produced.

'Harry, why are you dressed in a suit? Where are you going?'

'Where am I going?' Harry asked, incredulous. 'Where do you think I'm going? We've got all these people coming to the office today, upsetting the usual routine, which means no one will get anything done. And guess who has to deal with it all? Just get me a coffee. I need to steel my nerves!'

For a second Dora wavered. Had she got the day wrong? Maybe it wasn't Saturday. A quick glance at the calendar beside the door confirmed that it was indeed Saturday.

'Harry, it's Saturday. Since when are you going to the office on the weekend?'

He stared at her, then stood up abruptly to check the calendar on the wall.

'We're going to someone's retirement thing tonight at your boss's house. Remember? One of the other accountants is leaving.' Dora explained. She pointed at the calendar. 'There!' she said. 'JL's farewell, five pm.' Whoever JL is, she thought. She hardly knew any of Harry's colleagues.

Harry cleared his throat. 'Saturday,' he said baffled.

'Yes,' Dora replied. 'Saturday, today!'

Harry's eyes were on her lips, as if trying to decipher what she was saying. Irritated, Dora turned away from him to put two pieces of bread into the toaster.

Then a sudden flicker of realisation hardened his eyes as he pushed past Dora. Without another word he left the kitchen.

Shaking her head, Dora switched the kettle back on. Harry

must be terribly stressed. Maybe the thought of this upcoming get-together at his boss's place had bamboozled him. He didn't like social gatherings of large groups of people. Still, it was quite out of character for him to get his days confused. So much for a mathematical brain.

Minutes later, Harry returned to the kitchen, this time dressed in a pair of casual trousers and a polo shirt. 'I don't want to talk about it!' he said before Dora could open her mouth. Harry poured himself a cup of coffee, grabbed a piece of toast and disappeared into his study.

*

Dora was not looking forward to attending this party, either. Getting the days mixed up had stumped Harry and he had been monosyllabic all day. It had been hard for Dora to gauge his mood, which was something that always put her on edge. In a familiar feeling, her stomach had tensed up again. There was no knowing what he would be like at the party.

To add to her worries, she'd never heard of this JL who was retiring and for whom the boss was putting on a big farewell. She could only hope she didn't have to engage with him in conversation. What on earth could she possibly talk about?

Come to think of it, she didn't really know anyone Harry was working with, let alone their spouses. She had only ever been to one company Christmas celebration, and she had felt like a fish out of water. But this was an important get-together, as Harry had previously explained. The man who was retiring was a senior partner and everyone was expected to attend with their wives or husbands, respectively.

*

The boss's house was a concrete-and-glass monstrosity. A bunker with large windows and, just like a bunker, the concrete had been left in its raw state. Full of ridges and pimples and areas of honeycomb where the gravel shone through. Architect-designed, of course, cold and functional and modern. Spacious, yes, and luckily without any gun slits. Instead, lots of glass letting in the light. On the inside, it was minimalist with functional, expensive furniture only. No knick-knacks, no silly holiday souvenirs anywhere, no photos of grandchildren. Maybe he and his wife didn't have any. Again, Dora realised how little she knew about him, or any of Harry's other colleagues. The house made her shiver. She would not have liked to live here, day in, day out. You wouldn't want to make a mess in the kitchen, or drop pins and bits of cotton on the floor.

There was no denying, though, that the views of the ocean from the wide deck were spectacular. It calmed Dora's nerves and settled her heart, looking out onto the gentle movement of the waves, hearing the pebbles swishing forward and backward on the beach. The semi-dark created a particularly mysterious atmosphere. You could easily forget all the air-kissing and back-slapping that was going on behind her in the enormous living area.

Nevertheless, as she stood there with a glass of champagne in her hand, she tried to keep one eye on the ocean and one on Harry who was inside mingling with the crowd. Not an easy task, as there were quite a number of guests there. He seemed to know most of them but they were all strangers to her, apart from one or two vaguely familiar faces.

Everyone was walking to and from the buffet in the dining room, or wandering from group to group, with more back-slapping, laughing and chatting. Why was she trying to keep an eye on Harry? She answered her own question: because of the tension-filled day they'd had and the fact that he liked these occasions even less than she did. He found it difficult to converse with his colleagues on matters not relating to work, she was aware of that. Dora could see people walking away from him after just a quick exchange of words. He was not included in these chummy, we-know-each-other-outside-work groups.

Unexpectedly, Dora was suddenly approached by the wife of another accountant. Her husband, this woman said by way of introduction, had been in the firm for as many years as Harry, nearly a lifetime. Dora feared her short moment of peace on the deck was gone. Small talk, pretending interest in others and their families, and nonstop smiling and nodding exhausted her now more than ever. But she was pleasantly surprised when she discovered that this woman was a very charming person, easy to talk to. They even shared a stolen giggle at these important accountants. A woman she could possibly be friends with.

When Hannah – with an 'h' at both ends, she explained with a low laugh – asked Dora what she did with her time, she was fascinated to find out that Dora designed and made costumes. Quickly Hannah called over another handful of women and suddenly Dora found herself surrounded by a group of people who wanted to know all about her work.

She became quite animated when she talked about the cumbersome Baroque dresses or the sleek, elegant little numbers of the 1920s that she had designed. When Hannah heard that Dora had even made costumes for a couple of films, she wanted to know every little detail. Which films were the dresses for? Who were the actors and actresses who wore her creations? There were many more questions and Dora answered them as best as she could, all the while insisting that hers was only a very haphazard occupation. In thirty-plus years she had made only very few dresses for the screen.

In the meantime, the group around Dora had increased to nearly a dozen people without her noticing. She had even forgotten to keep track of Harry but suddenly spotted him standing at the back of her newly won fans. In contrast to all the others, who were wide-eyed and urging her to keep talking about her projects, Harry stood there scowling, a dark grey cloud hovering ominously over his head. Quickly Dora wrapped up her little exposé with the excuse that she needed a drink after all that talking. She had been quite elated, excitement coursing through her body as it always did when she thought about her work. It felt good to have an appreciative audience, but looking at Harry she now had a terrible sinking feeling in her stomach.

*

Sitting in the car next to him, she could feel the anger coming off him. He started the engine and straight away launched into a rant about how awful these get-togethers were. Nobody ever wanted to talk to him. As soon as he started on what he thought was an engaging topic of conversation they grabbed the first opportunity to get away. As he gripped the steering wheel, he talked himself more and more into a rage.

'I don't know why you can't have a proper talk to people anymore,' he complained. 'All they do is gabble on about their cars or holidays or playing golf or going fishing …'

'Well, it was a party and not a business meeting,' Dora ventured. 'People want to relax and enjoy themselves. Occasions like these are opportunities to find out something more personal about the people you work with, their families, their kids. Did you ask them about that?'

'They didn't want to find out anything about me either,' he growled. 'I told someone how I managed that problematic Sperloy account, but they weren't interested.'

Dora nodded, definitely not because she agreed with him but because she could imagine perfectly well what had happened. He had talked about how he was the only one who had known what was going on with the Sperloy firm. How he had spent weeks and weeks following up on some obscure paper trail leading to overseas accounts and how he had managed to … blah blah blah. She sighed. She would have run away, too, if someone had swamped her with that sort of conversation at a party. What complicated affairs social get-togethers were! Small talk was tedious and exhausting but serious conversation was a killer. She could appreciate the dilemma.

'But you obviously had a wonderful time!' Harry suddenly thundered. 'Standing there in the middle of gobsmacked admirers, going on and on about your fantastic work. Little do they know that it's all down to me that you can indulge in your hobby full-time! Who knows where you would be if it weren't for me!'

Dora shrank into her seat. Just when she was about to say something placatory, Harry had to humiliate her. He must be really angry, because he very rarely mentioned Dora's expenses. It was no good to remind him that she had occasionally earned some solid sums of money herself over the years. But, of course, 'occasionally' was the key word. Harry was right. Without his financial input, she would not have been able to 'indulge in her hobby'. So what could she say to counter his outburst? Nothing. Only that it was particularly mean of him to attack her like that. She was upset and angry, too, now. Her cheeks were burning and her breath coming in shallow bursts.

Dora turned her head and looked out the side passenger window. It was pitch black outside now, only the small chain of lights, the cat's eyes, faintly illuminated the edges of the highway. Those small lights were zipping past very fast. Dora suddenly wondered whether Harry was driving too fast. He was angry and he had had a few glasses of wine to drink at the party. It was a bad combination. Recently, she had noticed, too, that he reacted much more slowly in tricky traffic situations than he used to. At sixty-five, he was not young anymore. When the next overtaking lane approached, Harry continued straight ahead and overtook a few slower cars that had gone across into the left-hand lane to make way. Dora was convinced now that he was going much too fast.

'Harry,' she said carefully. 'Can you slow down a bit? I'm starting to feel a bit car sick.' No good telling him he was driving too fast. That would just make him accelerate even more to spite her.

'Serves you right,' he mumbled without looking at her. 'I saw you guzzle down those champagnes.' The foot stayed on the accelerator as they flew around a curve. A long straight stretch of road now lay in front of them. Dora could see a chain of cat's eyes on either side of the highway and a double chain right in the centre flying past, separating them from the oncoming lane.

They drove in silence, until suddenly the flickering of blue and red lights coming from behind them illuminated their car. Dora turned around and her heart stopped. A police car flashed its light, urging them to pull over. Where on earth had they come from?

'Pull over!' she urged Harry. 'Can't you see the police?'

Harry glanced into the rear-view mirror. 'Oh fuck! What do they want?' He jumped on the brakes and pulled over.

*

That was the moment their evening came to a horrible climax. As Dora had suspected, Harry had driven too fast. And his alcohol level was possibly over the limit, only just but still over. Two police officers approached the car. One walked around, checking the lights and tyres. The other, a middle-aged policewoman, leaned into his window and asked him for his licence. Harry pulled it out of his wallet and passed it to her through the window. Nothing unusual so far. Dora concentrated on her breathing. A forced smile played around her lips for the benefit of the policewoman who had only given her a quick glance. Then the policewoman asked Harry to step out of the car.

'What for?' Harry challenged her. 'The licence is valid, isn't it?' The petulant tone in his voice stopped Dora's breath as Harry pointedly threw himself back into his seat.

'Harry, do as she says and get out of the car,' she whispered between her teeth.

'Please, sir, I asked you to get out,' the officer insisted. In the meantime, her male colleague had approached and stood beside her.

That time, Harry reacted immediately. He grabbed the door handle and smashed the car door into her. All his pent-up frustration exploded out of him in a fraction of a second. It was all over by the time Dora managed to undo her seat belt and rush around the car. By then the second police officer had Harry on the ground and in handcuffs. What could have been just a fine for speeding and some demerit points for low-level drink driving had escalated into a full-blown case of assault on a police officer.

*

When his case went to court, Harry refused to acknowledge any guilt. He argued he had been asked to step out of the car and he had done exactly as he was told. Not his fault that the police officer was blocking the door. He ended up with six weeks in prison.

Not surprisingly, his boss at the accounting firm asked him to resign. The boss was prepared to keep the real reasons for Harry's sudden departure under wraps and instead announced to the other employees that Harry was taking an early retirement. At his age this was nothing unusual and it seemed no one was particularly surprised. Not even when the boss announced that there wouldn't be a farewell party. Someone in the company collected Harry's personal belongings and delivered them to his home, ending Harry's long working life as an accountant in the blink of an eye.

*

During several sleepless nights, Dora nearly managed to convince herself that some miracle might happen to prevent Harry going to prison, but it didn't. Nothing happened. Except that Harry wrote the requested resignation letter to his company and prepared himself to go to prison. It infuriated Dora hearing him talk about his prison sentence as if it were a banality, nothing major to worry about.

'It is something that can happen to the best of us,' he explained calmly to Dora. 'I'm the innocent victim of the stupid police.'

'This is not a joke, Harry! You've completely messed up your life!' Dora yelled at him as she thumped her fist on the kitchen table. Something she had never done before. 'I've never known anyone so stupid and stubborn as you! How can you pretend this prison thing means nothing?' She wanted to grab her husband by the shoulders and shake him, hit him on the head with her heavy cast-iron pot.

'Just pretend I'm going on a holiday,' Harry suggested with a smirk. God, she could kill him! Not just because he was so stupid, but because it was left to her to tell Andrew and Leah, and probably Stella Fulton as well. Without doubt, she would be the first one to wonder why there was no sign of Harry. Of course, she would also have to tell Luke and Boz.

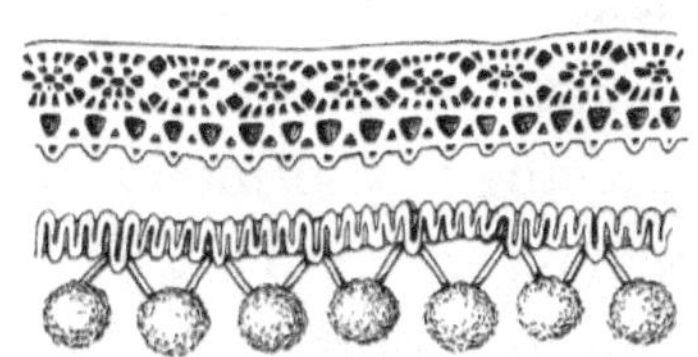

34

November 2019

Harry is going to prison

LEAH SAT NEXT TO DORA on the couch, holding her hands. 'Dora, are you alright? This is just terrible!' Dora's hands were freezing cold. She felt numb all over, her whole body as tight as a bowstring.

'No! Of course, I'm not alright! I just can't get this into my head. Harry is throwing everything away, everything! It's so out of character. I don't understand what's got into him!'

Dora stared out of the lounge window. Leah's chickens were squawking and squabbling over something on a patch of grass just outside the glass door. Stacked up against the shed wall were a few big bales of straw. For a second, Dora's mind was distracted.

Chickens fighting over seeds that fell out of the straw, she thought.

She had rehearsed what she was going to say in the car on the way down south. It was important to her to explain calmly and clearly what had happened and why. Until that point, neither she nor Harry had mentioned the incident with the police and the unspeakable consequences. Harry, probably because he thought it was no one else's business. Dora, because she had hoped until the last minute that something would intervene to prevent Harry's incarceration. Her plan had been to say her piece and then leave, but her in-laws' empathy had got the better of her. She had allowed hot anger to take hold of her.

Andrew stood up and poured himself a glass of water. 'He's just the biggest … I don't know what to say!' Andrew said angrily. 'But then nothing surprises me about Harry.' He shook his head. 'I have to say, I'm glad that our mother is gone. She would have been horrified.'

They had found Barb one morning, a couple of years ago. Sitting in her favourite chair, the shopping channel on the TV still advertising the wonders of some fancy kitchen implement. Barb's eyes were open, but blind to the advertisements, her ubiquitous glass of brandy spilled on the carpet next to her chair.

'She died doing what she liked best,' Harry had stated laconically. 'Watching TV and drinking her bedtime brandy.'

*

'Harry's gone to the mainland to do one last job before he retires,' Dora explained to Stella Fulton a few days after Harry's departure. 'I'll join him in a few days. We're having a holiday in Noosa to celebrate his retirement.' Lying was coming much more easily to Dora now than ever before. Well, she had been getting quite a bit of practice. Without blinking or blushing she looked straight into

Stella's eyes and smiled. She was glad she had decided not to tell her the truth.

'Oh, that sounds lovely!' the neighbour exclaimed. 'It's heavenly in Noosa. Always warm and sunny! You'll love it! I'll keep an eye on your house and collect your mail,' she determined.

Dora had decided that she would indeed go on a holiday. Harry's flippant comment had stuck in her mind. If he could go on a 'holiday' then so could she! She would escape, have a few weeks to herself pretending to celebrate Harry's so-called retirement.

In a moment of spitefulness, she considered going to Bali. Maybe Sophie would even come with her. Neither of them had ever mentioned the disastrous thirteenth birthday present again. They hadn't gone to Bali or Fiji then, but with Harry in prison they might just have a revenge holiday together now.

However, all of that had been such a long time ago. It was best not to warm up old resentments. Sophie had no time or inclination to go on a holiday with her mother, anyway, so Dora would instead escape to lovely, warm Queensland. All by herself. She'd always wanted to go to Noosa and now she would go. Stay in the best hotel and enjoy the fact that Harry was paying for it. This was not coming out of her emergency fund! For those few weeks, she would do nothing but walk on the beach and swim and lie in the sun. And not think of Harry. With a bit of luck, she would finally be able to sleep properly again, get a suntan and come back looking ten years younger! So there! Because at the moment, she looked like a wreck.

Next step: telling Luke and Boz. She didn't have to account for her movements to those two but she felt that it would be the right thing to do. Apart from the family, she felt more connected to them than anyone else. And why should they be wondering where she and Harry had gone? She might as well let them know. Going on a holiday. She and Harry were going on a holiday to

Noosa. Going for early morning swims and sitting under palm trees all day sipping cocktails. What could be better?

Looking across the road, she saw Luke sitting on the veranda. Might as well do it right now. She walked across the road and stepped into a front yard that just wouldn't clean itself up.

'Mornin', Mrs F,' Luke called out to her.

'Good morning,' Dora replied. Gingerly, she stepped onto the first tread of the five stairs leading up to the veranda. The second one was the one she had to watch out for. The timber looked rather rotten. The first time she had visited there she nearly put her foot right through it. Holding on to a splintery rail, Dora stepped straight from the first onto the third tread. That was better.

The front door opened just as Dora reached the top of the stairs.

'Thought I heard someone talking.' Boz stepped out of the house in his usual shorts and a torn t-shirt. He ruffled up his hair, flung himself onto the couch next to Luke and boxed his cousin on the shoulder. 'Hope we didn't make too much noise last night,' he said with a smirk.

Dora had just lowered herself onto the milk crate when she heard someone singing in the house. Huh, she thought. I understand!

With an effort, Boz got up from the couch. 'Bloody hell,' he mumbled as he opened the front door. 'Shut up, Amy!' he yelled and slammed the door shut again. The singing stopped abruptly. Boz threw himself onto the couch again, its base nearly touching the ground under this violent movement.

Dora shook her head at him. 'That wasn't very nice, young man,' she chided him. 'Your girlfriend needs a bit more respect, if you want to keep her.'

'She's not my girlfriend. We're just hanging.'

'Hanging?' Now what on earth did that mean?

'Hanging out, he means,' Luke explained. 'Just hanging out. You know, seeing each other, but without any commitment.'

'What you mean is a bit of sex now and then, when it suits,' Dora said rather prissily.

'Mrs F, what the …?' Dora suspected Boz was not easily surprised by anything, but she had made him sit up with her remark. 'The whole business suits her, too, you know,' he said rather defensively.

'What I know is that you should apologise. You were disrespectful. Besides, you should never stop anyone from singing. Singing is good for the soul. For the singer and the listener. That's what I know,' Dora insisted stubbornly.

'Right, then.' Boz heaved himself up off the couch again and yelled into the house. 'Sorry, Amy! Keep singing!'

The girl's reply came immediately. 'Arsehole!' Well, that was surely an appropriate response! If only she, Dora, had been brave enough to use that appellation with a certain someone. Except, her mother had put the fear of God into her when she tried to teach eight-year-old Freda to swear: swearwords might enter your head but a bar of soap in your mouth prevented them from going any further.

'Can't win with women.' Boz sat down on the top stair.

'No, you can't,' Dora agreed with a conspiratorial smile at Luke, who had remained silent during the exchange. 'But I didn't come here to talk to you about your "hanging" girlfriends,' she continued. 'I've come to tell you that Harry and I are going on a holiday, so you won't see us for a few weeks.' Dora suddenly stopped. She had wanted to tell them the same rehearsed story she had spun Stella Fulton but all at once she couldn't. Here she was, one minute lecturing those two about respect and the next she was lying to them.

Her pulse was fluttering in her temples. And the ridges on the milk crate were digging painfully into her behind and her thighs. She leaned across to pull a thin, not very clean cushion off the arm of the couch and put it under her. Why hadn't she thought of that before? That was much better.

She would tell them the truth. What on earth did it matter?

These two were not going to go around the neighbourhood telling everyone that her husband was in prison. For all she knew, they might have been in prison themselves at some point. Or at least know someone who had been.

'What I mean is, that my husband is going to Risdon for six weeks, and I'm off to Noosa for part of that time.' So there, she'd said it and the earth had not stopped moving. What had stopped moving were the brains of these two young men. They just stared at her uncomprehending, as if she'd spoken in a foreign language, trying to figure out what she had been saying.

There was a slight, if uncertain, flicker in Luke's eyes. 'Risdon? As in Risdon Prison?' he asked, a somewhat dumbfounded expression on his face.

Dora nodded. She grasped her sweaty hands tightly.

'Fuck me dead!' Boz exploded. 'Your old man is going to prison! Has he killed someone?'

The blood drained from Dora's face. 'Of course not! Don't be ridiculous. He wouldn't kill anyone!'

'So what's he done to deserve a holiday in Risdon?' Luke wanted to know.

In a few sentences, Dora summarised the events leading to Harry's arrest, starting with the boss's party and ending with the police pulling them up for speeding. They didn't need to know all the details. Harry's blistering anger over feeling sidelined at the party, his rudeness towards her, the fact that he had drunk too much. No, she kept that to herself. It was enough to explain that he had been too stubborn to acknowledge that he had been at fault when knocking over the policewoman.

'Fuck me dead!' Boz repeated. His repertoire of expressions of surprise was as limited as her daughter's, Dora realised, what with her constant 'wows'. Maybe it was a young person's thing. Not that these two were that young anymore. They would have to be in their thirties by now. Except that over the years nothing seemed to have changed in their lives. They still only worked when it suited them, neither of them had married and started a family. God, they even wore the same clothes they had all those years ago when she first met them. So, as far as she was concerned they were still young. Unable to grow up, obviously.

'I've completely underestimated your old man. He has principles.' Boz had a look of respect on his face that Dora hadn't seen before.

'Be that as it may. His principles got him into a lot of trouble.' Dora stood up and straightened her skirt. 'So, that's the situation.'

The two young men nodded. Something had clearly shifted in their perception of her husband. These two were not easily impressed but now they seemed to be in awe of him.

'Any work we can do for you while you're away?' Luke asked.

Dora shook her head. 'No, thank you.' She regarded the two men, slouching on their dirty couch, rubbish floating all around them on the ground. The paint was peeling off the weather boards on the wall behind them. The stairs leading into the front yard rotting. All of that seemed to be invisible to them. Or maybe they just didn't care.

A sudden thought occurred to Dora. 'Yes, actually, you can do something for me.' Frowning, she pointed at the stairs behind her. 'See those? Rotting and in danger of collapsing? If I'm to come over here occasionally, you'd better fix those stairs. I don't want to break my neck one day. Why don't you get to work on those?' she suggested. 'Just for starters. There's plenty more I can think of if you need any suggestions.'

*

Dora's holiday in Noosa was a disappointment. Not at all what she had envisioned. But the problem was not the place, it was her mind.

The weather was heavenly, just as her neighbour had predicted. The hotel was probably one of the most luxurious Dora had ever stayed in. The size of the room was generous, the furniture brand new, the view over the ocean unimpeded. She even had a small balcony where she could sit and read in the sun. She walked in the soft sand of the beach. She swam in the warm water. Everyone around her was in permanent holiday mode, relaxed and friendly.

But she was on her own, while all around her families and couples were strolling down the main road of Noosa or splashing about in the ocean together. For three weeks, she hardly talked to anyone, apart from the obligatory 'good morning' and 'lovely day today'.

Dinner by herself at a small table in a restaurant was excruciating. Dora had never felt this obvious and this deserted before. Because Harry had deserted her. He had set this whole awful chain of events in motion without sparing a single thought for her and the consequences she now had to live with.

At least she was able to sleep well. Walking and swimming tired her out pleasantly. When she fell into bed at night she slept soundly and without dreaming.

Returning home, she wasn't sure whether she looked ten years younger – highly unlikely – but at least she felt more rested than she had in the weeks previous. Outside her house, she asked the taxi driver to give her a few minutes, just sitting in the car, adjusting to being back home.

She had to compose herself before getting out of the taxi and taking the first few steps into her new life. That's what it felt like. Maybe not quite a new life but definitely a new chapter. Her world had been thrown into disarray by Harry and it needed a new order. From now on, he would be at home with her, day and night, a prospect she didn't fancy. Those valuable hours by herself in the house would be gone. Dora frowned. Maybe not. She should not allow that. That precious time should be fought for. She could not occupy herself exclusively with Harry. That was it. She needed to establish a new order in their day-to-day life. New parameters were needed. Indeed, she would set new parameters!

The memory of that day in the car when Harry had been talking about parameters made her laugh. So much had changed since then. What an innocent baby she'd been! And so trusting. Harry had been so knowledgeable about everything, and she had allowed herself to be guided by him. She had placed her life in Harry's hands. And look what happened! He had ended up in prison, and she had been wandering the beaches of Noosa all by herself, miserable and lonely. Another short laugh, tinged with bitterness, escaped her lips.

Astonished, the taxi driver turned around to her. 'You're alright?' he asked.

'Yes, yes! I just need another minute,' she said. Her eyes scanned her front yard and the house. Everything was as it should be. The blinds were still down on all the windows, the solid front door presenting a forbidding barrier. *Do not enter!* it signalled sternly. The house looked utterly lonely and deserted. Could a house be lonely? Dora wondered. Her car on the drive outside the garage was the only sign that anyone could possibly live there.

It must have rained while she'd been away. The bushes and flowers in the front yard looked green and healthy. Maybe Stella had watered them? Dora frowned and looked towards her neighbour's house. Unusually, there was no sign of her. Normally, the arrival of a taxi would have drawn her out to check who was visiting.

Turning slightly in her seat, Dora searched the dilapidated house across the road. She squinted against the sunlight and leaned forward. Something was different over there.

'Huh!' she exclaimed and slowly a broad smile spread over her face. Quickly she retrieved her wallet from her handbag and paid the taxi driver. 'Just put my suitcase on the footpath here,' she told him. 'Don't bother carrying it to the door!'

Without looking left or right, Dora crossed the road and stood by the low fence of Luke and Boz's front yard. There was no sign of beer cans or food wrappers or any other rubbish on the lawn. Everything had been cleaned up. Well, the bushes and trees still were in desperate need of a trim and the lawn was not really a lawn. It was still a mess consisting of all sorts of weeds interspersed with bare patches of dirt. But what a difference, anyway! Dora was speechless. And there, leading up to the veranda, stood a completely new set of stairs. The two not-so-young men had not simply patched up the one rickety step she had complained about. No, they had replaced everything, even the splintery rails on either side of the stairs. All the timbers were new, sanded and varnished.

In disbelief, Dora stared at the dilapidated house. That Luke and Boz had taken note of her request regarding the broken step moved her more than she would have expected. And to even clear up all that rubbish! She had imagined that once her back was turned, they would have called her an 'old busybody'. Someone who should mind their own business and not interfere with the life of others. It pleased her immensely to realise that they must value her sporadic company. Or maybe they just wanted to stay on her good side. After all, they had got a bit of money out of her for all those odd jobs. Her emergency fund had gone down dramatically once she had started employing them, but never mind that! Now it seemed quite conceivable that she could inspire them to do a few more odd jobs around their own house. Next, they could clean up the veranda. Sand the flaking paint of the weather boards and give the house a new paint job! Come to think of it, she had lots of ideas of what these two could do to freshen up their house.

Suddenly happy to be home, Dora crossed the road again, this time with a skip in her step. She picked up her suitcase and unlocked the front door of her house. First, she would open all the windows as well as the front and back doors. This house needed fresh air rushing through it, taking with it any suffocating staleness. Soon, Harry would be coming back. Today, she would put some life into this place. Afterwards, she would tell Freda how her whole existence had been turned upside down, thanks to Harry's stubbornness. She would add that after the initial shock, she had become much more decisive and single-minded than ever before. It was high time to acknowledge that she had been rather bloodless and demure for too long.

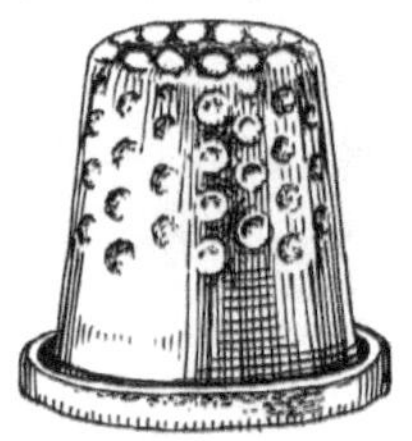

35

May 2020–October 2022

Harry returns from prison

MONTHS LATER, LONG AFTER HARRY had been released from Risdon Prison, Dora realised that the events leading to his arrest, and the stay in prison, had set off something in him that she couldn't yet grasp. She didn't doubt for one minute that something snapped in Harry when they were stopped by the police that night. He had never liked the police, or any sort of controlling authority, so being challenged by them the way he had been was putting him on the back foot, something he could not abide. By anyone. Of course, it was also possible that something had misfired in his brain well beforehand to cause his explosive reaction. His confusion that morning about what day it was, should perhaps have been an indication to her that something was not quite right with Harry.

Out of prison and back at home, he accused the police and legal system of having ruined the last few years of his life. He was furious, but something also had broken in him. He couldn't win this battle against the authorities, and it made him bitter.

*

The year 2020 turned out to be more unusual than expected. March of that year saw the beginning of a complete lockdown of Tasmania due to the Covid pandemic. Nothing and nobody was allowed in or out, no cruise ships, no planes, no ferries, no tourists swamping the island like a tsunami, and nobody could even hazard a guess at how long this lockdown would last.

Night after night, news reports broadcast horrific suffering and deaths all over the world. After weeks of being bombarded with these news items, Dora had had enough.

'Harry, I really don't want to watch the news anymore. It's all about death and dying and those horrible hospital scenes everywhere. It's making me ill.'

Amazingly, Harry got up and switched off the TV. 'We're having our own lockdown. A lockdown on the news! For the wellbeing of us citizens in this crisis!' he declared, his voice strong and convincing, as if addressing the whole population of Tasmania. The Premier couldn't have expressed it any better.

Following Harry's announcement, they sat silent and uncomfortable in front of the blank TV screen. 'What do you suggest we do instead?' he finally said, turning to Dora.

'I'm going to read my book. And you … you could sort all those photos we've always thrown into shoe boxes. Put them into albums.' What a good idea! That would keep him busy for weeks! Sophie, of course, would have laughed at the notion of photo albums. Most of her life, including her photos, seem to be stored up in the cloud somewhere. Well, Dora couldn't be bothered with that sort of thing. Scanning and copying, downloading and uploading. No, a photo album or two would do just nicely.

'Where are the shoe boxes?' Harry wanted to know.

'In the wardrobe of the spare bedroom. Shall I get them?'

Harry shook his head, pushed himself off the couch and shuffled into the hallway.

Dora pulled her book off the side table. *The Catcher in the Rye*, a book she had retrieved from among Sophie's old school things. Decades ago, she had read the book in her English class, but she only had a hazy memory of it. J.D. Salinger, American author, 1919–2010.

Carrying three shoe boxes in his arms, Harry shuffled past the lounge room door.

'Harry!' Dora called out. 'I'm not at all bad with numbers, you know! I can remember nearly all the birth and death dates of the authors I've read!'

Harry stuck his head in through the door. He shifted the boxes from one arm onto the other. 'If you're that good with numbers, tell me what the square root of 289 is?'

Annoyed, Dora slammed her book shut. 'I think you should sort the photos in your study, not here in the lounge.' Why did he always have to challenge her? 'I don't want them lying around here for days on end!'

'Just what I thought!' Triumphantly, Harry slammed the door of his study behind him.

*

All things considered, Dora enjoyed the lockdown. Finally Tasmania was a proper island again, inaccessible from the mainland and overseas. That is, if you overlooked the haphazard food deliveries from the mainland. In Dora's opinion, this should have been an opportunity to try out if Tasmania could survive as a self-sufficient entity, but no one asked her opinion.

All in all, Dora felt safe. If you couldn't feel safe on an island at the end of the world, then you couldn't feel safe anywhere!

Life had become peaceful again. Bird song and the whistling wind had taken over from roaring car engines. Apart from the odd furtive shopper, the streets were deserted. Dora dared herself to cross the forlorn-looking Channel Highway with her eyes closed. It was thrilling, taking your life in your hands!

If she met someone on the narrow path along the beach, she jumped into the bushes to let the other person pass so they wouldn't get too close to her. Nobody touched anyone anymore. Even Stella kept herself away from the fence. Instead, she raised her voice when talking to Dora, so that even Luke and Boz across the road on the veranda could hear every word she said.

*

When the first vaccines became available, Dora booked herself into the community centre to get her anti-Covid jab. Six months later, she got the booster injection. Harry refused to have anything put into his body that had been developed in a rush and not been tested properly.

'For all I know ...' he said. 'For all I know these injections could have side effects that are worse than this Covid thing. It's just pharmaceutical companies raking in the money. We should have bought shares!'

Many shops were closed. How enlightening that life could continue without clothing boutiques, jewellery stores, game shops and travel agencies. No one could travel! People discovered how nice their immediate environment was. Dora had always appreciated her backyard. Yes, she quite liked how this pandemic had brought everyone's life back to the basics.

The only drawback was having Harry home all day long, bored and restless. Not that that was due to the pandemic. If he'd still had his job at the accountancy firm, at least he could lock himself away in his study and work from home, like everyone else. But his being under her feet from the moment he woke up changed the rhythm of her day considerably more than the pandemic.

Normally, once Harry had left the house to go to work, she would head straight to her sewing room and start on her dresses. But now they both lingered, first over breakfast, then during that agonising half hour before Harry finally decided what to do with himself. Often, because he had nothing urgent to do – there had been absolutely no progress in regard to the 'photo sorting situation' – he engaged Dora in conversation. Big rants, she called them to herself, over something that had annoyed him, his mobile phone not working properly or the country's new defence policies which he didn't agree with. Defence policies! Good God, Dora should have had her own defence policies to ward off these unwanted verbal bombardments, these red-hot missiles flying through the air.

She dodged these missiles, his tirades, by washing the dishes, something she would have normally left until lunchtime or even until dinner. Or by thinking about something else, while occasionally nodding in Harry's direction. With one ear, she listened to Harry while trying to work out how best to sew the frilly neck on that dress that was nearly finished. All she wanted to do was try it out and see whether or not it needed adjusting. Instead, she was listening to the faults in the proposed defence policies!

Well, there was another major drawback to this whole Covid situation. She, Dora, had no work to do! Nobody was getting married, all plays and performances had been stopped, no one wanted a dress or a costume. So she kept herself busy, first by sewing face masks for everyone she knew. After all she had several bags of left-over fabrics in her sewing room that were ideal for small projects. Andrew and Leah received a few masks; Stella got some, which she paid for with some fresh vegetables. Dora made a few extra colourful ones for Luke and Boz, which they wore even when they were just sitting on their veranda. 'Just for the heck of it!' Boz had yelled across the road as a thank you. Harry refused to wear a face mask. It struck Dora as completely unfair that he, who refused to get vaccinated or wear a mask, never even caught the virus!

Then Dora decided to make a patchwork bedspread for Sophie. She couldn't be sure that Sophie would like it, but it told her that her mother was thinking of her, despite not being able to visit her. Finally, she made a dress for herself, something with a frilly neckline that would hide her wrinkles. The neckline she thought about when Harry was going on and on about defective defence policies.

Still, there were moments when she wondered how to occupy herself. The house had been rigorously cleaned, every tiny weed in the garden eliminated and the car washed, even though it wasn't necessary. She certainly did not want to stand by the window like Harry sometimes did. He stood rigidly staring at … she didn't know what. That faraway look in his eyes told her that his mind was somewhere else altogether. During those moments, he seemed morose, sullen, making her fear he might fall into a depression. Making her wish he had something important to do or something annoying to expostulate about.

*

It hadn't been that easy to set parameters after all. They both needed to adjust to their changed circumstances. It did annoy Dora that she had lost the solitude she appreciated so much. The leisurely time to work as much or as little as she pleased, to eat when it suited her. Now Harry's presence demanded her attention and regulated her day. It was obvious to her that Harry had suffered a great loss and she felt for him. Losing your work was the number two catalyst for depression, right after the death of a loved one, she'd read somewhere ages ago. When he was wandering from one room to another trying to find something to do, pity welled up in her, at times to be replaced instantly by anger. It was his own fault, after all, that he found himself in this situation.

'I have been confronted with things in that prison that you will never experience,' he pompously stated one morning while he was drying the dishes. Drying the dishes! Life was full of surprises.

'Well, I should hope not!' she snapped back at him. If it was a medal he wanted for going to prison – and that's what it sounded like to Dora – he certainly wouldn't get it from her.

A solution to these slow and wasted mornings came to her when she was walking past the newsagency one morning. The newspaper! She cursed herself for not having thought of it sooner. There had always been a newspaper in Harry's office. Dora had no idea whether he had ever read it but this was something she could try. Straight after arriving home from shopping, she rang the *Mercury* and placed a subscription for the following three months. Just long enough to see whether Harry would read the paper in the mornings.

It worked! Every day now, before breakfast, he walked down their drive and picked up the newspaper. The delivery man simply threw it out the window of his car and it usually ended up in the bushes somewhere. It gave Harry another reason to grumble but so what? Her strategy worked. Straight after breakfast, he now immediately withdrew into his study to read.

Dora's mornings were saved. Not only did Harry read the paper, he also did the crossword and the sudoku. That surely appealed to his mathematical brain and kept his mind occupied. Dealing with numbers, putting them into sequences – the sudokus were just perfect for him! Occasionally, he triumphantly showed her a particularly difficult sudoku he had successfully finished. Dora feigned interest but only gave a cursory glance. She thanked whoever had invented them from the bottom of her heart.

Harry had even started writing letters to the editor, none of which were ever published. All of those activities took up a good two hours or more. And when he finished with the newspaper he seemed to find something else to do in his study. Books were being sorted, folders checked and discarded, the furniture rearranged. At tax time he started doing tax returns for friends and neighbours. He even took up walking again. Initially along the beach just behind their house. Then he ventured further to rediscover the Alum Cliffs track.

Dora rang the *Mercury* again and extended the subscription for another year. She started to establish a new order in their life. New parameters had been set after all. They were working.

*

Still, it took the whole of a beautiful second summer to arrive at a comfortable arrangement. It brought to mind a puzzle. All those pieces that needed to find a place and fit in with each other to produce a more or less pleasant result. Grateful that Harry was now busy in the mornings, Dora did as much of whatever work she could find around the house before lunchtime. Sometimes she just sat in her sewing room in the sun and indulged in some reading. Very rarely did Harry disturb her. And she, Dora, conceded to have lunch with him, every day at the same time.

They had agreed to buy a dishwasher so the problem of when to wash the dishes was solved. The afternoons were 'free', but then, that was a misnomer because there was always something that needed to be done. The garden needed attention. One or the other of the cars needed a service.

Harry, Dora noted as the restrictions began to ease, had become a very mild-mannered person. Most of the time, anyway. Despite everything, he seemed unusually content. She had even heard him whistle! At times his placid mood made her a bit suspicious. It brought to mind his relaxed manner after those visits to the *house of ill repute*. Even though those visits had stopped a long time ago, she caught herself keeping an eye on him. She liked to know where he was and what he was doing. You just never knew!

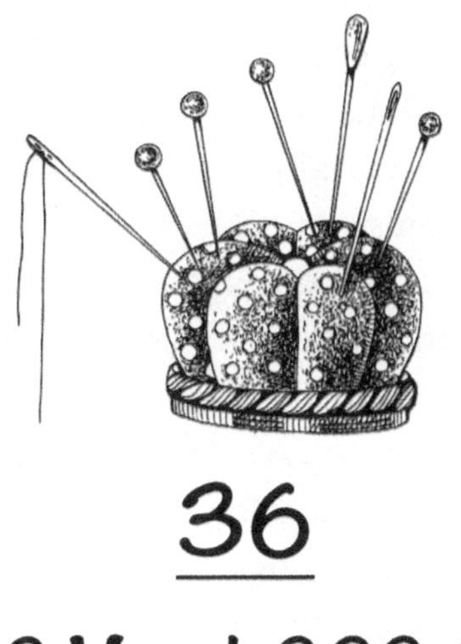

<u>36</u>

2 March 2024

Five days after Harry's death: Dora visits Luke and Boz

DORA DECIDED IT WAS TIME to go across the road and talk to Luke and Boz about Harry's old recliner chair. Offering it to them served several purposes, she had figured out. First of all, she wanted it gone. The corner it sat in could be used for something much more pleasant. A little side table maybe, with a lace tablecloth. She could see a vase of fresh flowers on it. Yes, much better than that wretched chair.

Secondly, the chair could be a symbolic gesture she was making to herself. Instead of *acquiring* things, she was now giving something away. For free. It was like paying a penance, making up for bad deeds in the past. The thought of stealing a handbag from the lovely owners of Homewares and Moore still made her feel uneasy.

It was incomprehensible what she had done. Whenever she used that particular handbag she had to fight a guilty conscience. Her feelings weren't quite as strong when she remembered the *acquisition* of the expensive buttons in that horrible fabric store. Nobody working there gave two hoots about any of the items they sold, but be that as it may, Dora had decided to do the right thing and from now on pay for everything. That was just what Freda would have advised. Even though, truth be told, her darling sister didn't always adhere to rules and conventions either.

Reason number three: she needed to find out what Luke and Boz had told the police. Offering the recliner chair was really only a pretext for her visit across the road. But it could nicely lead into other topics of conversation.

Later in the evening Dora heard the roar of a car just outside her house, then the screeching of brakes. Car doors slamming, someone calling out something at the top of his voice.

Aha, she thought. They're home! Through her lace curtains she saw the two not-so-young men from across the road unlock their front door. A few moments later, they appeared on the veranda, plonked themselves onto the old saggy couch and opened a can of beer each.

Harry had made a point of not looking at the house when driving past. 'What a bloody waste!' he used to complain. 'These bloody idiots are losing money every day by neglecting that house! And so is everyone else, what with that decrepit thing in our street.' He never realised that Dora had a special relationship with these 'bloody idiots', and because he avoided looking at the house, he hadn't noticed the improvements these 'bloody idiots' had made. The stairs leading to the house, the new timber floorboards of the veranda, the sanded and painted front wall, the more or less tidy front yard. Maybe they had even done something inside the house, but how could she know? She had never been invited in.

But now she was slipping into her thongs and on her way to

talk to them. When she approached their veranda Luke waved and called out to her. 'Mrs F, sorry to hear about your old man.'

'Thank you,' Dora said. She stepped onto the veranda and regarded the two men. Both had white paint on their hands and their clothing. Luke even had a few streaks of paint in his brown hair. Boz sat slouched into the back of the old couch. His shorts were covered in paint but he had taken his t-shirt off and now sat on it. His bare upper body was covered in strawberry coloured hair, as shiny as the red curls he sported on his head. It made her feel a bit uncomfortable looking at this half-naked man who rubbed his stomach in a very uninhibited manner.

What sort of a name is Boz? Dora thought. Even though she had had dealings with these two for quite a while now she had never asked. Was it short for Boris? Or something made up? Young people seemed to give each other all sorts of names.

She stepped over his stretched-out legs and lowered herself onto the plastic milk crate.

'You want one?' Luke asked holding up a can of beer.

'No.' Dora shook her head. She smoothed her skirt out over her knees.

'Sorry about your old man.' Boz repeated Luke's words. He took a long sip from his can, then flung it off the veranda into the open recycling bin.

'The police were here,' Luke said.

'Were they?' Dora pretended to be surprised. 'Why did they come to you?'

Boz's steel blue eyes fixed on her. 'They told us what happened to your old man. Fell off a cliff or something,' he said. 'Apparently you told them that we saw you coming home from the shops that morning he died.' Dora quickly lowered her eyes. Did Boz question what she had said to the police? Having to look at his naked upper body really disconcerted her.

'Ah yes, that's right.' Dora wondered whether they could see through her 'confused widow' charade. Of course, she had known that the police would be talking to them. 'That's right. I did. I told them I saw you sitting here on the veranda so you must have seen me, too.'

'Sure, we did see you that morning.' Luke also flung his empty can off the veranda but missed the recycling bin. Dora's eyes followed the can awkwardly rolling down the dried-up grass in the front yard, until it came to rest next to a wild rosebush. So much for a tidy front yard.

'We told them we're the unofficial neighbourhood watch team!' Luke broke out in loud laughter. 'We see everything that's going on here.'

'Yeah,' Boz confirmed, nodding vigorously. His strawberry curls followed every movement of his head. 'Like that crazy woman next to you, yabbering and singing in the garden all day. Drives you crazy! Makes you glad to go to work occasionally.' He ripped open another can of beer. 'Or your old man,' he nodded towards Dora. 'Always used to put on his jacket when he jumped out of the car.'

Surprised, Dora looked at him. She hadn't known that. She had always assumed Harry had driven home from work with his jacket on. Why would he put it on when he arrived home, only to fling it over the kitchen chair a few seconds later?

Would he really have done that just to annoy me? she thought, suspicion rising in her. He knew exactly how much she hated that bloody jacket hanging over the kitchen chair. When he actually walked past the hallstand on his way to the kitchen and could hang it up himself. What a man! Once, she had deliberately 'accidentally' smeared a bit of jam of the sleeve hoping it would give him a message. But no. He hadn't even noticed, and she was the one who had to wash the jam off the jacket. So much for that!

Huh, she thought. The things you find out! And to think all of that happened years ago.

She turned to Luke. 'So what did you tell the police?'

'We told them you came home with two shopping bags. Bloody heavy ones. We nearly came over to help you carry them inside.' He laughed again.

Dora stiffened. Yes, she did remember that they had called out to her, offering to help with the bags! Thank God, they hadn't come over. No, she knew they wouldn't have. They only came when she asked them to do a job for her. As a rule, their bums were either glued to that old couch or they were hiding inside the house. Unless they went to work. But then they jumped into their ute and were gone. She had never seen them walk along the road.

No, everything was fine. She just needed to stay calm, and she needed to look unconcerned. 'Did they want anything else?' she asked.

Both shook their heads. 'Nope,' Boz said. 'They left straight away.' He lifted his backside awkwardly and pulled the crumpled t-shirt from underneath him. Dora breathed a sigh of relief when he slipped it over his head. Now she was able to fully look at him.

'Lucky we sat outside.' Luke gave his mate a meaningful look. 'Wouldn't want them inside to see what's growing there!' They gave a laugh.

Dora didn't want to see inside, either. She had her suspicions of what was growing inside. Several times she had come over and knocked on their door to be hit by a sweet but pungent smell. She wasn't born yesterday. She knew exactly what the smell was.

'So do you think your old man fell, or someone knocked him off?' Luke asked.

'Maybe you knocked him off,' Boz speculated with a sideways glance at Dora.

Dora felt herself blush. Her bottom lip quivered. 'Heavens, no!' she cried out. 'No, no! I would never kill my husband. Never!'

Luke kicked Boz in the shin. 'You've upset her, you nong!'

The lady doth protest too much, she suddenly thought. Who had said that? Was it in some Shakespeare play? Was she protesting too much? Making herself suspicious? Shakespeare, English playwright, 1564–1616.

'When you're as married as long as we were, you do feel like killing each other occasionally,' she quickly said. 'It's only normal. Doesn't mean you're going to do it. God, no!' She rubbed at her temples. The last thing she needed now was a headache! No, she needed either a glass of wine or a good cry just to get rid of that tension. But not in front of these two. She had to compose herself.

'Actually,' she said in attempt to change the topic. 'I've come here to ask if you wanted my husband's recliner chair. Sooner or later it has to go, and I thought of you.' She glanced at the saggy, dirty couch.

'You mean one of those that tilts back?' Luke asked surprised.

Dora nodded. 'You can have it for nothing.'

'The Judge's chair!' Luke grinned widely. 'S'pose he won't be needing it anymore,' he said, nodding his head towards Dora's house. 'Yeah, we'll take it.'

Dora looked at him in surprise. 'The judge?' She shifted herself into a more comfortable position on the milk crate. It was digging painfully into her backside and thighs. Where had that cushion gone that she usually used? 'You thought he was a judge?'

'Always dressed in a suit and tie, polished shoes and that stick up his arse. Yeah, we called him 'the Judge',' Luke explained.

'And with that look on his face that makes the trees shake in their roots!' Boz added. The two of them collapsed in a fit of laughter at this seemingly hilarious play on words. Boz threw another can into the front yard but this time he, too, missed the bin. The can rolled down and came to a stop right next to its companion. If they kept this up it would look like a rubbish tip again in no time at all. Well, it wasn't her problem!

'He's not a judge. He's an accountant,' Dora sat up straight on the milk crate. 'Was,' she added. 'Was an accountant.'

'An accountant, fuck me dead! That explains his problem with money!' Boz slapped his bare thighs.

Dora had to admit that she quite liked these two not-so-young men. They didn't use big words and convoluted expressions. They told it as it was. Even the occasional swear words didn't worry her anymore. No doubt, they were a helpful and efficient means of communicating.

So they could have Harry's recliner chair. She did like them. They were deserving recipients of that chair. And she thought they liked her, too. Otherwise they wouldn't come back and work for her, would they?

This is what has made us into accomplices, totally unlikely accomplices, Dora thought. Money and lies and deception. Dora did feel the odd twinge in her conscience but it was not as if they had committed a murder together. It was something so very banal. It had all started with the garden gate all those years ago. It had been Harry, after all, who had asked her to find a gardening service.

37

November 2022

Harry wrestles the washing machine

CAREFULLY, DORA WRAPPED THE FINISHED dress in tissue paper. Over the top, she folded firmer wrapping paper. This parcel would go to Sydney soon. It was a relief to have completed yet another project, one of the very few she had had since the end of the pandemic. Hopefully, the payment would be on its way soon! She would love to see the opera singer in it, but didn't know when and where exactly the opera would be performed. Well, it didn't matter. She couldn't follow all her dresses around the country.

All of a sudden, a horrible noise broke through her thoughts. Dora knotted the string around her parcel and listened. The noise seemed to emanate from the laundry. A smashing, banging, slamming kind of noise, as if the washing machine was out of balance, its drum banging hard against the walls, like the sound of an out-of-control jackhammer. Dora frowned. She hadn't put on any washing. She stood up and placed her parcel on the stool in the corner.

As she approached the laundry, the noise level increased. *Clonk, clonk, bang, bang!* Hurriedly she flung the door open and stopped dead in her tracks. The drum in the washing machine must have been completely unbalanced, making the machine jump erratically from side to side like a big metal monster trying to loosen its chains.

And there was Harry! His legs spread wide to support himself, he had pushed his whole bodyweight against the machine, embracing it as best as he could with both arms. Holding the machine as if it were an oversized, unwilling lover. His face bright red from the exertion, he turned his head towards Dora.

'Harry, what on earth are you doing?' Dora shrieked.

'I'm trying to steady the machine!' he yelled back at her, all the while increasing his grip on the sides of the machine. 'This fucking thing is completely out of control!'

'Press the button, the off button!' Dora screamed at him.

'There is no off button! Can't you see?'

Dora pushed her way into the laundry and reached across Harry's body to the controls. The machine beeped gratefully as she pressed the button, then came to a rumbling halt.

'The on and off button is one and the same thing, Harry! Press once and it's on. Press again and it's off! Just like on the TV remote!' Surely, he could have worked that one out by himself. Finally, with a big sigh of relief, Harry let go of the washing machine.

'Last week the machine worked perfectly well,' he defended himself. 'I turned it on, it did its job and then it switched itself off!'

'What do you mean "last week"? You weren't using the machine last week, Harry. You've never used it!' Taken aback, Dora frowned at him.

'I washed my handkerchiefs last week when you were out. It seems to me that there are a number of things I have to do myself these days!'

Dora chose to ignore that last remark. Rather, she tried to remember when she had been 'out' the previous week. She hardly went anywhere. Then it came to her, her old school friend Cindy had rung her! No wonder she had pushed that afternoon into some dark corner of her brain. After decades of living on the mainland, Cindy had returned to her hometown in Tasmania, divorced, penniless and bitter. She had wanted to meet with Dora in a café, possibly to rekindle their old friendship.

'You made the right choice, marrying a rich man,' Cindy had said to her in that acerbic tone of voice she had practised as a teenager. Squinting her eyes, she took a deep drag on her cigarette.

I did not choose Harry, he chose me, Dora had wanted to reply, but she stopped herself. Instead she had come out with some feeble romantic riposte. 'Surely happiness is more important than money.'

'Maybe.' Through the cigarette smoke Cindy had looked at her with narrowed eyes. 'But happiness only lasts a nanosecond. And I can assure you, it's easier to be unhappy with a rich man rather than a poor man. You're leading a nice comfortable life, wanting for nothing. Sheltered from adversity.'

After that, Dora was sure she did not want to rekindle her friendship with Cindy.

*

'Harry, you don't even know how to use the washing machine. Just look what's happened right here, right now!'

'Of course I know how to use the machine! How dumb do you

think I am? Set the temperature on hot, the water level on high, push the "on" button and the machine does the rest!'

'Don't tell me you did all of that just for a handful of handkerchiefs?' Incredulous, she stared at her husband. Harry stared right back at her, their eyes locked as if in combat.

'Good God, Harry! What on earth is this? Why are you doing the washing all of a sudden?' Dora glared at Harry, hands on her hips. This really was too much!

His arms aching from holding onto the bucking washing machine, Harry fell back against the wall. Then he bent down and pulled a dirty bath towel out of the wash basket. Breathing hard, he wiped the sweat off his forehead.

'I'm washing my pillow,' he explained, still struggling for breath.

'What do you mean? Why? Which pillow?' Dora snatched the bath towel out of his hands and threw it back into the wash basket.

'The one with the feathers! My favourite!'

'For heaven's sake, Harry! That pillow gets dry-cleaned, not washed in the machine. What on earth were you thinking?'

Harry grumbled something unintelligible.

Holding her breath, she opened the lid of the washing machine, fearing what she might find in there. 'Look Harry, this pillow is squashed into one half of the drum.' Dora breathed in deeply to steady her voice. 'No wonder the machine was unbalanced. You need to put more things in so the weight is evenly distributed.' God, it was hard to appear patient when all you wanted to do was pull your hair and scream.

'You would think by now they had developed machines that deal with that sort of problem,' he grumbled.

'They have!' Dora replied exasperated. 'They are called front loaders. Next time we'll buy one of them!'

Harry shook his head. 'No, too expensive,' he declared.

'Whatever!' Dora was fuming. 'Just don't wash any more pillows. Leave that to me! In fact, leave all the washing to me! All of it!'

She bent down to pull at the heavy, sodden pillow but the sheer weight of it made her drop it straight back in.

'Don't just watch me! Pull out that pillow!' She turned to Harry impatiently. You bloody idiot! she added quietly to herself.

With a groan, Harry pulled at the pillow and swung it into the laundry tub.

Despite herself, Dora burst out laughing. The pillow looked like a sheep that had fallen into a lake. All wrinkled up, dripping wet, curled into itself and weighing a tonne.

'Why are you laughing? What's so funny?'

'Nothing, nothing!' Dora looked away from him. The frazzled expression on his face would only want to make her laugh even more. All of this nonsense had made her feel quite hysterical.

'What do I do with it now?' Harry frowned.

'Squeeze it out as best as you can and then put it in the rubbish. We'll buy you a new one!'

In a huff, Harry shuffled down the hallway towards the front door. Before he slammed the door shut behind him, he called out to Dora, 'I shall stick to what I know best and sort my stuff in the garage!'

'What a good idea,' Dora muttered under her breath, even though she could not quite think of what there was in the garage that needed sorting. It would only take Harry five seconds to check his small toolbox that contained all of five or six tools and a couple of glass jars with nails and screws. The dozen or so boxes with his old files already stood neatly stacked on the sturdy shelves that Luke and Boz had put in not too long ago. Whatever Harry kept those old tax files and company reports for, Dora didn't even want to guess at. Some of them were decades old.

Judging by the sounds emanating from the garage, Harry was

taking down the boxes and dropping them onto the floor. What on earth was he planning to do with them? To get away from the noise Harry was producing in the garage, Dora decided to go into the backyard and do some weeding. It had rained the previous night, therefore the horrible clay soil in their garden, which often set like concrete in the dry, should be a bit softer now. Hopefully she could clean up her neglected flower bed.

When she was back inside the house an hour later, she caught a glimpse of Harry through the kitchen window wheeling the big recycling bin onto the footpath. Good heavens! she thought surprised. Has he thrown out all those old files?

'Harry, what were you doing in the garage?' she asked him when he slumped onto a kitchen chair minutes later.

'I've thrown all that paperwork out,' he said. 'It was all old stuff that no one wants to look at anymore.'

'Wasn't there sensitive material in there? I mean, tax records, people's personal information? Shouldn't that have been shredded, rather than just put into the bin?'

For a moment Harry looked perplexed, as if that thought hadn't occurred to him. Then he said brusquely, 'What do you think they're doing at the rubbish tip? Looking through all my files and noting down some stranger's personal information? Just forget it, Dora! You worry about your stuff and I'll worry about mine!'

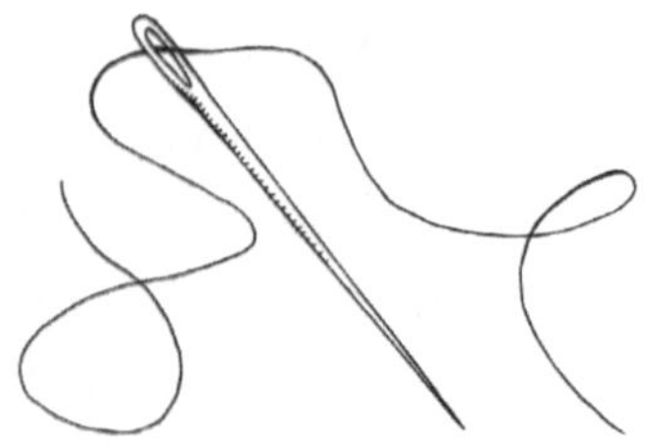

38

March 2023

What is going on with Harry?

'**D**ORA, I WANT TO RUN something past you,' Leah said as she stepped into the house. She had driven from Cygnet to Kingston to go for a walk on the beach with Dora. Harry was ensconced in front of the TV, his feet up on the coffee table, a cup of coffee precariously balanced on the arm of the couch.

'That had better not fall off there!' Dora regarded him disapprovingly. If it did, he would have to clean up the mess himself. Yes, she was glad to escape the football noise and go for a walk on what probably would be one of the last nice days in the season.

As usual on a sunny, still day, the beach was packed with people. On the northern end, on the dog beach, a large number of dog owners watched their much-loved pooches run around, chase each other or jump into the water after a stick.

Dora avoided the dog beach. She had never felt comfortable with dogs around her and certainly couldn't understand why people treated them like they were their children. Several times she had heard dog owners calling themselves 'Mum' and 'Dad' as if they were indeed the parent of their dog.

I wouldn't want to see you give birth to that monster, she thought disapprovingly, when she heard a stick-thin woman call out to her oversized St Bernard, 'Come to Mum!' It sent shivers of disgust and imagined pain down Dora's back.

Not wanting to be anywhere near the dogs and their indulgent owners, she suggested to Leah that they head the other way, towards the rowing shed. Halfway there, they had to dodge four teams of beach volleyball players. The look of the fit and tanned young women in their bikinis made Dora sigh with envy.

Enjoy your beautiful bodies while they last, she was tempted to call out. Both she and Leah had long ago lost that trim, firm look their bodies once had, as well as the flawless smoothness of their skin. Wrinkles and dimples had appeared out of nowhere over the years. Extra pounds of fat had found their way into unwanted places of her body. Even Leah's body showed signs of ageing. Though still slim, there was no denying the widening of her hips and upper thighs. Her translucent skin had not been spared, either. The Tasmanian sun had dulled her English sheen and sprinkled freckles all over her face and her arms. For the first time, Dora noticed that Leah's deep copper hair had been lightened by streaks of grey.

Both women had taken off their shoes and walked on bare feet near the edge of the cool water.

'Dora,' Leah said. 'You know how Harry came over to our place the other day?'

The slight hesitation in Leah's voice made Dora look up. 'Yes?'

'I had told him that we had to go to Hobart and could be late back, but that he could let himself in.'

Dora walked into the water to feel the cold on her feet. 'Yeah?' In the light breeze her skirt played pleasantly around her legs. She was glad she'd put on her lovely new georgette skirt.

'The key is always under the geranium pot by the shed. You've both used it before, remember?'

Dora nodded. The cold water on her feet felt delicious. She walked in a bit further so it completely covered her ankles.

'Well, Harry was sitting on the front step, waiting for us when we came home. I can tell you he was more than a bit annoyed that we hadn't been there. Not only had he forgotten that we said we would possibly be late home, he had also not been able to find the key.'

This surprised Dora. Harry had always known about the key.

'Do you know what he said?' Leah continued, glancing at Dora. Without waiting for an answer she forged ahead. 'He said the snails had taken the key!'

Dora stopped dead in her tracks. 'The snails? What does that mean?'

'He said he checked under all the pots but could find nothing. The snails had taken the key. First I thought he was joking. But I can tell you he wasn't.' Leah threw her arms up in the air. 'He said snails had been known to carry things away. Where on earth did he get that from? It sounds like something you would see on children's TV.' She had a sceptical look on her face when she asked, 'He doesn't watch kids' programs, does he?'

'God, no! It's always sports, not kids' programs!'

'Well, Andrew thought he'd had a heatstroke. You know, sitting in the sun waiting for us.'

'Good heavens, I don't know what to say.' Dora was perplexed. 'Are you sure he wasn't joking?'

Leah shook her head. 'No.' She sounded very definite. 'No! He was dead serious. Anyway, the important point is that he couldn't remember where the key was. It's been in the same place for donkey's years!'

The two women took up their walk again. 'I know he wasn't joking because something similar happened later,' Leah explained. 'We were in the kitchen, having a drink, when Harry pointed at our electronic clock. You know the one that automatically changes the date every day?'

Dora nodded. What on earth was going on with her husband? He had been behaving differently for a while now, but she thought it was because he had to adjust to life without work. Being at home all day with her. It couldn't be easy.

'He asked if he could take it home and repair it.' Leah brought Dora back to the present.

'Repair it?' Dora couldn't have been more surprised. 'Harry can't repair a thing!'

'Exactly,' Leah agreed emphatically. 'But that wasn't the point. He said the date was wrong.'

'The date was wrong? Well, was it wrong?'

'No, of course it was right, but he insisted it couldn't possibly be 2023. And when I asked him what he thought the year was he got all confused and defensive and then mumbled that he wasn't sure.'

'Huh!' Dora was lost for words. What had gotten into Harry?

'Dora,' Leah said carefully, 'I think Harry is showing signs of dementia.'

'Good God, don't say that!' Dread was rising up in her like that little whip snake she'd seen slithering up her lemon tree. 'He's much too young for that, isn't he? He's only sixty-eight! No, I think he was just being silly.' Harry must have been annoyed and was taking his revenge by saying silly things. Yes, that would have been it. Even though it was hard to imagine Harry being silly. The whip snake disappeared.

On the other hand, he had been forgetting people's names and what day of the week it was. Well, that happened to her, too. Only recently, though, he had searched outside in the front yard for the newspaper when he'd already brought it in half an hour earlier. Did that signify anything? It was hard to know what to think.

'No.' Leah was unaware of the conflicting emotions racing through Dora. 'Unfortunately he's not too young to get dementia. Some people get it in their fifties, maybe even earlier.' Leah regarded Dora closely. 'There is support for that, you know? Maybe you should get him tested.'

Dora grimaced. 'Can you imagine me suggesting to Harry that he should be tested for dementia? He would hit the roof.' After a few moments of silence she said, 'I'll wait a little while and observe him. Once there is no doubt, I'll get someone to come in to test him.'

'Don't wait too long. They can do things to slow down the process.'

Dora gave a deep sigh. She would have to watch Harry even more closely now. Dementia. It was a frightening prospect. Her only hope was that Leah was wrong, but she could already feel a little seed of suspicion growing in her.

39

May 2023

Harry is behaving strangely

SLOWLY, THE WEATHER WAS GETTING colder and more unpredictable. One day it would be mild, then cold the next. One dreary afternoon she became aware for the first time that Harry had started walking differently. She could hear him moving from the lounge room into the bedroom. No, not walking, shuffling. *Shrup, shrup, shrup.* And back again, *shrup, shrup, shrup.* Quietly talking to himself.

'Harry, why are you dragging your feet?' she called out to him from her sewing room.

Shrup, shrup, shrup, Harry approached her room. 'My feet are feeling heavy. I think the earth's gravity is getting stronger,' he explained.

Dora swung around on her chair. 'What do you—' she started but when she saw Harry she stopped. For the time being the earth's gravity had lost its importance. Harry looked … dishevelled, upset, red in the face as if from exertion. Breathing erratically, he was wrestling with his clothing. Over his neatly zipped-up padded puffer vest, he had tried to put on a jumper. One of his arms was stuck in his favourite grey jumper, the rest of it hung down on one side, dragging along on the ground.

'Harry, what's with the jumper?'

'You're asking me?' he replied, his voice rising. Accusation was written all over his face. 'What have you done to it? It doesn't fit any more. It's my favourite. You've ruined it!'

If there was one thing Dora couldn't stand, it was to be accused of something she had not done. For decades – decades! – she had taken particular care when washing Harry's expensive shirts and jumpers. It was unfair and most annoying to be accused of carelessness now.

Dora stood up abruptly. 'I've done nothing to your jumper,' she insisted. 'It's perfectly alright. If you wear it properly, that is,' she added. A mother talking to her child.

She approached Harry and pulled the jumper off his arm. 'Now, take off that puffer vest and put the jumper on first,' she ordered him. She held the jumper while he was unzipping his vest. Then she passed him the jumper.

'Right,' she said impatiently. 'Jumper first, then the vest over the top.' Why on earth could he not figure that one out for himself? It wasn't the first time he had worn those two pieces together.

Suddenly, like a bolt of lightning, Leah's words shot through her. Dementia!

'Harry, you worry me sometimes.' She shook her head. 'You don't usually have a problem with your clothes.'

'I don't know,' he replied. 'The jumper just didn't fit.' He turned away from her and *shrup, shrup, shrup,* he was gone. That sound would drive her mad. She could just tell.

*

'Sophie, I need to talk to you about your father.' This time it was Dora who did away with the niceties. No 'hello, how are you?' or 'what have you been up to?' Instead she came straight to the point. If her daughter could do it, so could she. And anyway, she was too preoccupied to engage in some meaningless chatter. Harry was off on his usual walk, which presented Dora with the rare opportunity to speak to her daughter without him listening in.

Phone in hand, Dora stood by the kitchen window, looking out onto the street. Harry had just disappeared around the corner. All was quiet. Stella Sticky-Beak was nowhere to be seen and across the road the veranda was empty. The two cousins must have gone to work.

'What's wrong with him? Is he sick?' Sophie asked.

'He's not sick. I mean he's not physically sick,' Dora replied. She took a deep breath. 'I can't help but think that he's mentally not quite right.' Good God, she could have expressed that differently. She had made it sound as if he was a lunatic. 'What I'm saying is that I suspect he's got the beginnings of dementia.' There, she'd said it.

'Dementia? Dad? What makes you say that?'

'He's doing and saying weird things. Things he wouldn't normally do and say.'

'Like what?'

This was the part of the conversation Dora had dreaded. What should she tell her daughter without feeling that she was betraying Harry? It felt sneaky, speaking behind his back about his problems.

'Well, a few weeks ago he couldn't find the spare key to Uncle Andrew's house and—'

'Mum, not finding a key is not a sign of dementia,' Sophie interrupted her. 'You remember my friend Mei?' Dora nodded into the phone. 'She loses her keys all the time, and she's a genius!'

'You didn't let me finish,' Dora admonished her daughter. 'He couldn't find the key and explained to Uncle Andrew and Aunt Leah that the snails had carried it away.' Dora exhaled loudly.

'He was joking! You don't get his jokes!'

'And he told them that the electronic clock they have in the kitchen was showing the wrong time and date.'

'Honestly, Mum! That still is no reason to think someone's brain is melting!' Dora could feel Sophie's exasperation zipping through the phone line.

'He offered to fix their electronic clock.' Maybe this one would convince Sophie. There was silence on the other end of the phone.

'Fix it? Dad doesn't know a lawnmower from a washing machine!' This time Sophie's voice sounded a lot more tentative.

Exactly, Dora thought. Don't I know it! Except that she had seen him change a tyre once. He had done it unwillingly, but he had done it. And the tyre hadn't fallen off.

Now that Sophie sounded neither exasperated nor impatient, Dora felt encouraged to keep going. She might as well let Sophie in on another few of Harry's peculiarities, if that's what you could call them.

'The other day he tried putting on his jumper *over* the puffer vest. As if that would work! He stands by the window looking at nothing. He doesn't walk properly anymore. It's shuffle, shuffle, shuffle all day long. He watches sport and only sport, because he can't follow the story line of a movie anymore.' Dora wasn't quite sure whether that was actually the reason he watched so much sport but she had her suspicions.

And he used to visit prostitutes, she felt like adding while she was running down a list of his misdemeanours. But no, she wouldn't mention that one. That didn't concern her daughter and as far as she knew it was not a sign of dementia.

'He spent six weeks in prison!' The words flew from her mouth before she had decided she was going to say them.

There was sharp intake of breath on the other end of the phone. 'He what? Mum? He what?'

For an excruciatingly long moment, there was silence on the phone. Then Sophie's voice came through the ether, gently this time, but with an ominous undertone. 'Mum,' she said slowly.

Dora nearly smiled. She could just see her daughter facing one of her students who had been uncooperative in class. Next, Sophie would say, *Now listen carefully to me. When I say …* Yes, Dora could imagine it very well. This student would pull her head in and do exactly as her daughter, the popular maths teacher, had demanded.

'Mum,' Sophie's repeated. 'Mum, listen to me.' Huh, didn't she know her daughter well! 'Mum, don't take this the wrong way, but I'm starting to think that *you* are the one who may have dementia. You're making things up. Dad has never been to prison. I would know.'

'No, you wouldn't,' Dora replied sweetly. 'Parents don't tell their children everything.'

'Tell me then, why was he in prison?' The challenge was unmistakable. As if trying to catch her mother out, making up stories.

'Speeding and injuring a police officer, refusing to pay a fine. Refusing to admit he was at fault.' Dora didn't have to think about this or make anything up. That incident was burnt into her brain forever. There was some satisfaction in enlightening Sophie about her father's misdemeanours. Again, a sharp intake of breath on the other end of the line. But before Sophie could say anything Dora continued. 'Why don't you ask him yourself? He's just gone for a walk, but you could ring in an hour or so.'

*

Harry stood in the garden watching the birds. The cockatoos had settled in his favourite tree again, flapping their wings, spitting pine kernels onto the lawn and screeching. Dora stepped out onto the lawn to join him.

'Anything happening out here?' she asked casually, her eyes on the cockatoos.

'No.'

'No?'

'Sophie rang,' Harry clapped his hands to shoo the birds away but they ignored his futile efforts.

'Did she? What did she say?' Discreetly, Dora scanned his face for any signs of annoyance or indignation. She knew exactly what Sophie would have said.

'She asked me if I thought that parents should tell their children of any momentous events in their life. Events that have a huge impact on everyone.'

Clearly, Dora had not known exactly what Sophie had planned to say. Her daughter was cleverer than she thought. Rather than challenging Harry, Sophie had approached the topic in a round-about way that was very uncharacteristic for her.

'What did you say to her?'

'I said, of course not. Parents were allowed to have their secrets. And not every momentous event impacts on everyone.'

'You're making a lot of sense today, Harry,' Dora acknowledged. Surprised, he turned to her.

'I always make sense,' he insisted.

'Come, let's go inside. The breeze is a bit cool,' Dora said. She wasn't going to get involved in a discussion about Harry making sense or not. 'And then you can tell me what Sophie said.' They stepped into the lounge room.

'So, what else did she say? Sit down.' Dora pointed at the couch. She took an empty cup of coffee off the table and sat it on the floor beside her. Then she straightened the tablecloth, brushing out some creases with her hands.

'I would be grateful if you didn't put your feet on the tablecloth, Harry,' she said with a frown. 'I'm doing enough ironing already. I don't need any more.'

Harry pulled a face but ignored her. 'Sophie wanted to know whether I'd ever been to prison,' he said calmly. 'She thought something like that would be a momentous event that the family should know about.'

Dora spun around to face him. 'And?' she wanted to know. Yes, that was the sort of direct question she would have expected from her daughter.

'I told her yes, I'd been to prison.'

'What did she say?'

'You keep asking me the same questions!' Harry started to lose his patience. '"What did she say? What did you say?" She asked me why I had to go to prison, and I said I couldn't remember.'

'You couldn't remember or you didn't want to say?'

'Couldn't remember! Didn't want to say! It's all the same to me!'

'OK, ok, calm down! Then what?'

'Then she wanted to know what the capital city of Portugal was. Which didn't make any sense to me at all because it's nothing to do with going to prison.' He shook his head.

'And what …?'

Irritated, he turned to Dora. 'I said I couldn't remember. I couldn't remember the capital city of Portugal. Then she hung up. Are you satisfied now?' Harry was fuming, but Dora didn't care. Even she knew that Lisbon was the capital of Portugal. Surely everyone knew that one.

'Are you serious? You couldn't remember?'

'Yes, I couldn't remember. So what? I can't keep every little bit of information in my head! Let's stop this silly conversation!' Harry put his feet on the table and without further ado pressed the 'on' button on the TV remote.

*

The following day, Sophie rang Dora to give her strict instructions to watch Harry like a hawk. It was possible that Harry had just been contrary and pretended he didn't know the capital of Portugal. This fact seemed to have been more upsetting for Sophie than Harry's stay in prison. But if he really hadn't remembered either of those two, then something was seriously wrong with him.

'I am watching him. That's all I seem to be doing these days!' Dora felt exasperated with both her husband and her daughter. Harry's behaviour was slowly wearing her out. At times it was even a bit frightening. And Sophie? Well, it was always easy giving good advice when you were removed from it all. Yes, I will go and see someone if it gets any worse. No, I don't need any more advice from you, she thought when she finally managed to get Sophie off the phone.

God, she was exhausted. And a tiny little bit scared. If Harry got any worse, she could possibly have thirty years of looking after him. At the moment she managed well. His mental state was not too bad. A lot of silly things he said and did were things that most people occasionally said and did. And everyone forgot things, times, dates, names … Maybe a mentally fit person did not forget why they had been to prison. What she would do if Harry's frame of mind deteriorated didn't bear thinking about.

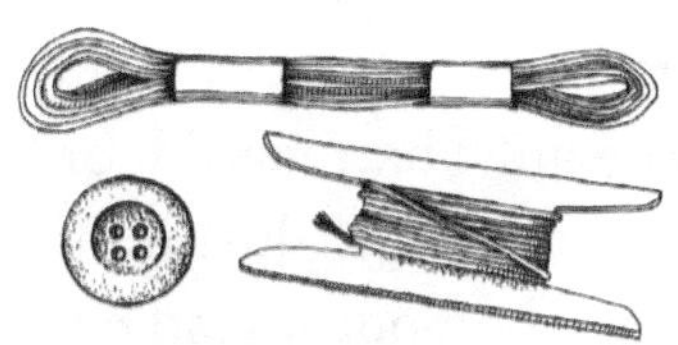

40

3 March 2024

DORA STOOD IN FRONT OF Harry's recliner chair, casting a critical eye over it. Should she give it a wipe with a damp cloth before Boz and Luke came over to pick it up? There was some dust in that gap where the arm of the chair met the seat. The footrest could do with a wipe, too. Sometimes Harry lay on it with his shoes on. But no, Boz and Luke wouldn't notice a bit of dust. In any case, the chair would be covered in biscuit crumbs in no time. She could save herself the effort.

A car stopping outside brought her to the kitchen window. The Indian police sergeant, dressed in full uniform – on a Sunday! – slammed the car door shut and walked up the drive. Dora frowned. Presumably the police could not afford to take the weekend off if someone had died in mysterious circumstances. Quickly she brushed her fingers through her hair. From the kitchen drawer she pulled a rubber band and tied her hair into a tight knot. One quick pull at her skirt and a deep breath to settle her heart. It had started to hammer crazily.

Don't smile, she told herself as she opened the door. *You must not smile. You're a widow now.*

'Mrs Freeman,' Sergeant Sharma said. She took off her police cap and stepped into the house. 'I just wanted to check how you are and keep you updated on our investigation.'

'Please, come through.' Dora was glad she was leading the way into the lounge room. Right now she did not want Sergeant Sharma to see the frightened look on her face. My God, she thought, there is actually an investigation! Are they really thinking …?

Dora pointed at a chair and the sergeant sat down. She hadn't noticed before that Sergeant Sharma had beautiful dark eyes and a rather sensual mouth. She had been too upset by the events to take any notice of her, except that she was Indian.

Dora narrowed her eyes, taking in the sergeant's uniform. That stark uniform was probably hiding a perfectly well-shaped body. She should be wearing a sari. Particularly on a Sunday! Yes, Dora could see her in a sari. She could sew her one. Nothing easier than that. Just one long rectangular piece of some lovely light fabric that would envelop her body from shoulder to foot. Something yellow or orange. And in place of that painfully tight bun in the back of the neck, her thick black hair should be flowing freely down to her waist.

Dora had no problems with clichés or stereotypes. There was some comfort in the knowledge that you would get exactly what you expected. Like that movie about the young woman whose dress she had been sewing. Struggling with the harsh conditions in the outback. Going from being poor and desperate to becoming rich and beautiful and happy. It would have been obvious in the first five minutes of that film where the story was headed.

And what was wrong with dressing in a sari if you were an Indian woman? The Indians must have always known that a sari was so much more suitable for the women in their country than a police uniform. But then, this lovely sergeant was no longer in India. And maybe female police officers in India weren't wearing saris to work either.

'Would you like a cup of tea?' Dora asked, but Sergeant Sharma shook her head.

Dora folded her hands in her lap and looked up expectantly at this young woman. She really was beautiful. It probably didn't make her job any easier looking like this. Dora could just imagine the comments her colleagues would be making behind her back. And all those criminals she had to deal with! Many of them violent, cold hearted and possibly misogynists. It was unthinkable. They probably wouldn't take her seriously. What a difficult career she had chosen.

'I just wanted to let you know that we have nearly completed our investigation,' the sergeant said gently. There was that word again! Dora gave a little start. An investigation!

'It's purely routine,' Sergeant Sharma reassured Dora. 'You must understand. In a case like this we always have to make sure that there was no interference …' She noticed that Dora gave another start and left her sentence unfinished. 'What I mean is we have to ask a few questions.'

'Of course, of course. I understand,' Dora said. 'If you don't mind I might make myself a cup of tea. I'm still very shaky,' she explained. 'To think that Harry is gone. And how he left us. I can't quite fathom it.' She blinked away a few tears.

When she returned to the lounge room Sergeant Sharma had disappeared. Through the open door of the sewing room, Dora spotted her leaning closely into the pin board. Obviously, even Indian police officers were curious people.

Sergeant Sharma turned around. 'I hope you don't mind. I saw those photos.' Then she looked around at the room, taking in the two mannequins, one still wearing a half-finished costume, the other one naked. Her eyes fell on the large table, covered in shiny fabrics, several boxes of colourful sequins, pins, needles, paper patterns.

'You're a dressmaker,' she said. It was a statement, not a question.

Dora nodded. 'Sort of. I used to make mainly wedding dresses or special occasion clothes, but for a long time now it's been nearly all costumes for theatre or opera companies.'

'That's a very niche occupation, isn't it? I can't imagine many people doing that,' the sergeant said. 'Does it pay well, if you don't mind me asking?'

'When I get a contract from a big company then, yes, it pays well. But they don't keep me busy eight hours a day every day, so there are times when I earn very little or nothing. As a matter of fact, in the last few months or more there has not been much work for me at all. Just the odd piece. Most of the costumes come from China now.'

'So I assume your husband was the main breadwinner and you will inherit everything now that he has passed?'

Dora nodded. She took a hasty sip of hot tea. It burnt her mouth and made her eyes water.

'I'm sorry,' Sergeant Sharma apologised, mistaking her moist eyes for tears. She turned back to the pin board and pointed at a photo showing Harry and Sophie on the beach. 'What was he like, your husband?'

'He was a good man,' Dora answered. 'Generous, great with our daughter.' She approached the sergeant and stared at the photo. 'Had a bit of a temper at times but I would say nothing unusual.'

'Nothing unusual?' Sergeant Sharma repeated. She fixed her big dark eyes on Dora. 'Except that we saw in our system that he had a conviction for assaulting a police officer.'

The blood rushed into Dora's face. In her trembling hand the teacup was rattling in its saucer. Quickly she put it on her sewing table. Of course, the police had done background checks on Harry. She should have expected that.

'Yes, yes,' she said, her voice shaking. 'It was a terrible night. Harry was out of his mind.' Dora sank onto her chair. 'That Saturday had started badly with him thinking it was a work day. I don't know what was going on with him. He never got his days mixed up.' She reached for her cup but, realising her hand was still shaky, she just pushed the cup further into the middle of the table.

'Then that same night we went to the farewell party for one of his colleagues at his boss's place …' Sergeant Sharma nodded. Obviously, she had read about that in Harry's statement.

'He wasn't very good in social situations,' Dora pushed on. 'They often made him a bit anxious but not angry. No, not angry. He did lose his temper at times but nothing like on that night. I don't understand what was going on with him.' Well, she did know. He had been jealous of her. People at that party had been interested in her and her work. They had not been interested in him.

'Was he ever violent with you or your daughter?'

'No,' Dora lied. 'Never. He wouldn't lay a hand on us.' He had only hit her once and then never again. So maybe that didn't count. It was nothing the sergeant needed to know. And he certainly had never laid a hand on Sophie.

41

July 2023

Harry is struggling with the firewood

FOR WEEKS, DORA HAD BEEN watching Harry closely for any more signs of dementia, but apart from small lapses of memory or the occasional vacant look in his eyes, he seemed his normal self. Dora started to think that Leah had been exaggerating. Everyone forgot things. She often forgot what she'd had for dinner the previous day. Sometimes she couldn't remember someone's surname. At times she, too, stood by the window and stared into space. It was called 'being in the moment'. Giving your brain a rest. All of that was normal. Admittedly, there had been the incident with the key and the snails that had set off alarm bells in Leah, and that business with the jumper he didn't know how to put on. And forgetting the capital of Portugal and why he had been in prison, which Dora suspected he hadn't forgotten at all. She wouldn't put it past him to try and hoodwink them. Yes, she thought: look at all those little smirks he made when he thought she wasn't looking.

With winter arriving, Harry spent most of his time indoors. Winters in Tasmania could be fierce. Vicious winds alternating with rain and deceptive sunshine. Sometimes, looking out the window on a calm, sunny day, one could be forgiven for thinking that it was warm outside, but put one foot outside the door and your ears would freeze off. In the distance, snow-covered Mt Wellington could be clearly seen from Kingston, but rarely did the snow come down all the way to this beachside town.

So, first thing in the morning, Harry lit the fire in the wood heater. It didn't take long to get the fire going, because usually the coals were still glowing from the night before. By the time they finished breakfast, the house was nice and cosy. Harry still spent the mornings in his study, reading the paper, doing the sudokus and rummaging around with whatever kept him busy until lunchtime.

If anyone had ever asked Dora, she would have said that she and Harry lived quite comfortably together. It seemed the new pattern of their life worked well for both of them and she was pleased that Harry was a lot calmer than he had been when he was still working. There was only one thing that got her hackles up. The blasted TV! When he was young he had always switched the remote to 'mute' and watched the sport without sound. He couldn't bear the inane comments the sports reporters made. But now it was the opposite. Sometimes the noise was unbearable.

To her dismay, he turned the TV on as soon as he woke up from his afternoon nap. More often than not he watched sports. Football, cricket, golf … She'd even caught him one afternoon watching the gymnastics championships. There had been times when he made fun of gymnastics but obviously, his attitude had changed.

Again, she suspected Harry watched sports because he couldn't follow the story line of movies and documentaries anymore. When she asked him about it, he waved off her concern, claiming that those programs were so repetitive and predictable, they made him want to put his foot through the screen. She had to agree that in that case, sport was preferable and left him to it. Except that even in her sewing room, with the door closed, she could still hear the noise coming from the lounge room. All that cheering and whistling and shouting. Those sports commentators yelling themselves into an apoplectic fit.

Dora was not a fan of sport, but she understood that Harry, a former football player himself, enjoyed it. She, on the other hand, hated football. She couldn't stand the aggression on the field, the physicality of it all. Overly fit and muscular men running after a ball that wasn't even round. Pushing and shoving each other, jumping on each other's backs, flinging themselves on each other's sweaty bodies. She could just imagine what the smell was like. No, she hated the whole rawness of it all.

Having escaped into her sewing room one afternoon, she was finding it hard to concentrate on this dress. As was the case so often, she had to sew on a number of buttons. Very small buttons, so it was a fiddly job. She put a floor lamp right behind her shoulder so it shone onto her hands and the fabric. In winter it got dark early.

Someone must have kicked a goal. The noise coming from the TV in the lounge room had increased dramatically and Harry was shouting something unintelligible. The football players were probably all lying on top of each other right now, kissing and hugging each other ecstatically about their goal.

Inevitably, this made Dora think about sex. Not that she had ever shouted in ecstasy, but hers and Harry's sex life had been quite satisfactory in the early years. Or so she thought, because she had no comparison and had never talked in detail to anyone about it. Just the thought made her blush.

She had never admitted to anyone that Harry had been the one and only man for her. She still remembered the surprise and proprietary pleasure when Harry discovered on their wedding night that she had never had sex with anyone before him. *Now you're truly mine*, he had said after their first night together. How could she forget that? She didn't want to be anyone's. Not anymore.

While she had been reminiscing and concentrating on sewing on these tiny buttons, she hadn't noticed the silence in the lounge room. Harry must have turned the TV off. Instead, she heard him opening the squeaky door of the shed, which was stacked full to the brim with firewood.

Huh, she thought. He must be filling up the wood basket. Dora kept one ear on Harry, who had come back into the lounge room but was now passing by her closed door and heading towards the kitchen. She heard some banging and clanging noises in the kitchen, then Harry passed her door again. Dora stood up and walked to her window. There he was, coming out of the shed with another armful of firewood. Heading through the lounge room and back into the kitchen. Heavens above! What was he doing? With a sigh Dora went to investigate.

As soon as she entered the kitchen, Harry turned to her. 'Why is there never enough room in here? What is all this stuff?' He nodded at the open refrigerator, looking exasperated. In his arms he was still holding a couple of logs of wood. Dismayed, Dora stared into the refrigerator. Harry had pushed all the pickle jars, the butter and jams, a tray full of meat and whatever else onto the bottom shelf. The two top shelves were now crammed higgledy-piggledy with firewood.

'Harry, for God's sake! What on earth are you doing?' Dora screamed. 'What is all of this?'

'That's what I want to know!' Harry yelled back at her. 'I can't fit anything in!'

For a few long seconds they eyed each other off like two boxers, each waiting for the other to make the first move. Dora's head was humming. What was going on with Harry? Was he sleepwalking? Had there been some malfunction in his brain? Synapses misfiring for example? A mini stroke maybe? Would that make a person do such strange things? Why on earth was he thinking that firewood belonged in the fridge?

She put out her hands. 'Harry, pass me that wood. I'll carry it to the wood basket,' she finally said.

'The wood basket?' he repeated, looking incredulous. 'What wood basket?'

'Come, I'll show you.' Harry was still firmly holding on to the firewood, so Dora took him by the elbow. Dear God, she thought. Maybe Leah was right after all!

'Come,' she said again. Harry suddenly lost all resistance and followed her into the lounge room like an acquiescent child who knew that all resistance was futile.

'Here, put it here.' Dora pointed at the basket. Harry looked confused but obediently followed her instructions. 'We need to get all that wood out of the refrigerator now and put it here,' Dora said. 'Okay?'

Harry nodded and trotted off into the kitchen. When he was out of sight, Dora shifted the box with the old newspapers that served for lighting the fire. As usual there were too many papers in there. Harry just stuffed them into the box when he'd finished with them, without considering whether they needed them or not. Dora pulled a handful of newspapers out and dropped them onto the floor. They would have to go into the rubbish bin.

One of the papers had fallen open on the puzzles page and Dora grabbed it to fold it back up. She quickly glanced at the crosswords, a large 'find-a-word' and two sudokus. Harry had done them all. Not bad! But then Dora narrowed her eyes. Her brows creased in disbelief as she had a closer look at the large sudoku. What on earth had Harry done there? Dora scanned the vertical and horizontal rows. Even someone who'd never done a sudoku could see straight away that all the squares and rows had been filled in with random numbers. There, that square in the middle had the number six in it three times. In one of the rows, going down the left-hand side, each small square had an eight in it. Every single one!

Dora checked the crossword. Eight down, five letters: 'famous opera by Puccini'. Harry had written 'none' into the first four squares and put an 'x' into the last square. Good God!

Frantically, she rifled through the other newspapers, searching for the puzzles pages. Here, too, the sudokus had been filled in with random numbers. The crosswords were filled in with letters that didn't even constitute words. It was all just nonsense!

A wave of weakness threatened to overcome her. She held onto the mantelpiece to prevent her legs from buckling. Recently, that silly business with his puffer vest and the jumper. Before that, the incident at Andrew and Leah's place with the snails … Now this! Did Harry really have dementia? These crazy acts, the confusion and the distant look in his eyes occasionally. Shouldn't that tell her something? When she added up all the strange things he had done … Could she really deny any longer that there was a problem? Where should she go from here?

Distractedly, she bundled the newspapers together in her arms just as Harry came trudging out of the kitchen with a small log of wood.

Dora dropped the newspapers onto the hearth. 'Is that the last bit of wood?' she asked.

'Yes, but the … the …' Harry looked at her blankly.

'The what, Harry?' She supressed an irritated sigh.

'The …' He tilted his head sideways towards the kitchen. 'The … cupboard is quite dirty now.'

'The fridge, you mean?'

'The fridge, the cupboard!' His voice rose. 'What's the difference?' The log of wood dropped into the wood basket with a dull thud.

'I'll clean the fridge. The fridge! Go and have a rest on the couch!' she snapped.

Dora snatched the TV remote from the coffee table and pressed the 'on' button. She flicked through a few channels until she'd found the sports channel. 'There!' she told Harry. 'Watch some football!'

Maybe her sister Freda could help. She was a very down-to-earth kind of person. For starters, it would be best to write to Freda and get her opinion. When she'd finished cleaning the fridge and sorting all the jars into their places, Dora pulled out her writing pad and began a letter to her sister. There, just writing 'Dear Freda' was making her feel better already!

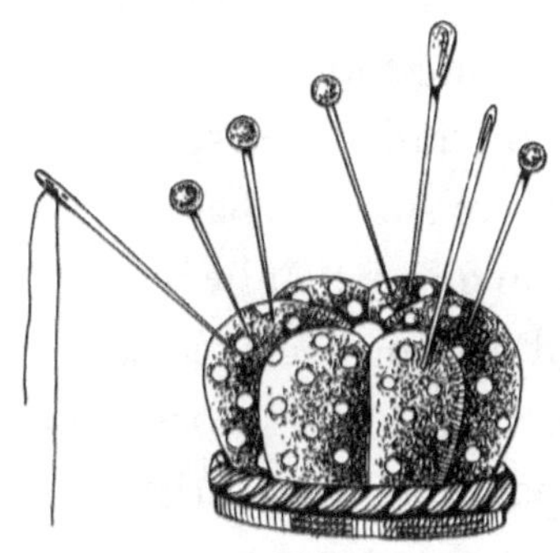

42

December 2023

Sophie makes an announcement

THERE HAD BEEN NO MORE major incidents with Harry for a number of months. Dora called them major incidents because she didn't know what name to give that strange behaviour Harry sometimes displayed. It was unfathomable to her that Harry's mind was relatively clear for most of the time but then he'd do something inexplicably silly.

So she had done nothing. She had not looked for any help from … whom? Their doctor? Some dementia service? She didn't even know the correct name of such a service or where they might be located.

'Look it up on the internet,' Sophie had said. 'Everything is on the internet. You'll find anything and everything about dementia on the net.'

But apart from watching Harry like a hawk, she had done nothing. Except to ask him whether he was still reading the newspaper and doing the sudokus. 'Yes' to reading the paper. 'No' to doing the sudokus. 'It was getting too boring,' he had claimed. She had checked the recently discarded newspapers next to the fireplace. None of the crosswords or sudokus had been attempted, so at least he wasn't pretending anymore that he was doing them. She could only hope he was still reading the articles.

So the last month of the year proceeded as it always did in their household. Preparations for Christmas were well underway. Dora had cleaned the house from top to bottom, even though it had hardly been necessary. Luke and Boz had given the garden a once over and put up some fairy lights in the grevillea bush. Harry had gone and bought the Christmas tree, which he had then put up in a corner of the lounge room. Dora had bought presents for Harry, Sophie and herself. Everything was as it should be, even Harry. So maybe Dora had been over-anxious. Seeing problems where there weren't any.

Dora often thought that the month of December was something people on the mainland would shake their heads about. It was meant to be summer but in Tasmania that meant nothing. One day it would be pleasantly warm, the next day Mt Wellington was covered in a lace blanket of snow. Rain and gusty wind could make you think you lived on Macquarie Island, somewhere deep in the Southern Ocean. Then, another hot day would make you wonder whether you had imagined the previous miserable days.

Christmas itself was a quiet affair. Sophie had gone off with friends for a few days to celebrate Christmas on some island somewhere.

'Tasmania is an island!' Dora had pleaded with her.

'Not a tropical island,' was Sophie's response. Well, you couldn't argue with that. So she and Harry had been on their own until Boxing Day when they drove to the farm to visit Andrew and Leah. It had been a pleasant but uneventful visit. Dora had felt thoroughly let down by the festive season and the unpredictable start of summer – until Sophie's phone call.

*

The melodious tinkling of her mobile phone was only just audible over the pelting rain and the rattling of the sewing machine. As there had been nothing better to do, Dora was altering one of her favourite skirts. Horrified that the skirt didn't fit over her hips anymore, she had decided to let the side seams out.

Dora took her foot off the pedal and looked around. Where was the phone? There, just behind her on the shelf. She got up and grabbed it just in time before it stopped ringing. She really needed to find out how to extend the number of rings before the calls cut out.

The display said 'Sophie'. Dora's heart always gave a little skip when Sophie rang, which was not very often at all, truth be told.

She pressed the green answer button. 'Sophie, darling, how lovely—'

'Mum,' Sophie interrupted her. 'I'm getting married.' Then, silence. Dora pulled out her stool from behind the door and sat down.

'What was that, darling?'

'I said I'm getting married,' Sophie repeated. There was just the slightest hint of impatience in her voice. 'You know, man and woman, ring on finger.' No, this was more than just a hint of impatience. Typical Sophie. That's what she was like. Never one for a bit of chit chat first. No gentle preparation for what was to come. Just a straight, raw announcement without unnecessary preliminaries, just like Harry. He always came straight to the point. It was either yes or no, black or white, right or wrong. Maybe that sort of thing happened if you had a mathematical brain. Even though Dora suspected that Sophie would have argued against those simplistic assumptions of her mother's. There were a lot of grey areas in mathematics and a lot of unsolved problems.

'Well, I'm lost for words,' Dora finally managed to say. She shifted uncomfortably on the small stool. She really didn't like surprises. 'Who are you marrying?'

'Tom. Tom Jenkins. We met at some conference in Canberra.'

There now, there was a bit more information. The stool made a horrible screeching noise as she manoeuvred it closer to the wall so she could lean against something. She did need a bit of support right now.

'Well, that's quite something,' Dora said. 'Do you want to tell me a bit about him?'

'About my height.' Sophie was quite tall, unlike Dora. 'Same age, lives in Launceston but mainly works in Canberra. Never married before, no children.'

'That's good to know.' Dora groaned inwardly. Oops, that silly comment said more about herself than this Tom! She tried again. 'How long have you known each other?'

'About eight months. Or seven months and twenty-five days in the biblical sense if you know what I mean.' Dora could hear a little guffaw on the other end of the line. Her daughter obviously thought she was too nosey and needed to put her in her place. Well, she hadn't asked for that sort of detail!

Dora tried to keep her voice on an even keel. 'Can I ask what he does? Do you work together?'

'No, I did say he works in Canberra. He's in cyber security.'

Dora didn't like to be pulled up by her daughter. Surely she couldn't be expected to remember every detail of this colossal announcement.

'Cyber security?' she repeated. What did that actually mean?

'You know, keeping all your info safe that's up there in the cloud. Preventing your money from disappearing mysteriously from your bank account. Or preventing kids from being stalked on the internet by perverts. Keeping governments safe from being infiltrated by cyber criminals. All that sort of stuff and more.'

Strange jobs people have these days, Dora thought. Of course she'd read about all of that in the papers. And there was always some mention of it in the news at night. If she recalled correctly, the news was mainly about this cyber security not working particularly well. There were always hackers stealing some company's data or people's personal information, and there always seemed to be someone who knew someone whose bank account had been emptied by one of these hackers. As far as she knew, there had never been a news item about the perfect solution for any of this.

It seemed to Dora that many of the jobs young people were involved in these days were about preventing things from happening. Stopping cybercrimes, stopping climate change, stopping air and water pollution, stopping exploitation of lowly paid workers ... there seemed to be no end to it. Wasn't anyone creating anything anymore? Producing something constructive? Apart from consumables that no one needed? Maybe she was getting old. It was hard to keep up with what was going on in the world.

'Mum, are you still there?' Sophie's voice snapped her out of those muddled thoughts.

'Yes, yes, of course,' Dora replied hastily.

'I'll send you a photo of Tom and the details of the wedding. Sometime soon.'

'Are you getting married for a reason?' Dora suddenly asked. She grasped her phone a bit tighter.

'No, Mum! I'm not pregnant if that's what you mean. People are getting married again, you know. Committing to something.

Not like when you were young and you hippies cringed at the word 'marriage'. Anyway, there are too many people on the planet already. I don't think we'll be contributing to that number.' There was a moment of silence on the line. 'Mum, I'm really busy. Talk to you again soon.' Click.

Well, Dora thought, a bit stung. I was too young to be a hippy and I certainly didn't cringe at the word marriage. It just didn't happen the way I had imagined. But how could Sophie know? She had told her daughter nothing about her own youth and how different it had been from what Sophie assumed.

So why was Sophie getting married? Dora wondered. Getting married just made things so much more difficult if you wanted to separate later. Why on earth did she, Dora, get married? She should have stuck with free love and flowers in her hair. Except that she never even experienced that when she was young.

She switched the sewing machine off and walked into the lounge room. The TV was running without the sound. Thank goodness! Harry lay rolled up on the couch, snoozing.

'Harry,' she said. 'Harry, wake up!'

Slowly he opened his eyes and uncurled himself. 'What?' He yawned loudly. 'What?' he repeated.

'Sophie just rang. She's getting married.'

Harry yawned again. Dora had always imagined that she would be thrilled out of her mind about her daughter's momentous announcement. She would be laughing and cheering and hugging Harry, overcome by excitement and the anticipation of the big event. But instead she felt deflated. Maybe because her daughter had been so nonchalant about it all, so unemotional, as if she had been telling her mother that she would be acquiring a cat and not a husband. It was possible, of course, that it was all one and the same for young people these days.

Or maybe because she had not imagined sharing this announcement with a husband who lay half-asleep and dishevelled on the couch. Whose first reaction to this life-changing announcement of their daughter's was a big yawn.

'Who's she marrying?' Harry finally asked. He sat up on the couch and brushed his fingers through his thinning hair.

'Some fellow called Tom. From what she said he seems to be some mathematical genius.' Dora knew full well she was exaggerating but maybe that bit of information would create some enthusiasm on Harry's part.

'Well, that's good,' Harry said. 'I'm glad she's not a lesbian after all. When's the big event?'

Dora shook her head. 'I have no idea. She was not very forthcoming with any information.' She was wondering how Harry felt about losing his daughter to another man. Not that they had been particularly close in the last few years. Since Sophie chose to work in a school, rather than a university as Harry had hoped, he had not shown that much interest in her life. But then, when she really thought about it, he had not shown much interest in anyone's life. Apart from his walks, he spent a lot of time inside the house, busying himself with … well, mainly the TV.

Anyway, she would write a short letter to Freda about Sophie's brilliant news. Freda might even consider coming home for the wedding. Maybe. If she did, she could help with the preparations for the big event. Yes, the wedding would be the most urgent issue to deal with at the moment. Every little detail would have to be planned. It would occupy her mind for months! Dora pulled out her note pad and began writing.

43

Early January 2024

Stella Sticky-Beak's letters are disappearing

ACOUPLE OF WEEKS INTO THE new year, another incident happened, finally convincing Dora that she could no longer ignore the problem. It was all to do with their neighbour, Stella Fulton.

It was hard to avoid her at the best of times. Dora would leave the house or come home from somewhere and her neighbour would pop up over the fence out of nowhere. One minute the coast looked clear, but the next, as soon as you thought you were safe, there she was! It always seemed to be a coincidence that she just happened to be watering her vegetables or doing some weeding when there was some movement outside Harry and Dora's house. Smiling and waving and engaging you in a conversation over heaven only knew what triviality. Every now and then, Dora thought of parking her car around the back and sneaking into her house through the garden, but pride – or stubbornness – forbade her from doing that. She had a perfectly good driveway which allowed her to park her car off the street, virtually right outside her front door, and that's where she would park it!

This time it was clearly not a so-called coincidence that her neighbour was in the front yard. Her body language left no doubt that she had been waiting for Dora. She stood tall and straight by the fence between the two properties and did not even try to pretend she just happened to be there. Her arms crossed, a scowl on her face, she watched Dora climb out of the car.

Dora was in no mood to talk to Stella. She had just had a meeting with Michelle about a new dress design. The meeting had lasted longer than expected, so that Dora had missed an appointment with her hairdresser. As if that had not been annoying enough, halfway through the meeting the director of a play had rung. In order to include Dora in their discussion, Michelle had put her phone on speaker so they could have a three-way conversation. The connection hadn't been the best, with some terrible crackling noises and dead spaces. At the best of times Dora disliked phone conversations. She preferred to see the facial expressions of the person she was speaking to. Visual clues helped her interpret the real intentions and emotions of the other person.

Due to the bad connection, a number of times the three of them had either spoken on top of one another or left big gaps in the conversation, waiting for one or the other of them to speak. It had been nerve-racking for Dora. One of the reasons she liked working with Michelle was that Michelle made the effort to come to Kingston and speak with her in person. Between the two of them, face to face, they had always managed to sort out the dress designs and contractual matters. Having a third person involved made matters much more difficult.

Then, towards the end of the conversation, Michelle intimated that this new design would probably be the last. Ordering costumes from China was more cost-effective, everyone needed to save, et cetera, et cetera.

Therefore, Dora was tense, exhausted and terribly disappointed. She was not looking forward to sewing wedding dresses again. Maybe she would have to give up altogether and find a new occupation. Reinvent herself, like so many people seemed to be doing. But right now all she wanted to do was to sit quietly at home and consider her options. She did not need a neighbourly chat with Stella Sticky-Beak.

She got out of the car and with a silent sigh walked over to her neighbour, who was visibly upset.

'Dora.' Stella started without a greeting, her voice unusually high-pitched. 'I don't want to make a big fuss over this, but it's been going on for a while now and I need to say something.' She stopped to take in a big gulp of air.

Taken aback, Dora opened her mouth to inquire what had upset her neighbour but before she could get the first word out, Stella continued hurriedly.

'Purely by chance, I noticed something very disturbing a couple of weeks ago. Your husband, Harry …' She took another deep breath as if to steal herself before a big revelation. 'Your husband has been taking the mail out of our letterbox!' she burst out.

'Your mail?' Dora repeated stunned. 'Are you sure?'

'Am I sure? I'm very sure! I saw him take the mail, read the envelope and then throw it into your rubbish bin.'

'Our rubbish bin?' A headache was taking shape now, spreading into every crevice of Dora's brain. She couldn't tell whether those flickers of pain were impairing her hearing. They certainly prevented her from thinking clearly.

'Yes, your rubbish bin!' Stella confirmed emphatically, nearly triumphantly. 'No wonder we haven't had any mail for a couple of weeks. I had to ring the electricity company to get another bill sent and I had to go to the bank and ask them to reissue our statements. Dora, this cannot continue!' Expectantly she looked at Dora.

'I don't understand why Harry would do that. Dora was puzzled. This was indeed a very curious thing to do. She rubbed her temples. God, her head was buzzing.

'You need to talk to him. This cannot continue!' her neighbour repeated. 'I can't stand by the window all morning and watch our letterbox just to make sure your husband doesn't get there first and snatch our mail.'

It annoyed Dora that she made Harry sound like a thief. 'Stella,' she said, piqued, 'I will talk to Harry and make sure this doesn't happen again. I'm sorry it happened but I wish you had said something earlier.'

'Well, I didn't want to make a fuss. We've been good neighbours so far.'

Dora nodded and without another word disappeared into the house.

*

As he so often was, Harry was sitting in front of the TV watching a cricket match. Grateful that the sound was off, Dora sat on the couch next to her husband.

'Who's playing, Harry?' she asked as she eyed her husband. His hair was dishevelled and it looked like he had forgotten to shave that morning. Stubble covered his chin and cheeks. He looked comfortable in his track suit. As usual he had his feet on the coffee table. An empty chips packet was lying on the carpet. Well, for the time being she would not comment on his unshaved face, his feet on the table or the empty bag.

'Australia, can't you see?' Harry responded. 'Green and gold stripes on the shirts.' He pointed at the TV. 'They're our national colours.'

Dora nodded. Yes, she did know that. 'Who are they playing?'

'They're playing …' He hesitated. 'New Zealand, I think.'

Not that it mattered who they were playing. That was not what Dora wanted to talk about.

'Harry,' she said after a moment of silence. 'Harry, have you been checking next door's mail and throwing it into the rubbish bin? I just spoke to Stella next door. She said you've been taking her mail and throwing it in the bin. Tell me that's not true.'

Anxiously she regarded Harry. There was still a skerrick of hope that their neighbour had made a mistake. She supressed a sigh. But it seemed highly unlikely that Stella would make such an accusation against Harry without reason.

Harry looked at her blankly, his mind probably still on the cricket. 'What mail?' he finally asked.

'Next door's.' Dora vaguely pointed behind her. 'You know, old Mr Tomlinson's place.'

'Ah, yes, Tomlinson!' Harry nodded and smiled in recognition. 'I'm checking Tomlinson's mail while he's in hospital. It's not a big deal. Most of the letters were not addressed to him anyway so I've thrown them in the rubbish bin.' He nodded again at Dora, pleased that this small riddle had been solved. 'Yes, that's what I've done.'

'Harry,' Dora started but immediately closed her mouth. In despair she regarded her husband, who had turned towards the TV again. None of what Harry had said made sense. Mr Tomlinson hadn't lived next door for absolutely ages. It was true that he had been in hospital for a while, and during that time Harry had kept an eye on the house and the garden, which had included collecting his mail.

Had Harry's mind suffered some sort of time lapse? How could he forget that nearly fifteen years had passed since Mr Tomlinson had been in hospital and died there?

Leaning into the back of the couch, Dora closed her eyes. She needed an aspirin. And she needed to think carefully about how to approach this matter of their neighbours' mail with him. Dora rubbed her temples. She had to be clever about this. Pretend it was not a big deal. Despite her thrumming headache she suddenly struck upon an idea.

Dora cleared her throat. With a neutral expression on her face and a level tone of voice, she asked, 'Harry, has there been any mail for Mr Tomlinson recently?'

'No,' he answered without turning to her. 'Only for someone called Fulton. That's why I have been throwing it in the rubbish.'

'Harry, the Fultons … that's Stella and her husband. They live in old Tomlinson's house now. Don't you remember? We often call her Stella Sticky-Beak.'

'The Sticky-Beaks? Do they live there? Why is that?' Puzzled, he turned to Dora.

'Because old Mr Tomlinson died some years ago and he left the house to Sophie in his will. You must remember that, surely!'

Instantly, Harry's face lit up. 'Yes, of course, I remember. Sophie owns the house. It's rented out and she's getting quite a bit of money for it. She's doing well out of it!'

'Exactly!' Dora let out a deep breath. Trust him to remember anything to do with money! His accountant's brain was still working. Anyway, she needed to focus on the matter at hand.

'And the people who are renting it are the Fultons, so the mail is theirs.'

Dora regarded her husband while he was absorbing the information. Patience, she needed patience.

'Therefore you don't need to check it again. What do you think?'

'Yes, of course,' Dora heard Harry say. He'd already turned back to the TV. 'They can collect it themselves.'

'So you won't do it again?' Dora needed to hammer this into his brain.

'No,' he replied. 'It's nothing to do with me!'

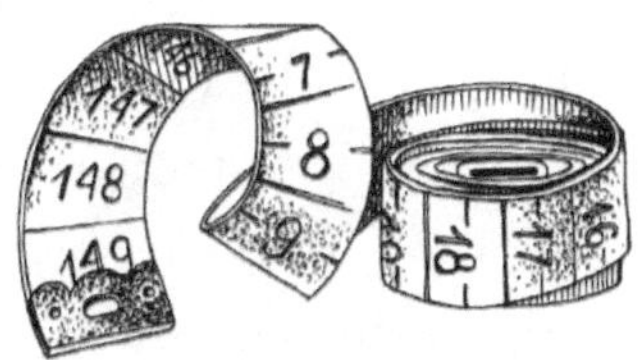

44

Late January 2024

The intelligence test

DORA LAY AWAKE AT NIGHT thinking about Harry. Listing in her mind all the incidents which had occurred over a number of months, if not years, and which pointed to a problem in Harry's thinking and behaviour. Most days he was perfectly normal, reading his paper, going for walks, complaining about silly little things, getting impatient with her. Yes, all of that was nothing out of the ordinary. As a matter of fact, it was quite a relief when he acted like that.

But then, out of the blue, he would do something extremely disconcerting. Stealing the neighbour's mail, stacking the firewood in the fridge. What would be the next thing he'd come up with? It was not simply a matter of forgetting names anymore, or dates. No, what he had done and might possibly do in the future pointed to a much more severe problem. It was time to accept Leah's advice, relinquish all pride, and get in touch with the Dementia Support Service.

Yes, Sophie, she thought with a sigh. Now I know the name. I did look it up on the internet! But like she had that day with Stella Fulton's mail, she would have to be clever about it. She couldn't just tell Harry he needed to get tested for dementia. A strategy was needed.

'Harry,' Dora said at the breakfast table the following morning. 'We're both getting older and certain things have been getting harder to do.'

'Have they? Like what?' Harry had his eyes on his boiled egg, which he was peeling very carefully. With a knife. After weeks of behaving 'normally', he was doing something … something odd again! Dora supressed a groan. *Like peeling eggs with a knife for example,* she wanted to scream. No, yelling and screaming and being facetious wouldn't get her anywhere. It was patience that was required, not sarcasm. Patience!

'Harry, it's easier if you use your fingers. Or I can do it for you.' If it hadn't been so ridiculous she would have admired the dexterity of his hands. God, sometimes he drove her crazy!

He quickly looked up and shook his head. 'I can do it myself.'

Dora took a deep breath and decided to ignore the matter of the egg. 'So anyway, I've been thinking it would be a good idea for us to get tested, you know. Both of us. Just to see how well our brain cells are working. Like an intelligence test, you know. What do you think?' An intelligence test! She was glad she'd thought of that. Harry's competitive personality would like that. It would give him an opportunity to prove how clever he was.

The egg was completely de-shelled now. Harry cut it up into neat slices and placed the slices carefully onto his piece of toast.

He looked up. 'I don't need an intelligence test,' he replied. 'But I still think that it's a very good idea.'

Dora was taken aback. She was expecting firm rejection, not easy acquiescence.

'Really?' she asked.

'Yes,' Harry confirmed emphatically. He took a large bite of his toast, crumbs floating onto his lap 'You have been saying some strange things lately, so I think it's a good idea you have your head checked.'

*

The woman from the Dementia Support Service introduced herself as Claire. She looked to be in her mid-fifties and had a friendly and direct demeanour. Her greying hair was done up in a French knot, leaving her colourful earrings free to dangle from side to side with every movement of her head. A casual suit consisting of a blue jacket and slacks was matched with a comfortable looking pair of flat shoes. Lively eyes took in the surroundings as she stepped in through the front door.

Introductions over and seated at the dining room table, Claire pulled a folder out of her briefcase. Inside were loose sheets of paper.

'I'll give you a sheet at a time,' Claire explained. 'You'll get one each, of course. There are different tasks to complete, some to do with words, others with numbers.' She smiled encouragingly at Harry. 'I hear you used to be an accountant and always good with numbers.'

Instead of answering, Harry pressed his lips tightly together.

'I should explain that these are not tests,' Claire reiterated, unperturbed by the tension emanating from Harry. She pointed at the sheets and smiled again. 'You're not getting marked. Just do whatever you can and when you're finished with one sheet, I'll give you the next one.'

Despite Claire's assurances, Dora felt her stomach contract. What if *she* couldn't do the exercises? She wasn't too bad with words, but there was always that irrational fear of numbers. She could only hope that these exercises wouldn't be too hard.

She glanced across at Harry, who looked downright hostile. Dora's stomach was shrinking into a tight little ball.

'First we're going to do a cloze exercise,' Claire explained. 'You can see that there are two short paragraphs on this first sheet and that there are words missing in both. Below the first paragraph is a box of words. Just pick the ones you think belong in the empty spaces.' Automatically, Dora nodded, even though Claire's eyes were on Harry.

'There are no words for you to select from for the second paragraph. Choose any words you think fit best and fill them in. Alright?'

Harry took one look at the paragraphs and started writing straight away. Every so often he crossed out words from the box under the first paragraph. Pleased that he was taking this seriously, Dora concentrated on her own sheet. Harry passed his sheet to Claire well before Dora did and sat waiting, his arms crossed in front of his chest.

Claire quickly scanned Harry's sheet before she put it in her folder. 'This is our number sheet.' She handed a fresh sheet to Dora and Harry. 'There are incomplete sequences of numbers. You are asked to add another three numbers to every one of the five rows you can see here, following the same pattern.'

Nervously, Dora stared at the rows of numbers, but she realised with relief that the patterns in the sequences were quite easy to figure out. Multiples of three in one row, adding four to the previous number in the next row. And so on, easy! She finished her sheet just as quickly as Harry.

'One last one,' Claire said.

The third sheet showed several round clock faces, numbered

from one to twelve, but the clock hands were missing in each one of them.

'Look at the first clock and draw in three o'clock for me,' Claire instructed.

'Half past six on the next one.'

'A quarter to eight on the third clock.'

'And one last one: ten past nine.'

'I don't really think I should be doing this kindergarten stuff!' Harry mumbled with a scowl as he drew in the clock hands.

Finally, Claire placed the sheets in her folder. 'Thank you. That's all we're doing for today. I hope it wasn't too painful.' She stood up. 'Mr Freeman, would you show me out?'

Harry jumped up, relief spreading over his face, and accompanied Claire to the door.

'I have to be in Devonport in an hour,' she said casually to Harry. 'Hope there's not too much traffic.'

'No,' Harry shook his head reassuringly. 'Not at this time of day. It shouldn't be a problem.' The tests over, his demeanour had instantly changed. All charm and friendliness, he opened the door for Claire.

Dora had followed Harry and Claire to the front door. She had overheard the exchange and was perplexed. What was Harry talking about? He had driven to Devonport hundreds of times for work and knew it would take closer to four hours to get there rather than one. But when she saw Claire nodding, she understood what was happening. Harry was being tested. Except that she wasn't altogether sure whether Harry thought in all seriousness that it only took one hour to drive to Devonport, or whether he had caught on to the fact that Claire was testing him. Was he toying with her?

At the bottom of their drive, Claire stopped and looked around before unlocking her car. 'This is a lovely area,' she remarked to Harry. 'Have you got nice neighbours?'

He nodded. 'Yes, we do. An elderly gentleman, Tomlinson.' Was there a flicker of uncertainty on his face as he turned to Dora? 'It is Tomlinson, isn't it?'

'Mr Tomlinson used to live there. Now it's the Fultons,' she replied with a quick look at Claire.

'Yes, I know. Just testing you,' Harry replied nonchalantly. Then he pointed across the road. 'I can't tell you who lives in that last house over there. Dora, do you know their names?'

'No. They only moved in very recently. A young couple, I think.'

'But I can tell you who lives next to them,' Harry addressed Claire with a dismissive wave of his hand. 'A couple of losers, two cousins. They are letting the house go to wrack and ruin. They do nothing but sit and drink beer!'

'Harry, that's not quite true!' Dora objected. It upset her more than she would have thought to hear Luke and Boz called 'losers'. 'Those two young men have done a bit of work for us. They're quite skilled. And they do have casual work with a builder friend, I think,' she added in their defence. Harry harrumphed but desisted from saying any more.

Claire unlocked her car. 'I'll be in touch with the results,' she said before driving off.

*

The following day, Claire rang Dora to tell her that she could not justify an official diagnosis as Harry hadn't done any of the tasks she had given him.

'Didn't he?' Dora asked surprised. 'But I saw him doing all the exercises!'

'He did. He wrote 'dumb' into every single gap of the cloze exercises,' Claire replied. 'He completed the number sequencing with zeroes, and on the clock sheet he drew every hand to six o'clock.

Without exception.' She waited for a moment to let her words sink in. Then she continued. 'It could mean that he felt extremely patronised and upset about these tasks and that was his way of telling me. Or it could mean that he really didn't know what to do.'

Dora was lost for words. She suspected it was probably a bit of both. It was hard to know with Harry.

'And because I can't be sure whether he was just being contrary, I would need to do more testing.'

'What about those questions you asked him about Devonport and our neighbours?' Dora insisted. 'Surely, that must have given you some indication.'

'Yes, it did. But that alone is not enough. For an official diagnosis and support from our services, more testing is required,' Claire repeated.

'Thank you!' The tremor in Dora's voice was audible. 'I'll have to let all of this settle first before ...' Dora was unable to complete her sentence because she just couldn't envisage what the next step could possibly be. She took a deep breath. 'So far we're managing alright,' she finally said. 'We don't need any support at the moment, but when the time comes I'll definitely be in touch.'

'Please do. It might happen sooner than you think.'

A heartbeat passed. 'Before you hang up,' Dora said hurriedly. 'Can I ask you something? Something unrelated?'

'Yes, of course.'

'I've been wondering ...' Dora's voice faltered. 'I've been wondering why adults would steal. You know, shoplifting.' Her hand holding the phone trembled.

'Is that what Harry is doing? Shoplifting?'

'Oh no, God no! Not Harry!' Dora was quick to protest. Then, after moment's hesitation. 'A friend of mine. A grown woman.'

'I see. Well, there could be several reasons. Some people steal out of necessity. They might not have the money to buy the essentials they need, but that is not very common. More often than not, people steal because it gives them some control over their actions when otherwise they feel they have no control over their lives. Also people who feel overlooked or excluded or whose emotional needs are not met or who are in some emotional turmoil. It could be any one of those, or a combination.'

There was silence while Dora considered what Claire had said. Did any of those apply to her? She felt deflated and ashamed. Were her emotional needs ignored? Was she in turmoil? Was she really one of those people Claire had described? In her defence, she hadn't *acquired* anything in a long time.

'Thank you,' she finally said.

'There are counsellors who specialise in that area. Maybe your friend would consider seeing one of them?'

'I'll talk to her about it. Thank you so much!'

*

Still holding the phone in her hand, Dora leaned against the kitchen cupboard. Did she need to prove she was in control of her life? Was she disregarded and overlooked? Claire's words tumbled around in her head. Yes, yes, all of the above applied to her, but surely they applied to everyone at some stage in life. The gravity was not such as to suggest she had a mental illness.

So why did she steal? It had happened only occasionally when she was young. The odd bar of chocolate disappeared inside her clothing but she only did it to see whether she would get caught. It was a thrill. Even though it was just a small thing it got the adrenaline coursing through her body. Making her feel so alive. No different from jumping into the blowhole in Blackman's Bay before they put the cyclone fence around it. Not that she was ever one of the brave ones who did jump down.

Dora still remembered the look on Harry's face that day in the car when she pulled the bar of chocolate out of her coat. If he had known she'd stolen it, he would not have married her, she was sure of it. Upright law-abiding citizen he'd been, successful role model for all the up-and-coming young people and look where that had gotten him. He had been the one to end up in prison, so there!

Later in life Dora had ever only stolen that handful of buttons in the oversized, impersonal fabric shop. She felt no guilt over the theft. No one in the store cared about the goods in the store and in any case, thefts were most likely built into their pricing, but she had had no reason for stealing those buttons. It was more that she had wanted to outwit that contemptuous shop assistant with the tarantula eyelashes. To show her who was the smarter one. Even though she had had to keep that triumph hidden, it had made her feel good.

That business with the handbag in that lovely old shop in Huonville was a different matter. Every time she used the handbag she was assaulted by pangs of guilt. Not that it had been an outright theft. After all she had paid something, a bit more than half the asking price after switching the price tag with that of a cheaper bag, but why had she done it in the first place? There had been no need to outwit anyone.

Again, she thought of what Claire had said about being overlooked. Somehow that stuck in her mind. Was that true in her case? Well, yes. Sometimes she did feel overlooked by Harry, who thought her work as a designer and dressmaker was just something she played around with. He gave no indication that he appreciated her skills and her artistic talents. Maybe that was one of the reasons she had stolen the bag. Did that mean then that she was so desperate for his approval? After all, other people appreciated her work. Michelle obviously did, or she wouldn't have recommended her again and again to these stage and film directors for a dress.

Except that even that aspect of her work was about to finish. Leah was another person who loved her work. She had said so often, and particularly that night in Sydney. Dora wasn't sure what Sophie thought about it all. She did not have much time for artistic pursuits. Like father, like daughter. Well, it looked like Dora would have to give up her 'artistic pursuits' soon anyway.

Why on earth was she thinking about all of that now? She needed to concentrate on what was going on with Harry's mind, not her own. That could wait. Would Harry agree to be tested again? Dora doubted it. Unless he forgot during the next few weeks that he'd already been tested. Which would be a bad sign in itself. Good God, what a dilemma!

45

4 March 2024

Seven days after Harry's death

THE LOVELY INDIAN SERGEANT PAID Dora another visit the following day. Feeling slightly uneasy, Dora invited her into the sewing room. She had just been sewing in some threads on a sleeve by hand and wanted to quickly finish the job. Why had the sergeant come again? Was she still not convinced that Dora had nothing to do with Harry's death, and she needed to make further inquiries?

Outside, the white cockatoos were screeching again. One of them was sitting on the lawn pecking away at something. Just a few days ago Dora had sprinkled a few grass seeds into a bare spot in the lawn. Silently she sighed. That was probably exactly what this pest of a white cockatoo was pecking at.

'I just wanted to make sure you're alright,' the sergeant interrupted Dora's thoughts.

'Oh, yes,' Dora hastily replied. 'I still can't fathom it all but I'm trying to keep my mind occupied, as you can see.' As if to erase any doubt as to the truth of her words, she lifted up the nearly finished sleeve.

Sergeant Sharma smiled. 'Despite what your husband said about your work in the car that day when he was arrested, he must have been proud of you, surely,' she said. She walked up to the half-finished dress hanging on one of the mannequins. 'Not everyone is asked to make period dresses for the stage and for films, I assume?'

Dora nodded. 'Yes, it is a niche occupation, and as I said before it certainly isn't regular work.' Wistfully, she looked across at the mannequin. She knew this would be the last dress she ever made, but the sergeant didn't need to know that.

Dora smoothed her skirt down. 'Whether Harry was proud of me? I don't know. To be proud of someone, you must believe that they did something extraordinary. Something that is to be admired. I don't think Harry ever admired anyone. If he did he'd fall off his pedestal.' The bitterness in her voice made Sergeant Sharma raise her eyebrows.

'I suppose I should qualify this,' Dora added hastily. She didn't want to speak ill of Harry. She never had when he was alive. 'He was proud of Sophie, our daughter. She's got a doctorate in mathematics. So, yes, Harry was proud of her.'

Sergeant Sharma's face lit up. 'I remember you telling us about that, the first day we came here. The value of each angle in a hexagon: one hundred and twenty degrees. I don't think I'll ever forget that!'

Dora blushed. 'I'm sorry. I was beside myself that day. I didn't know what I was saying.'

She was silent as she considered what to say next. 'It took me a long time to figure out that Harry had a problem with people who excelled at something.'

'If you don't mind, I'd like a cup of tea.' The sergeant looked at Dora. This was obviously going to take longer than either of them had expected.

'Of course, of course! Come into the kitchen with me.'

Once seated, Sergeant Sharma encouraged Dora to continue. 'So tell me about Harry and successful people.'

Dora turned to the sink and filled the kettle. 'Rather than admiring people who knew a lot about certain things, he would ridicule them or make disparaging comments. As if he couldn't bear that someone was better than him in certain regards, no matter what it was.' There, now she had spoken ill of him after all.

'I think he was brought up in his brother's shadow. Andrew was so popular and so easygoing. Everyone liked him. Likes him,' Dora corrected herself. 'As a child, Harry must have felt he had to prove himself, so I suppose over the years that became a habit. Outdoing his brother and outdoing others.'

Dora got two cups out of the cupboard and placed them on the table. Analysing Harry's character when she knew nothing about psychology was embarrassing. It probably told the sergeant more about her, Dora, than Harry.

But Sergeant Sharma did not seem to be worried. While Dora talked, she listened and looked around the kitchen. It was a neatly appointed kitchen. Everything was in the right place. The kettle on the bench close to the water tap. The fridge only a couple of steps from the stove and work bench. A food processor in the corner. No superfluous gadgets that stood in the way. An efficient kitchen that was easy to work in and easy to clean. There were no dirty dishes in the sink, no breadcrumbs on the table, no stale food smells. Dora always kept it smelling fresh and clean. The lace curtain was slightly drawn to one side, giving a clear view of the street and the houses across the road. Sergeant Sharma's eyes fixed on the photos on top of the fridge. Standing up to have a closer look she asked, 'Who is this?' She pointed at a photo showing a couple and two little girls.

'Oh, that was taken a very long time ago,' Dora replied. 'That's my parents, my sister Freda and myself. We must have been ten and twelve, I think.'

'You all look very happy? Are your parents still alive?' The sergeant nodded at the photo.

'They died in a car accident, on the way home from the cinema one night.' Good God, it was still hard to talk about. Her parents had been so young. She, Dora, had been so young, only in her twenties. Too young to lose her parents. And Freda, her poor sister Freda! She had been even younger than Dora.

The young policewoman rested her kind eyes on Dora. All of a sudden, Dora's mouth felt as rough as the scouring pad she used for cleaning her pots. She grasped the edge of the kitchen bench to steady herself.

'I'm so sorry.'

'Thank you.' Dora blinked away tears. 'Apparently they died instantly. At least they didn't feel any pain,' she answered, her voice choked up, her legs weakening and melting. 'It happened only one year after Harry and I got married.'

For a few short moments, both women looked silently at the photo. Finally, Sergeant Sharma moved back to her chair.

'I'm sorry to have to ask you this again, but do you think that Harry could have committed suicide? Had he ever talked about taking his own life? Or was there any other evidence that he could have considered that at all?'

The noise of the boiling kettle gave Dora a few minutes before responding. She stood up gingerly, relieved to have something to do, and filled the teapot.

'I can't be sure about that,' she answered slowly, her back to the sergeant. 'He never spoke about taking his own life but …' She hesitated. 'I don't think his mind was all that sharp anymore. There were moments that made me think Harry might have suffered the beginnings of dementia.' Good move. She didn't have to think about her parents and Freda anymore.

'Dementia? What makes you say that?'

Dora sat down opposite Sergeant Sharma. 'There were several incidents that made me wonder.' She struggled to find the right words. 'First it was all the usual things, you know, forgetting what day it is or what month, not remembering people's names. But I thought nothing of it. Sometimes I forget those things, too. We all do occasionally, don't we?' She looked for acknowledgement to the sergeant, who nodded at her encouragingly.

Indian people were just lovely. Those dark brown eyes were full of sympathy and understanding. Just like the young Indian taxi driver had been. He had seen her in a state of emotional upheaval and remained calm and considerate. The police sergeant displayed the same empathetic demeanour. It was a relief to share all these difficult family issues with them. Dora wondered whether these two knew each other. After all, the taxi driver had said they were all one big family. But that was not important now. She had to get back to her suspicions regarding Harry's dementia.

'One time there was a more serious event,' Dora said. 'Months after Harry left work, he decided to deal with some of his old boxes of papers. There was quite a number of them stored in the garage. Old tax records, receipts, old payslips and whatever else, I don't know.' She took a sip of tea. 'Well, I was afraid he might be sorting through them again, but surprisingly, he just threw them all into the rubbish bin. Just like that. I don't think he even looked at them. They went back decades and he'd always insisted that you should never throw out your paperwork.'

'That sounds just like what a conscientious accountant would say,' the lovely sergeant confirmed.

'But then a few weeks later I heard him rummaging around in the garage. Then he came inside furious, asking me what I had done with his boxes. I don't think I could convince him that he had thrown them out. He had completely forgotten. And this was surely not a small thing that you could just forget.'

'Did your daughter notice any unusual behaviour of his?'

'No, not really. Not to start with anyway. She's lived in Launceston for a number of years now. We don't see her that often.'

Anyway, there was no need to tell the sergeant about the other incidents, the more serious ones. The ones that should have definitely woken Dora up to the fact that there was a problem. The ones she had pushed aside.

There was concern in the sergeant's voice when she asked, 'Did you have him tested?'

Dora cradled the teacup in her hands. 'I tried a few months ago, because I thought if he really had dementia, sooner or later I would need some support.'

'So what was the outcome?'

'There was no outcome. Not officially anyway, because he refused to be tested.'

Sergeant Sharma raised her eyebrows. 'Really?'

'Well, I have to qualify that too. First he agreed to be tested, mainly because he thought I was the one with the problem. So I got someone to come, a very efficient lady from the Dementia Support Service. But when she attempted to do the tests, Harry refused to do them properly. The cloze exercises and the number sequences … Oh, he just wrote nonsense! And the clock test, you know, where you have to draw the hands into clocks to certain times? He drew them all in at six o'clock. He behaved like a stubborn child who refused to participate, and sat there looking smug. He must have thought the whole thing was ridiculous.'

The sergeant nodded in sympathy and for a short moment neither spoke.

Dora took a sip of tea, then leaned over the table towards her. 'Claire, the lady from the dementia place, was clever, though. When she walked out the front door she just talked to him casually. You know, "lovely day today", real casual. Then she looked at her watch and said, "I'm off to Devonport now. Hope I'll be there in an hour."'

'And how did Harry react? Did he realise you can't get there in an hour?'

'He said that that shouldn't be a problem.'

'Could he have just played along with Claire to humour her?'

Dora shrugged her shoulders. 'There's no knowing, is there? He would be clever enough to do exactly that, I think. Then,' Dora continued, 'Claire pretended to be interested in the neighbours and asked Harry who lived next door. He said Mr Tomlinson did. Well, he used to live there but hasn't for a long time.' She shrugged her shoulders. 'So Harry pretended he was testing *my* memory. Whether I knew who lived there! The point is, I can't work out whether he had these memory gaps or not. At times he was so clear and knew exactly what was going on.'

Sergeant Sharma shrugged her shoulders. 'I can see the difficulty here. Your husband could have responded to the test and Claire's comments in the manner he did because he really was of an unsound mind. But to me it sounds rather like a very clever ruse, wanting to show you how all that testing was beneath him. In my capacity as a police officer I've had too many dealings with people who've lied, deceived, cheated to take anything at face value.'

But Dora knew Harry's behaviour had not been a ruse. There

were too many examples to prove Harry's mind was 'unsound'. Not that the nice sergeant needed to know about all the other incidents. No, there was no need to expose all of Harry's deficiencies. If you could call them that.

Moving towards the door, the sergeant nodded thoughtfully. 'Before I forget: your husband's body will most likely be released next week. We will officially confirm that it was death by misadventure. There is no evidence that anyone was involved in his death.'

Dora clasped her hands to her chest. 'Oh, thank God! Thank God!'

'As you probably know, most murders are committed by someone known to the victim, so you were our main suspect. After checking the timing of your movements that day, though, we have concluded that it would have been impossible for you to follow your husband, go to the shops afterwards and return home. There just wasn't enough time.' Sergeant Sharma all at once sounded very official. The case was closed for her.

'And we have those witnesses confirming more or less exactly when you left the house and when you returned. As you know we got a statement from Mrs Fulton next door, Luke Wilson and Bernard Miller, as well as the young couple next to them.'

'Bernard?' Dora was lost for words. Did she mean Boz? Bernard sounded so ... so harmless and so conservative. It didn't fit at all with the image of an ill-mannered and loutish young man that he was presenting to the world. No wonder the poor boy changed his name to Boz.

'Yes,' Sergeant Sharma replied. 'Those two think the world of you, you know?'

'Probably because I have given them a lot of work around the garden and the house,' Dora said. 'They're very good. Better than you would think, when you consider how they appear,' she added with a slight chuckle.

'They do look a bit rough.' The sergeant smiled. 'But they definitely like you.'

'What about the young couple next to them? They only moved in a couple of months ago, so I haven't met them. You talked to them?' Dora asked surprised.

'We talked to everyone in the neighbourhood,' the sergeant said. 'The couple saw you come home from the shops, too. Apparently they work from home and they happened to look out the window when you arrived. They could even give me the exact time they saw you. So all in all, everyone confirmed what you told us.'

Her lovely neighbours had confirmed everything in her favour, yes. But again Dora thought it very strange, if not negligent, that the police had never asked her for any shopping dockets. If she were a policewoman that would have been the first thing she'd do. Check the facts, gather tangible evidence, collect proof, or whatever they called it, to make sure her alibi was watertight.

Stepping onto the driveway the sergeant turned to Dora. 'I won't have to talk to you again.'

*

When Dora returned to the house, she went straight to the fridge and for a long time stared at the photo of her parents and Freda. The accident had been such a long time ago, but Dora could still feel that painful contraction of her heart when she thought about it.

'Freda,' she said to the photo. 'You heard the sergeant. I'm in the clear. Harry's death was an accident. Which is exactly what it was, but as I wrote to you in my letter, it would have been hard to prove that I had nothing to do with it.'

Carefully, she took the photo off the top of the fridge. 'There are a few things I shall do,' she said while looking at her sister. 'Get rid of the dead dinosaur in the lounge. Hang up that painting that has been hiding for decades behind my filing cabinet. Dissolve my emergency fund. And do something with your letters, dear Freda.'

Holding the photo in her hand she walked into her sewing room. Quickly, she opened a drawer of her filing cabinet, flicked through all the different envelopes holding her patterns. When she had found the right one, she stuck the photo in and slammed the drawer shut again. 'I'll deal with you in a minute.'

She pulled out the painting from behind the filing cabinet and placed it on the table. The paper it was wrapped in had yellowed over the years. Dora ripped the paper off and regarded the swirls of blue that she had found so irresistible such a long time ago. The colours were still as vivid and captivating as they had been when she'd first brought the painting home. Keeping it wrapped up had protected it from fading. Yes, she would finally hang the painting up in the lounge room where it belonged. Where it always should have been.

In the garage, she found the box with Harry's tools. It was a small box, and it only held the most necessary tools, a hammer, a spanner, a wire cutter, a collection of nails and screws. If nothing else, this was sufficient evidence that Harry had not been a handyman. It was impossible to look after a house with this sad collection of tools.

Dora selected a nail, grabbed the hammer and marched into the lounge. She hammered the nail into exactly the same spot where its predecessor had been. Then she hung up the painting. Yes, she thought with satisfaction as she scrutinised it. This is where you belong.

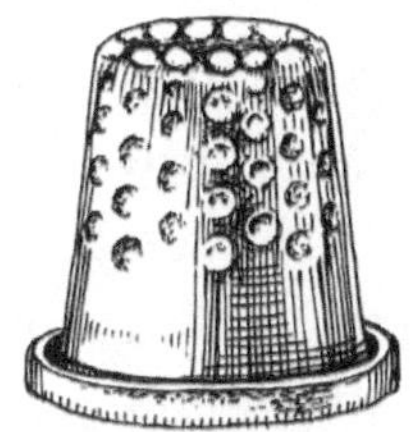

46

5 March 2024

Eight days after Harry's death

LUKE AND BOZ HAD PICKED up Harry's green chair and heaved it across the road. It now sat on their veranda, taking up what little space there had been.

'I hope you're not going to argue over this chair,' Dora said, looking from one to the other with a school mistress look on her face. She had been invited by the two young men to inspect the new seating arrangements.

'Nope, we won't argue. We're cousins. We get on like a house on fire,' Luke replied.

Boz had already taken over the chair, fitting his body into the unfamiliar shape.

'You got any cousins?' Boz asked without looking at Dora. He was fiddling with one of the side levers while holding an open can of beer in his hand. Suddenly the back of the chair plunged into a near-horizontal position sending a spray of foamy beer over his t-shirt. 'Fuck!' he called out and pulled the lever again.

Dora reached out to help him but then withdrew her hand. Let him figure out how it works, she thought. He's old enough. Instead, she retrieved the only cushion from the old couch and placed it on the milk crate.

With a screech, the back of Harry's chair suddenly flipped up again. 'You have to do it a bit more gently,' Dora instructed him. 'And no, I don't have cousins. My mother had a brother, but he and his wife didn't have children. And my father was an only child.'

'Tough shit,' Boz grumbled distractedly. Now he was fumbling with a small lever on the other side of the chair. The footrest flew out, knocking into his calves.

'I have a sister, though,' Dora continued, her eyes fixed on Boz. Bernard. No, Boz suited him better. She could see that.

'A sister?' Luke asked. He opened a can of beer and turned to Boz. 'Have we ever seen someone visiting that looks like Mrs F's sister? She must have flown under our radar!' Both laughed.

'How come we've never seen your sister, Mrs F?' Luke insisted. 'You've never even said you had one. Have you been hiding her from us?' He took a big swallow of beer.

Dora wriggled uncomfortably on the milk crate. 'Well, she doesn't live here. She's ...' Dora had her head down, picking at the corner of the cushion. The two young men looked at her expectantly.

She lives on the Galápagos Islands, Dora wanted to say. She lifted her head to meet their eyes. *Freda, that's her name, moved there a long time ago to look after God-only-knows-what animals. I write to her regularly. The mail takes ages to get there, weeks if not months. Ringing is nearly impossible, too. The connection is terrible and it costs a bucket of money. That's why I haven't spoken to her for a long time. The internet doesn't exist on the Galápagos Islands, so you can't just shoot off a quick email and expect an instant reply. And I have no idea when she will be coming back.*

But Dora didn't say any of those things. She didn't know how long the mail took or how expensive it was to ring the Galápagos. The internet had probably reached there by now, too. Every god-forlorn country in the world had the internet, so those islands way out in the Pacific probably did, too. And she knew that Freda would never come back.

'She's what?' Boz's voice cut through her thoughts. 'She's what, Mrs F?'

Dora's eyes swam. It was impossible to continue making up stories. Her whole life had been shrouded in secrecy and deception and falsehoods. She didn't want to tell any more lies.

'She's dead. My sister is dead,' she managed to say. 'She died in a car accident together with my parents. She was only in her early twenties.' Dora's shoulders were heaving, tears flowing fast. 'Yes, she's dead!'

'Fuck me dead!' Boz's voice was only just audible. He had stopped fiddling with the levers on the chair and stared at Dora.

'So my whole family was gone, only a year after the wedding, and Harry's family became my family. I hadn't even wanted to marry him! I wanted to marry his brother, but he already had a wife.' Words and tears came tumbling out together fast. Everything Dora had tucked away in the back of her mind came rushing out unchecked, like water gushing uncontrollably out of a burst pipe. Swamping everything and everyone in its path.

'Mrs F, you don't make much sense.' Luke leaned forward and fixed his eyes on her. 'But you did marry the Judge, didn't you?'

'Oh yes, of course I married him. We were so young and so silly. Sometimes I can't believe how everything just happened.' Dora pulled a handkerchief out of her skirt pocket and blew her nose with force. 'Things just seemed to happen all by themselves and I don't even know if Harry ever loved me. I never sensed much affection. In all the years we were married he never acknowledged what I did around the house and he never once said he was proud of my achievements.' She lowered her eyes to her clasped hands. 'I mean my work. He just took no interest in what I was doing. No interest at all.'

'Fuck! I hope I never get married!' Boz said under his breath.

'You mean your costumes?' Luke asked, ignoring his cousin's comment.

Surprised, Dora dabbed at her eyes with the damp handkerchief and stared at him. 'How do you know?'

'We're the neighbourhood watch team, that's how!' Grinning, Boz slapped his thighs.

Luke shot Boz a warning look. This was not the moment for smart comments. Then he turned to Dora. 'We painted your sewing studio not that long ago. We had to move everything out, remember? Your table and the machines, and all those boxes, and the two naked dolls.' Boz grinned again but this time abstained from making a comment. 'That's how we know what you do.'

Dora scrunched the handkerchief into a small sodden ball and stuffed it into her skirt pocket. 'The mannequins, that's what they're called. Yes, of course I remember. Oh God, my brain is so muddled. These last few days have been just horrible.'

'I bet you wish your sister was here now.' If he had intended this to be a sympathetic comment, Boz had failed. His words only caused another sudden flood of tears in Dora.

'Shit!' Luke thumped his cousin in the shoulder. 'You've made her cry again, you nong! Go and get her a cup of tea!' Turning to Dora he asked, 'Would you like one? A cup of tea, I mean? You're strung out. It might help.'

Dora had never before been offered any tea by these two. The surprise instantly stopped her flow of tears. She wiped her nose on the sleeve of her blouse.

'Yes,' she mumbled. 'Yes, a cup of tea would be nice.' She blinked away remnant tears.

Boz swung his legs over the chair and disappeared into the house. As soon as he had closed the door behind him, Luke flung himself into Harry's chair.

Only a few minutes later Boz returned, holding a cup of tea in one hand. A chipped cup, Dora noticed immediately, even though her vision was still a bit blurry from all that crying, but she didn't really care. She hadn't exactly expected Royal Doulton.

In his other hand, Boz carried a plate of chocolate brownies. He held it out to Dora. 'Home-made,' he said. The two cousins exchanged a quick glance as Dora accepted a brownie.

'Home-made by whom?' Dora asked.

Luke nodded towards Boz. 'He makes the best chocolate brownies,' he explained. 'But that's where it ends. Apart from that he can't cook to save himself. Oh, and the tea. He can make a cup of tea.' He laughed as he relaxed back into Harry's chair.

The world is full of surprises, Dora thought. She stared into her cup. Green tea, indeed. Not her drink of choice, but if she remembered correctly, green tea was meant to be good for your health.

'It's got honey in it,' Boz said. 'To sweeten it.'

'You two surprise me!' For the time being, Dora was sufficiently distracted from thoughts of her sister. 'Green tea and chocolate brownies! Well, I never …' She lifted the cup to her lips and took a sip. It tasted … unusual. Quite pleasant, though. Not exactly what she had expected but it was lovely and sweet. It had a subtle flavour she couldn't identify but how could she? She hadn't tasted much green tea in the past. Nevertheless, it reminded her of something – something from her youth – but she was upset, her head fogged up from crying and she couldn't be bothered thinking about it. She took another sip. A pleasant feeling of spaciousness and clarity spread slowly through her body. Crying and pouring out her heart to these two had clearly released something in her brain. Dopamine! Didn't the brain release dopamine after a session of intense crying? Or was it this lovely fragrant tea that made her feel so mellow and light? Yes, she hadn't felt this light in a long time.

Luke and Boz had just finished their second brownie. No wonder that couch was always covered in crumbs, Dora thought. The way those two got stuck into biscuits and chips and whatever else!

Luke held out the plate and she took a second one herself. And another sip of that delicious tea. Dora stretched out her legs and regarded the two cousins.

'I'm sorry for behaving like a cry-baby,' she apologised.

'Not to worry,' Luke reassured her. 'Losing your sister is a tough one.' He exchanged another mysterious glance with his cousin. 'Finish your tea,' he suggested. 'Finish it and you'll be fine in no time at all.'

'Oh, I'm feeling much better already.' Dora wriggled her toes. 'You've been very kind.'

'You wanna tell us what happened to your parents and your sister?'

Dora swallowed the last of her tea and without thinking passed the empty cup to Boz. 'A car accident, as I said. My sister Freda was driving. You don't know what she was like, always laughing and talking. Talking, talking, talking! She failed her first driving test because she was talking nonstop. When you talk too much, you don't concentrate on the traffic, she was told by the licence examiner, so she failed the test that first time.' She gave a slight giggle. 'No surprise there!'

Dora cleared her voice. 'Then, that day with my parents in the car, she drove straight into a lamp post. It was at night, by the way. They were all coming home from the movies. The light of that lamp post must have attracted her like a moth to flames.' Dora was silent for a moment. 'Oh,' she then cried out. 'It was such a long time ago!'

It felt good to talk about it. Not that it had ever been a secret. Harry had known about it, Andrew and Leah and Barb and John … Everyone in Cygnet had known about it. People looked you in the eye and you knew that they were thinking of the terrible accident. Or they avoided looking at you. All of them feeling sorry for you.

This was the first time Dora had told someone who didn't know her family. After she and Harry had moved to Kingston the accident was never mentioned again. Nobody in Kingston had known them and what had happened. It had been a relief. Like a new beginning.

Oh, she felt so much lighter now. The proverbial burden had been lifted off her shoulders. If she wasn't careful, she would be floating away. She smiled at these two young, lovely men who had freed her from carrying this burden. Should she go and hug them? To thank them? They looked so content and comfortable in their skin. Both regarding her attentively and smiling. Boz's hair shone like fire in that one ray of sunlight that sneaked through the crack in the alsynite porch roofing. What beautiful hair he had!

And Luke in his paint-spattered t-shirt … Why on earth had she ever wrinkled her nose at these colourful bright dots and streaks of paint? They literally seemed to dance on that t-shirt every time he moved. She was so happy to have these two as her friends. If she hadn't gone across the road all those years ago to ask them to work for her, where would she be now? Well, she didn't know where she would be, that was for sure!

All at once Dora noticed the silence around her. Nobody had said anything for such a long time. Boz sat on the old couch, his eyes closed now but a smile still playing around his lips. Luke was half-lying in Harry's old dinosaur chair, watching her.

Dora gave a little giggle. The dinosaur had finally ended up in the jungle. Because this place was a jungle. Stuff everywhere. You couldn't find your way around this jungle. Impenetrable, it was. She wouldn't be surprised to find herself in some thick, mysterious greenery, should she ever venture into the house. Another giggle escaped her lips.

'Could I have another one of those nice … what do you call them?' she asked. Boz's eyes snapped open, exchanging another glance with his cousin.

'Brownies. Maybe you've had enough,' Luke suggested. 'They are quite strong.'

Dora looked from one of the cousins to the other. What a strange description! She had never before heard anyone call a brownie 'strong'. 'Sweet' maybe or 'rich' but 'strong'?

It seemed a bit rude to her, too, to refuse her another one. If they had been her home-made brownies or biscuits or whatever, she would have been happy to offer another one to her guests. Well, it didn't matter. These two cousins had different ideas about lots of things. Like most young people. So why not about food?

'Mrs F,' Luke suddenly said. 'How about I take you home? You look like you could do with a rest.' He levered himself into an upright position and jumped off the dinosaur. Dora just couldn't stop giggling about Harry's dinosaur. Why had she never noticed before how silly this chair was?

She held out her hand to Luke and allowed herself to be pulled off the milk crate. 'You'd better help me down the stairs,' she asked. 'I think my feet have disappeared.' She looked down. 'Wrong! There they are!'

'Come on, Mrs F, I'll hold you. Hang on to the rails. That's it, slowly now. Down we go.'

'I'll have a little lie-down in the lounge room,' Dora said as Luke led her through her front door. He helped her onto the couch and covered her with a blanket.

'Leave your door unlocked,' he said to her. 'I'll come over later and check on you.'

'Oh, but don't steal my furniture,' she mumbled before she fell into a delicious deep sleep.

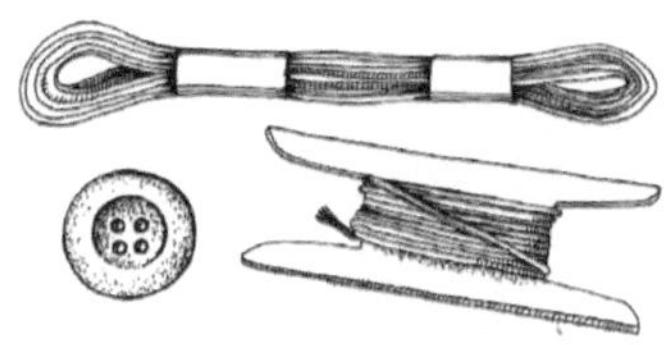

47

6 March 2024

Nine days after Harry's death

DORA WOKE UP IN A lounge room flooded in bright sunlight. She squeezed her eyes together, then yawned. Opening her eyes she realised that she was lying on the couch, fully dressed and covered in a blanket. Slightly dazed, she looked around. What on earth was she doing on the couch? What was the time? She threw the blanket off and stood up gingerly. There was a slight pinch in her back. Maybe a stretch would get rid of it.

The position of the sun told her that it must be mid-morning. Had she spent the whole night on the couch? She stumbled into the kitchen to check the time. Good God, after ten o'clock already. Slowly the memory of the previous day came back to her. She had been visiting Luke and Boz to admire Harry's recliner chair in its new home. There had been tea and chocolate biscuits. No, brownies. Luke had taken her home. That was it. He wanted her to have a rest on the couch. Had she said something about furniture to him? She couldn't remember.

Dora shook her head. What she needed was a nice shower and a hearty breakfast. God, she was hungry!

*

Walking into her sewing room after breakfast, she went straight to the filing cabinet and pulled out the envelope marked 'EF'. She carried it to her table and tipped it upside down. Out fell the photo of her parents and Freda, a large number of letters and an even larger number of hundred-dollar bills. Brushing the money aside, Dora opened the ribbon holding the pile of envelopes. Every single one was addressed to Freda and every single one displayed a date in the top right corner where the stamp should have been. There was no need for Dora to pull out the letters and reread them. She knew exactly what they said. And it was time to forget what she had written.

Back in the lounge room, she opened the door of the wood heater. Kindling was stacked up nicely in a pyramid over some scrunched-up newspapers. Dora's breath stopped for a second. Harry always cleaned the wood heater at the end of winter and set the fire ready to go when the first cold days arrived in late April.

With her free hand she pulled a box of matches from underneath the wood heater. Then she lit the fire. The neighbours would think she was crazy, lighting a fire in the middle of summer. When the wooden pyramid caught fire and crackled away nicely she placed the letters into the flames, waiting until each one had turned to ash before she placed in the next one. After the last letter had disappeared she sat and watched until the fire had gone out.

'Goodbye, Freda,' she said. 'You've been a good sister to me. But now I'm on my own.'

Finally, she pushed herself up and breathed a sigh of relief. The time had come to look ahead and give her life a new direction. Just recently she had seen a lovely colourful advertisement in the newspaper. A cruise ship company was offering specials on cruises to Alaska. Alaska! She, Dora would go to Alaska! Leave one of the southernmost inhabited places on earth to go to one of the northernmost inhabited places. Right across the world, from the bottom to the top. From the South to the North. Who knew what might eventuate on the journey?

48

26 February 2024

The day of Harry's death

'I'M OFF ON MY WALK,' Harry yelled out. Dora opened her mouth to reply, but the door had already slammed shut and he was gone. Through the kitchen window she saw him walking down their long drive, as usual in his old saggy track pants and a sloppy t-shirt. As he had grown older, he had thinned down quite a bit but was still wearing his old shirts and jumpers. His body now only held a vague memory of his once solid football player's physique.

But look at how well he walks, Dora thought, more than a bit miffed. Not a hint of that *shrup, shrupping* he does in the house. All day long, shuffling from one room to the next, wearing the carpets out. How come he can lift his feet up like a gazelle as soon as he is outside? He knew the shuffling annoyed her and she strongly suspected that he was doing it for exactly that reason.

Harry was headed to the Alum Cliffs, like every Monday. Dora hated the name. Alum sounded so chemical, so artificial, when in reality this walk was one of the most beautiful and serene walks in the area. Even though she had had the best intentions, over all the years they'd lived in the area, she had never bothered to look up the origin of the name. It was most likely that she didn't actually want to find out.

Harry passed their neighbour, who was tending her already immaculate front garden. Since the incident with Stella Fulton's mail, he had become persona non grata for her. At the most she condescended to a quick nod but generally she ignored him, which suited him just fine. Well, Harry had managed to get away again without even a proper greeting. He stood at the bottom of the drive, then turned left, took a step forward and stopped. He looked right, then left again.

Dora frowned. What was he doing? To get to the Alum Cliffs track you had to turn right. There was nothing on the left but thick eucalyptus bush.

Finally, Harry turned right and disappeared from her view. Dora breathed a sigh of relief. Well, she for one was glad he still went for his walk *and* found his way back! As regular as clockwork he went on his Monday morning walk along the cliff tops. Always carelessly dressed in what he called his 'sports outfit', always the same walk, all the way up onto the cliffs, with the ocean on his right. Usually he walked until he came to a certain point on the path that he had marked with a stone cairn as his finish. There, he would turn around and make his way back home.

If you walked all the way from their house, which was nestled in behind some trees in a quiet cul-de-sac not far from the beach, the walk to Harry's stone cairn took about thirty minutes one way. If, on the other hand, you drove up the Channel Highway and parked in one of the side streets, you could start the walk from there. Not only did it save you time, but you could also avoid the first part of the steepest section leading you to the cliff top. Harry's pride forbade him to shorten the walk. He could still manage the initial steep part which took him to the top of the cliffs. Which was surprising, considering all that heavy-footed shuffling he did at home.

Dora pulled the blinds of the kitchen window down. The sun had been streaming in and the expected heat, forecast for later in the day, was already tangible in the air. She should really use this time alone in the house to continue work on the latest costume. Michelle was expecting it to be ready in a fortnight, but Dora's restless thoughts kept returning to Harry. It was annoying how Harry could prevent her from getting stuck into the work when he wasn't even there. Her last dress. Already she could feel grief tugging at her insides. She'd spent nearly her whole adult life in her sewing room, designing and sewing, and now that was to come to an end. It was a loss, a heavy loss.

Dora wondered if Harry had felt that loss, when he had to give up his job. He'd never said anything. Well, he never said much about anything she thought was important.

Out of the blue one day, a few weeks ago, she had asked herself if Harry really did go for a cliff walk every Monday morning. How would she know? She had never gone with him or, heaven forbid, followed him. What if he veered off in a completely different direction once he was out of sight of the house and spent the morning in a pub? But there was never any evidence of alcohol on him or that all pervading universal pub smell of fried foods and insufficiently aired rooms. She didn't think Harry had been to a pub since his days at university.

Maybe he would go and visit some woman? Would he go to a lover in his old track pants? The thought made her smile. No, he wouldn't. He couldn't stand the idea of looking dishevelled or underdressed when he was visiting. If you weren't dressed right, people would take advantage of you or not take you seriously. He was convinced it would put him on the back foot. Having a secret lover would definitely make him dress properly. She was sure of it. Aside from that, he'd already done the 'lover thing'. Or, to be correct, she should say the *visiting a house of ill repute* thing. No, he was too old to bother now.

It suddenly occurred to Dora that maybe it wasn't a good idea anymore, to let Harry go for a walk by himself. Yes, he had always come back, but his dementia – if that's what it was – wasn't getting any better. Maybe it was completely irresponsible to let him go up on the cliffs all by himself. What if he couldn't find his cairn one day, his marker that told him he'd gone far enough? Kids sometimes kicked over cairns, just for the fun of seeing all those stones tumbling every which way.

What if one day, he walked all the way past his stone cairn towards the Shot Tower, a historic old tower, and couldn't find his way back? What if he snuck behind a tree to relieve himself and got lost in the bush?

On a sudden impulse, Dora grabbed her handbag, rummaged through the bits and pieces in there and found her car keys, right at the bottom, as usual. She slipped into her thongs and opened the garage door. She would go and find her husband.

And there she was, Stella Sticky-Beak, standing right by the fence near the garage, waving. Dora groaned inwardly. Now she would have to talk to her.

'It's going to be a scorcher today,' Stella said. 'I've been up for ages, watering the garden.'

'Yes, I suppose that's the best thing to do.' Dora really wanted to jump into her car. She jiggled her keys, hoping that her neighbour would get the hint.

'I saw your husband go for his walk,' Stella continued. 'Bird watching again, I suppose. And where are you off to in this heat?' So she did get the hint.

Snooping on my husband because I can't trust he will find his way back home, she wanted to say. But no, that would not do.

'Just doing my usual Monday morning shopping,' Dora explained, keeping her expression neutral. 'Before it gets too hot.'

'I see, but remember to take your shopping bags.' Stella stared at Dora's empty hands. 'Too many people just buy new bags every time. Such a waste!'

Dora forced a smile on her face. She pointed behind her at the car in the garage. 'Already in the car!' she assured her neighbour. 'I'd better be off. See you later!'

Stella's eyes followed her even as the car rolled down the drive.

*

Dora breathed in deeply as she accelerated towards the main street, glad to have escaped her nosy neighbour. She had decided not to follow Harry, but to drive up the highway, which ran parallel to the walking track. She would stop at the old brickfields and walk down the path that intersected with the Alum Cliffs track. Then she would walk south, heading towards Harry. That way she couldn't miss him. Unless he'd already turned back at his usual spot, but considering that he'd only just left a few minutes ago, that seemed unlikely.

*

Dora turned right off the main street onto Channel Highway and drove all the way up to Bonnet Hill. At the crest of the hill, just before the highway descended towards the seaside suburb

339

of Taroona, she turned off towards the brickfields, a short-lived convict brickworks from the mid-1800s. A grassy area just at the top of it had become an unofficial car park. Really, it was only a wide, weedy verge.

'This short-cut is for the lazy halfway walkers,' Harry had once pronounced with derision. 'Those who can't be bothered to do the full walk from end to end.'

Well, now he couldn't manage it from end to end anymore either.

*

If her timing was not too far off, she should be able to catch up with Harry before he got to the suicide spot. What a horrible name. But that's where he always had a little break before continuing on. The suicide spot. It was all her fault they called it that. She remembered it well.

As soon as she stepped out of the car, she realised that her thongs would be absolutely useless in the bush. A couple of steps and her feet were already rolling on the uneven ground. This would only get worse once she got onto the path, which was dusty and slippery, randomly strewn with small rocks and criss-crossed with ankle-breaking tree roots. Not only were her thongs completely inappropriate, she had also forgotten her sun hat. She usually wore it religiously, in order to protect her pale skin. Her mother had drilled sun protection into her from a very early age and now she had forgotten something as basic as a hat. At least she had managed to grab her sunglasses.

But clearly, she had not thought any of this through. Harry would be pleased that he had been proven right again if he had known about this stupid spontaneous excursion of hers. It upset him that she always got herself into situations on the spur of the moment, without considering the consequences. They tended to be not only to her own detriment but also to others. By which he generally meant himself.

Like that time she spontaneously decided to see Sophie in Launceston. A two-and-a-half-hour drive, there and back easily done in one day. She just had to go. An ominous feeling in her stomach that morning when she woke up, something she called a motherly premonition, made her cancel an appointment with the dentist she had that day and jump in the car to see Sophie instead.

Her motherly premonition had failed her completely. Dora had sent Sophie an anxious text asking her how she was and telling her that she was on her way to Launceston. But Sophie was well and happy. She taught her maths classes at the high school until midday and afterwards the two of them enjoyed a relaxed lunch, followed by a walk in the city park. How could Dora possibly have known that her car would get a flat tyre on the way home? Only thirty-something kilometres from Kingston! And why was there no spare tyre in the boot? Of course, Harry came with a spare and laboriously changed the tyre, but he was certainly not happy about it. It was a wonder that he even knew how to change a tyre! He was still wearing a thundercloud on his face when they both arrived at home in their separate cars half an hour later.

And here she was again, a victim of her spontaneous actions, in a long skirt, for God's sake, and a sleeveless shirt. Her arms would be burnt in no time. How could she have gone out without a sun hat and wearing those silly thongs? This half-hour walk through the scraggly bush and along the cliff top would be torture. Knowing her luck, she would probably have to climb over some trees that had fallen across the narrow path during the vicious storm a few weeks ago. Or maybe she would stumble and fall and not be able to get up again. And Harry or someone else would have to rescue her once again.

Already she felt anxious and sweaty, and she hadn't even left the car park. At least there were no other cars there and no one to see her in this utterly inappropriate get-up, wondering what on earth she was up to.

She checked that her car was locked and hid the keys just above the front tyre, behind the metal covering. Gingerly she made her way across the grassy car park to the start of the walk. Well, grassy was not the right word as the grass and weeds had shrivelled up into a thousand crunchy, prickly needles. Catching her breath under a very dehydrated-looking gum tree, she considered for a moment that it would be best if she just turned around. She could just pretend this little adventure of hers had never happened. Harry would never know. What was she actually doing there? It almost felt like some sort of spying mission. Making sure her husband had really gone for his usual walk? Or that he was not lost in the bush? How would she find him anyway, if he had gotten lost? What on earth was she thinking?

He certainly wasn't visiting a secret lover. Whatever had made her think that? Surely at the age of sixty-nine he could not be bothered with that anymore. Of course, sex was one thing, she could see that, but the logistics of organising it all, the lies and the secrecy … his life was much too comfortable and sedate to contemplate any of it. No, she could dismiss that.

What had happened years before with his secret excursions into the city was something she didn't want to waste any thoughts on anymore, particularly since it sometimes felt like the whole thing had been her fault. She should have never told Harry about that long-dead uncle of hers. Once a week, for decades, this uncle had visited his lover, always on the same day. And all of this with the full knowledge of his wife, as well as the rest of the family. Everyone knew about it and no one ever said anything. Certainly not after her aunt categorically refused to leave him, even though several of her many sisters had offered to take her in. No, the aunt had insisted she would not be a burden on anyone. She had married this man and she would see this marriage out.

So the affair continued until the lover, the mysterious woman, died. By this time her uncle was already in his eighties and his wife had not only gotten used to his regular absence but actually enjoyed those few hours she had to herself. She was most upset that he was now at home every day all day long and she had lost those short moments of freedom that she had had for over forty years.

They had only been in their mid-twenties when Dora told Harry this story of her uncle and aunt. They were both in love, or so she thought anyway, and it was unimaginable to them what could possibly lead a relationship down that path. They had laughed, but Dora had felt a lot of empathy for the aunt. Whereas Harry had guffawed and slapped his thighs. 'The old geezer! He obviously knew what was good for him!'

No, she should not have put those ideas into Harry's head.

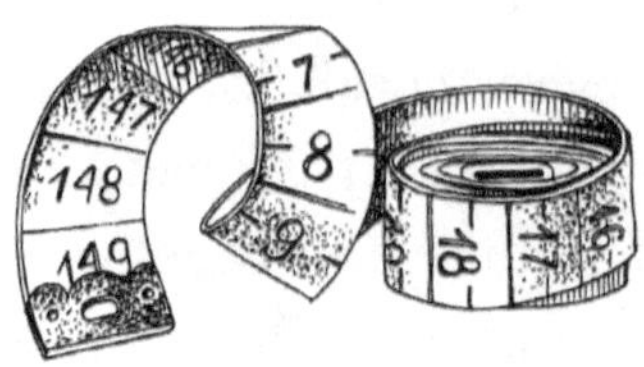

<u>49</u>

26 February 2024

The morning of Harry's death

BY THE TIME SHE REACHED the actual brickworks, the tops of her feet and ankles were stinging. She might as well have walked barefoot across the dry, stubbly grass! Dora licked her fingers and rubbed some saliva over the stinging skin. This did not bode well!

At least there was a bit of shade now, right at the head of a set of wooden steps. Years ago, the council had built those wooden stairs leading through the old brickworks site. Whether it was to protect the historic site or to make the start of the path, a rather steep section, easier, Dora didn't know. To her left stood a big sign with faded pictures explaining the history of this long-forgotten convict site. In the past, Dora had carefully read the information on the sign but she couldn't remember a thing and right now she didn't care, so she walked straight past without another glance.

Thankful for some scraggly gum trees which offered her a bit of shade now, she cautiously descended the wooden steps and finally stepped onto the dirt track. Where the narrow path met up with the Alum Cliffs track, she stopped and wiped the sweat off her forehead. She was not looking forward to the constant up and down that lay ahead of her, until she would at last meet up with Harry on the cliff top. To allow a bit of air onto her legs, she tucked the skirt into her underpants so it sat just above her knees. Hopefully that would help.

Dora left the shade of the gum tree and started making her way up the first incline. It was quite a gentle rise, really, easily managed in proper walking shoes. But as she had predicted, she was slipping and sliding in her thongs, even though her toes were desperately gripping onto the toe post, trying to hold the thongs in place. Not only that, but she could feel every tiny rock poking into the thin rubber soles. Angry determination coursed through her. She was here now, and she would struggle up to the top. She would not turn back. Once she was on the flat part she would take a quick rest in the shade again, find Harry and pretend that all was well with her already sore feet.

She reached the cliff top out of breath and sweating. Her thin cotton shirt was glued to her body. Sweat was running down her back and between her breasts. Her hair, which had once been white-blond, was now streaked with grey but still thick and curly. Now loose strands were plastered to her forehead and shoulders. She viciously tore a rubber band out of her tangled curls and brushed her fingers through her hair. Then she tied it into an unruly knot high up on her head to allow what little air there was to cool her neck.

*

Faster than she thought, she reached the suicide spot. Once on the path, and after a short break in the shade, walking had been easier than she expected. Even though there were rocks and tree roots everywhere, at least the path was level. Thank God, there was no more slipping and sliding in her thongs. Coming around a corner she could see Harry sitting on the wooden bench, staring out onto the sea. His hands on his knees and his back straight, he sat without moving.

He had indeed gone for a walk, as he said he would, and he was by himself. No secret lover sitting next to him. Dora was relieved beyond belief that he had not got lost in the bush or was off somewhere with another woman. Good God, she could be so silly sometimes. And it was too late now to turn around and hope he hadn't seen her.

When Harry heard her footsteps nearby, he turned his head, the indifferent expression on his face changing to a scowl.

'What on earth are you doing here?' he called out to her as she approached him. 'Just look at the state of you!' With one glance, he took in her dishevelled appearance and the tucked-up skirt. Self-consciously she pulled the skirt out of her underpants and then wiped the sweat off her face.

She sat down next to him. 'I suddenly thought how nice it would be if we were both doing this walk,' she said apologetically. 'But I didn't take the time to get changed. If I had, I would have missed you and you would have been way down the path.'

Harry shook his head. 'You're lucky you didn't break your legs in that get-up,' he said, his eyebrows knitted.

She waved away his concern. Was it concern? Or was he upset with her for having followed him?

'Ah, it's alright,' she replied, purposely casual. 'Even though I have to admit that thongs are not ideal for this.' She had disrupted his walk. His time of quiet contemplation, as he had once called these strolls. A sideways look at him told her nothing about the mood he was in. He turned away from her and again looked straight ahead at the sparkling water. Dora wondered what he was thinking about. What did people with dementia think about? Sometimes it worried her more to see him so placid and indifferent. At least when he was angry she knew how to deal with it. She'd had many years of practice.

For a while they sat quietly side by side. The leaves were swaying gently in the sea breeze. A lizard crawled out from under a pile of sticks and slid up onto a rock, warming itself in the sun.

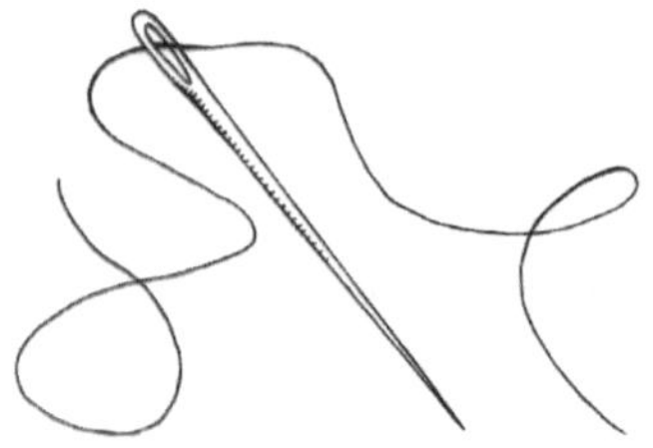

50

26 February 2024

Minutes before Harry's death

'I'M REALLY LOOKING FORWARD TO Sophie's wedding in May.' Dora broke the silence. It was the only topic of conversation she could think of that might cheer Harry up. 'It should be great fun. Of course, we have to get through all the preparation for it first, which will be a pain in the bum. Booking a venue, finding the right dress, the invitations, the flowers and all the rest of it. I assume it's the parents of the bride who do all of that? What do you think?'

'Hrumph,' Harry grunted.

'Maybe it's all different these days. I wouldn't be surprised if Sophie wanted to do it all herself.' Dora sounded disappointed.

'She might.'

'We haven't been to a proper party for absolutely ages. Just think how nice it will be. Good food, dancing. I can't wait.' Dora smiled in anticipation.

The days of going to big noisy parties were long gone, but she still remembered with fondness all those get-togethers they used to have when she was a student. Random parties for no particular reason, just for the fun of it. The loud music, the dancing … how she had enjoyed that! There was always a lot of alcohol, even though she never needed to drink in order to enjoy herself. People were still smoking in those days, filling up the rooms with clouds of smoke, and they were not always the cigarettes you could buy in a shop that were passed around during those long nights.

Dora knew that parties would not be like that again, not this one at the wedding anyway, but still, there would be music and dancing, happy people with big smiles on their faces, because it would be such a special day. Dora could already sense the excitement and anticipation that would be in the air, infecting everyone with positive energy.

'Just imagine, our daughter getting married. I can hardly believe it. She's still a little girl to me.' Dora elbowed Harry lightly in the side. 'You'll have to give a speech.'

Harry looked at her sideways. 'I'm not going,' he said impassively and returned his gaze to the ocean.

What was it Harry had just said? Dora wasn't sure she had heard him. He wasn't going?

'What do you mean, you're not going?' Dora frowned as she looked at his profile.

'I mean, I'm not going!'

'You're the father of the bride, so you'll have to go. And the father of the bride always gives a speech!'

'You're not listening to me,' Harry responded impatiently. Again, he turned to look at her. 'I said, I'm not going. I'm *not* going to the wedding.' His face was pinched, his eyes somewhat dull.

Dora stared at him, stunned. Was this the dementia speaking? For a moment her mind went blank and she was lost for words. Yes, it must be the dementia speaking. Maybe Harry didn't realise what this was all about. It was quite possible that there was a link missing in his thinking. Probably he hadn't made the connection between his daughter getting married and his obligations as the bride's father. Yes, that's what it was. That wretched dementia. It must be worse than she had thought. Right, she needed to be calm and patient.

'Harry,' she said. 'Sophie, our daughter, is getting married. You're her father and it's your job to give a speech.' She looked at him beseechingly. 'We can write the speech together. It's not really a big deal and it doesn't have to be long. Just some funny things about Sophie's childhood to make everyone laugh. Of course, we have to say how happy we are that she is getting married to this lovely young man.'

The lovely young man. They hadn't even met him yet, for heaven's sake! Sophie had sent some photos of him but that meant nothing. What can a photo possibly tell you? She had no idea whether he was lovely.

Harry shook his head repeatedly. 'I'm not going. That's all there is to it.'

Despite her best intentions, Dora lost her patience. 'What do you mean you're not going? How can you not go to your daughter's wedding?' she cried out and grabbed him by the arm.

Harry replied slowly but firmly. 'I'm not going, and I'm not giving a speech, because that is the job of the bride's father. As you just confirmed.' He shook off her hand. 'So let the bride's father do all of that,' he added.

A rushing started up in Dora's ears. All at once she couldn't hear the birds anymore or the gentle rustling of the leaves in the breeze. What on earth was going on with Harry?

'You are the bride's father!' she screamed through the noise in her ears. 'What in God's name is the matter with you?' She moved closer to him. Suddenly she wanted to hit him. Box him in the chest, slap his face, throw him onto the ground. Beat the dementia out of him and bring him to his senses.

Harry leaned away from her. 'How do I know I'm her father? You tell me! Do you really think I don't know what went on with you and Andrew all those years ago? That night on Bruny Island? When you and he went to that crappy film and nine months later Sophie was born? Do you think I'm stupid?' Words and rage were flowing out of him as if a dam had burst. A dam that had held something back for over thirty years.

'Why did we never have a child before that blasted holiday? Why never another child after Sophie was born? Do you really think I haven't thought about that?'

Dora stared at him, aghast. All around her, the birds had taken up their chirping again. The leaves of the eucalyptus trees were rustling in the breeze. Down below, at the bottom of the cliff, waves were gently slapping against the rocks.

The sun was burning more fiercely than before, stinging Dora's face with its heat. She noticed she had stopped breathing. With one big gulp she took in enough air to expand her lungs to near bursting. Expelling the air forcefully, she faced Harry.

'I have never, ever slept with another man the entire time we have been married. Or before, as you well know! Neither with Andrew, nor anyone else! Ever!' She was fully aware of how she looked, perched on the edge of the bench. Red face, dishevelled hair, dust-covered feet and skin damp with sweat. Every fibre in her body so taut that she was in danger of snapping in half.

'So what about that night on Bruny Island then?' he repeated. His voice was a challenge, letting her know he had definitely not forgotten about it. 'I remember the two of you coming home with sand in your hair and on your clothes. That did not happen while watching a movie. So don't tell me that nothing happened. Blind Freddy could see what was going on!'

There was no sense in asking meekly, 'Which night?' Dora, too, knew exactly which night Harry was referring to. It had been early on, a long time ago. Probably only the second or third time they'd all gone to the shack together. She and Harry, Andrew and Leah, Barb. All of them.

Yes, she knew exactly which night. And something nearly did happen between her and Andrew, but it hadn't. She was the one who'd stopped it. She'd stopped it for what? For being unjustly accused now? Over thirty years later? Had Harry really thought for all those years that she had been cheating on him? With his brother? Oh, if Freda could hear him now she would be shaking her head. When Dora had told her about that night in one of her letters, she knew exactly what Freda would have said and done had she been in Dora's place. Right there on the beach and stuff everyone else!

'Harry, let's stop being silly. Everything has been set in motion for this wedding and Sophie is expecting us. It is important for her that we be there and share this with her.' Dora was forcing her voice to be calm and steady, but she could feel a hot seething mass of thick liquid erupting from deep inside her. She was being accused of something she had not done. Harry had carried this with him for over thirty years. Over thirty years he had believed that she had cheated on him.

Hot lava. Bubbling. Like the pictures of a recently erupted volcano she had seen on the news. The thick heavy lava was spewing out of the top of the volcano and then slowly rolling downwards, smothering everything in its way. That's how she felt. Hot vicious lava boiling and inexorably moving up her insides and exploding out into the world. There was no way she could stop it. She was ready to explode and smother Harry, stop him from saying these stupid things and make him shut up.

'Nothing happened!' she yelled. 'I did nothing! Nothing!' She took in another big gulp of air. 'Unlike you! You were the one who strayed. You! Do you really think I don't know that you went to that place, that … that brothel for years on end? Telling me you were playing cards? Telling me about the people in your card group? People who didn't even exist? The old lady with the pink hair? The autistic boy? You made it all up! Don't you talk to me about cheating and lies and whatever else!'

Slowly Harry turned his head to face her. A thin smile played on his lips.

'Well, you can go to the wedding by yourself. I've had enough of the pretence. It's time that everyone finds out what has been going on all this time. What sort of person you really are, and who Sophie's father really is!'

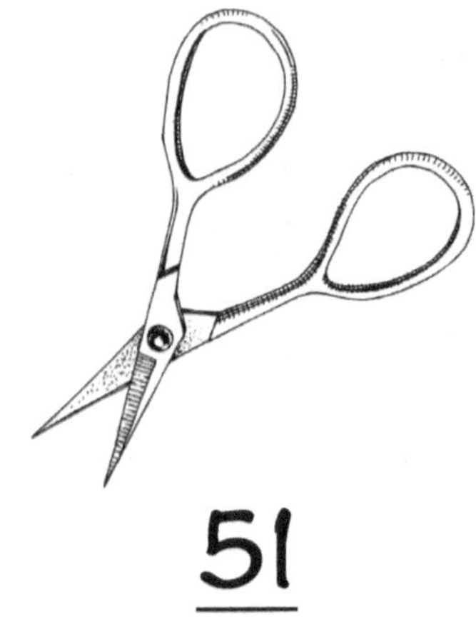

<u>51</u>

26 February 2024

Harry's death

DESPITE HARRY'S OUTLANDISH PRONOUNCEMENTS, DORA thought he had sounded surprisingly coherent. There had been no sign of confusion at all in what he said. There was no truth in it, no, but he had expressed his thoughts clearly and coherently. Strangest of all, he was not upset or angry. Rarely had she seen him this calm when they had a disagreement or an argument. Usually, she was the one who tried to keep everything on an even keel and take the heat out of an argument. Now, it was the other way around. She was out of control, yelling at her husband and hardly knowing what she was saying, whereas he spoke calmly and succinctly. But she didn't like the indifference in his voice. The disconnectedness. He spoke as if nothing really concerned him anymore. Not her supposed infidelity on Bruny Island, not Sophie's wedding, not the ridiculous notion that he wasn't Sophie's father. He spoke as if he'd made his point and come to terms with those past events that hadn't even happened.

The cacophony of thoughts running through her head paralysed Dora. It seemed impossible to convince Harry of the truth. He had carried his suspicions with him for so long that they had calcified in his brain for good. Never to be softened or removed. Once his mind was fixed on something, nothing and nobody could shift him. Dora had long ago given up trying.

Incredulous, she now watched Harry as he got up and moved towards the edge of the cliff. Those old floppy track pants he wore disguised the shape of his legs. There was no telling whether they were still strong and muscular as they used to be, or whether they had morphed into the stick-thin, withered legs of a much older man. Of course, she knew that they had morphed. The shirt, too, hung off his shoulders, looking two sizes too large. There must have been a point sometime in the last few years when Harry had given up on looking neat and sharp. Sometime soon after he had to leave work, Dora assumed, but she couldn't remember.

'Harry,' she called out gently. She slid to the edge of the wooden bench. They needed to get home, calm down, and talk about this business in the comfort of their home. It served no purpose continuing this silly argument there, in the middle of the bush, in the heat and on the edge of a cliff. She certainly shouldn't be yelling and screaming. This situation needed to be controlled.

'Harry, let's stop this. We need to go home. Come on.'

Harry moved his shoulders up in slow motion, rolled them back, then dropped them down again. As if to release some stiffness from the joints.

'Please come away from the edge, Harry! Come on!' Dora pleaded. It frightened her to see him so apathetic. Why did he not react?

But then he turned around slowly, facing her. 'Are you scared I might fall?' He gave a sharp laugh. 'That would suit you very well, wouldn't it?' To Dora's horror he spread his arms wide and moved them up and down as if he were a bird. Then he started rocking on his feet, at the same time making a terrible '*brrrrr*' sound. With his back still to the edge of the cliff, he swayed from side to side.

He's pretending to be a plane! He wants to frighten me! In his mocking eyes, Dora saw a recklessness that made her insides contract. Except for her bladder. It felt big and soft and uncontrollable. The bladder did not want to contract. It wanted to let go.

Like a disappointed child whose parents didn't acknowledge his efforts, Harry suddenly lowered his arms. He stood unmoving, watching Dora. Very slowly, Dora lifted her body off the bench. Desperate to get Harry away from the edge of the cliff, she moved closer to him. In order not to frighten him, she placed one foot in front of the other, very carefully like a first-time gymnast on a beam. She was close enough to touch Harry when he smiled at her.

'Or maybe,' Harry said with a malicious spark in his eyes. 'Maybe I should push *you* over the edge!' Dora stopped dead. All blood drained from her head to her feet.

'Do you know how much I've done for you over the years?' Harry sounded threatening. 'And how little you've done for me? Tell me, what have you done for me?'

Dora's pulse was throbbing in her temples. She held out her hand to Harry. 'Come,' she said, her voice shaky. 'Take my hand and come away from the edge. And then we'll go home.'

Harry reached out towards Dora and in one quick movement he grabbed her upper arm and pulled her close to him. Both of them now stood perilously close to the edge. Too scared to move and dislodge the gravel breneath her thongs, Dora stood stock still. The lapping of the waves against the rocks below her had turned into a thunderous noise in her ears. A group of seagulls circled and screamed overhead in a deafening chorus. Watching these two small figures from high above. Urging them on. *Go ahead, it's easy to fly.* Or warning them. *Don't take another step!* It was hard to tell the difference.

'Harry, let go of me. Please!' Dora whispered.

'Oh, but I can't,' Harry replied. 'If I do you may fall. Fall, fall, fall, a long way down,' he sang.

Dora's bladder was full to bursting. Its weight was pushing against her urethra. I've got to stay calm, she told herself desperately. Stay calm, Dora!

With her free hand, she gently tried to unpeel Harry's fingers from her upper arm, with the terrible result that Harry only tightened his grip on her.

Distract him, Dora told herself. You have to distract him! She looked around frantically. There was nothing, nothing that she could see or do that would help her. There weren't even other walkers on the path she could call out to. The track was completely deserted. Only the seagulls, still circling and screaming, watching with their beady eyes. A whole flock of them, swirling round and round in the sea breeze.

Then, out of nowhere it came to her. Her only chance to get away from Harry. If she stayed calm she might be able to pull it off. She raised her face towards the sky, slowly turning her head from left to right, as if she were following the movement of an object. Forcing what she hoped was an astonished, reverent look onto her face, she managed a smile.

'Look, Harry,' she said, her voice soft and soothing. 'Oh, look, there's a sea eagle!'

Harry and his fascination with sea eagles.

With her free hand Dora pointed up into the sky beyond Harry's shoulder. Automatically, he turned his head to follow her hand. Without realising, he had loosened his grip on her arm. Giving a strangled scream, Dora tore herself from Harry and jumped back from the edge.

The momentum caused by her sudden drawing away propelled Harry towards her in an uncontrolled stumble. For a short moment he teetered on one leg, then he instinctively jerked his body back to regain his balance. He took a step back to distance himself from Dora and … was gone.

*

Later, Dora thought that there were moments when time seemed to stand still. One minute you were busy doing or thinking something and the next minute a wide space opened up, making room for all sorts of things to happen, unthinkable things, outrageous things, terrible things. Then the space would close up again, slowly and irreversibly, until it disappeared and there was no evidence of it ever having been there. Everything was as it should be. You were still doing or thinking the same things and all that was left was a vague sensation that something extraordinary had happened, but you couldn't quite put your finger on it.

You would look around and notice the lizard still sitting on the rock sunning itself, the leaves on the trees still swaying in the breeze. The sunlight flickering through the trees like before. Apart from the waves crashing into the rocks below and the seagulls above, there was no other sound to be heard, and yet something had changed. Harry had gone.

It was strange. One minute he was standing next to her, the next he had disappeared. Dora turned towards the path and looked up and down it but no, he was nowhere to be seen.

The sudden shrieking of seagulls shot through her body like a burning arrow. The cliff! Harry was gone! And then her bladder let go, hot urine gushing down her legs. Dora sank into the dirt and gravel and curled herself around her knees.

'Oh my God!' she moaned. 'What has just happened? What on earth have I done?' She covered her face with her hands. Her skin was burning, sweat was running down her cheeks and her back.

After what seemed an eternity, Dora looked up. She couldn't stay there. What if other walkers came past and saw her squatting there? Looking sweaty and dirty, behaving like a crazy woman. Smelling of urine. Good God! They would call the ambulance, or worse, the police. No. She needed to clean herself up and decide what to do.

Dora's body felt stiff all over as she stood up awkwardly. The urine had pasted some of her skirt to her legs. It was disgusting. She tore the soaked underpants from her body and threw them under a bush. The she patted her wet legs with the edge of her skirt. Parts of the skirt were wet and dirty already so a bit more wouldn't matter.

In the hope of drying the skirt a bit, Dora stood and flapped it around her with both hands. What now? Should she just walk home, pretending nothing had happened? Heaven help her, but should she look over the cliff edge first to see whether Harry was really lying down there? No, definitely not! She would not do that! If she did not see him, she could still pretend that none of this had happened. No, she did not want to see Harry dead.

Dora let go of her skirt and combed her fingers through her hair. If anyone walked past she needed to look as normal as possible. A woman taking a rest after an exhausting walk in the heat. More importantly, before anyone could possibly see her, she needed to leave. *If you're going through hell, keep going.* Now, where had that come from? And was she, Dora, going through hell right now? It certainly felt like it.

She stood up and looked around the area for any signs of what had happened. There were scuff marks in the dirt where she and Harry had struggled. She needed to get rid of them, get rid of any traces that anyone had been there. Near the wooden bench she found a branch that must have dropped recently. The leaves at the end were still green and supple. It would do as a broom. A quick sweep, then she threw it over the cliff.

Dora scanned the area. A big wet patch where she had … dear God! But that would dry in the sun. To make sure, just in case, she kicked some dirt over the patch. What else? She tended to leave her sunglasses lying around everywhere but they were still glued to her nose. Full of smudges from when she'd put her face in her hands. It was a wonder they hadn't come off in her struggle with Harry.

Then she remembered her underpants. She couldn't leave them there. If anyone found them and for some obscure reason could trace them back to her, they would know she'd been there. The thought alone made Dora squirm with embarrassment. She walked over to the bush and bent down to retrieve the underpants. Not only were they wet and smelly but also covered in detritus from the bush. Disgusted, she shook off small twiggy bits and dried leaves. There was nothing she could do about the sandy soil that clung to them. She held the underpants up with two fingers. She had no choice but to curl her hand around them and hide them as best as possible.

Finally, Dora took one more look at the scene in front of her. Everything looked just like it should. An empty bench, a few footprints – they could be anyone's – ants running up a blackened log. The lizard had disappeared.

In the distance she could hear the engine of a boat. It was time to go. At first she walked deliberately slowly. Not only because her feet were hurting in those thongs, but because she needed to calm herself. Walk slowly and breathe in deeply, she told herself.

It didn't take long for her heartbeat to settle. She breathed in the faint aroma of eucalyptus from the gum trees. Being in the bush always calmed her. Everything was so serene, so eternal. Everything was the way it was meant to be.

In the dappled shade of a gum tree, Dora stopped for a short moment, and with the back of her hand wiped the sweat off her forehead. She shook out her hair, then gathered her long skirt in one hand to make walking easier. She didn't mind at all, walking home alone. Just for this short space of time, while she was in the bush, on her own, she felt overwhelmingly blessed.

It was only when the path curved around an outcrop of rocks that she realised she was not far from the car park. Soon she would have to face whatever it was that was going to happen. All at once she was seized by panic. Harry was gone. Nobody knew about it except her. She knew exactly what had happened. There were consequences to face. Sooner or later. Gripped by panic, Dora started to run. She needed to get to the safety of her car before anyone saw her. Run, Dora, run!

Acknowledgements

A handful of people have been kind enough to help me shape this novel.

Particular thanks go to Susan Young and Kat Richardson, whose sensitive editing added life and movement to the story. Dawn Keer proofread the first draft and offered ongoing support over many months and many thousands of miles. Sue McNeill found gremlins in my writing that were completely invisible to me.

George Cresswell's enthusiasm for this novel was truly humbling. Several times he walked the Alum Cliffs and brought back the most beautiful photos of the cliffs.

I have Shirley Storey to thank for getting me started on this project. If only she could see the result!

And then there are the two most important men in my life. You know who you are.

Thank you, all of you!

C.Z.